Dawn of the Red Sun

by

Michelle O'Leary

The Sunscapes Trilogy, Book 3

Dawn of the Red Sun

Cover Art by *Debbie Taylor*

The Wild Rose Press, Inc.
PO Box 708
Adams Basin, NY 14410-0708
Visit us at www.thewildrosepress.com

Publishing History
First Fantasy Rose Edition, 2018
Print ISBN 978-1-5092-2136-3
Digital ISBN 978-1-5092-2137-0

The Sunscapes Trilogy, Book 3
Published in the United States of America

How did they always do this? Unpredictable and nimble, Sin and her brother ran rings around her. She could only go still and wait for the whirlwind to pass.

Sin's chin lifted and her gaze darted over Liaena's shoulder. Liaena's stomach muscles tightened with renewed anxiety. She had a horrible suspicion the whirlwind had just begun.

"What the hell is this?" A deep voice sliced through the serenity of Sin's home.

Liaena closed her eyes a moment to brace herself before turning to face Manakai Shay. As always, his impact drove through her all the way to her toes.

The dark scowl on his face underscored his dangerous good looks. With his careless toss of thick black hair, features as strong and handsome as a poet's dream, those devastating green eyes, and long lean body, he could put every male model in the galaxy out of business. Add his aura of predatory power and the man could make any female forget her own name.

He stalked toward them like a panther about to pounce, his gaze fixed on Liaena with narrow ferocity. He reminded her of an oncoming storm, dressed all in black like the last time she'd seen him, when he'd threatened to make her his hostage. She couldn't suppress a shiver of anticipation.

Dedication

To my family for their endless encouragement and
patience in helping me finish this series.
All my love.

Prologue

Liaena Griffin remembered with crystal clarity the day the Shays came to visit, fixed the fountain, and destroyed an entire art collection. She'd only met them once before, but they'd made an impression. She'd bruised Manakai Shay's shin for insulting her.

The day of the fountain, she met them again with a sense of disorientation. Years older, they hardly seemed the same children. Her resentful memory of them shriveled in the face of their impossible beauty and charm. Then again she was not the same either. Her fierce fire had faded, dampened by her father's endless cold lessons on proper behavior and obedience.

Their father, Ezekiel Shay, matched her memory, a tall lanky man with ink-dark hair and a reserved smile. His eyes held the same warm green twinkle as his children's, as if mischievous thoughts ran rampant behind his composed face. He spoke to Liaena's father with such amazing fearless ease.

Webster Griffin terrified everyone, including Liaena. She'd never seen anyone treat him with less than absolute deference. Didn't they know her father was dangerous? Or did they know something she didn't?

Her father's heavy hand on her shoulder startled her out of her fascination. "Daughter, be a good hostess and show the young Shays our Aqualyr." He turned away with Ezekiel Shay, leaving her alone with the twins.

She said nothing at first, unsettled by the adults' abrupt departure. Older, taller, and intimidating, the twins watched her with their unnerving cat-green eyes and identical faint smiles. She wasn't sure what to do.

"Are you going to kick me again?" Manakai asked with a tilt of his dark head.

Liaena straightened with as much dignity as she could muster, face burning. Remembering her father's lessons, she responded, "Of course not," in an even tone.

Sinsudee slanted her brother a quick look, smile deepening. "Aena, what's an Aqualyr?"

Liaena blinked, distracted. A nickname? Didn't people use nicknames when they liked someone? She wasn't sure; she'd never been around other children. "Um, it's the Water Room. One of Father's art collections. All the pieces are made of water or have water in them. It's this way."

She headed on uncertain feet down the corridor, gaining confidence when they followed. They moved with such silence she kept checking to make sure they still trailed her.

"I like art," Sinsudee offered in a soft lyrical voice.

"I'd rather slice," Manakai said. "Is this water room any fun?"

Liaena shot him a puzzled look. "Fun?"

"Yeah, fun. Like games, a slide maybe. Or hey, it'd be fun to chuck things at my sister. Got any water balloons?"

"You're a booger, Kai," Sinsudee declared, smirking.

2

Liaena reached the entrance to the Aqualyr, turning to them with a frown. "What's a water balloon?"

"What's a…?" He gaped at her, which should have made him look dumb but didn't.

"Close your mouth, Brother." Sinsudee studied Liaena, a shadow in her green eyes. "What do you do for fun, Aena?"

Having no answer, Liaena shrugged and opened the door, waving them through. She watched them as they entered, waiting for the usual gasps of amazement, awe, and avarice. The Shays only glanced around with mild curiosity at the hangings, sculptures, and framed art.

"Huh." Manakai stopped next to the ornate marble fountain in the center of the room, hands on narrow hips. He sent Liaena a grim look. "No slides."

"This one's pretty," Sinsudee commented, gesturing to a water sculpture held together by a film of glowing, multicolored energy. "It looks like an angel. But I don't get that one." Making a face over her shoulder, she pointed to a tangle of tubes with colored fluid bubbling through them. "Is it supposed to look like a pile of guts?"

A strange sensation moved in Liaena's chest, like a bubble trying to escape. It took her a second to recognize the urge to laugh, something she hadn't done in a long time. They didn't fear her father and his wealth didn't impress them. Her father flaunted this collection, but it bored and grossed them out. Crushed under a wave of youthful admiration, she swallowed her laugh and watched them with wide eyes.

"Your fountain's busted," Manakai announced, staring at the apathetic streams of water gurgling out of hidden spouts. His face brightened. "I can fix it."

Sinsudee winced and swiveled toward him. "Um, Kai…"

He bent, searching the base of the fountain. "Just have to find the control panel. Ah, here it is."

"We're not supposed to touch things," Liaena said with a surge of alarm when a panel slid open under his fingers.

"Seriously, Brother, this is not a good idea."

He knelt next to the fountain, studying the panel display with an absorbed expression. "Told you, I can fix it. Dad says I have a natural talent."

Moving behind him, Sinsudee bent and frowned over his shoulder at the display, her hair cascading forward in a rush of blue-black silk. "Dad was being nice. You break things more than you fix them."

"Oh, shut it, Sinsi. This thing reads like there's low pressure. I'll bet it's the regulator."

"It's slow, not broken," Liaena tried. "I'm sure maintenance could—"

"Why wait?" Manakai interrupted, shooting her a dazzling smile. "We're here now. Just have to find the regulator."

His sister reached over his shoulder and touched the display, pointing when a schematic of the fountain appeared. "It's right there. But I'm pretty sure the regulator's not the problem."

"Bet me." He closed the panel and sidled along the edge of the fountain, opening a different slot. "Who put his own slicer together from parts?"

Sinsudee scoffed, her tone full of contempt. "Oh sure, you did a great job. Does it fly yet?" She crouched, looking inside the fountain with him.

Manakai glowered at his twin and mumbled, "Bad parts." Then his expression lightened, eyes gleaming with triumph. "I found it! Okay, just a sec."

Liaena stared at the two of them, nonplussed. Her father had given her a simple order. How had it gotten so out of hand? Yet she couldn't stop watching them, absorbing everything about them. She'd spent most of her isolated life with adults who either ignored or avoided her. The exotic revelation of the twins blew her away. They glowed with energy like mini-Suns, fearless and vibrant. They reminded her of her mother's island, of the beaches that had been her playground, of warm light and life.

"There!" Manakai bounded to his feet with athletic grace and made a theatrical gesture. The fountain gave an odd rumble, the gurgle of water lurching to a foaming stream. "Your fountain is"—water exploded from the spouts, spraying in all directions—"fixed," he sputtered, turning his face away and lifting a hand to ward off the deluge.

Liaena clapped her hands over her mouth, staring in frozen horror at the catastrophe unfolding before her. The water pressure knocked sculptures off stands, hangings and frames off walls. It ricocheted off the ceiling and drenched the entire room. Cold water soaked her hair and clothes, dripping down her face like ice tears.

Sinsudee laughed. The sound held no malice, no ridicule, only pure humor and lyrical delight. She held out her arms, looking down at her water-logged self. "Kai, you're an idiot!" she chortled, stepping forward, angling her hand in one of the streams, and hosing down her brother.

He yelped in gleeful outrage and splashed her back. They chased one another around the fountain, laughter ringing through the room.

Liaena giggled behind her hands, shivering with terrified wonder. The Shay twins had taken disaster and turned it into a playground without a hint of fear for what they'd done. Weren't they worried what their father would say and do to them? Instead they were having…fun.

A small part of her remembered fun and stirred. Warmth spread through her, as though she danced on a beach again, listening to her mother's laughter.

"Aena, grab him!" Sinsudee called in a light breathless voice. "We'll show him 'fixed.' "

The door slid open and Liaena froze again, ice shooting like white lightning through her heart. Their fathers stood on the threshold, expressions blank with surprise. Liaena's father touched a control next to the door. The fountain gasped and died.

For a moment, silence held, broken only by the drip of water off every surface.

Then Ezekiel Shay said in a low rueful tone, "Oh, Sun's blood."

His children stepped forward together, their laughter gone.

"Sorry, Mr. Griffin, I was trying to fix—"

"I tried to stop him but he wouldn't—"

"Fountain wasn't working right, so I thought—"

"Never listens, he's always trying to—"

"Tweak it a little, it's a mess but—"

"We'll clean it up," they finished in unison.

"Web, I apologize for my children." Mr. Shay was gazing at the twins, hands clasped behind his back.

Liaena searched his features for disapproval, anger, or malice, but found only mild censure and furtive amusement. "At this age, they're twin typhoons. I'll reimburse you for any damages."

Liaena's father chuckled, casting an indulgent smile on the twins, but she saw the chill in his eyes and shuddered. "No need. We did send them off to entertain themselves, although this wasn't quite what I had in mind." His hard icy stare flicked to Liaena long enough to freeze her heart with the promise of painful punishment.

Ezekiel Shay made a sound of amusement, his twinkling gaze moving to her as well. "Don't be too hard on your daughter, Web. Not much can stop these two when they get rolling, and I doubt she helped."

"Oh, no." Sinsudee stepped forward, sending Liaena an anxious glance. "Aena didn't do anything."

Manakai stepped forward with his sister. "She told me to leave it alone."

"Well, there you go," their father said, mouth twitching with the beginnings of a smile. "Sin, Kai, apologize to your hostess for the trouble you caused her."

Liaena realized her hands still covered her mouth and dropped them, shuffling with nerves as the Shay twins approached. She tried to speak, to say they didn't have to apologize, but her voice failed her. Sinsudee reached her first, wrapping her in a gentle hug. Liaena made a squeaking sound, body stiff with shock.

"I hope you'll forgive us," Sinsudee whispered in her ear. "And if you want to kick Kai again, that's okay with me."

With a muffled snicker, she let Liaena go, stepping

aside for her brother. Liaena stared up at Manakai, wondering with dizzy horror if he would hug her too. Instead, he gave her a charming smile and clasped her hand, his touch shockingly warm.

"I'm really sorry, Aena. I hope you don't get in too much trouble." He bent and kissed her cheek, sending her world into a spin. "It was fun, though," he whispered with a mischievous grin and a wink.

Then they left her there, wet and dripping, full of unnamed emotion, etching the day on her memory in bright, unbreakable lines.

Chapter 1

"I must be out of my mind." Liaena Griffin stared out the view port at the command station for Shay Enterprises. Her transport ship circled the imposing structure, waiting for permission to dock. A thousand butterflies took up residence in her stomach. She'd spent years planning and waiting for this moment, but now it seemed too soon.

Don't be a coward. She stiffened her spine, taking a deep breath. She'd considered every possible outcome of this visit, and short of the Shays killing her outright she had nothing to worry about. But she strove for one particular outcome, and convincing the Shays wouldn't be easy. Years of distrust and animosity stood between them.

Liaena pictured the fountain to steady her nerves. *All things are possible.* One moment of warmth in her cold world, the glimpse of a different life through the Shay children, had kept her going, steeling her resolve. The twins had shown her what could be if she stayed strong enough to make it happen.

One fragile glimpse. The next time she'd met the Shay children, they'd lost their mother and their open warmth, watching her with eyes gone cool and wary. They'd still been charming but with a brittle insincerity, cutting right through her. Only the lessons she'd learned under the merciless hand of her father had kept her from showing the depth of her dismay.

Over the years, she'd endured a thousand more cuts from the Shays, becoming ice in self-defense. They painted her with the same brush as Webster Griffin, assuming she acted as his tool. True enough, she had to admit, but she understood them better than her father. *At least I hope I do or this trip will be a disaster.*

"We're cleared for docking, Lady Griffin," the pilot announced over the com, releasing another wave of butterflies in her stomach.

"Thank you. Proceed." Habit and training kept her voice cool and steady, her palms growing damp and apprehension clogging her throat. How would they receive her? She'd rarely spoken with them without her father looming close by. She'd never approached them on her own. The last time she'd seen Manakai Shay, he'd threatened to kidnap her.

Taking a shaky breath, she let it out with slow control as they entered the docking bay. A part of her half-hoped he'd follow through on his threat. The memory of it ambushed her; green eyes fierce, hard fingers manacling her wrist in fire. She banished it to a far corner of her mind. Becoming a hostage might make her life easier, removing all her hard choices, but it would not end well in the long run.

She had her own life's calling. Becoming a pawn of the Shays in their dangerous game with her father didn't mesh with her plan.

The enormous docking bay seethed with busy efficiency, ships flowing around her transport in a two-way river of commerce. This was only one of Shay Enterprises's many stations, rivaling her father's organization in wealth and size. She didn't think the galaxy had ever seen two commercial entities so massive as Shay Enterprises and Quasicore in all the millennia humans had colonized space.

She expected her pilot to angle toward the main entrance and land on the visitors' platform, but he headed for the far end instead. She'd studied the Shays' main hub of business. Her pilot set down close to the maintenance bay, where they housed their notorious black racing ships, the Shadow slicers. Out of the main flow of traffic, away from the central focus of the public eye.

The Shays did nothing by random. Why direct her transport to this quiet corner?

Rising from her seat, she moved toward the hatch with smooth control, hearing her father's cold lecture: *Griffins do not dawdle or rush. We arrive when we mean to arrive. One's will is one's power, Daughter.* Stilling the tremor in her fingers, she brushed a hand down the crisp line of her pants suit, touching her upswept hair to make sure it remained in place. Then she activated the hatch.

She had anticipated one or both of the Shays. Her stomach lurched at the sight of a stranger waiting for her. The smile on his pleasant face welcomed, his gray uniform sporting the sphinx Shay company logo on the left breast. He gave a deferential bow. "Welcome to Shay Enterprises, Lady Griffin. Right this way, please." He waved her toward the maintenance bay.

Keeping her face expressionless, she moved where he directed. "I assume the Shays are in residence."

"Yes, ma'am. Lady Shay sends her greetings and waits for you above. If you will follow me?" He led her through a large bay filled with organized machinery and vessels in various states of repair. Standing out like dangerous black gems against this mundane backdrop lay a double row of Shadow slicers, their sleek gleaming lines drawing her eye.

She gave them a cursory study, ignoring the sharp looks and whispers of the people in attendance. Her escort didn't pause, continuing to the back of the bay and an unassuming portal. Beyond this, they entered a lift to rise a few levels. Liaena pondered the purpose of bringing her through the back door. Insult, discretion, or both?

They disembarked into a room she recognized from various descriptions, an opulent reception area called the Gold Rooms. Expensive art and sculpture, ornate furniture, and luxurious seating all arranged to saturate the senses and disarm visitors.

She'd expected this reception from the Shays, so when her escort continued through the room without pause, Liaena couldn't suppress a small frown. She smoothed it away, but her confusion couldn't be dismissed. Where was this man leading her? It looked like a corridor to private rooms.

Sinsudee Shay waited for them at the end of the corridor. Liaena pinned a cool smile on her face, ignoring the pang of disappointment in her middle. Better not to have Manakai here. He would disrupt…well, everything. He always did.

"Lady Shay, I present the Lady Liaena Griffin to see you," her escort announced with sleek formality.

"Thank you, Paul." Sin nodded dismissal to her subordinate, mouth curved in an enigmatic smile. "Aena, what a lovely surprise. Won't you come in?" She half-turned, inclining her head and gesturing toward the interior, her every movement brimming with the silky feminine grace Liaena had worked for years to emulate.

"Thank you for seeing me on such short notice," Liaena responded, giving her own nod to the escort before stepping over the threshold. *If ever there were a lion's den.* Or in this case, a lioness.

She entered prepared for anything but she should have known, should have remembered. The cryptic Shay twins forever did the unexpected. She hadn't stepped into a secluded meeting room or even a holding cell as she'd half-feared. She stood in someone's personal living space, simple and graceful, elegant and soothing.

Liaena stilled for a moment, containing her surprise, before turning her head to meet Sinsudee's gaze. "These are your private quarters?"

Sin's cat-green eyes gleamed with what might have been amusement. "Yes. Welcome to my home, Liaena Griffin." She led the way toward a comfortable arrangement of sofa and chairs. "I was having tea. May I offer you a cup?"

"Thank you, you're very gracious." Liaena hid her uncertainty in precise movements; lowering to a seat, tucking crossed ankles against the chair, and folding hands just so on her lap.

Sinsudee poured amber liquid from a quaint little teapot into a delicate-looking cup, her smile widening as she slanted her visitor a knowing glance. "You sound surprised. Didn't you expect me to be gracious, Aena?"

Liaena hadn't thought she'd done such a poor job of hiding it. "You have always been so, Sinsudee. I would expect nothing less of you." She accepted the tea, tipping her head in thanks and cupping it in both hands. "But given recent events, I didn't expect to be welcomed into your most private space."

Her hostess' expression turned dry. "Hmm, yes. Recent events." She settled on the sofa cushions and tucked her legs on the seat beside her, sweeping her cup off a stand and taking a meditative sip.

In the pause, this woman's impossible beauty struck Liaena again. She'd met other women as lovely in appearance, enhanced through artificial means. Sin seemed as natural and exquisite as a piece of living art, dark hair lying in shining blue-black waves over her shoulders, features fine-sculpted and elegant, eyes such an arresting bright green. Her real beauty lay in her casual confidence and fearless grace, her unconscious aura of power. Even in a relaxed state, in her informal cream blouse and slacks, she radiated thoughtless predatory control, magnetic and dangerous.

Her brother even more so.

Liaena had been struggling to match these twins for most of her life. In moments like this, she seemed far from the mark.

"Well, Aena, if you've come to play your father's game, receiving you like this instead of giving you all the flash and bang"—Sin gestured with a wry hand back toward the Gold Rooms—"should cause you some discomfort. To my advantage I'd think. If you're here on your own, this setting might make you more comfortable."

Also to your advantage. Liaena looked down at her tea. *But what if it's both*? Raising the cup, she took a careful sip; ginger, honey, and something else she couldn't name, sweet and spice in perfect balance. It warmed, soothed, and did in fact make her more comfortable. Lifting her gaze to her hostess, she murmured, "It's delightful, thank you."

"My pleasure," Sin answered with a quick smile. "Now please don't keep me in suspense. Why are you here, Liaena Griffin?"

Butterflies bloomed again in her stomach, and she took another sip of tea to quell them. The cup shivered from the tremor in her hand. *Games within games*. All of them dangerous. But to do nothing wasn't acceptable.

"How is Dr. Draegen?" Liaena asked, lowering the cup to the cradle of her hands.

Sinsudee's smile sharpened, eyes narrowing like a feline sighting prey in the distance. "Cassie's well enough, cultivating a healthy hatred for your father. Being the victim of kidnapping will do that to a person. She believes you assisted in her liberation. She seems to like you, Aena."

A warm glow of delight formed in Liaena's chest. She allowed a smile, remembering her interlude with the refreshing and forthright Cassiopeia Draegen. "The feeling is quite mutual. My father was wrong to take her, and I only did what I could to rectify the injustice."

"Injustice," Sin repeated with a flash of hard humor in her eyes. "What an interesting word for it. But let's move on. I don't think you've come all this way to check on Cassie's well-being."

Liaena set down her cup and linked her fingers together in her lap, heart beating too hard. "The incident with Dr. Draegen has made me aware of several things. One is how far my father will go, as you put it, to play his game with you. Another is how far you and your brother will go to protect what you care for." She paused. "I assume you care a great deal for Cassie."

Sin said nothing, studying Liaena with disconcerting cool intensity. Her expression revealed nothing of her thoughts, but Liaena's nerves twitched at her silence. The Shays had always been quick, clever, and perceptive, which made them worthy opponents for her father but turned Liaena's current position perilous.

To deflect her, Liaena jumped forward a bit in her rehearsed overture. "I want to help you stop my father."

Sinsudee's eyebrows lifted. "You want to help us stop Webster Griffin," she said in a flat disbelieving tone. "Why?"

For a moment, the direct question held her immobile, frozen at the center of a storm of reasons to put an end to her father's reign. She drew in a slow breath to ease the pressure in her chest and focused on the one reason meaning the most to her. The one she was almost sure would gain their cooperation. "Because he has my mother."

She tried to remain alert to Sin's reaction, but saying it out loud after so many years of concealing her despair and worry almost shattered her. She looked down at her clasped hands, the knuckles turning white, and fought the bubble of emotion rising in her throat, either a sob or a hysterical laugh. She closed her eyes and pictured the fountain, drawing in those strong enduring lines with each breath.

"Your mother," Sinsudee said in a low voice. "I wasn't aware she was still alive."

Liaena waited until her voice steadied before lifting her head. "He keeps her in seclusion for her protection." She put more acid than she'd planned into the last word and paused to regain her poise, swallowing hard to rid her mouth of the taste of bile. She met Sin's gaze. True compassion softened those lovely features, startling her and sparking an almost painful gratitude.

Belief opened like a fragile flower, spreading tingling warmth over her skin. "I was hoping," she breathed like a prayer and trembled with it, "you would help me free her."

The Shay twins had lost their mother to despair; she'd ended her own life. They'd made it plain they blamed Webster Griffin for her death, before they learned how to emulate their father's discretion. When younger, Liaena hadn't understood why they blamed her father. When she did, fear for her own mother had turned her world to dust.

"In return," she tumbled on faster than she'd meant to in this sudden rush of emotion, "I will assist you however I can in your campaign against my father. As his daughter, I have access to many aspects of his business. I can and will open the very heart of Quasicore for you in exchange for my mother's safety and freedom. Sinsudee—" She snapped her mouth shut, clenching her jaw to stop herself from begging. So much more painful than she'd imagined, more difficult than she'd rehearsed. What would she do if they said no?

Sin surged to her feet, startling Liaena. She paced, measuring the room in a restless prowl, tension in the angles of her face. "You're offering to be our spy. You know how this sounds, Aena."

Liaena nodded with quiet acceptance. "You've

seen me as my father's instrument for so long. It's hard to imagine I would act against him. This looks like a ploy, another gambit in my father's game. But I know something he does not. Something he can't see, could never understand. I know, Sinsudee, for you this is no game. You are in deadly earnest. My father is a force that must be stopped. Let me help you."

Sin paused, studying Liaena again with a penetrating gaze, as if she could see through her skull into every thought and dream Liaena had ever had. "Aena," she said in an ominous tone, "when in the Sun's name are you going to start calling me Sin?"

Liaena blinked then cleared her throat, the skin over her cheekbones prickling with an unexpected blush. How did they always do this? Unpredictable and nimble, Sin and her brother ran rings around her. She could only go still and wait for the whirlwind to pass.

Sin's chin lifted and her gaze darted over Liaena's shoulder. Liaena's stomach muscles tightened with renewed anxiety. She had a horrible suspicion the whirlwind had just begun.

"What the hell is this?" A deep voice sliced through the serenity of Sin's home.

Liaena closed her eyes a moment to brace herself before turning to face Manakai Shay. As always, his impact drove through her all the way to her toes.

The dark scowl on his face underscored his dangerous good looks. With his careless toss of thick black hair, features as strong and handsome as a poet's dream, those devastating green eyes, and long lean body, he could put every male model in the galaxy out of business. Add his aura of predatory power and the man could make any female forget her own name.

He stalked toward them like a panther about to pounce, his gaze fixed on Liaena with narrow ferocity. He reminded her of an oncoming storm, dressed all in black like the last time she'd seen him, when he'd threatened to make her his hostage. She couldn't suppress a shiver of anticipation.

"Kai!" Sin barked, sharper than Liaena had ever heard her speak to her brother. Her voice lowered to steel and warning. "You will not be rude to a guest in my home."

He came to a sudden halt, gaze snapping to his sister. Something in her expression made an impact. He visibly reset, expression cooling as his gaze swung back to Liaena. When he advanced again, circling the seating arrangement, he still moved like a wildcat on the hunt. "Sorry, Sissa. Kneejerk reaction. When a Griffin shows up, you know, after they've kidnapped one of our own"—his voice dropped to a silky growl—"I get testy. How've you been, Lie?"

The callous play on her name still cut, even after all these years. A foolish and childish reaction but she couldn't help it. She'd never lied to them. She couldn't blame them for putting her in the same mold as her father, however. She'd done nothing to show otherwise, until now.

Putting aside the hurt, she focused on the reason behind his hostility. Once again proof they felt more for their people than any typical employer. Cassie had called them family. Manakai had risked his life to pluck the little doctor out of Webster's clutches. If capable of this much emotion, they might be moved to rescue her mother.

"Manakai," she murmured in cool greeting,

ignoring her racing heart. "I apologize for dropping in unannounced. If my presence is unwelcome, perhaps you would be amenable—"

He cut her off with a low snarling curse, dropping into a chair at the opposite end of the sofa. "Suns, woman, get the stick out of your rump before you hurt something."

"Kai." Sin sighed. "I'm sorry, Aena, we're going to have to cut this visit short, as my brother is being an insufferable jackass. When he gets over his foul mood and is slightly less obnoxious, rude, pig-headed, and offensive, I'll relay your proposal."

"What proposal?" Manakai asked with a frown. "And you forgot 'irritating.' "

"No, I didn't," Sin retorted, shooting him a disgruntled look. "I just don't have all day to list your sterling qualities."

His expression lightened, as if amused by his sister's insults and censure. Stretching out his legs and crossing his ankles, he rested his head against the seat. "Point taken. What proposal?"

Perplexed by the sibling exchange and unsettled by Manakai's smoldering stare, Liaena decided a retreat was in order. "I believe I'll let Sin explain. My time here is—"

He sat forward in an abrupt movement, startling her to silence. "Wait a minute. Did you call her Sin?" He shot an accusing look at his sister. "What did you do to her?"

"Water torture," Sin replied with a straight face. "Brainwashing with a bit of caning thrown in."

"So that's what it takes," he drawled, gaze returning to Liaena with scary glittering speculation.

She was almost sure they were kidding. But not one hundred percent. Clearing her throat, she rose to her feet with enough caution not to startle the predators in the room. "Thank you for your time and the wonderful tea. Shall I show myself out?"

"That stick has got to chafe," Manakai mused.

Sin ignored him, smiling at Liaena, putting a gentle hand on her arm, and guiding her toward the exit. "Paul will be waiting to show you back to your transport. Kai and I will talk, think on what you said, and get back to you. I'm glad you came, Aena. We should do this again. Maybe without the fate of the galaxy hanging in the balance?" Her eyes sparkled with warmth and amusement, mouth curled in a mischievous smile.

With an inner despairing sigh, Liaena responded to the irresistible Shay charm, lips curving in reluctant answer. "That would be lovely," she said and stepped away before she broke down and begged to stay.

"I'll bake you cookies next time." Sin's voice was light with humor.

Glancing over her shoulder with the smallest of smirks and a lifted eyebrow, she quipped, "You bake?"

Sin chuckled and stepped back into her home, the door closing between them with a quiet swish.

Aena stared at the barrier for a moment, caught in a wave of melancholy. She did want to stay. Though they distrusted her and often made her prickle with discomfort, they still put more color and life in the world than anything she experienced in her own home. Correction, in her father's home. For her, home was an island with an endless beach and her mother's warm smile.

She turned away, found her escort Paul waiting in

21

the Gold Rooms, and followed him down to her transport. After giving the pilot quiet instructions, she settled in her seat, closed her eyes, and relived the meeting in her mind. Very little of it had gone according to plan. She hadn't had a chance to go into detail, but at least she'd given Sinsudee the basics. What would they do?

Worrying over their response and trying to ignore nerves rubbed raw by Manakai's hostility, she waited on the edge of fitful sleep until the com chimed an imperious demand. Sighing, she straightened and accepted the incoming transmission.

Her father's stern face appeared on the viewer, eyes as gray as her own studying her with clinical chill. "You were faster than expected. What is the result?"

"They accepted my offer," she lied without a qualm. "As you predicted, Father. My assistance of the doctor's escape paved the way. They believed my horror at your actions, my plea to make what reparations I can for our family honor. The Shays now believe I am working for them."

"Well done, Daughter. I expect a full report on your return."

She bowed her head in demure submission. "Yes, Father."

Chapter 2

"You've lost your mind," Kai snarled at his sister, pacing around her living room. Her quarters seemed much too small all of a sudden.

"You aren't thinking straight. Which is why I saw her alone." Sin gave him a pointed look, driving another needle of irritation under his skin.

"I'm thinking plenty straight. She's a Griffin."

"She's not Webster."

"She's his puppet and you know it. Sun and Stars, you didn't tell me she was coming, you let her into our home—"

"Hello, you don't live here."

"—gave her Suns-damned tea, listened to all the krell dung she spewed. Then you let her leave. What the hell, Sin?"

"You'd prefer I took her hostage?"

He paused and scowled at her, not liking the patient humor on her face. "Yes. Sun's sake, you said you'd bake her cookies."

"I was kidding. I don't bake. Take a deep breath, Brother, and think. You know she always does this to you."

He spun away, aggravated. Liaena did always do this to him, but he didn't have to admit it. "Just tell me you didn't buy into her little fairytale."

"It doesn't matter what I believe. Whether she's

telling the truth or trying to play us, our answer should be the same. We can't pass up an opportunity like this, Kai. If Web is pulling her strings, we can feed her the same lies we feed all his spies. Keep your friends close, your enemies closer, and so on."

He snorted, leaning against the back of her sofa and folding his arms across his chest. "Holding her hostage would've kept her plenty close."

"And what would Webster Griffin do then? We aren't ready for full-scale war."

"Taking his bonded will set him off too."

"Not if he doesn't know it was us."

He made a rough sound in his throat. "If he even suspects—"

"So we make sure he doesn't. Seriously, Kai. She's dropping a gold mine in our lap. Even if she tells us nothing useful, we can use her to play him. There is no downside to this."

Yes, there is. He remembered cool silver-shot eyes. "It's a risk."

"Everything we do is a risk."

He shot a black look over his shoulder. "A risk we don't have to take. We don't need her."

She pursed her lips, assessing him with far too much knowledge in her eyes.

He looked away again in self-defense.

"Every advantage must be taken, no quarter given, or all will be lost," she murmured and he winced. She was quoting their father.

"Don't do that, Sinsi," he rasped, voice raw.

"I'm sorry."

At the honest contrition in her voice, he sighed. "Fine, but you take point. I don't want to deal with her."

"As much as I can. You need to at least apologize. You were bloody awful. Her opinion of you has to have dropped to a new low."

He clenched his jaw. "She took me by surprise."

"Yes, she does that a lot." She chuckled. "It's one of the things I like best about her."

Since his twin felt it was time to start poking at him instead of sparing his feelings, he muttered a curse and headed for the exit.

"Have a good night, brother mine," she called after him in a lilting tone, poking at him again. She knew how his night would be. He'd never discussed this particular problem with her, but as twins they could almost read each other's minds.

Grumbling about evil unsupportive sisters, he made his way across the Gold Rooms to the lift, debated for half a second, and then keyed it to rise. He could go down, take out his Shadow, and seek solace in the slicer's power and speed. But lately even his Shadow hadn't helped. Instead, he rose to the very top of the station, to the enormous atrium and his secluded quarters beyond it.

He didn't go to his home. His companion artificial intelligence, Basher, would have heard all about their visitor by now from Sin's resident AI, Mina. Bash would have something to say about it, and Kai needed solitude.

Moving through the lush greenhouse and arboretum with a prowling stride, he headed for the pool at its center, shaped to resemble a small lake in a woodland landscape. Arching above, the atrium's apex appeared to open into space, providing a stunning vista of velvet blackness and dancing stars. Kai gave the view only a cursory glance, stripping his clothes with rough speed.

Then he dove in, cleaving through the cool dark water like an arrow. He swam with deliberate intensity, working his body hard and trying to blank his mind. Trying to escape cool gray eyes. As usual, he didn't succeed. After a long while, muscles humming from the workout, he slowed and rolled over, floating in the water and staring at the vast expanse of sparkling stars above him.

With grudging admission, he faced what had chased him here to this quiet natural sanctuary. Or rather who. Liaena Griffin, daughter of their arch enemy, their opposition, his nemesis. And his secret obsession for as long as he could remember.

Stupid and useless to crave something he could never have. He'd cursed the obsession as senseless yet reacted every time he laid eyes on her, to his everlasting humiliation and misery. Thank the Suns his sister had stopped him from putting his hands on her this time, or Liaena's visit would have ended in disaster. Wouldn't Griffin have been delighted to have a Shay dangling on his hook?

Kai grimaced at the stars, aware of how easy it would be if Liaena ever made a real effort to seduce him. But she was the Ice Queen, always glacial and remote, thank the Stars for small favors. Neither Griffin seemed aware of his weakness. If Liaena suspected, she either didn't care enough to pursue it or found the idea repulsive. She stayed cold enough toward him. Webster often used his daughter to distract Kai but in a general sort of way. Any red-blooded male would find Liaena distracting.

He blew out a hard breath, unable to avoid the image of Liaena watching him with those silvery eyes, lovely face serene, fire-kissed mahogany hair captured in some complex weave at the back of her head, leaving her graceful neck bare. She'd been wearing a deep forest green today, enhancing the smooth cream of her skin, the businesslike suit hinting at a long sleek taunt of curving female perfection.

She seemed a maddening contradiction between ice and fire; cool eyes, warm hair, remote smile on lips shaped like pure sin. She could sit marble-still one moment and move like liquid silk the next, stealing his breath. Heat lurked somewhere under her cold exterior. He'd seen it and wished he hadn't. If cold permeated her through and through, maybe he wouldn't be so fixated. She might act like perfect ice, but her pulse tripped whenever he touched her.

He'd lived with it and dealt with it, avoiding her as much as possible and touching her as little as possible when he couldn't avoid her. He'd sought pleasure and companionship with other women to their mutual satisfaction. If a large percentage of them happened to be redheads, so what? He'd thought he was coping.

Until he'd stormed in to rescue Cassie and found Liaena by her side, cool as a breeze but with a new curve to her lips, a new light in her eyes, bright and unflinching. They'd never met in such a circumstance, only seeing each other at polite social events. He'd expected her to show some kind of distress, seeing him without a civilized veneer, realizing him capable of real violence. She'd been utterly unafraid, absorbing his furious energy with astounding calm. Even when he'd captured her wrist, anchoring her in place, her calm never wavered. She'd quivered in his hold, pulse leaping under his fingers, the light in her eyes flashing silver like heat lightning. Fearless anticipation.

He'd nearly stolen her then and there.

With a harsh sound, he smacked the flat of his hands on the water, sending a wave rolling away from him. So now his Achilles heel pretended a change of heart. Had she finally seen it in him? Or was this a horrible coincidence?

Kai flipped, diving down into the cool depths. The silky rush of the water, dark and heavy, set his mind on another path. His Red Sun teacher, T'Zai, had said they were reaching a focal point and Webster Griffin was making preparations. Liaena's proposal might be a diversionary tactic in some major offensive, Griffin using his daughter to blind them and sway them.

Screw it. Releasing a stream of bubbles, Kai shot to the surface and struck out for the shore, tired of worrying at it like a dog on a bone. Lunging out of the water, he stalked naked and dripping to his quarters. He greeted his AI as he stepped over the threshold. "Bash."

"Kai." His house companion's smooth baritone filled the room, threaded with mild amusement. "Did you lose your clothes again?"

"Mmm." Kai paused, running rough fingers through his hair to shake out water. "I need to do some work. Pull up whatever I was doing on my office unit today, would you?"

"How odd. I would swear it was someone's bedtime. My chronometer must be busted."

"I'll bust you one if you don't zip it," Kai responded without force, wandering into the san for a towel.

"Would this lack of charisma and sudden unseemly work ethic have anything to do with our recent delightful visitor?"

"Would this be your large helping of 'shut the hell up'? I do believe it is. Take as much as you want."

Basher chuckled, but it wouldn't be so easy to silence his friend. On a normal day Kai enjoyed their sharp banter. He didn't have the energy for it tonight, though.

Stepping out of the san, he ran the towel over his skin and waited for Bash's next salvo, staring out the window. It showed a holographic recreation of a peaceful pond, complete with a dock and wooden rowboat. The view complemented the interior of his home, a detailed reproduction of a log cabin, some real material, some holographic, the overall atmosphere warm and comforting, soothing after a long day.

"I don't have a taste for it now," Basher responded.

Puzzled, Kai tilted his head then remembered, *Right, large helping of shut the hell up.* No, he wasn't sharp enough to hold his own with Bash tonight.

"Griffin's daughter looked exceptionally tempting, don't you think?"

Kai fisted one hand in the towel and pinched the bridge of his nose with the other, trying to remember why he even had an AI living with him.

When he didn't answer, Basher tried another shot. "It sounds as though you'll be seeing quite a bit more of her now. Such a chore, spending time with—"

"Hey, Bash," Kai barked, tossing the towel back in the san with an aggressive flick of his wrist. "Sounds like you need an overhaul. I'll get Cass right on it, scour you good inside and out."

"Shutting the hell up now," Basher said in a meek tone.

"Smart boy." Kai stalked into his bedroom to snag a pair of lounge pants before striding into his home office, a room he avoided most of the time. He sat at his tidy desk and called up the day's workload on his viewer. If it didn't numb his brain and put him to sleep in under an hour, he was a lost cause.

He answered memos and jotted some of his own, signed off on a few requests from requisitions and accounting, and approved a new contract for the courier service. His mind kept circling back to where he didn't want it to go until he cussed under his breath and opened the Griffin files. He searched for anything they had on Liaena's mother, Zofie Griffin.

Her dossier seemed surprisingly slim. He would've expected his father to put the bond-mate of his arch enemy under careful scrutiny, assessing her potential as either a threat, weapon, or asset. The reports detailed her life early on, from her upbringing in a family of relative wealth to her political Sun-bonding to Griffin. Quasicore had been in its infancy then, but like all baby monsters, it grew fast and Griffin's influence grew with it. Zofie's family must have felt it necessary to appease this rising power with their daughter.

Subsequent reports of her painted a picture of a devoted docile accessory on Griffin's arm, at least in public. He found little documentation about the couple's private life. From all appearances, Zofie knew almost nothing of Webster Griffin's business dealings, her role in his life consigned to mere decoration.

Shortly after Liaena's birth, she and her mother

disappeared from the public eye and from Ezekiel Shay's covert sources. When Liaena returned to her father's side, Zofie did not accompany her. Kai's father had assumed Griffin had rid himself of a pawn outliving its usefulness, which would have been typical of their enemy's normal pattern of behavior. If Liaena had told the truth and her mother still lived, why had Griffin kept her hidden away all these years?

Kai called up a holographic image of Zofie Griffin and drew in a sharp breath. Lovely and appealing, she had a warm smile and sad eyes. She looked far too much like her daughter for his peace of mind. Liaena had taken after her mother in all but the color of her eyes and the more regal lines of her face, characteristics she'd inherited from her father.

"Bash, did Mina pass you a record of Liaena's visit?"

His AI chuckled. "Of course she did. We had bets going on how long it would take you to ask for it. You held out longer than either of us thought you would."

Kai scowled at the nearest sensor. "Watch it, pal, or I'll tune you up to a falsetto. Just play the thing."

Zofie's holo-still melted into an image of Liaena crossing Sin's threshold, cool as always but wary. Kai absorbed the visit, working to remain analytical, to see her only as their opponent. It should've been easier without the distraction of her light scent and gray eyes looking right through him, but somehow it wasn't.

She didn't follow her typical patterns. Hints of uncertainy and stress marred her familiar cool containment. She spoke to Sin without her usual veneer of distancing ice, and when they discussed Cassie, the new curve to her lips appeared again, furtive delight.

His stomach muscles tightened in response, and he breathed out slowly through clenched teeth, fighting to see the motive behind this new act. It fit Cassie's description of her time with Griffin's daughter, a subtly altered Liaena, reserve tempered with cultivated warmth. These overtures must be part of a grander plan, a prelude to a strategy of distraction and misdirection. Griffin wasn't so indirect, but maybe he sensed the Shays closing on him.

Kai curled his lip in a sneer when Liaena offered in such an earnest voice to help them stop her father. Then she said, "Because he has my mother," soft, broken, and genuine. Her reserve cracked in a flash of anguish, stabbing through his chest like a blade of ice. No wonder Sin had leaned toward belief. If Liaena was acting, she'd given the greatest performance of the millennium. He owed his sister an apology.

With a clenched jaw and bitter taste in his throat, he watched Liaena push for an alliance and hated her a little. Whatever genuine concerns she had for her mother, she used it to work them, to net them into whatever game she and her father were playing.

Kai watched his own entrance and winced. No wonder Sin had barked at him. Talk about obvious. He'd handed Aena ammunition, but she didn't look triumphant or calculating. She looked unsettled. His sister had called it; he really had been a jackass.

With a grimace, he flicked a glance at Bash's sensor. "Play it back with vitals, please."

This time his AI didn't comment, the hologram flickering and restarting with an overlay of physiological readings. It invaded privacy, and Mina wouldn't have scanned Liaena's vital signs without her permission unless Sin had required it as an infallible lie detector test. Kai watched again, disturbed when the readings reinforced her words and actions.

When he reentered the room on the holo, his readings flashing like a neon sign of hormonal stupidity, Kai caught his breath and went still. Liaena's heart leapt and raced, reacting to him with an intensity matching his own.

He swore through his teeth and killed the holo. Bounding to his feet, he measured the room with a prowling stride, trying to think around the fist of need in his gut. It changed nothing. She was still a Griffin, still playing her father's games of power and manipulation. He agreed with his sister; no matter what Liaena's motives they couldn't pass up this opportunity. They couldn't afford for him to think with his hormones.

Liaena Griffin courted an alliance, so he and his sister needed to play along, succumb and seduce in turn. They had their own endgame to play and needed to exploit every weakness and distraction to keep Griffin busy. *Every advantage taken, no quarter given.*

Blowing out a hard breath, Kai stalked back to his desk and sat, considering his options; overtures and apologies. A simple note wouldn't cut it. If they played this game, he needed more imagination.

"Never let it be said," he muttered, reaching for the com, "I can't play nice."

Kai contacted their favorite sculpting artist and commissioned a gift.

Chapter 3

"She did what?" Cassie goggled at Sin as if she'd announced all the Suns had gone out. "Liaena came here?" Her eyes widened and her head swung toward Kai. "Oh Stars, did you see her?"

"Yes, he did," Sin answered for him, mouth curling in furtive amusement.

Cassie didn't take her gaze off Kai, her features radiating mild horror. "Sun's blood. You locked her in your dungeon, didn't you?"

Kai lifted his eyebrows. "Nice embellishment, Cass. I don't have a dungeon, at least not one I'll admit to."

Sin snickered. "Liaena escaped without a scratch."

"Wow." Cassie took a sip of her coffee, glancing around Sin's quarters as if looking for traces of Griffin's daughter. "So what did she want?"

"She wants us to rescue her mother. In exchange, she'll spy on her father for us."

Cassie stared at Sin with her mouth hanging open. After a few seconds, she shook her head. "No, you're selling me a load of krell dung. What did she really want?"

"No doubt about it, you're a smart one, Cass," Kai drawled, flashing her a grin when she sent him a quelling frown.

Sin smirked behind her own coffee mug. "What

she really wants is a mystery. She seemed genuinely concerned for her mother, but I don't believe she could come here without Griffin's knowledge and approval. For now we'll assume she's her father's mouthpiece. We'd like you to go over the holo of her visit. Use your genius brain and psyche degree to analyze her behavior. She seemed, well, different."

"A-ha!" Cassie pointed her cup at the two of them, sloshing coffee on the counter in the process. "I told you. You didn't believe me when I said she was acting strange for a Griffin."

"You'd been kidnapped. I figured it was the trauma talking." Sin tossed a napkin over the spill without glancing at it. Cassie often talked with her hands, no matter what was in them.

Cassie lifted her chin and straightened on her stool, staring down her nose at them in mock affront. "I am a highly trained professional. I resent your implication I could be susceptible to such distractions."

Kai snorted and Sin lifted an amused eyebrow.

Cassie deflated. "Okay, fine. I was a little traumatized. But not by Liaena's part in it. Why is she worried about her mother?"

"Again, not sure. Here." Sin skidded a holo disc across the counter to her with a challenging gleam in her eyes. "Prelim exam and diagnosis, Doc?"

Cassie started the playback of Liaena's visit, taking meditative sips of her coffee as she watched. When Liaena pleaded for her mother's rescue, Cassie jolted, setting her cup down. At Kai's entrance, she made a squeaking sound and caught herself at the edge of her stool, sending him a quick startled glance.

Kai folded his arms and said nothing, keeping his

expression blank with an effort. He hadn't wanted to let Cass see his part in yesterday's fiasco, but they could use her analysis of Liaena. He'd have to suck it up and deal with the invasion of privacy.

When the holo finished, Cassie looked between them and blurted, "Holy crap."

Sin snickered and snagged Cassie's cup, refilling it from the warmer. "There's our highly trained genius." She handed over the drink with a wry look. "Any other riveting insights, Dr. Draegen?"

"Kai, you, um." Cassie pointed at the disc and fell silent, as if hunting for a discreet description for what she'd seen.

Kai narrowed his eyes, muscles tightening. "I what?"

"N-nothing." Cassie's wide gaze slid away.

Sin held up a hand. "Let's focus on Liaena. Your impressions, Cass?"

Cassie leaned on her elbows and laced her fingers together, staring at the disc with a faint frown. "If I didn't know she was a Griffin and if I didn't know I'd get an earful from you about being too trusting and gullible, I'd say she's in trouble. She's under stress, afraid for herself or her mother or both. I wish I had more detailed readings. Mina, did you do a full medical scan?"

"I'm sorry, Cassie dear, I did not," Mina answered with warm regret.

Cassie patted the air as if soothing the AI. "It's all right, Mina. The record you did get tells me plenty."

Sin made a humming sound and grinned at Cassie. "My own house companion loves you more than me. It's so cute how they all dote on you."

Cassie lifted her chin again. "Every AI on this station has excellent taste." When they made identical disbelieving sounds, she added, "Also, I keep them in top condition. So you know, love thy doctor and whatnot. Back to Liaena. I'll study this holo in more detail but prelim impression is she's telling the truth. What are you going to do?"

"We'll dance with her a bit, get more information. We weren't even aware her mother was still alive. We'll want to know more."

A sound came from the hallway to the back rooms.

Sin turned her head in a listening posture, her face softening and glowing with warm intimacy. "Hmm, I think we woke someone."

Sin's lover and soon-to-be Sun-bonded shuffled into the room in nothing but his sleeping shorts, face scrunched in a disgruntled squint. Rubbing the heel of one hand against an eye like a grumpy eight-year-old, Del mumbled something. Kai caught a couple of cusses plus the words early and coffee, and he smothered a laugh. This big man used to be an enforcer for the Core, dealing out pain and misery to any poor sap who'd crossed the line. Hard to imagine now, seeing him all sleep-fuddled and morning-cranky.

Cassie clapped a hand over her mouth, muffling a giggle. "Good morning, Del," she managed around her hand. "Can we get you some coffee?"

Del squinted at her like she'd turned into an alien fungus. He grunted and glowered, rubbing rough fingers through his short dark hair.

Sin chuckled, slipping off her stool. "Hang on. He needs to wake up." Sauntering over to Del, she slid a hand around the back of his neck and molded her mouth to his.

"That's just nasty," Kai muttered.

Cassie leaned over the counter and gave him an admonitory swat on the arm, but the two lovers seemed oblivious.

The grumpy eight-year-old grew up fast. Del's arms wrapped around Sin, pressing her close with a much more agreeable rumble in his throat. When she leaned back, he gave her a heated grin. "Now it's a good morning."

Sin chuckled and slipped out of his arms. "The man's officially awake. Now you can talk to him."

"Nice shorts, Giv," Kai commented with a smirk.

"Bite me." Del scrubbed a hand through his hair again and headed for the coffee carafe. "It's like what-the-hell o'clock. Why are we up?"

"Because torturing us is fun for them," a new voice answered from across the room. Nick Givliani, Del's brother and the Shays' liaison to the Federated Planetary Alliance, strolled in from the entrance. He paused, giving his brother's outfit a dubious look. "Nice shorts, bro."

Del sent a sour glance from Nick to Kai. "I'll get you both a pair," he drawled, toasting them with his coffee.

Kai shared a grin with the young inspector.

Nick sat on the stool next to Cassie and leaned close to her, expression heating. "Missed you, little dragon," he murmured in a low husky tone, brushing his mouth against hers.

Cassie melted toward him, her face radiant. "Tell me good morning."

He smiled like a wolf and kissed her again, slower

and deeper.

Kai turned a disgusted glance on his sister. "What is this, Make Kai Sick Day?"

She rolled her eyes and gave him a nudge with her elbow, eyeing the gooey pair with an indulgent smug smile, as if she were responsible for them getting together. How disturbing. His sister had never before exhibited matchmaking tendencies.

He turned back to Cass and Nick. They stared at one another as if alone in the universe, so much in love it nauseated him.

"Quit it," Del growled at them, clunking a mug of coffee in front of his brother. "Or go in the other room or something. What's this?" He gave the holo disc a suspicious poke.

"Our Sun-bonding contract," Sin answered with a sly grin.

Del flinched and she snickered.

"Just kidding. It's Liaena's visit. Cass was giving us her impressions."

Nick frowned. "Liaena who?"

"Liaena Griffin, Webster Griffin's daughter," Cassie answered, grinning at his thunderstruck expression.

"His daughter came here? What for?"

"When we figure it out we'll let you know, Inspector." Kai snagged the disc off the counter and tucked it in his pocket. Then he turned an expectant look on Sin. "Where's breakfast?"

"Waiting right here for you to cook it," she answered, patting the food storage unit.

He nodded, rolling up his sleeves. "Smart, waiting for the expert."

"Sure, the expert braggart, expert complainer, expert pain in my—"

Kai bumped his sister out of the way with a growl.

Shaking his head, Del escaped around the counter and sat next to his brother while Kai and Sin worked their magic in the kitchen. Creating a row of spicy omelets with swift artistic efficiency, he and his sister chatted in their usual cryptic exchange Cassie often called twin-speak. Del drank his coffee and ignored them. Nick stared at them with a pained expression, as if trying to understand but falling short. Cassie watched breakfast being born with gratifying anticipation. She hadn't been eating well, and Kai approved of her expressing an appetite. She'd been focusing too much attention on AIs and not taking care of herself.

Speaking of AIs, they could use an update. "What's the word from the lab, Cass?"

Cassie heaved a sigh, pushing her cup away and leaning on folded arms. "Nothing good. I told Marchand to send them all here. Every infected AI and the whole Federated Planetary Alliance lab staff. Consulting from a distance isn't working."

Nick's head swiveled, eyebrows shooting up. "You told Marchand? You gave the head of the FPA, my boss, an order?"

"Well, he asked for my help. This is how I can help. Somebody infected those AIs with a modified code of the virus I created. I have to see what it's done to them." She paused with a pained frown. "I have to be there for them. Since you all grounded me and I'm not allowed to leave the station ever again in this lifetime—"

"Does she seem sulky to you?" Kai interrupted.

"Funny," Sin answered in a drawl, "wasn't she the one duped into running off and getting herself stolen?"

Cassie sat back with a sour grimace, folding her arms across her chest and glancing at Nick.

He twitched a shoulder and gave her a sympathetic half-smile. "Pretty sure they're gonna hold that one over you 'til the end of time, Cass."

"Count on it," Del rumbled, leaning past his brother to level a reproachful frown on their resident genius. He'd been caught in the crossfire when she was taken. He didn't look ready to forgive her for it yet.

Cassie's cheeks reddened, and she looked down at the smooth surface of the counter. "Anyway, I'm the best chance those AIs have for recovery. They need me. Plus they're our best lead for finding Imago." She flinched as if saying his name aloud pained her. Pulling her braid over her shoulder, she began yanking on it. "Maybe they can help me make up for what I've done."

"Don't you take that on yourself," Sin snapped, pointing a utensil at her friend, green eyes flashing with righteous fire. "Don't you take what Imago did away from him either. The FPA followed his signal to the lab. His signal saved the other AIs." She brandished the utensil and almost smacked Kai in the face with it.

He twitched it out of her grip with mild irritation and flipped the omelets, ignoring her continued tirade.

"We made the call to send him in there, not you. Stop blaming yourself for not being able to fix him. You didn't infect him with the code."

"No," Cassie responded in a low defeated voice. "I didn't infect him. I created the only known virus circumventing an AI's hardwired safety laws, driving them insane. I made it possible to weaponize artificial intelligence. I deserve blame."

When Kai and his sister shot her dual black frowns, she pointed a finger at each in turn. "And I don't want to hear anything from you two about taking responsibility for other people's actions. You're like the king and queen of associative guilt."

Del's laughter rumbled through the kitchen, Nick chuckling right along with him.

Kai shared a look of wry tolerance with his sister. "I'm feeling picked upon."

"Me too." Sin sighed with a sly gleam in her eyes. "Makes me not want to share. How about you?"

"Dibs on these three omelets. You can have the rest."

"Deal."

"Aw, come on," Nick complained. "The fire breather slammed you, not us. My stomach is totally innocent of all charges."

"Traitor," Cassie accused, poking Nick in the side.

He flashed her a grin and a wink, capturing her hand and bringing it to his mouth. "You're my heart and soul, Cass, but a guy's gotta eat and these two cook like fiends."

For this compliment, Kai relented and dished out the meal, keeping an eye on their undernourished braincase. He frowned when she only stared at her omelet and twitched as if her skin itched all over.

Cassie sighed and slipped off the stool. "Sorry, I need to go. I have to make sure everything's ready for the AIs' arrival."

"Cass, you need to eat," Nick protested, brows pinched together.

"The lab's stocked with munchies. I'll be fine," she

muttered and bolted before they could call her on the lie.

Chapter 4

In Webster Griffin's administration center, Liaena sat beside her father with her best remote mask in place while he received his daily updates over the viewers. He'd said he wanted her aware of the workings of their company, but Liaena believed he liked an audience.

She tuned out the routine updates, mind chasing its own worries, fixed on her meeting with the Shays. *What will they do? Mother, I'm sorry. I think I failed you.*

A chime at the door turned them both from the viewers. With a flick of his hand, Webster darkened the screens, cutting off the images of his subordinates. "Enter," he said in the same tone as a judge would say, "Death sentence."

Her father despised interruptions unless he'd planned them himself. His displeasure sharpened her interest. Anything making him unhappy might be useful.

One of Webster's assistants stepped through the entrance, his head lowered and shoulders hunched. In his hands sat a small package. "Sir, my apologies for intruding. A courier just made an urgent delivery from Shay Enterprises. Your standing order regarding missives from the Shays—"

"Yes, yes," her father interrupted. "I assume it passed all security checks. Bring it here."

The man crossed the room with alacrity, offering the package to his boss. "Sir, it's addressed to Liaena Griffin from Manakai Shay." He bowed and scurried for the exit.

With a slight lift of his eyebrows, Webster looked from the box in his hand to Liaena. "Daughter?" Ice rimmed his voice.

Her pulse had begun to race, but she disciplined her expression to show nothing. "I don't know, Father. We didn't discuss how we would exchange information."

"He sent this openly. If they are ignorant of my involvement in your dealings with them, why would they send anything I would intercept?"

She gave her suspicious father a cool smile. "They know you are too clever and observant not to know my whereabouts at all times. We also didn't discuss what reason I would give you for visiting them. Perhaps they're sending something to cover for me, to distract you. We won't know until we open it." She held out her hand, palm up, and quirked an expectant eyebrow.

His eyes narrowed and mouth tightened. He didn't hide his loathing for her small rebellions, but she knew the line to tread between defiance and subservience. With an icy smile, he placed the box on her palm.

Liaena stared at it, heart thumping. What in Stars would Manakai Shay be sending her? A security field cushioned the object to protect it during transport, and she touched the tiny control disc to release the field. The obscuring glow of the field disappeared, revealing a smooth wooden box, the polished ornate container a work of art. The hinges and clasp invited her to open it.

When she lifted the lid and saw the small sculpture

inside, she stared for a moment in confusion. Then the corners of her mouth turned up before she could stop them.

"What is it?" her father asked in a sharp tone.

Tucked in the cushioned interior of the box, the statue steamed like ice. The figure had four hoofed feet, kicking out its back two, its long face comically stretched in equine tantrum, teeth bare and ears flopping. A hee-hawing donkey, perhaps, or a jackass.

Liaena pinched her lips together for a moment, crushing the urge to smile. Manakai Shay, forever doing the unexpected. His sister had called him a jackass. Was this an obscure apology then?

"What insult is this?" Webster hissed, leaning forward with a dark frown.

"I'm touched by your concern for my honor, Father." She spoke softly enough to take the sarcasm out of her words. "But this is no insult."

Something inside the statue caught her eye, a flash of muted color at the heart of the absurd little donkey. Curious, she scooped the figure out of its cushion, then started and almost dropped it when the ice statue flash-melted at her touch. Left with a mini fog bank around her hand and a small weight on her palm, Liaena waved the remains of the jackass away.

She stared at the object lying in the cradle of her palm, going very still. It was shaped like a flame and made of clear crystal, elusive warm color shifting in its depths, at its heart. The sculptor had created a beautiful delicate piece. The crystal's cool weight warmed on her skin. "Oh," she breathed and for the first time in her life forgot her father's presence.

She'd received jewelry and objects her father

deemed necessary for appearances and control. They hadn't been gifts. But this small crystal sculpture with secret fire inside was a gift in every sense of the word. She stared at it and everything inside her crumbled, chest constricting and throat closing, fine tremors running through her.

The flame shivered on her palm in response, flashing color. Voicing a wordless murmur, she stroked it with a fingertip. At her touch, soft music rose from the crystal, mellow instrumental chords weaving a simple pensive tune. Captivated, she tilted her head and listened, the music sinking into her like sunshine.

"System, title and composer of this music."

Her father's hard voice slapped her back to reality. She almost flinched, aghast she'd let down her guard. Dangerous to show emotion in front of her father. She kept her gaze on the sculpture and wiped her face of expression, hoping he wouldn't see the tremor in her fingers and the pulse racing at her throat.

The data system answered him in a toneless voice. "This sonata is titled *Contrition*, composed by Hans Wildref Vinslen."

"Contrition," Webster mused. "An apology then. For what, Daughter?"

"My visit surprised him. He was not as gracious as his sister. I assume this is an apology for any perceived rudeness." She paused, flicking her father an assessing glance. "Is this also a confirmation of his commitment to our new alliance, Father?" Asking his opinion, deferring to his authority, stroking his ego. And leading him away.

She had partial success with the ploy. He watched her with sharp eyes, regal face set in shrewd lines.

"Perhaps. But young Shay takes after his father in more than appearance. Ezekiel's children are almost as crafty as he was. I wonder, Daughter, would his courtship please you?"

Sun's mercy. He'd seen her reaction to Manakai's gift. No doubt he now wondered if she could be seduced into betraying him for real. Too close to the truth. She needed to tread this dance with her father with as much care and grace as she could muster.

Shooting her father a startled look, she glanced at the flame then plucked it off her palm, lifting it into the light and studying it. "Courtship? Do you think so? An interesting game." She let her mouth curl in cold amusement, looking beyond the sculpture to her father with a tilt of her head. "Would it please you, Father? Perhaps I could provide some small diversion."

His mouth pinched as though he tasted something sour, but he eyed the flame with a calculating gleam. His expression said her suggestion had caught his interest. A risk and a challenge, to pit his control over his daughter against the Shay charm, distracting at least one of the Shays in the process.

Her father and his old rival, Ezekiel Shay, mirrored each other in craft and guile. She knew he wouldn't agree outright to her suggestion. He'd let her dangle on the possibility, a control of a different sort.

"It would please me if you left the strategizing to me," he chastised, tone laced with contempt.

She bowed her head in submission, folding her hands in her lap. "Of course, Father. I would be grateful for your expert direction in this."

He made a scoffing sound. "A tad overdone, Liaena. I thought I taught you more subtlety. You are dismissed from my presence. Remember to send appreciation to the Shays for their unusual gift."

With a deferential nod, she grasped the wooden box and rose, slipping the sculpture inside as she walked to the door. At the threshold, she turned. "Good day, Father."

He'd already refocused on his viewers and ignored her.

Breathing a careful sigh of relief, she escaped and strode through the corridors at a measured pace. Webster might be preoccupied now, but she never knew when he would go through the security feeds. They recorded her every movement, everything she said and did, no moment private. She'd learned early not to trust being alone, not to cry or show any emotion. He would find out, ridiculing and punishing her for what he saw as weakness.

These days she had to be perfect. He watched her with the paranoid eye of a monarch perched on a precarious throne. She had to tread with utmost care. He couldn't suspect what she was really doing, or all her work would be for nothing.

The box warmed her chilled fingers and her mind's eye fixed on the gem inside. *He sent me a gift.* She told her tripping heart not to read anything into it; an elaborate apology fit the Shay style, methods they'd used over the years to dazzle and distract her arrogant father. But her heart continued to spasm in her chest with nerves, hope, and longing. *A gift.* Not some cold detached offering, but personal, intimate, responding to her touch. If only it were real. If only she could believe the charming rueful humor and the subtle seduction.

Her father had been right. It looked like courtship.

How else could she interpret the secret flame and its response to the stroke of her fingers? *Too cruel, Manakai.* She stepped into her quarters. Mindful of the watching security grid, she moved at a sedate pace into her kitchenette and settled on the cushioned seat in her eating nook. The holo-screen on the wall mimicked a window looking out on a serene lake vista with high snow-capped mountains in the distance. She would have preferred a tropical beach, but such an image, so reminiscent of her childhood home, would reveal too much to her father. Setting the box on the small table, she opened it, tucking her hands in her lap to hide their shaking.

Liaena stared at the little flame, trying to decide how to respond. It would be easier to send a recorded message, polite thanks with a subtle reminder that she waited for their answer. It would be easier not to face Manakai. *Don't be a coward.* She closed her eyes, picturing the fountain.

Taking a deep fortifying breath, she rose and moved into her bedroom, retrieving a necklace of fine crystal links. Returning to the box, she lifted the flame from its cushion. It sang again for her, and Liaena couldn't suppress a tiny pleased smile. Clicking the gem into the necklace setting, she fastened the chain around her throat then paused, working hard to school her expression. The cool weight of it against her skin drove the air from her lungs. *Fool.* But no matter what names she called herself, she knew she'd never remove it.

She moved to her com unit and sat, taking a moment to compose herself before keying in a request to Shay Enterprises. Her heart thumped an anxious rhythm in her chest. When she saw Sin's face, she let out a quiet gust of relief. "Sinsudee, thank you for accepting my call."

"Of course, Aena," Sin replied with an easy smile, tilting her head to one side. Blue-black hair spilled over her shoulder in a silky river. "What can I do for you?"

"I wanted to thank you again for welcoming me to your home, and to thank you both for the lovely gift." She touched the flame at her throat, releasing the music once more.

Sin's smile altered, gaze flicking to Manakai's gift with a teasing gleam. "Kai does have his moments, good and bad. I'll relay your thanks and you're very welcome on both counts, Aena. It was a treat to have you here. You're welcome to return anytime. Maybe we'll finish the conversation we were having."

Liaena's heart knocked in her chest. "I would be delighted. I've heard your station boasts some of the finest eateries in the galaxy. Would you care to prove the rumor over lunch tomorrow?"

"A challenge, is it?" Sin purred with the arching of a dark eyebrow. "You're on. We'll take a culinary tour and fatten you right up."

Liaena suppressed a smile. "Well, doesn't that sound…alarming. Will there be chocolate?"

"Of course. No proper fattening can be done without it. Have I discovered your weakness, Liaena Griffin?" Her grin held an unnerving sharpness.

"As if I would admit such a thing to you, Sinsudee Shay."

Sin's melodic laughter tugged at Liaena, spilling warmth in her chest and curling the corners of her mouth upward.

"Another challenge. This will be fun." Her twinkling green eyes dropped down beyond the frame of the viewer and dimmed. With a grimace, she continued, "I'm sorry, Aena, I'm out of time. I have to go corral my lazy brother into a meeting. Say a prayer for me." Sin flashed a smile and a wink, then disappeared from the viewer.

Startled by her abrupt departure, Liaena blinked at the blank screen and sat back. That had gone well. Too well? What was Sin up to? Suddenly Liaena had the entering-the-lioness'-den feeling again. "System, replay last communication, audio only."

When the data system complied, Liaena closed her eyes and listened, baffled all over again by Sin's ability to run rings around her. When the record came to the end, she caught her breath.

Say a prayer for me.

It seemed an odd comment coming from Sinsudee Shay, especially when followed by an abrupt end to the conversation. Neither Shay struck her as pious. A message?

Mindful of her watched status, she didn't replay the communication again nor did she search the database for anything religious. Instead she went into her kitchenette and busied herself with a hot meal, thinking hard. What had Sin meant? Did they want her to go to Temple? Griffin had no Sun Temple on this station, but several resided close by within their current solar system.

She worried over the theory then discarded it. Too many possibilities. While she ate her meal, she considered Sin's comment might not have been a message. Too obscure. Or she needed another clue. She paused, staring down at her food as an idea struck. Manakai's gift had come by a courier owned and operated by their company. Would the courier have left more than one item?

Discarding the remains of her meal, Liaena tidied the kitchenette first before heading to her data retrieval station. Sitting down, she paused, touching the flame at her throat. The soft music played. She listened with a blank expression, not showing how her stomach fluttered and toes curled. After it finished, she searched the station's database for the composer, sifting through the artist's titles and history but finding no other reason for Manakai's choice in song besides the obvious.

She moved on to the real object of her search, the courier, hoping her father would see it as a logical step in exploring her gift. She didn't have access to the ship's manifest but confirmed the courier delivered nothing else and spent very little time on the station. Here and gone, a quick professional delivery.

Liaena paused to curse in the privacy of her mind before searching for the ship's delivery route. The station's sensors had recorded the courier's arrival and departure from this solar system. The courier had arrived through the star-way, the transportation network allowing fast space travel between solar systems using the Suns as their power source. The courier had then flown to the Griffin station, made a brief stop at a commerce hub planet-side, and headed back through the star-way.

A tingle zipped down her spine and she stood. Her father should still be in admin meetings. If she moved fast enough, he wouldn't stop her and she could make some explanation afterward. Her instincts told her she needed to explore the courier's second stop right now.

Leaving her quarters, she strode through the station at her usual measured pace, ignoring the urgency tightening her muscles. She wanted to hurry, but patience and time had always been her allies. Breathing through the need to rush, she made her way to the docking bay and requisitioned a private transport. A pilot scrambled to her side and escorted her to a ship, a middle-aged man with an ingratiating smile. "It's an honor to serve you, Lady Griffin. May I know our destination today?"

"The surface, please. Hub nineteen."

"Shopping for anything special?"

She gave him a cool look and didn't answer. He took the hint and shut his mouth, hustling into the pilot's compartment. Liaena settled in a seat and considered her next move. She had to be cautious. Half the people in this solar system reported to her father with the other half willing to pass information to him. Her father would track her movements and hear of any line of inquiry she made.

When they landed, she thanked the pilot and asked him to wait for her return. Then she exited the ship and headed for the nearest docking assistance station. The automated system told her the courier had left the docking bay by exit arch eleven, returning through the same arch and flying his ship out of docking.

Liaena headed for exit arch eleven. Stepping out into sunshine, she took a moment to assess her surroundings, enjoying the warmth on her skin. Her father didn't allow her to leave his side often, and he spent most of his time on his space stations. The warm bright light and colorful chaos of this busy market thrilled her senses. The sight of the Blue Sun Temple in the distance sent an even greater thrill down her spine. *Say a prayer for me.*

But if she went to the Temple, her father would make the connection. She had to stay her course. Stepping out into the quaint open-air market, she moved to the nearest human-manned booth and signaled the proprietor for attention.

He hurried to her side, bobbing in frantic deference. "Lady Griffin! What an honor." His narrow face and quick movements reminded her of a chicken. "I would be delighted to be your guide today, if it please you. Dare I ask you to begin at my booth? I offer the finest—"

She held up a hand, silencing him. "Thank you, but I'm looking for information, not merchandise. A courier from Shay Enterprises stopped here not long ago. Did you happen to notice him? I would like to know where he went."

"Apologies, Lady Griffin, I didn't see him," he answered with a crestfallen look. Then he brightened again. "But I can find out for you, ask around and such so you don't have to bother. It'd be no trouble."

"You're very kind."

"Leave it to me." He grinned and scampered away.

Liaena moved on, enjoying the sights and sounds of the market. Several thoroughfares led off this open space, funneling shoppers into rows of small shops with larger buildings behind, housing many levels of commerce. The Blue Sun Temple dominated the skyline down one of the thoroughfares, the commercial buildings a respectful distance from its graceful interlocking arches. At the apex of these arches, a holographic miniature Blue Sun shone benevolent light over the surrounding area.

Liaena spent no more time studying the Temple than any other aspect of her surroundings, but her mind fixed on the structure. She needed a reason to approach it, some excuse her father would accept for entering a Sun Temple. Webster Griffin regarded the Temples and Sun Orders with vast contempt and loathing. He'd never allowed her to visit one before.

She spent the next short while exploring the booths in the market at a leisurely pace, keeping her demeanor tranquil as if she were only killing time, her mind circling the problem with ferocious intent. In her preoccupation, she didn't at first notice the figure hovering at her elbow.

"A mythical creature appears before me, ethereal and filled with power," a soft voice intoned at her side.

Liaena twitched, spinning toward the short figure. The woman smiled, meeting her gaze with direct brown eyes. Her long hair gleamed an odd bronze color, confined in numerous braids hanging down her back to her waist. She wore a simple tunic of faded blue, a teardrop tattoo in the same color at the corner of her left eye. A Blue Sun ascetic.

"You flatter me," Liaena answered with as much composure as she could muster. The woman had seemed to appear out of nowhere, her gaze much too knowing for comfort.

"Creatures of myth need no flattery, only recognition. I see you, winged gryphon. Do you see me?"

Liaena blinked. "You are a Blue Sun priestess. To what do I owe the honor?"

The priestess gave her a wry look. "I also need no flattery, but thank you. I carry the entreaty of another creature of myth. Will you hear me?"

Liaena's heart picked up speed. The ascetic had named her a gryphon, the insignia of Quasicore. The Shays had chosen the sphinx as the insignia of Shay Enterprises, another mythical creature. This priestess must have the Shays' message. "I will," she answered in a low voice, disciplining her expression to show only cool politeness.

The woman studied her for a moment, full mouth curling with secretive humor. Then she reached out, touching a fingertip to the gem at Liaena's throat. "Where is your heart's desire, creature of flame?" she murmured in a husky tone, eyes warm and inviting.

Liaena's face tingled with an unexpected blush, and she fought the urge to sidle away. Blue Sun ascetics had a promiscuous reputation, but she doubted the woman was trying to seduce her. *Where is your heart's desire?* She thought of Manakai and her blush deepened.

Then her mind cleared, offering a more rational thought. What did she wish for most in her heart? Her mother's freedom. With a sharp indrawn breath, she met the priestess' gaze and whispered the location of her mother's island.

"Ah." The woman sighed, shifting back with an air of reluctance. "Perhaps it's for the best. Water and fire don't mix." She touched the teardrop tattoo at the corner of her eye then gestured to the flame at Liaena's throat. "You appear to follow another path. Yet there is grace and wisdom in each of the Suns, yes?"

With an elegant bow, the woman turned and faded

into the crowd. Liaena stared after her, feeling idiotic. Ascetics of the militant Order of the Red Sun wore a red flame tattoo at their throats. So was Manakai's gift truly an act of contrition, a romantic overture, or another declaration of war?

Chapter 5

"Beauty and brains," Sin drawled as she watched the message from the Blue Sun Order scroll across their viewer. "You sure know how to pick them, brother mine."

"Stow it, Sinsi." Kai concentrated on running Zofie Griffin's location through the database. "If Aena didn't know how to play the game, Griff wouldn't keep her around."

"Aena? I was talking about the priestess. Wasn't she one of your conquests?"

"No, and shut up. I'm trying to focus here."

"You're so cute when you pretend to be all conscientious and hard-working."

He snorted and initiated a three-dimensional holographic image of the planet where Zofie lived, leaning on the desk to study it. "Stop trying to be irritating, Sissa. You know I do it better. Look, her mother's right at the corner of no and where. Not quite in the Fringe, nothing around her but space. The planet's mostly water with habitable islands, a great location for spousal imprisonment. If Aena isn't lying and leading us into a trap." He grimaced. "Remind me why we're doing this."

"So you can be Aena's hero and win her undying devotion." When he shot her a dark look, Sin grinned and added, "Also, stealing Griff's bond-mate right out from under his nose would be super satisfying."

"Sold." Expanding the image to show the surrounding systems, Kai traced the route he meant to take, finger pausing over uncharted space. "I'll rendezvous with the militia in the Fringe, get them up to speed. Then I'll scout the locale and make sure little Lie wasn't handing us a load of krell dung. Do you have Marchand's ear?"

"I will have by the time you get done playing around out there. Don't forget to raid Cassie's toy box. She tweaked her security jammer. I do believe its range is now half the galaxy. Do you think she means to take over the universe?"

"Naw, she's too busy playing with her AIs and her pet inspector." He zoomed in on the island, studying the layout. "Speaking of, are you saddling me with Nick again?"

"No, this one's off the grid."

"Good." Kai downloaded Zofie's location onto a personal datapad and wiped the main system's memory. "Let's keep it that way."

"Mm-hmm." His sister laid a hand on his arm and studied him, all humor gone. "Surgical strike, in and out. No one knows you, no one sees you. If Griffin finds out we took his mate, everything else falls apart."

"Tell me something I don't know," Kai growled, shaking off her hand. "This is a huge risk we don't need to take."

"That's almost blasphemy, coming from my reckless brother. It's only a risk if you screw up. Are you going to screw up, Kai?"

He swiped at her and she danced away, snickering. "I'll get it done. You keep your new best friend busy.

Maybe get her drunk." He paused, trying to picture it. Icy controlled Liaena Griffin tanked. He couldn't do it. "It'd be a sight to see."

"I'll do what I can." She tilted her head with a sly glance. "Did I tell you she's wearing your gift?"

As if she didn't know he'd replayed their conversation and seen for himself the flame lying against Aena's creamy skin. As if she didn't know what it did to him. "You're a rotten sister," he informed her. "You get the evil twin award today."

"You're giving up your title? This is a momentous occasion."

He snorted and snagged her into a rough hug. "I so wanna be an only child right now."

"You'd miss me," she mumbled against his shoulder.

"I suppose." He let her go and headed for the exit. "Watch your step with the Griffins, Sissa."

"You too, brother mine."

****

Butterflies multiplied in Liaena's stomach again. She was returning to the Shay station, almost as nervous as her first visit. This time they'd granted immediate permission to dock, giving her no time to settle her nerves. The pilot landed the transport on the visitor's platform in the midst of the bustle and rush instead of the quiet end near the maintenance bay. This would be a public meeting, then. She wasn't sure why, but this made the butterflies even more frantic.

With measured breaths, she moved to the exit and smoothed a hand over her outfit before releasing the hatch. Sin stood waiting for her with an easy smile. The sight loosened the tightness in her middle.

"There you are," Sin greeted with a flashing grin. "Ready to eat until you burst?"

Answering humor tugged at Liaena's lips. "Bursting sounds unhealthy." The formality of their first meeting had somehow evaporated, victim of the mercurial Shay will. She told herself it didn't mean she was safe, but she couldn't help responding.

Sin looped a casual arm through Liaena's, startling her. "The fun stuff usually is," she drawled with a pointed arch of her eyebrow and tugged Liaena into motion. "How was your trip?"

"Uneventful."

"And your father?"

"My father?" With a twinge of alarm, Liaena studied Sin out of the corner of her eye. Was this meeting to be some sort of interrogation?

"Yes, your father. Remember him?" Sin met her gaze for an assessing moment before her face lit with amusement. "Relax, Aena. It's only small talk. We're supposed to chit-chat about easy things. How've you been, how's the family, what's the weather like, before we get to the serious stuff."

"Serious stuff." Should she be amused or terrified?

"Oh, yes," Sin answered with a solemn expression. "We're going to have to delve. By the time you leave, I expect we'll know each other's most embarrassing moments, the first boy we ever kissed, maybe even—" She paused, eyes widening, voice lowering to a whisper. "Our worst bad-hair day ever." She gave a theatrical shudder then grinned. "It'll be great."

"I see." Liaena tried not to show how out of her depth she felt. Sin's playfulness enchanted her, but she had no experience to match it. "In that case, how've you been?"

Sin's eyes gleamed. "Great. You?"

"Very well. Your brother?"

"His usual obnoxious self. Your father?"

"The same," Liaena answered with a wry look, triggering a low burst of laughter from Sin. "I don't suppose you've had any weather to speak of." She gestured around at the space station.

"Haven't been planetside in a while. You?"

"There was sunshine." Liaena's voice softened, a furtive smile sneaking over her face. "Warm and lovely. I've missed it," she blurted and cringed inside. Now she knew she wasn't safe. This new familiarity had a horrible loosening effect on her tongue.

Clearing her throat, she looked away, then slowed at the sight before her. She hadn't noticed where Sin led her, too charmed by their banter. Now the Reception Hall captured her full attention.

In the vaulted ceiling far above, a holographic representation of the galaxy spun in vast splendid indifference. The black marble floor, polished like a mirror, reflected this magnificent sight, humbling visitors from above and below. Seating arrangements and artwork scattered throughout the enormous space in a calculated balance between comfort and opulence. Her father would have appreciated this room, not for its beauty and refinement, but for its crushing power. It dwarfed and reduced. Even for someone like her, used to wealth and strategy, it made an impact. As intended.

Liaena paused, swiveling her head to take in the vast expanse. She turned and leveled a cool look on her escort.

Sin twitched a shoulder in an unrepentant shrug. "I

know. Total overkill. It gets the job done, though." She pointed toward a distant archway. "The station commons, the food courts and shops, are through there. Come on, the hike will work up our appetite." Arm still linked with Liaena's, Sin urged her forward.

Few people had ever touched her for so long. Sin's arm through hers should have felt intrusive and overbearing but somehow didn't, her touch gentle, courteous, and almost affectionate. It had the oddest calming effect. As if she weren't on treacherous ground.

Drifting along at Sin's side over the wide expanse, Liaena frowned at her reactions, worried she might be seeing or feeling only what she wanted. She lifted a hand to hover over the flame in the hollow of her throat, reminding herself the Shays often had reasons within reasons for whatever they did or said. Even a gift shouldn't be taken at face value, though the last time they'd sent something to her father, the message had been quite clear.

Liaena's head lifted when she remembered what they'd put on display here in the Reception Hall. "Sin, I wonder…" She trailed off, concerned she might overstep propriety. Her father had meant to insult them with the gift after all. Softening her voice, she asked, "May I see the Enua?"

Sin tilted her head, studying her with a quizzical expression. Her mouth curved in a wry smile. "If you're sure it won't kill your appetite, I'd be pleased to show you. This way." Sin guided her on a right angle to their previous course, leading her across the vast area, stars gleaming overhead and at their feet.

They approached an ornate recess lined in black

velvet, the interior glowing with hidden lighting. The sculpture within floated and pivoted with slow grace against its black backdrop, the clear crystal structure reflecting light in a dazzling sweep and flash of color. The artist had nearly reached perfection, creating a flower of such delicate detail and fragile beauty it hurt Liaena's heart to look on it.

Her father had sent this gift to Sinsudee, but at the time a vine of thorns had trapped the Enua flower; not a statement of affection but a declaration of domination. The Shay twins had responded by freeing the flower from its confinement and sending the shattered pieces of vine and thorn back to her father.

Liaena curled her hand into a fist, remembering how her father had responded to their defiance. Her fingers and palm still bore fine scars from the shattered crystal. But when she looked at the clean graceful lines of the Enua flower, fragile and free, she decided it had been worth it. "It's so beautiful," she whispered, blinking away unexpected tears. "So perfect. I see not a single restoration mark."

"He's a gifted artist, the same one who created your pendant."

Without thinking, Liaena stroked a finger along the flame at her throat, mouth curving at its soft pensive music. Then she clasped her hands together and schooled her expression. Clearing her throat, she pulled her gaze from the dazzling flower to her waiting hostess.

As she feared, Sin watched her with a piercing look, as though she could read Liaena's every thought. They saw too much, these Shays.

"Thank you. It's a stunning piece of art, and I'm

glad to have seen it."

Sin didn't respond for a moment, studying Liaena. Then she gave another wry smile. "My pleasure. But Aena, if you become any more polite a guest, you'll implode. Come on, let's get you some chocolate. See if it doesn't unwind you a bit."

Liaena blinked but didn't resist when Sin linked their arms again and guided her away from the display. "Unwind me. Sounds ominous."

"It should. Did you want to start with sweet or lunch first?"

"Meal first then dessert. I'm a traditionalist."

"Oh boy, do I have my work cut out for me. Have you ever tried a supernova?"

Liaena shot her a dubious glance. "Never. The alcohol content is practically lethal."

"Cassie said the exact same thing. Do you mind if she joins us, by the way?"

Liaena allowed a small smile. "Not at all. I would be delighted to see her again."

"She's looking forward to seeing you too."

They paused in the entrance to the station commons, looking up at several levels of food markets, eateries, shops, and business offices, rising in concentric rings. The center stood open, a large marble fountain at the base performing a fanciful extravagant display of liquid and light.

Liaena caught her breath. The shape and style of the structure reminded her of her own fountain in the Aqualyr but with more color and light, as if her subdued gray fountain had transformed into this dazzling white work of art, like a butterfly emerging from its cocoon. "Sin, do you remember?" she whispered, an ache in her chest.

"Of course I do. Don't worry, Kai's not allowed to touch this one." Sin moved her forward with gentle pressure on her arm. "Shall we start the tour on this level and work our way up?"

Liaena nodded, unable to speak past a lump in her throat. Eyes stinging, she blinked and swallowed hard, taking measured breaths and berating herself for her lack of control today. She couldn't make mistakes or break down. Her mother needed her to be strong. So many things depended on keeping a stern focus and iron will. She brushed at her outfit, touched her upswept hair, and lifted her chin. Her goal was poise, grace, and dignity, but she'd settle for getting through this visit without damaging her plans.

Sin led her around the first level at an unhurried but steady pace, pointing out unusual wares and edibles. Several proprietors greeted Sin with easy familiarity, and she answered the same way, with an air of casual warmth. Liaena couldn't picture her father doing likewise; even at social engagements when he wasn't domineering, people treated him with respect and deference but no friendliness. Is this how the Shays created such fierce loyalty among their people?

As they ascended to the next level, Sin glanced at her, a questioning crease in her brow. "You're awfully quiet. Have I bored you into a coma already?"

"You've been anything but boring, Sin. I apologize if I seem withdrawn. Your station is very different from what I'm used to. If I admit to being in awe, will you still respect me?"

Sin gave her a dry look. "Overdoing the flattery a little, Aena. What you see here can be found on almost any commerce hub across the galaxy."

"The wares are not what impresses me. Everyone is so…content here."

Sin's mouth twitched at the corners. "How gratifying," she responded in a bland tone. "How often do you get out and see regular people, Aena?"

Liaena acknowledged the gibe with a tilt of her head. "Seldom." The soft word held a world of regret. Liaena looked away to escape Sin's shrewd gaze and caught sight of Cassie hurrying toward them.

The doctor wore a smile so bright it lit her face like a Sun. "Liaena! Welcome to Shay Enterprises." She clasped both of Liaena's hands in hers. "It's so good to see you again."

Startled by this warm greeting, Liaena blinked and went still, managing a belated, "Thank you."

Cassie ignored the awkward pause, letting go of Liaena's hands and waving them forward. "It's probably rude of me to say, but can we eat now? I'm starving."

"Of course," Liaena responded, glancing at Sin askance when her hostess gave a soft snort.

"Cassie has atrocious eating habits," Sin declared with a look of censure for the petite woman. "She forgets to eat then gobbles whatever's available, usually something unhealthy."

Cassie made a face at her boss. "Food is just fuel."

Sin smirked. "Unless it's chocolate."

"Chocolate isn't food; it's divine sustenance. We're going to Horizons, right?" Cassie raised enquiring eyebrows at Sin, then grinned when Sin nodded. "Liaena, I think you'll like this place. The food is good but the show is even better."

Liaena had trouble containing an answering smile to Cassie's infectious grin. "Is it music?"

Cassie sent her a sly look. "Different kind of show. You're not afraid of heights, are you?"

"Not that I'm aware," Liaena answered with a trill of alarm. What were they planning? Had she been foolish to come here without protection?

"Don't let Cass scare you." Sin sent an amused glance at the brunette. "Horizons is perfectly safe. They offer a unique service—"

Cassie shushed her. "You'll spoil the surprise."

"Surprise?" Liaena lifted her eyebrows, but both women only smiled and ushered her onward. Feeling a bit like a lamb on its way to slaughter, she followed where they led.

Horizons appeared innocuous at first glance with its sparse decor. Round tables peppered the open dining area, hover discs laden with meals zipping around the engrossed diners. The expressions of delight on many of the customers' faces didn't match the simplistic atmosphere, and Liaena turned to Cassie with a questioning lift of her eyebrows.

Cassie grinned and led her to an empty table. On the way, Liaena noticed an odd shimmer around each seating arrangement and solved Horizons' riddle; the diners were experiencing a holographic display of some kind as they ate. Liaena turned to her companions, but Sin caught her eye and gave a small furtive shake of her head, eyes gleaming with indulgent humor as she glanced at Cassie. Liaena guessed Sin didn't want her to spoil Cassie's surprise.

Smothering a smile, she sat and turned to Cassie with an attentive air.

Wearing a gleeful expression, Cassie touched a control tablet in the center of the table. "Ready? You might want to hold onto something. The first few seconds are unnerving."

Liaena nodded, prepared for a slight visual disorientation, switching from reality to hologram. The ground disappeared from under her, and she sucked in a breath, grasping the edge of the table in instinctive response. Then she stared in wonder.

They appeared to be floating in a vast sea of clouds, light from a trio of Suns shining through the amorphous stuff, turning their surroundings a million shades of pink and orange. A huge pitted moon hung in the sky above them, looking close enough to touch.

"Amazing," Liaena breathed, stretching fingers toward the clouds. "I can almost feel the moisture."

"She's not afraid of heights," Cassie commented in a smug tone.

Sin chuckled. "She hasn't looked down yet."

Liaena glanced at their expectant expressions, then couldn't resist the urge to look past her feet. As if on cue, the clouds parted, revealing a long drop leading to a magnificent ridge of snow-capped mountains, ablaze with sunset colors. The perspective sent a wave of dizziness over her, but she steeled her nerves and lifted her head with a cool smile. "A lovely hologram. Very well done."

Sin assessed her with those penetrating green eyes, mouth curling in faint amusement.

Cassie's brow creased. "Oh no, you think we're testing you," she blurted, then waved her hands and shook her head. "I picked this hologram because it makes me feel free, like flying with no wings. I'm sorry, Liaena. I really wasn't trying to work your nerves. We can switch this if it bothers you."

Liaena blinked. Cassie's intuition and honesty both unsettled and gratified. She eased her smile into a warmer expression. "It's delightful, truly. The color and detail is astounding."

Cassie sagged a bit, the worry draining from her face. "I'm glad you think so."

"She helped tweak the holograms for Horizons," Sin volunteered, mouth still curled in a faint smile. "Their customers will never be the same."

Cassie pursed her lips. "Sounds like an insult, but I'm too hungry to care. Sorry, I have to be rude again." She leaned forward and tapped the control, calling up a holographic menu. "I like their pastas, but if you want something lighter, all their soups and salads are fantastic."

Liaena waited for her to finish ordering, then considered her options. The eatery had a wide array of dishes, from appetizers to full course meals, but her stomach lurched at the idea of a heavy meal. Following Cassie's recommendation, she chose soup and salad.

Sin ordered as well and then looked from Cassie to Liaena, her expression somber. "All right, ladies, this is where it gets serious. It's time to delve. We may need alcohol."

Cassie snickered. "Hell, no. The last time you got me drunk, I tried to go swimming in the fountain with my clothes on. Not again, Sinsi."

Liaena stared at her, bemused. She hadn't heard this nickname for Sinsudee since they were children.

"Better than stripping naked to swim in the fountain," Sin countered with a quirk of her lips. "My

71

brother, the exhibitionist."

Liaena's breath stuttered in her throat. The image of Manakai naked in the fountain would now star in every one of her fantasies.

Cassie grimaced. "I don't think Kai would appreciate us telling embarrassing stories about him."

"Are you kidding?" Sin snorted. "He's proud of that story. I'm not sure it's possible to embarrass my brother."

Cassie snickered and glanced at Liaena. "Have you done anything embarrassing while drunk?"

Liaena went still. When she didn't answer right away, Sin's eyebrow rose in mute challenge. "I don't drink enough to impair my judgment."

"Wow, you never get drunk?" Cassie looked impressed.

Sin hummed, eyes narrowing. "Evasions won't help you, Ms. Griffin," she drawled. "I see a story in your eyes. Cough it up."

"Oh, she has a story," Cassie exclaimed, leaning forward with bright eyes.

Under their keen regard, heat climbed Liaena's cheeks. "I have no story. Nothing of interest."

"Move along, nothing to see here?" Sin murmured, face filling with humor.

Cassie sat back with a light frown and turned to Sin. "She doesn't want to go first, so you have to. You did bring it up, Sinsi."

Instead of balking, Sin propped her chin on one hand with a thoughtful expression. "Hmm. An embarrassing story."

A hover disc interrupted, lowering their food to the table. Cassie made ecstatic noises as she grabbed her dishes, much to Liaena's amusement. Liaena claimed her own dishes, arranging them in front of her. The soup steamed an inviting fragrant scent, tweaking her appetite.

"I was sixteen," Sin remarked, her mouth curling in a reminiscent smile as she sliced meat on her plate. "We were attending a boring party with lots of stodgy people, too much champagne, and nothing to keep us occupied. One of the chancellors had a son." Sin glanced at each of them, her eyes gleaming. "Glorious blue eyes, built like a swimmer. He and I made our own party in the garden."

Liaena watched her, fascinated, forgetting her soup. She'd had almost no contact with people her own age when growing up. What contact she did have was under the watchful eye of her father. She'd never done anything so bold.

"We were playing games with the champagne. I drank too much. As we were getting to a good part, I got sick all over his pants."

"Oh, no," Cassie half-groaned half-laughed, covering her mouth with one hand.

"Oh, yes," Sin responded with a wry smile, "but it gets better." She took a meditative bite of her food.

Liaena remembered her soup.

"Have I ever mentioned what remarkable timing my brother has? Right after I got sick, he saunters up, as casual as you please, and inspects the damaged pants. Then he turns to the boy and says, 'I don't know why you're mad. You weren't wearing them,' and walks away."

Cassie choked on her drink and burst into laughter.

Liaena realized her mouth hung open and shut it,

staring at Sin. "This is not a real story," she said in a low voice.

Sin's eyes gleamed with rueful humor. "Sadly, it is. And you haven't heard it all. So there I was, feeling unwell and underdressed, the boy standing next to me poking at his pants with a stick of all things, when my father and his father come striding around the corner. Needless to say, champagne and I have not been friends since."

Cassie chortled, wiping tears from under her eyes. "Wow. I have not a single thing to top that. I got the hem of my dress stuck in my undies for half a day, which is why I don't wear dresses. Other than that, I'm out."

Sin paused with her fork suspended, giving Cassie a quizzical look. "No boy stories?"

The little woman shrugged. "No boys. By the time I hit puberty, I was already working on my doctorates."

"Impressive," Liaena commented.

"But not much fun," Sin added with a pointed look at her friend. "All work and no play is bad for the soul."

Cassie rolled her eyes. "Says the woman who hasn't taken a vacation ever."

"I have too much fun at work," Sin responded in a silky tone, turning a glittering glance on Liaena. "Feel like sharing your story now, Aena?"

She set her spoon down with care and folded her hands in her lap. Oddly she did feel like sharing. But would it be wise? She'd never spoken of it to anyone, but no harm could come of it now. The other person involved was already dead.

"I've only been intoxicated once in my life. I don't understand the appeal of it. I felt out of control and made errors in judgment."

"Those are the reasons why people drink," Cassie said with a twinkle in her eyes. "What'd you do?"

"I seduced my security guard." Liaena tilted her head, surprised the words had come out with such ease.

"No kidding?" Cassie's eyes went round.

Sin's eyebrows lifted. "Why, Aena, you little devil," she said in a bland tone. "But I'm not hearing anything embarrassing."

Liaena looked down at her half-eaten soup. How could she tell them she suffered more shame and guilt than embarrassment? Because of her mistake, the man had died. Her father had made him disappear. "I'm not proud of it. I should not have been drinking."

"Why were you?"

Liaena pressed her lips together. She'd resorted to drink, hurt and furious after yet another painful encounter with Manakai. He'd implied she was cold in bed, lacking in passion. She couldn't recall his exact words, but he'd christened her Ice Queen then. Determined to prove him wrong, she'd swallowed enough liquor to bolster her courage and coaxed the security guard into her room. Her first and only sexual experience, full of awkward missteps and discomfort. It ended in humiliation for them both, she proving Manakai right and he unable to finish. She'd thought the humiliation the worst of it until the man disappeared, wiped out of existence by her father.

Webster Griffin hadn't even been angry, just disgusted. "Save your female charms for someone important, Daughter. Don't waste them on trash. Trash is only meant to be disposed of."

How could she sit here and banter while her father

made such things possible?

A light touch on her arm startled her. Sin watched her with shadowed eyes. "Where did you go, Aena?"

Liaena stiffened her spine. "I apologize for my poor company and even poorer conversation. I'm afraid my memories aren't as colorful as yours."

Sin smiled, the shadow remaining in her eyes. "Colorful is a kind way to put it, and you're being too polite again. I'm sorry I made you uncomfortable."

Liaena blinked at her, then glanced across the table. Cassie leaned forward, a frown of concern creasing her brow. What had they seen in her face to bring them both to such seriousness?

"Liaena, don't you have any good memories?" Cassie asked in a soft earnest voice. "What about your mother?"

"My mother?" She flashed a glance at Sin who gave her a cryptic smile. "Ah yes, we spoke of her before, didn't we, Dr. Draegen?"

"Call me Cassie and yes we did, during the fun adventure I had in Griffin-land." A sour look passed over Cassie's face.

"I've been remiss. How are you feeling after your ordeal, Cassie?"

Impatience flickered in her brown eyes, but she answered in a level voice. "I'm fine, thanks for asking. You're avoiding the topic of your mother."

Before Liaena could respond Sin interjected, "Cassie is aware of our previous discussion, Aena, and this holographic display has privacy shielding. No one will hear us."

Liaena inclined her head. "Thank you for the courtesy. I have not seen my mother in a long while."

"Why not?"

After a small hesitation, Liaena answered, "My duties do not allow much free time."

Sin gave her a veiled look and Cassie's expression soured. "He doesn't let you see her, does he?"

"I beg your pardon?"

"Your father," Cassie clarified. "He keeps you apart. Does he use her against you, Aena?"

Liaena's hands tightened around one another in her lap. "My father is quite adept at exploiting every advantage."

"Understatement," Sin murmured, settling back in her seat and sipping from her drink, watching Liaena over the rim with shrewd eyes. "Do you fear for your mother's wellbeing?"

Liaena looked down, a cramp in her chest restricting air. Cold invaded her limbs. She gave the tiniest nod without looking at either of them.

"Why? Has he threatened to hurt her?" Cassie asked in a sharp tone.

Taking a careful breath, Liaena cleared her throat, her voice reduced to a near whisper. "He has not needed to. There are many ways to harm someone. When isolated, a person can fade, the soul withering." She thought of the Shay twins' mother, Juliette. So much regret and horror could make any strong soul falter. Force a person to wrestle with those inner demons alone, and how could anyone stand a chance?

"Tell us about her," Cassie coaxed. "What do you remember of your time with her?"

Emotion still clogged her throat. She had to swallow hard to speak. "When I was a child, we spent nearly all our time on the beach in the Sun. I remember her laughing. Now when I visit, we talk on every subject but her laughter is gone. When I leave..." Her voice whispered away, a black wave of despair shredding it to nothing. Her eyes stung and her throat ached with the threat of tears.

"I'm sorry, Aena. Sin, maybe we should—"

"Continue the tour," Sin finished for Cassie. "I agree. We have a rendezvous with a chocolatier."

Liaena drew a deep breath, composing herself before she lifted her chin and met Sin's gaze. When she opened her mouth, Sin made a sharp gesture, expression turning stern.

"No more apologies from you. This one's on us for pushing you so hard." She glanced down at Liaena's half-eaten meal, mouth twisting. "And for not fulfilling my promise to fatten you up. It's time to test your legendary willpower, Aena."

The constriction around Liaena's chest eased, and she managed a small smile. "Legendary?"

"Would you prefer infamous?" Sin tapped the tablet in the center of the table and returned them to Horizons' spare reality. "Let's move along. We have so much more indulging to do."

Grateful for the change in subject and atmosphere, Liaena wondered if she'd furthered her cause to save her mother or damaged it. In true mercurial form, Sin's demeanor had changed to light-hearted hostess again, leaving the heaviness of Liaena's predicament behind as if it hadn't happened.

Cassie rose to her feet with an uncertain expression, her crooked smile vying with the anxiety in her eyes. "But shouldn't we—?"

"Timing is everything, Cass," Sin interrupted with

a sly glance at the smaller woman. "And dessert shines new light on the darkest of issues. Shall we?" She led them toward the exit, glancing over her shoulder at Liaena. "What's your downfall, Aena? Dark chocolate? White? Caramel, toffee, truffles…?"

Liaena considered with a thoughtful hum. "All of the above I'm afraid."

Cassie snickered, giving her a gentle nudge as she drew alongside in the corridor. "My turn to ply you with goodies. After you taste the fudge at Dark Decadence, you'll be willing to spill all your secrets. Right, Sinsi?"

"Absolutely," Sin drawled, flashing Liaena a wicked grin. "Let's see, we've done embarrassing moments. What else was on the list?"

"I believe you mentioned worst hair day," Liaena commented, moving between the two women as they headed for a lift.

Cassie gasped. "Oh, no! Too cruel, Sin. Let's stick with easier stuff, like favorite color and what type of person you're most attracted to. I like indigo and smart dark-haired men with dark eyes and lots of muscles." When she grinned, a dimple of mischief appeared beside her mouth.

Sin loosed a lyrical laugh, something Aena hadn't heard since the incident with the fountain. She couldn't contain a bemused smile.

"She's playing with you. Cass lost her heart to our current FPA liaison. You met him briefly."

Liaena nodded, glancing at Cassie's beaming face with a twinge of envy. "Nicholo Givliani. Quite handsome and heroic."

Cassie's joy faltered. "And not available."

"My loss, I'm sure," Liaena murmured, working hard to contain her own amusement as Sin laughed again. "I regret I don't have a favorite color or type," she lied with smooth practice, stepping out of the lift with them and moving at a sedate pace along another corridor farther up the commons. "It does bring a story to mind. Sin, do you remember the luncheon we attended at the Bethwell fundraiser with the delegate from Plyn and the White Sun ascetic?"

Sin cocked her head in quizzical thought a moment before her face lit with a sudden grin. "Oh, yes! The fool who couldn't pronounce your name. I don't think Cassie has heard this one. Will you tell it?"

A warm scent wafted around them like melting chocolate, and Liaena took a deeper breath. They approached the chocolatier, Dark Decadence. "Perhaps you should, Sin. You're the better storyteller, and I've a feeling I'm soon to be distracted."

Sin chuckled and complied, glancing beyond Liaena to Cassie. "From the moment the Plyn delegate saw Aena at the luncheon, he was smitten, couldn't leave her alone, monopolizing her attention. He kept calling her Leanna, despite several attempts from others to correct him. It drove the White Sun ascetic mad. You know how Whites are, so focused on truth, order, and perfection. Finally the ascetic grabbed his face and said very slowly, 'Lie—*ey*—nuh, you moron! Drink less, listen more, and stop ogling her cleavage. This is a fundraiser, not a singles bar.' Then she snatched his drink out of his hand and stalked away. I nearly applauded."

While Cassie snickered, Liaena studied Sin out of the corner of her eye. She hadn't thought the incident so memorable, yet Sin had quoted the White ascetic with striking accuracy. "Do you remember the ascetic's name? I found her quite formidable."

"K'etarci. We made sure to be on her good side afterward." Sin winked and slipped her arm through Liaena's, leading her to a lustrous display of sweets.

A man hurried toward them behind the counter, hovering in alert attendance.

"Marcel, we'll need one of everything in this case for starters."

With a wide smile the man began assembling delicacies.

"You're in jest, of course," Liaena said in dubious alarm, watching the pile of sweets grow.

Sin checked a discreet chronometer on her wrist. "You'll need the fortification, Aena."

Liaena couldn't prevent a small crease in her brow. "Fortification?"

"To stave off nerves. My brother should be finding your heart's desire right about now."

Liaena's heart leapt in her chest, knocking against her ribs like a trapped bird. She sucked in a sharp breath, knees wobbling. Manakai was on her mother's island?

Sin's arm steadied her, those piercing green eyes watchful. "Easy," Sin murmured and lifted a truffle. "Let's start with this one and see where it leads us." With a wry smile she tipped the chocolate into Liaena's trembling fingers.

Chapter 6

Kai's Shadow made a shushing sound as it slid from the water onto the island's beach. Kai heard it through the Shadow's sensors, but the lapping waves would cover any incidental sounds he made, and the thick darkness of a moonless night would hide him from view. The occupants of the sprawling bungalow in the center of the island remained unaware of his approach. He monitored them anyway, the sensors tracking their movements—half a dozen armed personnel and one unarmed female, Zofie Griffin and her guards.

The scattered positions and random movements of the guards suggested they hadn't seen much action on their watch over the years, growing lax in this assignment. Noting the many gaps in their protection, Kai figured he could ace this rescue even without Cassie's toys and his militia. No sense taking further risks, though.

He sent the number and position of the guards to the militia waiting out of sensor range. Then he slid from his Shadow, taking his workbag with him. Setting the bag on the sand, he opened it and retrieved a small device. It looked like a tiny helo-flyer or a winged bug.

"Time to wake up and take over the universe, Cassie-bot," he muttered and touched the control pad. It whirred to life, launching off his palm and arrowing over the dunes toward the bungalow on the rise. As it disappeared into the night Kai drew on a mask and gloves and settled night-vision lenses onto the bridge of his nose. The lenses also penetrated solid objects, so he'd be able to monitor the positions and activities of everyone on the property.

Shouldering his bag, Kai set off at a loping run across the beach toward the house in the distance. Cassie's flying security jammer would be his vanguard, covering his approach by preventing the building's security systems from detecting him. Once he reached position, it would shut down all of the building's security functions, detection and deterrent systems, locks, and lights. The only thing it couldn't do was pluck Mother Griffin from her confinement and carry her off. No wonder Marchand seemed so taken with their resident genius; he must drool every time he read Cassie's reports on her new inventions.

Considering the enormity of this operation, Kai hadn't left much to chance. He wore a light-refraction suit, much like the skin of their Shadows, allowing him to blend into any surface. In the dark it made him invisible. The militia provided distraction and a cover story for Zofie's abduction, but he'd brought his own weapons and accessories in case this mission didn't run according to plan, plus a fine selection of Cassie's toys. After their father had been surprised and killed while hunting for intel on weapons runners, Kai and Sin had vowed to be prepared for any contingency.

When he neared the bungalow, Kai crouched and prowled forward at a more cautious pace. No alarms blared, no defense systems activated, and no personnel came running. Circling the building to Zofie's location, he signaled the militia to make their run on the property. It would take them a few minutes to reach the place, so Kai settled against the outer wall, turned off the night vision, and glanced through glass doors off the veranda into the interior, assessing the layout.

Zofie Griffin sat alone in what appeared to be an old-fashioned library. An amazing number of archaic printed books lined shelves on the walls. Zofie perched in an armchair in a halo of light, a book open on her lap. She didn't appear to be reading it, her features blank as she stared into the distance. Despite her elegant posture, her shoulders slumped and her mouth turned down at the corners. Something about her struck him, a grayness in contrast to her colorful attire and well-groomed appearance. She looked as though she were waiting for something unpleasant.

He scanned the room. No hidden surprises.

The militia's ship arrived in a roar of engines and blaze of light at the front of the bungalow. Weapon's fire sounded, and Kai signaled the Cassie-bot to kill the building. Turning on his night vision, he watched Zofie startle and drop her book in the sudden darkness. Stepping to the veranda glass doors, he pushed them open and strode in without fanfare.

He kept his voice low and stayed back so he wouldn't frighten her too much. "Zofie Griffin, please come with me. Your daughter sent me to retrieve you."

She sucked in a sharp breath, then stared in his direction with blind eyes through the dark, features slack with shock. "Z-Zeke?" she whispered.

Kai went still. As far as he knew, none of the guards bore the name. She could only be referring to his father, Ezekiel Shay. She must have known him from before her long confinement. Kai took after his father in looks but hadn't known he also sounded like him. How would she remember his father's voice after all these years?

He moved forward on silent feet. "No, ma'am. It's time to go." Clasping her arms in a gentle hold, he lifted her to her feet, ignoring her shuddering tension at his touch.

"W-what's going on?" she breathed, twitching in his grip at the sound of violent weapon fire echoing through the building.

"I'll explain later. We're out of time."

"Lady Griffin!" a muffled voice sounded from outside the room, accompanied by a flurry of noises as the man bumbled his way through the dark toward the library.

"Stay here," Kai muttered and moved to the door, watching the man's outline stumble closer beyond the barrier.

"Please don't kill him," Zofie whispered in a frantic tone behind him. "He's just doing his job."

Kai gave a silent snort but didn't respond, waiting until the guard reached the door. Kai opened it and jerked the man inside, ripping his weapon out of his grip. With a hoarse cry the guard stumbled to his knees and rallied, turning toward his attacker and lunging. He never made it to his feet. Kai clubbed him unconscious with his own weapon.

"Oh, Suns," Zofie moaned, staggering back and huddling against a shelving unit.

"It's all right." Kai moved on swift feet to catch hold of her again. "He's not dead, just knocked out. We need to hurry. Come on."

"W-wait, I can't go without…" She fumbled along the row of books until she came to a short table and a small object displayed on it. She gripped the object in her fist and turned back to him. "I'm ready."

Kai stared for a second before he clasped her arm and guided her toward the veranda. He'd expected more resistance and confusion. He could have been lying to her about Aena sending him. He could be any number of bad guys looking to score big by abducting such a wealthy woman and ransoming her, exactly the cover story the militia would soon circulate for him.

The sounds of fighting decreased. Moving Zofie at a swift pace toward the water, Kai contacted the militia leader. "Trash the place. Take anything of high value. Destroy what you can't take but leave the guards where they lie."

"Aye, sir," the leader barked over the com in Kai's ear.

With luck they'd make it look like a random robbery, with Zofie's abduction as an afterthought. The guards could attest to the attack but would lack key details due to the darkness and absence of the building's sensor readings. A bogus splinter group in the Fringe would claim responsibility and demand ransom for Griffin's bonded.

Aena's mother scrambled to keep up with Kai's loping run, huffing and wheezing beside him. He decreased his pace but kept her moving, wanting to get off this rock and as far away as possible before Griffin discovered what had happened. He might have reserve defenses and personnel in the area.

As they crossed the beach to his Shadow, he signaled the Cassie-bot to return and removed his mask and gloves, stashing them in the bag.

"You'll be riding with me, Mrs. Griffin. It won't be comfortable, but it's the fastest way out of here."

"Call me Zofie," she whispered, eyes searching the dark in his direction. "You must be Manakai."

He paused, snatching the little security jammer out of the air when it whirled into reach. He turned it off and stowed it, tossing the bag into the interior of his Shadow. In the distance the bungalow's lights flickered to life.

"Time to go, Zofie." Without waiting for her to respond, he scooped her in his arms and settled into the Shadow with her across his lap.

She made a muffled sound like a swallowed yelp but didn't resist.

"Watch your head." He shut them in and started the slicer, keeping a wary eye on Aena's mother and wondering if she'd protest the close quarters.

She looked around the interior with wide eyes. "This is quite a ship." She stayed stiff, bracing an arm on the back of the seat, keeping her upper body from touching him. A fine tremor ran through her limbs; reaction, he guessed. She didn't seem nervous or frightened, only uncomfortable.

Connecting with his Shadow in a rush of power and sensation, Kai slid the slicer off the beach and back into the water, disappearing under the surface. If the building's security grid had come to life along with the lights, it would detect any ship in the air. Submerging, Kai retraced the path he'd traveled to reach the island until they'd gone out of reach of even the most rigorous house security system. Then he burst from the ocean and shot for space, his Shadow growling in a rush of exhilarating power.

Zofie shifted her position across his thighs. "You said my daughter sent you?"

He said nothing for a moment, studying her profile. Her resemblance to her daughter struck him even more in person. The same shape of her eyes and mouth, the same hairline and mahogany tresses with gray streaking her hair and warm blue coloring her eyes instead of silver-gray. She couldn't match her daughter's cool poise.

"Yes, ma'am. Try to relax," he added when her arm buckled from the strain of holding her upright. "We're stuck in here for a while, and I swear my intentions are honorable."

She grimaced, shooting him an odd glance, part humor and part wariness. "You look and sound so much like Ezekiel," she murmured, easing closer until her shoulder rested against his chest. She smelled of ocean and tropical flowers. "It's uncanny."

"You knew my father."

"Yes," she said with a strain in her voice. "I knew both your parents. I'm so sorry for your loss."

He frowned. From what he'd read of her she remained innocent of her bond-mate's transgressions, but Griffin might still use her as a pawn to play him and his sister. He couldn't afford to allow her under his guard. "Kind of you. Try to rest. We can't use a star-way. Slicers are too small to handle a star-way wormhole's forces, so we're stuck taking the long route."

"Where are we going?"

"Somewhere safe."

"Is Liaena there?" She turned her head, meeting his

gaze with an ocean of hope cresting in her eyes.

"I'm sorry, no."

Disappointment shadowed her face. "Is she well, though? I haven't spoken with her in so long."

"She's fine. You'll speak with her soon."

She studied him out of the corner of her eye. "I don't mean to sound ungrateful, but why are you doing this? Unless something drastic has happened since Liaena and I last spoke, you and my—and Webster are still in conflict. Am I your hostage?"

Kai almost smiled. The direct approach. What a refreshing change for a Griffin. "At this point our plan is to keep you safe. We'll try to make you as comfortable as possible, but you'll be as isolated as you were on your island. It might feel like switching one prison for another." He tilted his head, catching her gaze with a wry twist of his mouth. "Sure you don't want to go back?"

She shuddered, her face paling. "No," she whispered. "Take me hostage, use me if you must. But please don't ever return me to Webster Griffin's control."

With a twinge of concern he patted her on the back. "That's a promise."

"Thank you." She took a shaky breath, letting it out on a sigh. "How did your father die, Manakai? Liaena wouldn't tell me."

He stiffened, startled by both the direct question and the veiled emotion in her voice. She seemed strangely interested in someone who should have been only a social acquaintance from her distant past.

"Criminals killed him, a group of weapons dealers."

"Oh, sweet Suns," she choked, covering her mouth with one hand. Her eyes filled with tears. "Why?"

"He was in the wrong place at the wrong time."

"That's horrible. Manakai, I'm so sorry. Were the criminals brought to justice?"

"In a way. They're all dead."

Her eyes went wide, studying him. "Dead? H-how?"

"Not by my hand," he answered with a grim smile. "How well did you know my father, Zofie?"

She blushed and turned her face away. "Not as well as I wanted to. I confess I was deeply in love with Ezekiel Shay. He was everything Webster Griffin wasn't. But he was devoted to your mother, and I loved her as well. She was a sweet soul and had the most generous heart."

Kai stared, at a loss for words. Zofie Griffin wasn't just direct but brutally honest. Her admiration of his parents twisted something inside him. He always had trouble discussing his fragile mother and stubborn father. Their deaths weighed on his soul like chains of black acid. At her words a burning pit opened in his core.

When he said nothing Zofie fidgeted and shot him a quick glance.

"Forgive me, I spoke out of turn. You barely know me and I'm getting far too personal. My social graces are rusty. I haven't had the freedom to speak my mind in so long, I'm afraid I've begun babbling."

"You're forgiven," Kai murmured. "Your guards weren't the chatty types?"

She grimaced. "They were pleasant enough but kept their distance as you can imagine. Webster didn't allow fraternization. He watched us, monitored every word and action. The only privacy I found was on the beach, and even then his people stayed close." She folded her arms against her chest as if she felt a sudden chill. "He watches my daughter too. Have you seen her? Does she look well?"

"She's fine," he said again, preoccupied by her words. The idea of Griffin watching his family with such controlling paranoia didn't surprise Kai, but he hadn't considered what it might be like for them. Then again this poor woman had been on the receiving end of Griffin's manipulations for decades and kept in isolation. Could he take anything she said at face value? "She's on the Shay station right now. You'll be able to contact her soon."

"Thank you," she breathed and put a hand on his chest, eyes glossy with tears and expression earnest. "I'm so grateful for what you've done for me. I can never repay you, but if there's anything I can do you only have to ask." Then she blinked, looked down at her hand, and snatched it away with a pinched look. "This is a lovely ship but a bit cramped. Am I crushing you?"

He chuckled. "Not at all, ma'am, you're light as a bird. This is a slicer, built for single-person racing. This model is called a Shadow, the fastest most powerful slicer in the galaxy. Its speed and stealth make it the perfect ship for daring rescues. Or dastardly abductions as the case may be."

She slanted him a wry look. "I prefer to think of this as a rescue. I've never seen a slicer before. I'm not much for sports. Do you race on the professional or amateur circuits?"

"Neither. Haven't found the time. Did your Sun-bonded ever visit you on your island, Zofie?"

She looked startled by the abrupt subject change but answered without hesitation. "Very seldom." She glanced down, lifting her arms and staring at the scrolling bond marks etched around her wrists as if they were golden manacles. "As long as I didn't cause trouble he left me alone. Do you suppose I could have these removed now?" She tilted her wrists toward him.

He caught sight of the object clutched in her fist, the thing she'd taken from the bungalow. "What do you have there?"

She opened her fingers, her face warming in a soft smile. "Memories of my daughter, the only thing I care to keep from my time there. Would you like to see?" Without waiting for his answer she touched the side of the octagonal crystal. A hologram flickered to life above it, a still image of a child running along a Sun-washed beach, laughing over her shoulder at the holographer, bare limbs kissed golden by the Sun. Her red hair streamed behind her like a banner.

Kai stared with a sense of displacement. Reconciling this image with the Liaena he knew seemed impossible. But he remembered a girl very like the one in the hologram, kicking him for making a joke at her expense, which turned out not to be so funny. He remembered and ached deep inside. Without thought he reached up and turned off the holo-image. "You should get some rest."

She made a face, fingers curling around the crystal. "No offense but traveling like this isn't restful. Besides I'm too anxious to sleep, looking forward to seeing my daughter and worrying about you. Webster Griffin will retaliate. He doesn't love me but he does consider me his property. He won't ignore what you've done."

"Griff won't know it was me. Another group will claim responsibility and demand ransom."

A crease formed in her brow. "Won't his security grid show you there?"

"I killed it. He'll have only the guards' word on what happened. The people helping me will make it look like a robbery."

"Who were the people helping you?"

He gave her a dry look. "Just think of them as guardian angels, your anonymous heroes."

She nodded. "I understand. You're protecting them." She paused, watching the crystal turn in her fingers. "My daughter speaks highly of you and your sister. You seem to protect others quite a bit. Who protects you?"

Maternal bias must be coloring her memory. Kai couldn't imagine Liaena speaking highly of him. "We take care of ourselves."

"Tough competent Shays. You perform miracles without batting an eye. No wonder she—" Zofie stopped short, turning her face away and pressing the crystal to her chest. "I'm babbling again. Soon you'll regret rescuing me if you don't already."

"No regrets," he responded with ease, but he would have given a lot to have her finish what she'd started to say. He guessed she spoke of Liaena. No wonder she...what?

Chapter 7

No wonder I'm always scrambling to keep up, Liaena thought with rueful anxiety, watching Sin shop and herd them around the commons with ruthless ease. Her hostess acted as though no other matter concerned her but entertaining Liaena. As though her brother weren't in the middle of a dangerous rescue mission. Liaena would've thought he'd send people to whisk her mother away, not perform the feat himself. She should have guessed what he'd do, considering what he'd gone through to retrieve Cassie from her father's grasp. But she'd still been focused on whether or not they would consider helping with a rescue attempt. She'd never dreamt they'd leap into action.

The sheer audacity left her breathless. Her own life had been one long patient wait and endless planning. This abrupt decisive action shocked her and his peril terrified her. She also worried for her mother; the guards on the island would never harm her on purpose, but anything could happen when violence came calling.

After dropping this emotional bomb, Sin proceeded to act as if nothing had happened, evading Liaena's questions and leading her through a succession of sweet shops, eateries, and clothiers. Overfull and preoccupied, Liaena had let Sin talk her into purchasing a flowing fern-patterned sundress and sandals, a wild deviation from her usual attire. When she tried on the dress,

Cassie had become so enthusiastic Liaena felt obliged to acquire it.

Now for the first time in her life she stood on the threshold of a Sun Temple, about to step in and unsure how they'd come to this circumstance. Sin may have issued an obscure challenge. Liaena couldn't remember the exact phrasing. She also couldn't remember her vague response, yet here they stood, outside the Red Sun Temple at the apex of the commons.

"How odd," she murmured, staring at the rough wood and stone of the temple front, as primitive as the station was advanced. "Why do you have a Red Temple here?"

"They chose to be here," Sin responded with a thread of amusement in her bland voice.

Liaena sent her a cool look for the evasion, but Sin only flashed a grin and ushered her inside. Liaena entered and paused, waiting for her eyes to adjust to the dim lighting. The antechamber appeared lit by flickering firelight, casting strange patterns over the interwoven slabs of wood and stone. Large stone doors barred the way to the interior of the temple, decorated with intricate puzzling marks. Next to the doors a simple stone bowl squatted on a plain pedestal.

While she absorbed the plain yet powerful atmosphere, an ascetic approached, a young woman with serene features and a red flame tattoo nestled in the hollow of her throat. The ascetic gave Liaena a small smile, her gaze dropping to the crystal flame on its fine chain. Then she bowed and waved them toward the interior doors. "Enter and be welcome."

"Thank you," Sin answered, her tone solemn.

Liaena followed Sin to the doors, but Cassie

deviated from course, stopping at the bowl and touching its bottom. At Liaena's quizzical glance, Cassie whispered, "A blood offering," with a tiny grimace.

"Should I—?"

"You are welcome, sister," the ascetic interrupted. "No offering is necessary."

Her hand rose without conscious thought, touching the flame at her throat and setting off its music. The ascetic must think her part of the order because of Manakai's gift, so similar to their tattoos. "Forgive me, but you misunderstand."

Sin caught her elbow and urged her inside. "Trust me, she doesn't misunderstand a thing. She's giving you a pass, Aena. You should take it." She sounded so confident, too comfortable with this forceful atmosphere.

A flicker of irritation stiffened Liaena's spine. "And you? Why aren't you making an offering?"

Sin chuckled. "I've given enough blood to this place. Stop giving me the evil eye, Aena. You're missing the show."

Liaena faced forward and teetered to a stop. A Red Sun loomed over her, roiling with unimaginable power, its corona reaching out into the temple air in unspoken demand for attendance. It hovered a man's height above the stone floor in the center of a large circular room ringed by columns of stone. The sheer majesty of it rendered her mute.

Cassie gasped next to her. "It's incredible. Which red giant is this?"

"Bain in the Shantai system. It's in real time," Sin answered, her tone thoughtful.

"The holographic detail is amazing." Cassie drifted forward like a dreamer.

Liaena clasped her hands together, feeling foolish. Confronted by the red giant, she'd almost thought it real. Even knowing it was holographic, its presence overwhelmed like the penetrating eye of a god. She pulled her gaze from its mesmerizing surface, glancing around the room. Several ascetics sat on mats at the base of the columns, either gazing at the Sun or bending their heads in meditation.

"You've brought me a creature of flame, pupil," someone said on the other side of Sin.

Sin chuckled in response.

Liaena turned and met the piercing gaze of an older man, white-haired and light-eyed, the smoldering light of the Sun obscuring the exact color of his eyes. "Greetings," she said with wary respect, not knowing how to address him. "I fear my necklace is misleading. I'm not part of—"

"I was referring to your hair, dear lady. Of course you're not in the order. I am T'Zai. Follow me, please."

He set off past the Sun without looking back as if their cooperation were a foregone conclusion. Sin ushered Liaena forward, the rueful humor on her face made mysterious by the Sun's brooding light.

Cassie snorted at her side. "He has more arrogance than a Shay."

"Watch it," Sin growled, though a fleeting grin curved her lips.

"Where are we going?" Liaena addressed them both. They passed out of the Sun sanctuary into a plain corridor lit with flickering light. More rough-hewn wood and stone made odd compelling patterns on the walls, ceiling, and floor.

Sin hummed, sly humor in her gaze. "We're following a wild-eyed priest into the bowels of a Red Sun Temple. We must be on our way to hell."

T'Zai sent a frown over his shoulder. "Impudent child."

"Thank you, Mendani," she responded with cloying sweetness.

His mouth twitched and he turned away with a snort, leading them through one corridor after another. Liaena wondered if they went in circles, her sense of direction thrown off kilter. After a while, they stopped in a small bare room. T'Zai touched a random stone on the back wall and a door opened onto a lift. Liaena blinked at it. After the primitive atmosphere of the temple, the smooth metal interior of the lift disoriented her.

Sin placed a kiss on the elder's cheek with an arch look. "We have unfinished business, Mendani."

He rolled his eyes and huffed a long-suffering sigh, a comical contrast to his air of monastic mystery. "Get on with you, child."

Cassie snickered. "Thanks, T'Zai."

He nodded to the doctor with a fond smile then turned to Liaena, his expression sobering and eyes turning fierce. "Young one, remember this: you rise anew like the dawn, full of potential. Don't doubt the promise of your soul." He raised a gnarled hand, palm toward her, and intoned, "Walk in the Light," before striding out without a backward glance.

Liaena turned to Sin with a lift of her eyebrows. "Should I be concerned or flattered?"

"Neither," Sin answered in a dry tone. "The man

turns melodrama into an art form. This way, Aena." She waved a graceful hand at the lift.

"And where does this lead? Don't say hell."

Cassie laughed, tugging Liaena forward. "I know this looks suspicious, but we're giving you a cover story. If anyone has been watching you today, they'll think you're taking a tour of the temple with us."

"So what am I actually doing?"

"Discovering the results of my brother's little adventure," Sin answered.

Liaena's heart leapt into her throat, stifling her breath. Wordless, she stepped onto the lift, brushing a trembling hand down her outfit as Sin touched the controls. White noise filled her mind, obliterating all thought, the same as when her father administered severe punishment.

"They'll be all right," Cassie said softly at her elbow. "You can count on Kai."

Liaena clasped her hands together and concentrated on her breathing. She'd never been able to count on anyone in her life. Aware of the keen regard from her companions, Liaena fell back on her usual protective behavior and went still, emptying her face of emotion.

Sin hummed low in her throat. "My brother may be a pain at times, but he does get the job done."

The lift doors opened onto a wild abundance of plants. At first Liaena thought it a holographic display, similar to her father's structured garden, until she inhaled a thousand organic scents from flower perfume to rich soil. The dome overhead mimicked a blue sky with a yellow Sun inching across the apex. "This is lovely. Though I'm afraid I don't understand why we're in this place either."

"Just passing through," Sin responded with a grin, slipping her arm through Liaena's and urging her forward. "Watch your step. Some of these green things can get overfriendly."

With an inner despairing sigh, she went where Sin led. It was becoming a dreadful habit.

They strode along a path through tangled woods broken by open areas filled with mounds of bright flowers. The moisture in the air kissed her skin and filled her lungs with a strange energy. Something in her eased, a knot she couldn't identify.

The path ended in an open area around a wooden structure. Horizontal logs formed the walls of the building, and the entrance boasted a handle. When Sin depressed the handle and swung the wooden door open Liaena blinked in surprise. This was a quaint old-fashioned log cabin, straight out of the storybooks her mother had read to her as a child.

A disembodied male voice greeted them as they stepped over the threshold. "Welcome, ladies."

"Hey, Bash," Sin responded. "Has Kai checked in yet?"

"Have you no manners? Introduce me, please."

Liaena moved into the space, looking around in bemused interest. The relaxed décor and intimate seating suggested someone's personal living space. It exuded warmth and comfort with the most delicious fragrance in the air, a mysterious spice she drew in deeper with each breath. Another residence of Sin's? If so, it seemed odd Sin would choose so masculine a space.

Sin snorted and turned to face Liaena, waving an impatient hand in the air. "Aena, this is Basher, Kai's

AI house companion. Bash, may I introduce Liaena Griffin?"

"It's a pleasure to make your acquaintance, Liaena," the voice said in a smooth baritone.

Liaena barely heard. Kai's house companion? This was Manakai's residence? She inhaled the scent again and her cheeks flushed hot. Being in his home and breathing his scent felt as intimate as sliding a hand up his shirt. She murmured something appropriate to the AI, ducking her face to hide her reaction.

"Now be good, Bash, and connect me with Kai."

"He's waiting for your call."

Liaena's knees wobbled. If Manakai was waiting for his sister's call, did this mean he and her mother were safe?

The holographic fireplace at one end of the living room flickered out of view, replaced by an enormous viewer. Sin moved toward it, Liaena and Cassie trailing her. Clutching her hands together to keep them from shaking, Liaena watched the viewer fill with color.

Manakai appeared, looking as devastating as always, no visible damage but wearing a disgruntled expression. "Took you long enough. Did you buy half the commons?"

"Only a quarter," Sin answered with a lazy grin. "How'd it go?"

"As advertised." He glanced to one side, his expression clearing. "Someone wants to say hello." He shifted out of view.

When her mother appeared, warm blue eyes filled with tears and mouth trembling in a smile, Liaena pressed her hands to her lips and stopped breathing. "Liaena, my sweet girl," Zofie whispered. "Are you all right?"

Conscious of everyone watching, Liaena managed to unlock her chest and dropped her hands. "Mama," she husked, then cleared her throat, taking a deep breath. "I should be asking you that. Are you well? Did you run into any trouble? Where are you?"

Zofie released a shaky laugh. "I'm fine, sweetie. Manakai spirited me away with hardly a hiccup. As to where I am, I'm not entirely sure." She glanced in the direction Manakai had gone. "I haven't been told. Somewhere safe it seems."

A cold trickle slid down Liaena's spine. She sent a sharp glance at Sin. "Are you holding her hostage?"

Sin gave her a look of mild disgust, but Zofie answered. "Liaena, don't. There's a difference between protective custody and incarceration. No matter how beautiful our island was, it remained a cage. Now I'm free, but your father will look for me. Don't fault the Shays for taking precautions."

Liaena inclined her head, taking a precaution of her own and keeping her opinion of the Shays' motives to herself. She sent Sin a guarded look out of the corner of her eye. "How soon may I visit her?"

"We'll do what we can to arrange it as soon as possible," Sin answered, her voice bland. "The logistics, as you might guess, will be a bit touchy."

She had a point. Liaena had been so focused on her mother and how much she wanted to be with her, she hadn't considered how she was going to do this without her father taking notice. "I understand. Forgive me for sounding ungrateful."

Sin waved her apology away. "It's an odd situation for us all. We'll need to return to the commons soon to keep your watchers from becoming suspicious, but would you like a few minutes alone with your mother, Aena?"

Her throat tightened. "I would, thank you," she managed past a lump in her throat. Of course, any privacy would be illusory. They could record everything she and her mother discussed. But the offer touched her. No one had ever asked if she wanted privacy before.

Sin nodded and moved toward the exit. "We'll be right outside. Bash, privacy mode, please." Cassie touched Liaena's arm and smiled before following.

Liaena met her mother's watery gaze and couldn't stop tears from filling her own eyes. "Mama, are you sure you're all right? You look wonderful, but it must have been so frightening."

"I'm fine, really. It was over quite fast. I hardly had time to be afraid. Manakai arranged it to look like a robbery and kidnapping for ransom. Some unknown group in the Fringe will be demanding compensation for my return. Your father won't have proof the Shays did this, but I'm worried about you. Won't he link your visit to the Shays with my disappearance?"

"He might question it, but I'm prepared to handle him. Don't worry, Mother. I've had a great deal of practice deceiving him. I just wish I could be there with you."

"I wish you could too, sweetie. I don't want either of us to go back to that man. Why don't you ask the Shays for protection as well? We could be together and as far out of his reach as possible."

Liaena shook her head, wistful regret weighing on her chest. "It would put the Shays in far too much danger. I will be more help to them standing at Father's side."

"My brave girl," Zofie whispered, reaching out to touch the viewer. "You take too much on yourself."

"Not bravery. Believe me, if I could leave this to anyone else I would. But I will visit as soon as I can, Mother."

Zofie nodded, worry lining her face. "Just be careful. Your father is not—forgiving. I would rather never see you again than have him take his anger out on you. If he even suspects you, I'm so afraid of what he'll do."

Liaena smiled with as much reassurance and confidence as she could muster. "He's just a man with blind spots and weaknesses like any other. I'll be fine. We're running out of time. May I speak with Manakai before I go?"

"All right." Zofie reached a hand toward her again. "I love you, Liaena."

Her smile wobbling on a surge of painful emotion, she mirrored her mother's gesture. "I love you too, Mama."

Zofie left and Liaena took a few deep breaths to compose herself, brushing at her eyes to remove tears and smoothing rebellious strands of hair back from her face. A movement on the viewer warned her, and she dropped her hands, clasping them again and stiffening her shoulders.

Manakai met her gaze with cool amusement. "Zofie says you want a word with me. Going to lecture me on the care and feeding of your mother?"

Her skin prickled with affront. "She's quite capable of feeding and caring for herself," she responded, somehow keeping her tone even. "I wanted to thank you for all you've done to free my mother." She paused, fingers tightening around one another. "But I don't know what to say. There aren't enough words to express my gratitude."

His amusement faded, direct gaze spearing through her defenses. "Thanks are appreciated but not necessary. You offered us a deal, Liaena, and we're taking it. As long as you hold up your end, we're on level ground."

Liaena held his gaze with an effort, doing her best not to inhale the delicious scent of him wafting all around her. "Of course. How may I be of service?"

His mouth twitched. "What a leading question. For starters you can be my alibi and tell Web I was on our station. But leave the rest for now. You need to go." He paused, gaze flicking down to the pendant at her throat. Something moved in his eyes and doubled her heart rate. "It looks good on you, Aena." Then he turned away and the viewer went black.

Liaena pressed a hand over her heart, the rapid beat vibrating against her palm. Had she imagined the look in his eyes, the dark heat in his voice? He'd flirted with her before at social functions but always with a maddening brittle insincerity, toying with her and chilling her to the core. He'd looked much more serious a moment ago. *It looks good on you.* The man was going to be the death of her.

With a shake of her head she moved through his attractive home, his warm spice teasing her senses with each breath. She shouldn't fantasize or dream about things that could never be. Her mother was safe enough in their hands; she could trust the Shays not to hurt her, even if they planned to use her in their wild game with Webster. So she'd play her own wild game with her father. She couldn't allow any distractions.

At the door she took a moment to study its configuration before mimicking Sin's earlier actions. When she depressed the handle and pulled, the door swung open with ease. Stepping out, she tugged it shut behind her, puzzling over sudden odd satisfaction. Perhaps the long strange day affected her, but it felt good to move the portal herself instead of it opening and closing on its own.

"Aena? Everything all right?" Cassie asked. The two women stood a short distance away, watching her.

"Will you please tell Manakai he has a captivating home? I didn't get a chance to mention it." When Cassie's expression turned quizzical, Liaena pointed at the handle. "I like the door."

Cassie made a scoffing sound in the back of her throat. "Sin, this is your fault. She's getting woozy from too much shopping."

"Fairly sure it's not the shopping," Sin murmured with a secretive smile. "Let's get you on your way, Aena."

They ushered Liaena back along the path through the arboretum, walking in silence for a few steps.

Then Cassie cleared her throat. "So Aena, Sin tells me you offered to help them stop your father."

"I did. I will help any way I can."

"Isn't that sort of a huge conflict of interest? He is your family."

"What he does isn't right. He must be stopped for the good of everyone."

"Huh. Well in that case," Cassie started in a

hesitant tone, pausing to glance at Sin. When Sin nodded she continued, "I have a question for you. What do you know about Imago?"

Liaena tilted her head. "What's an imago?"

Cassie's expression faltered, gaze dropping as they reached the lift. "He's an AI. I hoped you'd heard of him and knew where your father is holding him."

"My father hasn't shared anything about this AI with me. Shall I try to find out for you?"

"We would be grateful," Sin interjected, keying the lift to descend. "But be careful. He's gone through a lot of trouble to acquire Imago. He'll protect his investment."

"I understand." Dread tightened Liaena's stomach muscles. Her father had given no hint of any AI projects. If he still had this Imago, he kept it from her on purpose. The implied distrust and paranoia concerned her. He'd been so suspicious of late. Had he seen through her deceptions?

When the lift doors opened onto the temple once again, Liaena glanced at Cassie. "May I ask for background on this Imago? Any information would help my search."

Cassie's features turned almost haggard. "Imago was…is one of my AIs. I created him. I also created a code damaging to AIs, which allows them to circumvent the safety laws governing their behavior. I didn't give it to him, but Imago is carrying this code. He's not well, Aena. He needs to be home with us, not in some cold lab suffering your father's games and tortures." She paused, swallowing hard. "Sorry, I get worked up about him."

"It's all right," Liaena murmured, the cold knot

tightening in her stomach. Cassie connected to Imago on a personal level. Perhaps the Shays did as well. If her father knew, he would use it to his advantage without mercy. "I'll do my best to find him."

Cassie touched her arm with a wan smile. "Thank you."

Sin led them through the temple without another word, passing through the sanctuary and casting a thoughtful glance at the red giant's magnificence. Liaena wondered how many times she'd passed through here to look so casual about it. She nodded to the ascetic at the temple entrance. The young woman bowed to all three of them but stayed as silent as Sin.

They paused outside of the temple. Liaena had to blink at the sudden change in atmosphere from dim and brooding to bright and festive. The commons now seemed unreal, as if the temple and the Red Sun within held more truth than the cheerful commercialism below them. Her back itched as though the Sun still bored its red eye into her skin. Something about it called to her and repelled her at the same time.

"Well, I have to be rude again and leave," Cassie announced with a grimace. "I have lots of work to do, and my bosses are total slave drivers." Sin snorted but Cassie ignored her, clasping Liaena's hand. "I'm glad you came, Aena. Come back anytime to visit, okay? And good luck with your father." Before Liaena could respond, she hurried off as if her heels had caught on fire.

"And there she goes," Sin drawled with a shake of her head. "She's obsessive about her work. I'm surprised she lasted this long." She angled her head toward the commons. "Shall we make our way down?

Would you like a bag of truffles from Dark Decadence for your return trip?"

Liaena allowed a small smile. "I may become their most frequent customer."

"Not possible, that's my title. And I hold the home advantage, so you're out of luck." With a cheeky grin Sin ushered her forward.

They made their spiraling way down the commons at a steady pace with a few stops at places Liaena had most enjoyed from their first tour. When they reached the bottom, Sin escorted her through the reception hall to the docking bay and her transport.

"Thank you for coming, Aena. We should do this again soon."

"I look forward to it. You've been a delightful hostess, though I'm afraid I ate far too much."

"Then my work here is done," Sin said with a chuckle and wrapped gentle arms around Liaena. "Be careful," she murmured next to her ear.

Startled, Liaena whispered, "I will." No one besides her mother had ever shown her such open warmth and concern. It called to her like a siren's song, urging her to let down her guard, to drop all her plans and stay.

To counter the feeling, she eased out of Sin's hold and stepped into her transport. She settled in a passenger's seat and signaled the pilot to leave. Resting her head against the back of the seat, she let out a long breath, looking out the porthole. The docking bay slid past and the Shay station receded from sight while Liaena brooded on the day's adventures. As usual the Shays had run rings around her. But at least her mother was free of her father.

Michelle O'Leary

Her heart lifted, providing the energy necessary to lean forward and make a call.

Her father's face appeared on the viewer, cold and commanding. "You took quite a long time, Daughter."

"Yes, it was an interesting visit."

"Report."

She gave him an abbreviated accounting of her time on the Shay station, omitting her visit to Manakai's quarters.

"So they are feeling you out, testing your resolve. Where was Manakai?"

Liaena kept her expression serene and gaze fixed on his. "I spoke with him but he did not join us. I don't believe shopping was to his taste."

His expression soured. "His courtship seems remiss, if it's his intention. What did he say to you?"

Liaena's hand drifted to the flame at her throat. "He approved of the necklace. I believe your intuition is correct and he intends to pursue me. Is it your wish I play along, Father?"

He studied her with icy gray eyes. "We'll discuss it when you return. Did they ask anything of you?"

"Yes, they did." She continued holding his gaze, keeping her expression smooth and unchallenging. "They mentioned an AI you had acquired from them."

"What did you tell them?" he asked in a sharp tone, eyes narrowing.

"I could tell them nothing as I know nothing. Will you enlighten me, Father? My ignorance places me in an awkward position with the Shays."

His face set in uncompromising lines. "We will discuss it on your return."

"Very good, Father. I will see you soon."

He ended the communication and she breathed a soft sigh of relief. She'd introduced the subject at least. He hadn't balked or exploded as of yet. Now she had to lead him on a verbal dance until he told her everything. The next few days promised to be rough. Leaning her head back, she closed her eyes and prayed for the solace of sleep.

Chapter 8

Kai heaved a sigh as he approached the Shay station. He wanted a fast swim followed by several hours face down in bed. Instead he'd get a huge dose of irritating discussion with his sister. A necessary evil but one he wished he could forgo this once.

Zofie Griffin had been difficult to deal with. She'd been cooperative, but her constant disconcerting references to her daughter had nibbled away at his patience. She'd painted an unbelievable picture of Liaena, contrary to everything he knew of the woman, maternal bias in full swing. He'd been thrilled to leave her at her final destination, a small mining outpost in an obscure system. They'd taken several different transports to reach it from the waystation where he'd contacted his sister and allowed Liaena to speak to her mother.

The memory of Liaena's face on seeing her mother ambushed him, driving another spike through his chest. She hadn't faked the stunned euphoria. It worked on him in ways he fought to deny. He'd had to leave the room to dispel his reaction. When she called him back, he almost hadn't gone. His gift lying against her skin set him on fire despite her cool and maddening poise. He'd wanted to put his hands on her in the worst way, if only to shake some reaction out of her.

Clenching his jaw, he shoved those thoughts to the

locked space in the back of his mind where they belonged and concentrated on his entry into the docking bay. It stayed busy night and day, a testament to the success of their courier service, Last Chance. Kai settled his Shadow onto the landing pad and powered it down, removing the connector from his data port with another muffled sigh. Cutting his connection to the slicer's power and exhilaration pulled the plug on his own energy reserves, draining him. The world seemed grayer when seen with his own tired eyes instead of the Shadow's sensors.

Grumbling, he levered out of the Shadow, made his way through the maintenance bay, and entered the lift, keying it to rise. At the Gold Rooms he passed through them to his sister's quarters.

Mina opened the door before he reached it, allowing him to stride in without pause. "Thanks, Mina."

"You're welcome, Manakai. Sinsudee is in the kitchen with Adelmo."

"Not having sex, are they?" he asked in a louder voice as he approached. "'Cause that's just gross."

They turned, both seated on stools at the long kitchen counter, Sin with a smirk and Del with a scowl.

"They don't appear to be involved in sexual intercourse," Mina answered in her smooth voice. "As a non-biological entity I'm not familiar with this practice. Perhaps you could assess their condition, Manakai, since you have such extensive experience in this area."

Kai paused, glancing at the nearest AI sensor with raised eyebrows while his sister burst into laughter. "Why, Mina, are you flirting with me?"

"How strange. Do humans often equate flirtation

with insult? I will study this phenomenon."

"Why is she picking on me today?" Kai asked the other two, hard pressed not to join his sister's laughter and Del's snickering.

"You're pickable." Sin slid her drink toward him. "How is our not-a-hostage?"

Kai scoffed, downing the rest of the drink in one long swallow. "Zofie's all settled in, relaxing after her big adventure. Cassie's parents made her feel right at home."

"So the op went as planned? No hitches?"

"Are you kidding? With Cassie's toy it was a walk in the park. One guy came in the room with us, but I'd killed the lights so he couldn't see me. She took one thing with her, a storage crystal full of holos of her daughter. I don't think Griffin will notice. I left the militia orders to trash the entire building." He sank onto a stool next to his sister with a sigh. "The op was easy enough, but the woman's a talker. I don't think she found a lot of conversation on her island."

"I imagine not," Sin murmured, studying him with shrewd eyes. "I also imagine she'll pester us until she sees her daughter. Ideas?"

"Yeah, but I need to sleep on it. Did you plant Imago?"

"We baited the hook and dangled the line. Now we have to see what comes of it."

Kai brooded for a moment, staring down at the bottom of the empty glass. "She said she didn't know anything about him, didn't she?"

"As we suspected she would."

"Truth or lie?"

"She seemed genuine, but Liaena has always been

good at blurring those lines between truth and deception. She's had to be, hasn't she?"

Kai lifted his head, studying them both with a frown.

Del raised his hands in a gesture of denial. "Don't look at me. I wasn't there."

"I watched her today, Kai. If she's leading us, it's the most magnificent performance of all time. On the other hand, she has to return to her father and play his game to survive. So I still don't think she can be trusted." Sin's eyes held an odd darkness, her mouth pressed in a grim line.

Kai spun the glass across the counter with a hard flick of his wrist. "You've always been too soft on her, Sissa. You let her work you. It's a weakness both of them will exploit."

She narrowed her eyes. "I said I don't trust her." Then her expression lightened. "Besides I'm not the one who painted myself into a corner. You sent her a gift, brother mine, and opened a door."

He glowered. "You know it was the right play."

"Sure it was. Your pursuit of Liaena would give us plenty of opportunities to exchange information with her. We would hardly ever see her otherwise. Griffin wouldn't interfere, since he's been dying to trip you up for years now. But this puts you on point, Brother. You'll have to spend a great deal of time with her. You'll even have to woo her, at least in public. However will you live through the torture?"

He gave her a sour look and didn't bother to answer. "Did you get anything out of her, besides waves of sincerity?"

"Sarcasm puts such a vicious sparkle in your eyes,"

she drawled. "We'll sit down with Cassie tomorrow and go over the specifics, if you can handle an account full of girl talk and shopping."

He shuddered. "Mercy."

"None for you. Your name came up a few times."

Suspicion tightened his muscles. "Oh?"

"I mentioned the time you swam naked in the fountain. You should have seen her face. Go ahead, thank me."

Del chuckled. "This one I gotta hear. What happened to your clothes? And why the fountain when you got a whole lake at your place?"

Kai ran fingers through his hair with a reminiscent smirk. "Had one too many supernovas. The rest of the night's a blur, but I'm pretty sure I wasn't the only one in the fountain, and I know I didn't sleep alone that night."

Sin stuck her fingers in her ears and screwed up her face in a childish grimace. "Ick! No more, I'll get sick."

He rolled his eyes. "Clean the rest up tomorrow? I need some shuteye."

She nodded, then scooped him close with an arm around his neck. "Thanks for not screwing up and getting dead out there, Brother."

"Thanks for not holding my hand like a mother hen, Sister," he countered, kissing her temple.

Del chuckled and shook his head. "You two are a trip."

"Better than boring." Kai stood and moved toward the exit. "You have a good—you know what? Never mind. I don't want to think about what you'll do after I leave. Nausea's setting in already."

"Love you too, Kai," Sin called after him as he left.

Kai grinned at his sister's sardonic tone but couldn't stave off a twinge of envy. He hadn't approved of Del at first. No guy was good enough for his sister in his not-so-humble opinion. But the man made Sin happy and showed complete devotion to her, so Kai supposed he'd earned some tolerance. Besides, the big guy had started to grow on him. The idea of them being Sun-bonded, of accepting Del into their family, wasn't altogether horrific. He almost looked forward to it.

Heading to the lift, he rose to the level of the arboretum and his home. He planned a hard swim followed by a face-plant on any comfortable horizontal surface. Tomorrow would be an interesting day.

****

Liaena waited on pins and needles for her father's summons. Soon he would discover her mother's disappearance. His reaction would be swift and brutal but not passionate. He'd never cared for Zofie, treating her with the same cold contempt he showed Liaena. She only wondered whether he would take out his fury on her or focus it on the offending parties or both. While used to his icy rage and punishments, she'd never accept them as her due.

She sat in her quarters and studied material he'd given her on AI research, a false trail if she'd ever seen one. But it kept her occupied and helped her stay composed and focused. She had never been more aware of the constant watch on her person, her trip to the Shay station still fresh in her mind. Even knowing her father had spies among their ranks, she'd never felt as free as she had with Sin and Cassie. A purposeful illusion perhaps, a ploy to trick her into letting down her guard. If so, they'd done nothing to follow through on the gambit, nothing to hurt her. On the contrary they'd shown her respect and friendship.

A sigh tried to work its way out of her throat, and she swallowed it back, keeping her breathing even and regular. Her father had said little of Imago, giving her research notes from his subordinates. So far Imago hadn't been discussed in those notes nor the code Cassie mentioned.

Their discussion of Manakai's possible courtship had been more in depth, with her father contemplating all the ways in which such a situation could be used to their advantage. At the same time he watched her with careful eyes, his thoughts clearly running in the opposite direction. Kai's abrupt interest made him suspicious. She demurred to his decision on the matter, as he would expect her to.

When her com chimed she rose and moved toward it with all the cool poise she could muster. "Yes, Father?"

"Get up here now," he barked, his eyes glacial and savage.

She allowed her head to tilt in slight question but gave him an obedient nod and headed for the corridor. She needed to react with natural emotion to her father's discovery, compartmentalizing all she knew and absorbing what had happened as if it were new.

Your mother has been taken. How would you feel?

When she reached her father's administration headquarters, she entered and approached him with quiet deference, keeping her expression neutral. He stood at his viewers, hands clasped behind him. He seemed calm, but a muscle twitched in his jaw and a vein pulsed at his temple. At first he didn't acknowledge her presence, normal behavior for him. He often made her wait, putting her in her place and reminding her of his control.

She'd begun to wonder if he'd found out after all when he turned to face her, his pupils dilated and his skin white around his mouth. Rage rolled off him like a black toxic cloud. She recoiled before she could restrain herself. When he became this furious he always hurt her no matter what she said or did. After an initial spike of fear the knowledge settled her. Knowing she couldn't avoid it made it easier to focus on what she needed to do.

If she stood dumb before him he would grow suspicious of her involvement, so she asked, "Father? What's happened?"

"Your mother is gone."

She stood still and blank for a moment, then let the words fill her with abject horror. "Gone?" she whispered. "She can't be. She was so healthy and—"

"Not dead, you fool, missing. Someone has taken her."

She slumped, pressing a hand to her chest. "Missing. Who would do such a thing? How would they know where to find her?"

"What excellent questions, Daughter. Perhaps you would care to extend a theory."

She ignored his acidic probe, pushing him closer to violence. If he was going to hurt her anyway, she might as well use it to further the impression of her innocence. Clasping her elbows and shivering, she murmured in a broken voice, "She must be so frightened. Oh Suns, what if they hurt her?"

"Liaena, this emotional outburst is inappropriate.

119

You are a Griffin. Act like one."

Not responding to his words, she reached toward him, tears filling her eyes. "Father, you must get her back, please, get her—"

He moved so fast she almost didn't see it coming. The back of his hand cracked against her face hard enough to throw her off balance. She stumbled, then turned it into a collapse as if her legs had given out. Seated on the floor, she cradled her face with one hand, head bowed. She didn't have to fake the shaking in her limbs; the side of her face throbbed, fury and fear roiled in the pit of her stomach, and adrenaline rushed through her veins. She hoped her emotional reaction would allay his suspicions of her involvement. He'd threatened her enough with her mother's safety to know how she'd react to a real crisis involving Zofie Griffin. But had she done enough?

He loomed over her like a black shade from hell, and her heart climbed into her throat. Then he made a sound of deep disgust and turned back to his viewers. "You disappoint me, Daughter. I raised you to be a Griffin, not a simpering sow like your mother. Perhaps I should have removed her entirely from your sphere and severed this childish emotional dependence you have on her."

Liaena remained silent. He would never do it; Zofie had long ago become the perfect tool to control and manipulate his daughter.

"The island guards informed me a small group attacked the compound, ransacked the place, and removed your mother along with several valuable items. The security system failed at just the right time and didn't record the incident. This implies the use of technology unusual for common thieves."

Her heart jumped but she didn't react otherwise.

"On the other hand, anyone who would attack an armed fortified compound would have to be resourceful."

"What will you do, Father?" Liaena asked in a low voice, keeping her head bowed in submission.

"I will hunt them down, of course. I've already begun a search. They will die for their efforts, though I must compliment them on their bravery first. To take something of mine was quite bold."

Liaena rose to her feet and stood at his elbow with her hands clasped. Her cheekbone ached. She ignored it and spoke around the pain. "I can't believe anyone would risk your wrath. Perhaps they didn't know who she is. Perhaps they'll give her back when they discover her identity." She inserted a thread of hope in her tone.

"Either way they will pay for what they've done. Such insolent actions have consequences." He turned his head to study her swollen face. "As I'm sure you know. Attend to that unsightly mess, Liaena."

"At once, Father," she murmured and headed for the exit, heart thumping hard in her chest. He hadn't mentioned the Shays at all. Did this mean he didn't consider them as the perpetrators or was he playing it close to the chest, suspecting her involvement with them? *Insolent actions have consequences.* This game would hold consequences for them all.

Chapter 9

Kai stepped over the threshold of Research and Development Level Five into chaos. What seemed like five thousand voices echoed through the space, conversing, shouting, and vying with each other. The confused and maddened AIs rescued from Griffin were making themselves heard. People in lab coats hurried back and forth, faces grim and focused as if they were at a murder scene or a sick ward for the terminally ill. He didn't recognize many of them, personnel from the original lab that had housed the distressed AIs from Griffin's experiments.

Kai scanned the workstations for Cassie but didn't see her. Catching the arm of a passing technician, he raised his voice over the din. "Where's Dr. Draegen?"

The man pointed at the holo-lab and pulled free with an impatient tug, continuing on his way without a second glance. Kai ignored the rudeness given the circumstances. Working in this madhouse couldn't be easy.

Moving to the holo-lab's observation window, he took a moment to watch Cassie work. She stood in an intricate web of bright lines and flashes, a holographic representation of an AI's neural network. She looked as focused as the rest of the personnel but with a keen energy they lacked. She never gave up, always searching for answers even when they seemed impossible to find. Kai smothered a smug grin; Griffin's loss became their vast gain.

He tapped on the window to get her attention. Cassie glanced over and waved him in with a quick welcoming smile.

Stepping to the entrance, he eased over the threshold, blinking at the disorienting transition. The hologram dropped him in the middle of the flashing web, no floor or ceiling apparent, the sudden quiet startling. "Hey, Cass. Whose brain are you working on?"

"None of them have names, only designations. We wanted to wait until they have more normal functioning before we try out names. This one's designation is ten E seventy-eight. Ten, this is Kai."

A strange blast of noise hurt his ears and he winced. After a pause a fractured voice said, "Hello."

Cassie gave him a pained shrug. "We still have a lot of work to do. But I think I've found a solution to the code. Griffin's researchers found a way to duplicate the code I made, only theirs is simpler. My guess is Imago was too wild for them and they wanted a more controllable version." She faltered for a second, eyes dimming at the name of her lost AI. "He's too valuable to eliminate, right? He's the original source of the code."

"Griffin spent too much time and effort getting his hands on Imago. He wouldn't destroy him," he reassured her. "What's your solution?"

Cassie nodded with a preoccupied frown, fingers worrying at her braid. "Right. Well, this new code is attracted to an AI's personality matrix. I can use this attraction to trap it."

"You tried the same thing with Imago, didn't you? You only managed to confine the code, and judging by all these damaged AIs, it didn't stay confined for long."

"I know." She sighed. "Poor Imago, he must hate me."

"He agreed it was the best way, so stop kicking yourself for it. How is your new solution better?"

She brightened. "It's so simple, I wanted to smack myself when I thought of it. The code is attracted to personality, so I'll give it a mouse-trap, a Trojan horse, a doppelganger to wiggle into. I'll turn off the AI's core personality and insert a fake one complete with trap doors."

He stared at her. "Oh yeah, simple."

She gave him a frown. "So the idea is simple, but implementing it will be more complicated and take time. It's progress. Don't rain on my parade."

"Wouldn't dream of it. Did you tell your staff the good news? Because they all seem a tad under-enthused."

"I didn't want to get their hopes up until I was sure it would work."

"I hope it does, Cass. Sounds like a great plan. Can I steal you away for a bit? I have a new project for you."

She made a face at him. "Don't tell me you have to rescue somebody else now."

"Not exactly."

"I'll go but not for long. Ten and I have a big day planned. Right, Ten?"

Another blast of sound ricocheted around the lab. "Yes. Doctor fix me. Fix, fix…" The fractured voice trailed off, sounding confused.

Cassie sighed and gave Kai a wan smile. "As you can see, my patients need me. Don't keep me long, Shay."

"I promise."

Kai accompanied her out of the holo-lab and waited while she dropped off her lab coat at a work station. Together they weaved through the chaos of the main lab toward the exit.

"Hey! Where you goin'?" Nick Givliani dodged technicians like a ball player and caught up with them at the exit.

"Kai has another project."

"Another project he's going to keep from the FPA?" Nick asked with biting emphasis, his eyes narrowing on Kai.

Kai gave him a lazy grin. "What are you doing in the lab, Inspector? I'm pretty sure this is not your area of expertise."

"I'm Marchand's liaison and he's giving this case special attention. So this is me, liaising." He paused, widening his eyes. "You remember Marchand, right? Tall guy, face like a blade, wears First Marshal rank on his uniform, head of the FPA. FPA, as in Federated Planetary Alliance, defenders of law and order—"

Kai held up a hand. "Thanks, I got it, Mr. Sarcasm." He glanced down at Cassie. "What'd you feed him this morning?"

"Bacon," she responded with a straight face. "Are you two going to start sniping at each other? If so, you can get a room and I'll go back to work."

Kai caught her elbow and steered her out the door into the quiet of the corridor. "We can snipe on the move, can't we, Giv? We're talented like that."

"Sure, talented," Nick muttered, glowering at Kai's hand on Cassie's arm as they moved along the corridor.

Kai smothered a grin and didn't let go. For some reason Nick acted jealous whenever Kai came within three feet of Cassie. Odd, since she treated Kai with all the affection of an impatient long-suffering sister. He in turn felt only fraternal love for the little braincase, but he had fun harassing Nick.

"Don't know what you see in this big lug, Cass," he announced in a casual drawl. "But if you're set on him, why limit yourself? You could have us both."

"Kai, don't start," Cassie warned, pulling out of his grip.

Nick made his feelings clear without a word, growling over the top of Cassie's head.

Kai grinned. "Well, well, I think he likes me. How about a hero sandwich, Cass?"

"What?" they both yelped and stopped in their tracks.

"You know, sweet succulent flesh pressed between two big hunks—"

"Manakai Shay!" Cassie hollered, eyes as big as saucers, holding back a furious Nick.

"Of bread." Kai gave them both a bland enquiring look. "I was talking about lunch. Where were your dirty minds? Come on, time's wasting." He flashed a wicked grin and continued on, heading for the offices.

"I wanna hit him," Nick declared.

Cassie heaved a sigh. "No, it would only encourage him. The man has a pathological need to drive people bananas."

Kai shot a smirk over his shoulder. "Just one of my many talents."

She snorted. "What's this project you want me to work on?"

"We'll discuss it as a group. Sin and Del are waiting for us."

When they reached the offices, they found the couple sitting side by side on the big desk, watching a multitude of vid-feeds on the viewers behind it.

"Any sign yet?" Kai asked them.

Sin answered without looking away from the screens. "Griffin has mobilized forces in the area but hasn't reported Zofie's abduction to the authorities. Are we surprised?"

"Suns, yes. The shock may kill me. What are his forces doing?"

"Search pattern." Sin glanced over her shoulder with a quick smile for Cassie and Nick. "The militia hasn't checked in."

"And they won't," Kai reminded his sister. "Too dangerous."

"If he catches them—"

"Their job is to stay uncaught. They're good at their job, Sissa."

She tipped her head in wan agreement and went back to studying the screens. Del rose and rounded the desk, exchanging monosyllabic greetings with his brother. Kai smothered a grin and wondered what it would've been like to have a brother instead of a sister. Or in addition to Sin, she had her moments, but he wouldn't change their lives for anything.

Kai headed for the bar. "Why don't you tell them about your idea, Cass?"

While Cassie told the group about her potential cure for the crazed AIs, Kai pulled out beverages for everyone.

Sin wander over from the viewers, her features focused as she listened. "Sounds promising, Cass. Do you think it would work on Imago?"

Cassie grimaced. "I'm not sure. The original code is more complex, affecting more of his base functions than his personality. If it works on these AIs, it's at least a possibility for him."

"Good. When we get him back, I know you'll find a way to help him."

Cassie cradled her tea, settling on a stool and hunching her shoulders. "How close are we to getting him back?"

Sin turned to Kai with a slight lift of her eyebrows, offering him the spotlight.

"We're not sure," Kai responded. "So far our own avenues of investigation haven't gotten us closer to Imago's location. Liaena offered to look into it, but we need a way to communicate with her without Griffin getting suspicious. Griff won't buy Sin and Lie turning into overnight soul sisters, but he might go for a courtship, so it's my turn to make contact. Even if he doesn't believe it's real, he won't be able to resist hooking me in. We need a—"

"Wait." Nick leaned forward, dark eyes gleaming with humor. "Are you saying you're gonna make moves on the Ice Queen?"

Del snorted, mouth curling at the corners. "Man, watch how close you get. You don't wanna freeze off any good parts."

Kai lifted his water bottle in an ironic toast to the brothers, taking a long swallow to wash the acid from his throat. They didn't know how right they were.

Courting Liaena would be hell in so many ways.

"Cut it out, you two," Cassie lectured, frowning at the brothers. "Aena isn't cold at all; she's contained. Imagine being raised by a father like Webster Griffin. We're lucky she's not a raging psychopath."

"How do you know she's not?" Nick countered.

She narrowed her eyes on him. "Who's the doctor here? Liaena is exhibiting signs often associated with abuse: disassociation and discomfort with physical touch. I would bet my entire savings she has trouble sleeping and has frequent bouts of depression and anxiety."

A strange knot formed in Kai's stomach. "Describe these signs," he commanded, setting down his bottle harder than he'd intended.

Cassie gave an abbreviated clinical account of Liaena's visit, sketching an illuminating picture of her reactions from her automatic shrinking at each physical touch to her dissociative moments in the face of stress. "She exhibited aberrant verbal and physical responses to this type of social activity. She oscillated between over-formality and withdrawal. She's not used to normal social interactions we all take for granted." She looked between Kai and Sin. "You've always seen her at formal occasions, events her father no doubt trained her for. Those are what she's used to. My guess is she's never had a friend, let alone a girlfriends' day out."

Sin nodded. "I'll second her impressions. Aena seemed surprised by everything we did and said."

"Given this, my guess is Griffin keeps her under emotional and physical lockdown, complete isolation. She's his prisoner in every sense of the word."

Kai braced his weight on the edge of the counter,

sharing a solemn glance with his sister. She shook her head, and he looked away with a crease between his brows, thinking once again he should've taken Aena hostage. But he and Sin had already had this conversation; their war against Griffin wasn't ready for such a drastic action.

Cassie glanced around and exclaimed, "Why do you all look so surprised? Webster Griffin has never been nor ever will be father material. He's sadistic and evil. I don't know how she's survived him all these years."

"Feel sorry for her all you want, Cass," Kai responded with a warning glance. "Just don't take everything she says at face value. If she's as trapped as you say, she's more likely to be his puppet not less."

Cassie glowered at him and folded her arms across her chest. "I'm not arguing about this again. What did you want to talk to me about?"

"We need a way to hijack a holo-suite to get a communication signal in."

"We can't sneak Aena away to visit her mother yet," Sin added, "but we'd like to give them face-to-face time. It'll reassure Aena of her mother's well-being and keep her interested in working with us."

"Of course I can hack a holo-suite," Cassie responded, her features still dark with discontent. "But Griffin will have security on his holographic systems. He'll catch me at it and might even find out about Zofie."

"It'll be a public holo-suite," Kai amended. "We're inviting the Griffins to a Golden Sun charity. I'll persuade Liaena to leave the party and take a tour of the local fun. We stop at an entertainment suite, you do your magic, and she gets to chat with her mother. Plus it's a secure place for her to give me any info she's found on Imago."

Cassie's expression smoothed. "I thought Griffin wasn't attending social functions these days."

Kai gave her a grim smile. "I'm bait."

"Takin' one for the team," Del mumbled into his glass with a snicker.

Kai sharpened his smile and turned to the big man. "Sin's going to keep Griffin distracted. Want to take bets on which slinky dress she squeezes into to keep his attention?"

Del's humor soured. "Low blow, Shay."

"Just returning your serve, Giv."

"Play nice, boys," Sin told them in an absent tone. "Cass, do you think it's possible to make an undetectable program to search Griffin's network systems? Any info it retrieves couldn't be used as evidence but would point us in the right direction. Aena could introduce the program and retrieve it when it's done without doing the search herself. Less of a chance for her to get caught."

"Making a digger worm would be easy enough, but an undetectable one would take more time. When's this party?"

"Tomorrow afternoon."

Cassie shook her head. "The holo-suite hack is no problem, but I'll need more time for a sophisticated hunter program. Wait, I have an idea. Maybe something to give Aena some breathing room." She paused, chewing on the inside of her cheek, brown eyes growing distant and absorbed.

"Uh-oh," Nick said with a grimace. "She gets this

look and I don't see her for days. The AIs keep her busy enough, Shays. Call this off before her brain explodes."

Cassie didn't act as though she heard him. Sliding off the stool, she announced, "I'll work on it and get back to you." Then she spun on her heel and marched for the exit.

Nick sighed, shot Kai and Sin an accusing glower, and followed her.

Del snorted, watching them go. "They'll be camping in the lab again." He turned his head, glancing between Sin and Kai. "Pushing this kinda hard."

"Door's open," Kai said with a one-shouldered shrug.

"We can't ignore the opportunity," Sin added, her eyes shadowed. "This is the closest we've ever come to the heart of Griffin's operation."

Del made a noncommittal sound and scrubbed a hand against his stubbled jaw, studying his bonded-to-be. "How'd you swing an invite to this party? Seems like short notice."

"The Sun Orders are being scarily helpful these days. T'Zai's contact in the Golden Order, Berrabas, handled the invite."

Del's expression darkened. "So what slinky dress are you wearing?"

Sin sighed and sent Kai a look full of censure. "Thanks a lot, brother mine."

"All part of the service," he said with a wink.

Turning to Del, she curled her mouth in sly seduction. "I'll make you a deal. Whatever I put on for the party you get to take off afterward."

A sudden male grin lit his face, but before he could

respond a chime sounded from the viewers.

Kai frowned and rounded the bar, heading for the viewers with Sin and Del on his heels. "That better not be what I think it is." When he reached the viewers, he swore under his breath. "It's the militia," he told the other two. "They're going off script. Boasting they've stolen something valuable from Webster Griffin, using a general signal."

He turned his head and met Sin's grim gaze.

"General?" Del repeated. "Everybody in the sector will know where they are. Do they wanna get caught?"

"Seems like T'Zai is playing a different game from what we decided," Kai growled.

Del gave Kai a nudge to get his attention. "What's T'Zai have to do with this?"

"The militia is his."

Del swore and Sin nodded with a cold smile. "I believe it's time we had a chat with our sneaky Red Sun mentor."

Chapter 10

Liaena should be getting used to the sensation of butterflies in her stomach by now. But she never could predict Manakai Shay. He'd requested she join him at a Golden Sun charity function. Not a typical first-date venue but his invitation suggested courtship. The idea of interacting with him in such a way gave her fits.

Even if he meant it as a sham to fool her father, how could she handle him smiling at her, flirting with her, touching her? *Oh Suns, give me strength.*

She entered the event at her father's side, heart racing and stomach doing horrible flips. In all her planning and preparation, she'd never once considered the possibility of Manakai initiating a relationship with her. She'd dreamt of it, fantasized about it, but she'd never thought those girlish unrealistic fantasies would come true. Even worse, everything he said and did would no doubt be false and she had to go along with it, participate, and pretend to enjoy.

The worst torture her father had ever administered couldn't compare to this.

People filled the long hall, ascetics in their golden robes drifting from group to group in a spinning dance of obscure politics. The Golden Sun Order focused on the structures of society, the social interactions producing power and influence. She'd never understood why or if they had a specific goal in mind, but Golden ascetics gravitated to social intrigues. As natural diplomats, they catered to many different aspects of society. So this crowd ranged a varied slice of life, from politicians to artisans and everything in between.

This included corporate heads like Webster Griffin and the Shays. Liaena scanned the crowd but didn't see Manakai. She took measured breaths and tried not to appear anxious, moving at a sedate pace next to her father. She'd had a great deal of experience accompanying him to events such as this, standing in his shadow and being the good daughter. Sometimes her duties included distracting or entertaining someone for her father, but most of the time she was just an ornament. Some women would be insulted, but Liaena didn't mind playing the role, allowing her father to dismiss her as unimportant and underestimate her. If he didn't see who she really was, he would never see her betrayal coming.

A Golden ascetic approached, rotund and jovial. "Greetings, Lord and Lady Griffin! Welcome to Bahia. On behalf of our host, Grand Chancellor Marquist, I welcome you to his magnificent abode. I trust your travels were comfortable?"

"Berrabas," her father greeted the balding ascetic with bland dismissal. "Where is the Grand Chancellor?"

Berrabas made a regretful face. "He's on the planet below I'm afraid. His duties pulled him away. Running a world slows for no party, I imagine. I do hope you will be able to enjoy our humble hospitality without him."

"I'm sure," her father said, his tone doubtful with a hint of insult.

Liaena flicked a glance at him. Webster Griffin

Michelle O'Leary

despised the orders, offended by their metaphysical teachings. To take the sting out of her father's attitude, she gave the round ascetic a bow. "Thank you, Mendani Berrabas."

His smile softened and he bowed in return, his eyes taking on a mischievous twinkle as he glanced past her. "And if our hospitality lacks, I'm sure your company will provide."

Liaena started to ask what he meant when warm fingers curled around her arm.

"There you are," Manakai said in a low intimate tone, subtle satisfaction heating his voice. He stood close enough for his warmth to bake into her side, his delicious male spice teasing her senses.

Liaena forgot how to breathe. Berrabas had distracted her but now all her nervousness came flooding back, freezing her in place. Her heart jerked hard in her chest, then ran rampant. Goose bumps bloomed under his touch and spread down her arm.

"Griff, good to see you again," Manakai greeted her father, his fingers tightening a fraction on her bare skin before sliding down her arm to her wrist in a slow glide.

Her knees wobbled. She worried her heart would explode. The goose flesh spread over her shoulder and all the way down her torso.

"Manakai, a pleasure. And Sinsudee, how delightful to see you as well. You look stunning, my dear."

Liaena blinked and managed to turn her head, startled at Sin's appearance. She hadn't known both Shays would attend. Sin did look stunning, her deep red dress clinging to every sleek curve. Liaena felt

136

underdressed in her conservative slacks and short-sleeved pale-blue blouse.

Sin grinned at Webster, a sly gleam in her eyes. "Web, I was hoping to see you here." She turned to Liaena, her expression warming, and gave her a hug. "Aena, I'm glad you came. Did you recover from our food fest? How's your chocolate stash?"

As Sin released her Liaena managed to find her voice. "All gone I'm afraid."

"Tragic! Don't worry, I'll send you more."

Manakai sighed, his fingers still clasping Liaena's wrist in a loose hold. His touch burned like fire. "Sister."

"Oh, right," Sin responded, sending her brother a mischievous grin. "He'll send you more. Mendani Berrabas, well met." She gave the ascetic's round cheek a brief kiss.

His balding head turned bright red, and he sputtered, "Well met indeed. Pardon me, I've grown quite thirsty all of a sudden." He turned and scurried off.

"So that's how you get rid of the odious fellow." Griffin gave Sin an admiring glance.

She batted her eyelashes. "I don't think it would have worked quite the same way for you."

He laughed and Liaena thought it might be genuine humor. Hard to tell with her father; his eyes remained hard and cold.

"Griff, do you mind if I steal Liaena away for a dance?" Manakai asked in a casual easy tone, as if the question hadn't opened a pit at Liaena's feet. How could she dance with him? She could barely draw air in her chest, let alone move her feet.

"Of course," her father doomed her.

She could say no, but it would defeat the purpose. They needed a way to exchange information, the whole point to this charade she assumed.

"Aena?" Manakai murmured in his new intimate tone and slipped his fingers around hers. He shifted away, putting coaxing pressure on her hand.

Taking a deep fortifying breath, Liaena nodded to her father and Sin and willed her feet to move. Her weak knees held. Manakai led her through the crowd, large fingers still curled around her own.

"How are you holding up?" he asked in a low voice.

She turned her head, meeting his gaze for the first time. "Pardon?"

His heart-wrenching green eyes weren't mocking or seductive but sober. "You're trembling and you have traces of a bruise on your face. What did he do?"

His concern almost put her on the floor. She had to pause and steady her knees, head swimming. He paused with her, shifting close and baffling her with his heat. His stance implied protection, his fingers around hers possessive, though both notions seemed ridiculous. She assumed he only moved close so no one would hear them speak.

"I'm fine," she said around an odd lump in her throat. "Don't trouble yourself."

He snorted as if she'd said something idiotic. "Aena, did he hit you?"

She schooled her expression, glancing around to make sure no one stood in hearing range. "I can handle my father. Do you really wish to have this conversation here?" In retrospect, leaving the remnants of the bruise on her cheekbone hadn't been a good idea. She'd done it as a goad to her father, one of her small rebellions. He hadn't even noticed, however, and Manakai's frown would draw attention. "Didn't you mention a dance?"

He sighed and let her go. She mourned the loss until his hand settled on the small of her back, sending heat in waves all the way up her spine. "All right, little Miss Evasive, let's dance. But I'm warning you, we're not done here."

Wordless, she drifted forward under the gentle guidance of his hand on her back, so focused on his searing touch she didn't see the crowd around them. When they reached the dance floor, she blinked, keen disappointment giving way to profound relief. The music and participants formed a step dance, each group moving in graceful lines and twirls. Manakai would not be holding her close. At least she'd be spared that torturous delight.

"Hmm, this one looks complicated," Manakai mused with an undertone of humor.

She glanced at him. His features wore a bland expression, a faint curl lifting one corner of his mouth. Was he mocking her?

"I'll understand if you don't believe you can perform," she responded in a serene tone, clasping her hands together and sweeping her gaze over the dancers.

He made a muffled choking sound. "Ouch, another swift kick delivered. Wish you'd go back to aiming for my shins."

Her cheeks burned. She hadn't meant her comment as a sexual innuendo. Before she could reply, he ushered her forward and inserted the two of them into a dancing group with impressive grace and skill.

Conversation proved impossible, so she had a small reprieve. She concentrated on the steps and twirls of the dance, smiling with polite reserve for her various brief partners and watching Manakai with furtive delight. Suns have mercy, the man was poetry in motion, as self-assured and powerful in his masculine grace as a jungle cat. All his female partners brightened when they squared off with him, melting at his charming smile and warm touch.

He bestowed the same smile on her. He also shifted closer to her than his other partners, sending her thoughts scattering and putting off her rhythm. Thank the Suns she didn't forget the steps or tread on anyone's toes.

When it was done, Manakai returned to her side and lifted his eyebrows, a faint challenging gleam in his eyes. "Another?"

And watch him seduce another half a dozen women without trying? "No, thank you." Then she grabbed the bull by the horns. "I wish to speak privately."

"No kidding," he said in a dry tone. "Whatever for, Ms. Griffin?" When she only stared at him, he gave his head an impatient shake. "Let it play out, Aena. We can't rush it or it won't look authentic. How about a drink?"

She inclined her head in assent, subduing a frown. This confirmation of the falsity of his courtship sent a pang through her chest, but his attitude aggravated her more. He didn't need to treat her like a ninny. She assumed he had some plan, but he hadn't disclosed it. How was she supposed to play along when she didn't know the script?

His hand returned to her back as they moved through the crowd, and Liaena's breath stuttered in her chest. She understood why he touched her, to give the appearance of interest. But each time he did it grew harder for her not to be seduced for real. The strength and warmth radiating from the gentle touch on her back made her weak in the knees, made her want to feel his touch all over. Shocking, considering she'd never reacted to a man this way before in her life. Even full-on sex with her security guard hadn't turned her limbs this quivery, and all Manakai did was place a polite hand at the small of her back.

Maybe not so polite. Instead of a light fingertip touch, his hand made full contact, his palm and spread fingers warming her right through the blouse. At each turn through the crowd, his fingers would flex as if guiding her or pulling her closer. Whatever his intent, it drove her mad.

When they reached the bar, she realized neither of them had spoken a word all the way through the crowd to each other or anyone else. She'd been too preoccupied with his touch to pay attention to others. She sent a furtive glance behind them, wondering if anyone had noticed. No one was staring at least.

"What's your poison?" Manakai spoke in a casual tone but with a shuttered expression, almost grim.

Did he hate this pretense so much? In all the time they'd known each other, he'd seldom touched her, each instance burning in her memory. From his expression she deduced he didn't want to touch her. Hurt seared her throat and she stiffened against it.

"Perhaps we should try something else," she whispered, staring without seeing at the array of drinks.

"Not thirsty?"

"No, I mean this." She gestured between them, careful to keep her face averted. "It doesn't seem to be working."

He made a sound she couldn't interpret, but she didn't check his expression. After a moment he said in a careful tone, "Cassie explained your discomfort with physical contact, but we don't have much choice here. This is the most viable option."

Liaena turned her head, meeting his intense gaze with a crease between her brows. "What do you mean, discomfort?" He didn't seem to be describing the heat and weakness she experienced at his slightest touch.

"He hurts you." His eyes hardened and mouth tightened into a grim line, reflecting his flat voice. "So you flinch or freeze. I'm sorry for it, but we don't have—"

"What? I do not." She faced him with her affront. She always took care not to flinch, and when had she ever frozen around him? Melted sounded more apt.

"Yes," he stated with implacable calm, "you do." He brushed the backs of his fingers along her cheekbone under the faint bruise, his touch slow and tender.

Liaena went still, lungs collapsing and heart stumbling along in her chest. Her skin tingled and her throat closed with longing. What she wouldn't give to have him caress her like this forever.

His thumb made a slow pass over the faded bruise, then his hand fell away. He watched her with a shadow in his eyes, features calm but grim.

It took her a few moments to get her lungs working again, and a few more to jumpstart her brain. Not easy under his unnerving stare, with him standing so close, filling the air with his muscle-loosening scent. Trying to process what had just happened, she turned her head, gaze sweeping blind and desperate over the crowd. All right, so she did freeze under his touch or at least went still like a mouse under a cat's paw. But he assumed she abhorred physical contact. Unfortunately for her, when it came to him the opposite held true.

"Point taken," she husked, then cleared her throat. "But it's not relevant."

He made an aggravated sound, a deep rumble almost like a growl. "You're right, it's not. We started down this road already, princess. If we back out now, Griff will smell trouble. So what'll it be?"

Liaena clenched her jaw against a sudden urge to tell him to go to hell. He made the term princess sound almost as bad as the nickname Lie. Taking a deep breath and chilling her expression to glacial smoothness, she turned to him. "I can handle it if you can. I assume you have a plan."

His mouth twitched as if fighting a smile. "My plan starts with getting this look off your face or nobody will believe we're an item. I'm getting frostbite, Aena. Have mercy."

She flexed her fingers, searching for something to do with them besides hit him. "You are not as charming as you think you are," she retorted, leaning over the bar and grabbing the first glass in reach. Taking a large swallow, she coughed and blinked sudden tears from her eyes. "Oh, dear," she wheezed. "This is not punch."

"Now there's a good idea," Manakai drawled, taking an identical glass and raising it to her in sardonic salute. "If anything can melt the ice, this will." He

143

drained the glass in three long swallows without any visible effect. "Come on, Aena. Drink up. We have somewhere to be."

So he did have a plan. She took another sip then gave up, setting the glass down and giving him an expectant look. He held out a hand, a gleam in his eyes. Her stomach flipped over but she didn't hesitate, laying her fingers across his palm. Something softened in his expression, his hold gentle as he tugged her into the crowd.

He led the way, making a path through the groups of people. His grip shifted, his fingers winnowing through hers with an intimacy so powerful it made her stumble. She gulped, arm tingling, breath lurching in her throat, and heart thundering in her ears.

When she realized they were returning to her father, she understood he only held her hand for appearances, while this intimate connection made her heart ache. Her eyes burned but she lifted her chin and stiffened her spine. She said she'd handle it and she would.

Then he surprised her by releasing her hand and cupping her elbow, urging her forward as they approached her father and Sin. The two appeared to be in a lively conversation, both smiling, but something in the air between them made the hair rise on the back of her neck. She'd always felt the same thing whenever Sin and her father played their verbal games. It had taken her a while to understand; Webster had never been convincing in his courtship, but Sin played with him like a wildcat chases prey. Her games ran deeper and more predatory than mere flirtation.

Liaena had never understood how her father could

miss this undercurrent. She came to the conclusion his arrogance and overconfidence blinded him. He always spoke in dismissive terms about the Shay twins, as if they were poor reflections of their father's strength. He underestimated them and they played to it with breathtaking skill and audacity.

Manakai proved it again, sauntering over to the pair with a boyish grin. "All right, I'll admit it. I had an ulterior motive."

Webster turned from Sin with eyebrows raised, mouth curving in a bland smile. "Ulterior motive for what?"

"For dragging you both to such a stodgy party. This floating castle happens to be orbiting directly above one of the finest open air markets and entertainment galleries in the galaxy. Father Griffin, do I have your permission to escort your daughter below?"

Her father's smile widened while his eyes narrowed. "How quaint. And possibly dangerous. I hope you'll forgive me if I send along a man to watch over her."

Manakai didn't seem to see the insult, the assumption Liaena couldn't watch out for herself and Manakai couldn't protect her. He gave her father a sage nod, the corners of his eyes crinkling. "Very wise. And prudent to send a chaperone, though I swear my intentions are honorable."

"I'm sure they are," her father responded with a dubious arch of one eyebrow. "Do enjoy yourselves."

Manakai inclined his head with a roguish smirk, nodded to his sister, and turned Liaena with gentle pressure toward the exit. One of her father's bodyguards met them, saying nothing but falling in behind them as they made their way to the transports.

"Open air market?" Liaena asked to fill the silence between them.

"Hmm. Pretty trinkets and such. You women love shopping, don't you?"

She stared at him until she noticed the humor lurking around his mouth. "Are you antagonizing me on purpose?"

"Yes. I hear you had loads of fun with Sin and Cassie." He opened a transport and ushered her in, allowing the bodyguard to follow them aboard.

"It was an interesting experience. What sort of entertainment galleries?"

He sat beside her in the passenger seating and flashed a grin. "It's a surprise."

"I'm not fond of surprises. Will there at least be chocolate?"

"I can promise you chocolate," he answered with a solemn nod, his captivating eyes gleaming with a wicked light.

"Well then." She settled into the seat, sending the bodyguard a quick glance. "Won't this be fun?"

Chapter 11

Kai chuckled, wondering if Griffin's watchdog had a way to record them or if he would report their activities to Griffin later. Liaena seemed to understand they now stood on center stage, every action watched and scrutinized. She responded with a small smile, sending him a silvered look out of the corner of her eye. He wondered what she'd do if he captured her face in his hands and kissed the breath out of her.

Looking away out of sheer self-preservation, he requested the pilot take them to the surface. Stretching his legs out and crossing them at the ankles, he linked his fingers over his stomach to keep from reaching for her again. Once he'd started touching her, it'd become addictive and he had trouble stopping. Her smooth skin and supple muscles under his fingers went straight to his head like a strong drink, not to mention her delicate fragrance, so like peaches and blossoms it made his mouth water. He wanted more.

Out of the corner of his eye he assessed their chaperone with mounting hostility. If the man weren't here, they'd have more freedom to speak. He'd suspected Griffin would send someone to watch them, but he'd hoped they'd have more time in relative privacy.

Then again, maybe they needed a chaperone. Not only could the man report their actions but his presence would help Kai stay on mission. Liaena was one hell of a distraction. He turned his head to study her with frank admiration.

As usual she'd swept her mahogany hair into some intricate weave at the back of her head. She stared ahead with her typical serene poise, gray eyes distant, the regal lines of her face both elegant and fragile. The pale hint of a bruise on her cheekbone called to his fingertips. Like some lovesick idiot, he wanted to soothe it away. He also wanted to give Griffin matching bruises in more places than his face.

"You're staring," Liaena announced.

"I know," he murmured. "Does it bother you?"

She tilted her head for a moment, considering. She glanced at their chaperone, then turned her head to meet Kai's gaze with a faint curl of her luscious mouth. "So how is the weather on Bahia today?"

Kai turned a rueful look on the bodyguard. "Man, I hate you so much right now."

The man smirked, then seemed to remember his duty and blanked his features, looking away. Liaena made a sound like a muffled laugh.

Kai sent her a swift glance, his heart lurching in his chest. What would real humor from her sound like? He'd give a lot to see her relax enough to laugh. She'd recovered her poise, looking down at her hands clasped in her lap. Maybe he should have stayed at the party long enough for her to finish the drink.

"My sister tells me she spilled all my darkest secrets while you ladies were palavering."

She turned her elegant head, blinking at him. "I'm afraid not. She mentioned a dip in the commons fountain, but public indiscretions don't count. Do you have dark secrets, Manakai?"

"Repeat after me: Kai."

She raised a regal eyebrow.

He grinned. "Pretty please. Don't make me get the cane."

"Only you would beg and threaten in the same breath."

"Is that what I was doing? You still didn't say it."

She sighed. "You will be the death of me, Kai. Why do I put up with you, Kai? Tell me all your darkest secrets, Kai."

He sent her a wolfish smile, liking his name on her lips far too much. "Not on your life, sweet Liaena. You would run screaming."

"I think you underestimate me."

He softened his smile and tilted his head in acknowledgement. "No doubt. It feels like we've landed. Shall we?" He held out his hand to her again, gratified when she placed hers in his hold without hesitation. Mindful of her aversion to being touched, he kept his clasp light, though he wanted to tighten his grip, to savor the texture of her skin and her delicate structure, to bring her hand to his mouth. He wanted to taste the peach fragrance on her skin.

Letting out a long breath through his teeth, he rose and escorted her to the exit, ignoring the watchdog on their heels. The transport doors opened onto a bright sunlit landing platform, bustling with activity.

"The weather on Bahia is warm and sunny with a slight chance of clouds later in the evening," Manakai intoned, angling toward the exit arches, but Liaena resisted the forward motion.

"Wait." She turned her face skyward to the Sun,

closed her eyes, and sighed, a furtive smile lifting the corners of her lips. "So warm and lovely," she murmured.

Kai went still, holding his breath. Sun's blood, the woman stunned him. The Sun cast fingers of fire through her hair and set her skin aglow. With her head back the long curve of her throat beckoned to his fingers. The scoop neck of her blouse framed the crystal pendant sparkling against the backdrop of her alabaster skin. He drank in the sight, wishing he could keep this image somehow, to bring with him when he returned home alone. With an ache in his chest, he remembered the holo Zofie had shown him of young Liaena, kissed golden-brown by the Sun. He had the strongest urge to take her to a beach and lay her out on hot sand.

The shifting shadow of the bodyguard brought Kai back to reality, and he sucked in a bracing breath. Thank the Suns for intrusive chaperones.

"You keep this up and your nose will turn pink."

She sighed again and lowered her chin, blinking at him with light-blind eyes. "I freckle first," she confided. "I don't get out in the Sun as often as I'd like." She looked as though she'd add more but turned toward the watchdog and paused. "So will you show me this open air market?"

"I'd be delighted," Kai responded, shifting his grip to tuck her hand through his elbow and lay it on his arm. "Right this way, Lady Griffin."

She tensed but didn't pull away, adjusting her hold and staring at her hand on his arm. "Are you being polite or mocking me again?" she asked in a low voice, then twitched as if startled.

He didn't think she'd meant to say it aloud. He laid

a hand over hers, warming her cool fingers. "Neither. Come on, Aena. We have chocolate to find."

She glided at his side like a ghost, sending furtive glances at her trapped extremity. His chest constricted with sympathy but he didn't release her. They had to maintain an appearance of growing intimacy, or her father would get suspicious. Besides he loved the feel of her fingers gripping his arm through his shirt, loved the cool silk of her skin against his palm. He only wished she felt the same.

The open air market boasted extravagant expensive wares, but the point of their trip lay elsewhere. Kai spent an obligatory amount of time escorting Liaena through the colorful stands, making sure to stop at one offering a splendid array of sweets. Much to his amusement, Liaena took her time and chose a selection with solemn care, as if it were a mission of grave importance.

As she accepted her package of goodies with an air of satisfaction he said, "I see Sin's converted you to the dark side."

"The shop on your station has a fine selection of chocolates, but this vendor has candies I've never even seen before." She lifted the package and pointed to one of her finds. "He calls this one Spiced Heaven. Would you like a taste?"

"Of so many things," he purred, letting his gaze take a slow walk from her pointing finger along the silky skin of her arm and throat to her mouth.

Her lips parted and his whole body tightened with fierce need.

He tore his gaze from her to the waiting watchdog. "But now's not the time. Let's move on to the entertainment section."

She didn't move. He didn't know what he'd do if he looked into her maddening gray eyes, so he avoided her gaze and took her hand again, giving it a light tug. She eased into motion, her stride smoothing into its usual enticing grace as they continued. She said nothing and he shot her a quick glance, worried he'd gone beyond her tolerance level. Pink color kissed her cheekbones, her features blank and eyes hazy. She held the package in front of her as if still offering it to someone, but she seemed to have forgotten it existed.

Kai swallowed hard. If he didn't know better, he'd say his Ice Queen was reacting to him on a very basic level. He looked away before he did something stupid but couldn't resist twining his fingers with hers, firming his grip to press palm to palm. Without thought he shifted closer so their arms also twined together and their bodies brushed as they walked. *Suns curse it, this is the stupidest idea I've ever had.* This playact of theirs would be the death of him.

Instead of an extended tour through the entertainment galleries, Kai opted to cut their adventure short for the sake of his sanity and head straight for the target holo-suite. At the threshold he paused and glanced at Aena's watchdog with sly speculation. "Any chance I can talk you into waiting out here? It's a private suite, our choice of holo-films, and I'd appreciate some time alone with the lady."

The man hesitated, glance flashing to their linked fingers. "Ah, I can't—"

"Boris," Aena cut in, her voice smooth and cool. "Please sweep the interior for any hazards and then stand watch outside."

Boris blinked, as if he hadn't expected her to know his name or hadn't expected an order from Griffin's daughter. But he didn't hesitate. "Yes, ma'am." He disappeared inside the holo-suite.

"Nice," Kai murmured.

"Is this part of your plan?"

"Yes."

"If you'd told me before, I could've sent him back to the transport half an hour ago."

"But then I would've missed my excuse to hold your hand." When she sent him a sharp glance, he shrugged. "He'll have a good story to tell your father."

Boris returned and nodded to them both. "It's clear."

Kai slipped an arm around her waist and ushered her across the threshold, giving the guard a conspiratorial wink and grin as he passed. Boris shook his head, masculine amusement on his rough features. The small room beyond contained only a short row of luxurious seats and segmented plates lining the walls, ceiling, and floor, along with a control panel to activate their choice of holographic entertainment.

As soon as the door closed Kai stepped away and locked the portal. Then he walked over to the holo-suite control panel and pulled one of Cassie's toys from his pocket.

"What are you doing?"

"We couldn't bring your mother here, but this is the next best thing." He plugged the device into the panel and turning it on.

The room flickered and gained some furniture along with a new occupant. "Liaena!" Zofie cried and flew to her daughter.

153

"Mama," Aena gasped, opening her arms, but her mother's form brushed right through her.

The women looked down at their merging images and Zofie laughed. "Oh my, this is disconcerting."

Aena looked over her shoulder at Kai and he shrugged. "Next best thing. Go ahead, we have some time. I'll try to give you as much privacy as I can."

Her features warmed and her eyes flashed silver with emotion, tying a knot in his guts. "Thank you."

He nodded and turned away before he tackled her to the floor and gave her mother an interesting show. While the women sat in their respective seats and whispered to one another, Kai inserted a com link in his ear and tuned it to the holo-jack's frequency. "Cassie."

"Hey Kai, how's it going over there?"

"Your hack is holding. Not a flicker of back feed, no sign of alarm or overwrite."

"I told you there wouldn't be." She sniffed as if insulted.

"Yeah genius, you told me. How long do we have?"

"On my end I'm seeing a pretty shoddy security system in play. I overbuilt the jack, but I guess better safe than sorry. You could stay in there all day if you like. Or until a search party comes after you."

"Neither option is appealing. Besides we have Boris the chastity belt outside the door waiting for us."

"Chastity belt? How far did you take this game, Kai?"

He grinned to himself. "I have a reputation to maintain."

She made a sound like a hissing kitten. "Damn it, I told you about her. She can't handle—"

"You'd be surprised what she can handle, Doc. But don't throw a fit. I've been a perfect gentleman."

"Why don't I believe you?"

"Because you're paranoid and distrustful. Ease down, Cass. She already has one guard dog; she doesn't need another one. Did Nick do what he was supposed to do?"

"Yes, he contacted the First Marshal."

"And?"

"No luck. Marchand said he couldn't send backup for the militia, since the Fringe isn't official FPA jurisdiction. If a unit went in, Griffin would wonder why and dig. Marchand said to tell you if you run ops off-record they have to stay off-record."

Kai peeled his lips back in a silent snarl. "Big M and I need to have a talk when I get back."

"Keep me out of it. You creep me out when you play hardball with the FPA."

"Have you been able to reach T'Zai?"

"He's still not answering."

Kai sighed and ran a frustrated hand through his hair. "Back to the task at hand then. Run me through your project for Aena again."

"All right, here's how it works. You give her the injection. It's a subdermal micro-tab. To activate it she presses down on the injection site for a count of three. To deactivate it she presses on the spot twice in quick succession. It has a range of several meters but won't affect anything beyond this, so we're talking a room-sized grid."

"And the effects?"

"It sends an erroneous signal to nearby surveillance. Not a blank, they'd jump all over it if audio and visual signals drop out. It jumbles the image and sound, scrambling them into nonsense. It'll look like a recurring hiccup in their systems. I recommend she only use it in specific places and not move around from place to place while it's active, or they'll figure out she's the source."

"Have I mentioned lately how scary smart you are?"

"No, you haven't. You also haven't given me a raise in a long time."

"You want a raise?"

"I don't need one but still, you haven't offered. Never take your techs for granted, Shay."

"We never take you for granted, Cassie. We're too afraid you'll take over if we turn our backs."

She snickered. "Thanks, that's gratifying."

"I aim to please. Anything else we need to discuss?"

"How are Aena and Zofie doing?"

Kai leaned against the panel and folded his arms across his chest, slanting an assessing look at mother and daughter. Aena had her back to him so he couldn't read her expression, but Zofie glowed with delight and affection. Aena gestured as she spoke, something Kai had never seen her do before, her shoulders relaxed and lithe torso softening toward her mother. As he watched, Zofie reached for her daughter, then laughed and shook her head when her fingers passed right through Aena's hand.

"They look like they're enjoying themselves. You did a good thing here, Cass."

"Thanks. Did Aena say anything about Imago?"

"Not yet. Too many listening ears."

"Right." Cassie sounded disheartened.

"Don't worry, as soon as the family visit is over I'll grill her."

"Is that what they're calling it these days?"

"Whatever are you insinuating?"

She made a derisive noise. "Watch your step with her, Kai."

"Always. Your hack is still holding here. How's it look from your end?"

"Smooth sailing. The second I see the tiniest blip I'll pull it."

"All right, keep watch, Cass. We'll check in later."

He ended the connection, removing his com link and turning toward the Griffins. They both sat watching him. He raised his eyebrows in silent question.

"How secure is my mother's connection?" Aena asked with a faint crease between her brows.

"Cassie's on it. You're in good hands. She'll cut it at the first sign of trouble."

"Cassie Draegen?" Zofie brightened. "I feel like I know her already. Her parents speak of her nonstop."

Aena glanced at her mother. "You're staying with Cassie's parents?"

Kai sighed. Well, he hadn't expected to keep this particular secret buried forever. "The Draegens have the same problem as your mother. They're perfect leverage. Griffin would love to find and use them to force Cassie's cooperation."

"I see. So you keep them in seclusion as well."

He nodded, studying her features. The information didn't seem to sit well with her; the crease in her brow had deepened. "Your mother is safe. We'll make sure she stays that way. Do you ladies need more time?"

Zofie's smile dimmed into sadness. "I would ask for the rest of our days if I could. But I understand you have other obligations to attend to."

"We need to stay in here for a while longer anyway for appearances."

Zofie's expression grew sly. "Yes, Liaena tells me you're romancing her."

"What I said was," Liaena interjected, sending her mother a quick frown, "you are courting me as a cover for exchanging information and to divert my father's attention."

"Well, I think it's a lovely idea." Zofie reached out to brush a strand of hair from her daughter's temple, tsking when her fingers couldn't make contact. "I'm glad you're spending more time together. I once hoped the two of you would—"

"Mother." Liaena stiffened, features a mask of tension, staring at Zofie.

Intrigued, Kai approached and leaned his forearms on the back of the seat next to Liaena. "The two of us would what?"

Zofie cleared her throat, hands fluttering in her lap as she looked from her daughter to Kai. She gave him a weak smile. "Become friends. Along with Sinsudee, of course. How is your sister?"

Kai smothered his amusement at her awkward sidestep but didn't force the issue. "Sin's doing fine. She's running interference, distracting Web for us."

Zofie's eyes widened, mouth turning down at the corners. "Oh, dear. I hope she's being careful. He's quite good at seeing through other's deceptions."

"She's had lots of practice," Kai responded and left it at that. Neither of them needed to know the details of

Sin's complicated dance with Griffin.

Zofie nodded, features still concerned, then brightened when she glanced at her daughter again. "Well, I'm sure the two of you have much to discuss. I don't want to be in the way."

"Mother," Aena said again in the same quelling tone.

Zofie ignored it, turning to Kai. "Will we be able to do this again soon?"

"As soon as we can arrange it."

"Thank you, Manakai. This was a very kind gesture. Please don't put yourselves at risk for me. I would never forgive myself if something happened because of this."

"Think nothing of it."

"Mama, don't go. He said we have more time."

Zofie turned such a warm and loving smile on her daughter Kai's chest tightened to an ache. His own mother's love was a distant memory, tainted with sorrow and complex guilt.

"I love you, little Sunbird." Her holo form flickered and disappeared.

Aena sighed, shoulders sagging as she looked down at her lap.

A twist of sympathy wound through Kai's gut. To distract her he asked, "Sunbird?" in a dubious tone.

She twitched and slanted him a wary sideways glance. "An endearment from when I was small. Didn't your mother have names for you?"

He moved around the seats, settling in the one next to her. "None as sweet. Your mother's diverting."

"I'll assume you mean it in a good way," Aena responded with a dignified lift of her chin. She hesitated then continued in a softer tone without meeting his gaze, "Thank you, Kai. It means a great deal to spend time with my mother. She seems so much more relaxed. She hasn't smiled or laughed this much in a long time."

Kai studied her profile for a moment, wishing he could afford to be drawn in. He wanted to ask her questions about her life, wanted to absorb her world. What was the other Liaena like, the one who flew over hot sand and laughed? Was she still in there somewhere, hidden like a secret flame?

Clenching his jaw, he resisted the impulse. "I'm glad for you both, but don't thank me too hard. This was part of our bargain. Gifts go both ways, little Sunbird. What do you have for me?"

She straightened, features cooling to their usual serenity, her gray gaze meeting his, distant and assessing. A pang of disappointment went through him at this return of the Ice Queen, and he shifted in irritation at his reaction. Better for them both to remember their roles, to remember their situation.

"Father assumed you would ask something of me on my last visit. I used the subject of your AI to fulfill his assumption. You may see this as a betrayal of your trust, but since I know nothing of this Imago or AI coding, I can excuse any search for information as prudent curiosity."

He nodded, keeping his expression neutral. He and Sin had guessed she'd go in this direction. Her candor impressed him, though; he hadn't expected her to admit she'd told Griffin of their request. He also admired her efficient strategy, no time wasted, using her own ignorance as both a shield and a tool.

"I'm sure it won't surprise you to hear he's given

me nothing of value. He buried me in reams of information about his AI research projects, none of which mentioned Imago or Cassie's coding. I will need to look further. At the moment Father is preoccupied with Mother's disappearance, and confronting him would not be prudent." Her hand rose, fingertips touching the fading bruise on her cheekbone.

Kai tensed, hands wanting to snap into fists. He took a measured breath. "Tell me what you can about Web's hunt for Zofie."

"He's made no announcement, of course. He's concealed her existence and he'd want to exact his own justice on the ones who took her, so he wouldn't bother reporting the abduction to the FPA." She paused, her mouth thinning to a grim line as she studied him. "The group claiming responsibility has not been as careful as I would have expected. It's almost as if they wish to be caught."

"They're acting against my orders for reasons of their own," Kai responded in a clipped tone. "I would never ask anyone to be a sacrificial lamb."

Some of the grimness eased from her expression. She tilted her head. "Whatever their reasoning, it's kept my father's attention firmly on them. He hasn't mentioned you at all."

He accepted this with a nod. "Small comfort. Griffin's confident he'll catch them?"

"Yes."

Kai swore in a low voice. She said nothing, her gaze drifting away across the empty room.

With a sigh he ran stiff fingers through his hair and straightened in his seat. "All right, is there anything else you can tell me?"

A faint crease appeared on her forehead. "I'm afraid not. I regret I've not had as much to give you as you've given me. Will you retract our bargain?"

He snorted. "I said we don't ask for sacrificial lambs. I wasn't expecting instant results, Aena, especially when dealing with your father. You should be more careful," he admonished, his hand lifting without conscious thought to brush against her bruised cheek. She went still and he drew his hand back with a muffled sigh. "Cassie has her own gift for you. It might help with your search as long as you use it sparingly."

He explained the injectable micro-tab, repeating Cassie's description and instructions. Aena watched him, eyes widening and slim form going statue-still. At one point she even seemed to stop breathing.

When he finished he frowned and asked, "What's the matter?"

"She gave me privacy," she whispered. She blinked rapidly and looked down at her hands. They'd tightened on one another until her knuckles whitened. "I know this is a tool," she said, speaking each word with slow care. "It will help in our efforts against my father. But having a few moments of privacy, where I don't have to watch every word or expression for fear of reprisal from my father, is a treasure beyond words. How did she know?" She swallowed hard. "Please thank her for me."

Kai lurched to his feet and paced to stop himself from hauling her into his arms. If she was plying for sympathy, trying to get under his guard, it was working like a charm.

"Kai? If you inject right here, I'll remember where it is." She pointed to a spot inside her left forearm.

He moved closer. A pale freckle adorned her smooth skin, so light he may not have noticed if she hadn't called attention to it. Pulling the small injector wand from his pocket, he bent over and clasped her arm, breathing in her maddening scent with an inner groan of despair. Touching the business end of the wand to her skin, he depressed the other end then removed the device, unable to resist running his thumb over the site in a soothing pass. "All right?" he murmured.

She met his gaze, her eyes steady and watchful. "I'm fine, thank you," she responded, her voice fraying from its normal smooth tenor.

Mouth curving in a slow smile, he crouched and studied her appearance. "Hmm, you look too neat and composed. Boris won't buy it."

She lifted her chin. "What am I supposed to look like?"

"Like I've had my hands all over you," he purred with a wicked grin. "I have a reputation to maintain, Lady Griffin."

She raised an eyebrow. "Are you trying to say you're actually proud of this reputation?"

"Let's just say it's well-deserved. We have to muss you up. Take down your hair."

She frowned. "No."

Of course he wouldn't get so lucky. "Aena, you're supposed to look at least a little ravaged, or even a thickhead like Boris will get suspicious."

She leaned away from him, her expression shimmering with wariness. "Ravaged?"

"You should try it sometime," he said in a dry tone, standing and tugging her to her feet, urging her toward the exit. "Come on, Aena. Think of it as stage makeup. Unless you want me to actually ravage you. I'm happy to volunteer."

She crushed his ego a tad bit, jerking out of his grasp and reaching for the intricate braiding in her hair. She fiddled with the clasp for a minute. "There, I loosened it."

He gave a wry shake of his head. "It looks the same. You'd better let me do it." He reached for her, but she sidled away with a quelling stare.

"Do not pull it down," she ordered. "Father doesn't allow me to have my hair down."

He paused, sobering as he studied her. "He punishes you if you wear your hair down?"

"Yes."

Shaking his head, he reached for her again, easing strands of hair from their neat confinement. "Aena, why do you stay with him? I would've killed him by now."

"None of your business. Not too much, please." She brushed strands from her temples and tucked them behind her ears.

He untucked them. "Stop fixing it. You made it our business when we became partners." He paused, assessing her with a critical eye. "Hmm, better, but you need color. And you don't look kissed."

"Boris wouldn't be able to tell if you've kissed me," she scoffed.

He blinked. "If you believe that, your men haven't been doing it right. Chew on your bottom lip."

"You chew on women?" She was looking at him as if he'd grown a second head.

He closed his eyes and prayed for patience. "Aena, your lips need to be red, swollen, and moist. If you don't take care of it, I will."

"I'm chewing," she mumbled.

He watched her nibble on her bottom lip and took a slow deep breath. He badly wanted to do the job for her. Instead he adjusted her blouse at the shoulders so the scoop dipped lower along her chest. "You also need color in your cheeks."

"I'm not slapping myself," she retorted.

He chuckled. "I don't think we'll need to go so far." Slipping a hand around the back of her neck, he leaned close and whispered in her ear, describing what he imagined she would look like stretched naked across his bed. He kept it brief, the image inflaming him almost more than he could stand.

Releasing her, he eased back and admired the gorgeous rose color seeping over her cheeks, down her throat, and across her chest. "There it is," he murmured. "One last thing." He gave in to the overpowering urge to touch her flushed skin, tracing slow fingers along the links of her necklace and circling the crystal flame. At his touch the pendant sang a new song, no longer contrite but full of bright energy.

"Oh," she breathed, eyes widening.

"Perfect. Here we go, Aena." He strode to the control panel, yanked the jack, and tucked it in his pocket. Then he slipped an arm around her waist and ushered her out of the holo-suite.

Chapter 12

Kai kept his hungry gaze on Aena, but as they left the entertainment suite he caught Boris' double-take at her disheveled appearance.

She didn't seem to notice her watchdog at all, fingers lifting to caress the crystal pendant. When the new music danced in the air, she sucked in a sharp breath and glanced at Kai. Her eyes glowed like soft mist, wide with wonder. "It's beautiful. Is this the same composer?"

"Yes."

"Does it have a title?"

"Rejoice."

Her eyes blurred. She tucked her chin down and said nothing more. She didn't pull away from his arm around her waist, matching his easy pace through the entertainment sector, but he sensed a sudden distance. When he asked if she'd like to explore the market further, she shook her head.

"I should return to my father."

He nodded and escorted her back to the transport. On the return trip she seemed to recover her poise, responding to his casual conversation and allowing him to hold her hand without flinching.

When they left the transport and approached the entrance to the event, she hesitated and brushed strands of hair back from her face. Her mouth tightened. "I should wait for my father in our transport. Will you convey my regrets to your sister?"

"Of course. I'll see you to your ship."

She thanked him, busy fingers smoothing and tucking her hair back under control. At the threshold of her transport, she clasped her hands together and gave him a small cool smile. "I had a lovely time. Thank you for the charming tour of Bahia."

Her return to chilly formality needled him, and he shook his head in amused irritation. She was putting a lie to all the groundwork they'd laid so far, giving him a glacial brush-off at the end of their date. No matter the reason—relief the date was over, nerves over her father's reaction, or something else—this wouldn't do.

He moved close, brushing his knuckles along her jawline, ignoring how she stiffened at his touch. "I'm glad you enjoyed yourself. Want to know my favorite part?" He slipped his fingers around the back of her neck, keeping her from pulling away as he leaned in to whisper in her ear, "Relax, or Boris will think something went wrong."

A shudder worked down her spine, but she stopped trying to move back.

Kai lifted his head and gave her a heated smile, trailing his fingers on a slow path along her hairline and jaw to cup her chin. She was so soft and fragile he wanted to keep going, to discover every angle and curve, to learn every one of her secrets. "Kiss me, Aena."

She twitched, eyes going wide. "W-what?" she whispered.

"It's tradition. All first dates end in a kiss."

Her gaze flicked, quick and panicky, toward the

guard. The man earned Kai's deep abiding affection by spinning on his heel without hesitation, giving them his back and a measure of privacy. Kai grinned, enjoying the alarm and flush of reaction on her features. The Ice Queen and her insufferable poise were gone. Her mouth moved as if to speak, but he wasn't about to let this opportunity pass him by. He'd been dreaming of doing this with Aena since he was old enough to know what kissing was.

He bent his head, mouth brushing hers in light tingling contact. He paused, savoring the sensation and breathing her in. The scent of peach and blossoms filled his head, sweet and dizzying. His heart thudded hard, pulsing at his temples.

She quivered in his light grip. He expected her to duck away and break their tenuous contact. Instead she whispered his name on a broken exhale.

His heart rate doubled, lust diving deep and taking merciless hold. He firmed the pressure of his kiss, exploring her lips with rising hunger. As soft and lush as it appeared, her pliable mouth gave under his, responding to his slow nudging glides and nibbles with tentative interest. Her reaction sent spikes of need and heat straight to his groin, erasing all thought. Unaware of his hands framing her face with gentle desperation, he sank into her, mouth demanding instead of teasing and coaxing. She was a fire in his blood, driving him mad with her ready responses, giving and taking in an ever more sultry dance.

He'd taken his first taste, his tongue sliding along the seam of her lips, gathering her sweet flavor with a groan of insatiable hunger in his throat, when reality intruded. The guard coughed, a false sound meant to remind them of his presence.

Kai lifted his head with aching reluctance, body throbbing and urgent. Suns, what he wouldn't give to back her into the transport and lock them in for several hours, even if only to kiss. Her mouth was perfect, sublime, and he didn't think he'd ever get enough.

He met her gaze and his breath locked in his throat, heart thundering in his ears. Her eyes gleamed molten silver, heavy-lidded and sensual. She watched him through long lashes with a devastating intensity, vibrating in his clasp like a tuning fork. She clung to his forearms with the same desperation as he'd framed her face, breath and pulse racing right along with his. Her aversion to being touched must have taken a backseat; he saw no fear or reluctance, only sweet heat and a need matching his own.

The guard cleared his throat, once again reminding them they weren't alone.

Kai took a deep breath and let it out slow, tracing a thumb over her lower lip. It took every ounce of training and discipline not to pull her closer and finish what he'd started. "Aena," he rasped then swallowed hard, trying to ease the rough desire in his voice. He let her go, taking a step back. "Dinner next time?"

She blinked, her eyes as dazed and unsteady as he felt. Then she gave him a slow nod.

With a wry smile he clasped her arm and passed his thumb over the injection site, lifting his eyebrows a fraction. Her gaze cleared and she stiffened before giving him another nod, this one smaller but more alert.

"'Til then," he murmured and moved away, inclining his head at the guard on his way by. Boris looked startled to be acknowledged but nodded in

169

return.

At the entrance to the building Kai paused, leaning on the outer wall and pressing the heels of his hands against his eyes. *Suns, give me strength.* He was in no condition to approach Griffin. They wanted the man to pursue control over Kai, not consider the job done. Griffin would take one look at him right now and celebrate his victory.

Kai sucked in a deep breath and blew it out hard, striving to get his unruly physical reaction under control and clear his mind. Picturing Webster Griffin's smug countenance helped. So did locking all thoughts and images of Liaena under the mental file "Torture Yourself Later," and focusing on what needed to be done next.

After a few minutes, he ran rough hands over his face and through his hair then straightened, schooling his expression. He strode through the entrance at a sedate pace, giving the room a casual sweeping glance. As he suspected, Griffin and Sin had positioned themselves to watch for his and Aena's return. Both caught sight of him and turned in his direction, Sin smiling in welcome and Griffin's eyes narrowing with veiled suspicion.

Kai gave them both a crooked smile. "Did we make it back before curfew?"

"One of you seems to have not made it back at all," Griffin noted with a raised eyebrow.

"Aena is waiting for you in your transport. I think I wore her out."

Sin's eyes gleamed with furtive humor. "How was the market?"

"Productive. How's the party?"

170

"Like watching paint dry. Thank goodness Web was here to keep me entertained." Sin sent the man a flirtatious smile, and he inclined his regal head. "Now that you've returned, we should head back home. Time marches on and our to-do list grows ever longer, Brother."

"So true," Kai responded, holding out his elbow for her to slip an arm through. "Griff, good to see you again."

"Likewise."

With identical charming smiles, Kai and his sister spun around and strode for the exit. Sin waited until they'd settled in their own transport before giving him an inquiring look. "Any problems?"

"No, the hack worked like a charm and their visit went off without a hitch."

"Did Aena have bad news?"

"She didn't have much for us yet." He gave her an abbreviated accounting of Aena's report and reaction to the surveillance micro-tab.

"It's what we expected." Her brow creased in a light frown. "So what was the trouble?"

"No trouble, it went fine. Why?"

She skewered him with a level stare. "Your face says otherwise."

Kai made a disgruntled sound. He'd known he couldn't fool his twin but he'd hoped she wouldn't dig at it. "Courting Aena is going to be problematic."

She winced, her expression turning sympathetic. "How problematic?"

Without answering he shook his head, leaned back against the seat, and closed his eyes.

"Oh, Sun's blood," she said in a low worried voice.

171

"Is it her or you?"

"Both."

"Damn. Kai, we don't have to continue with this. I don't want you to get hurt."

He snorted. "Stop mothering me, Sissa. It's too late to back out now anyway."

She subsided with a sigh and leaned a shoulder into his in empathy. The rest of the trip passed in heavy silence. At Shay headquarters they headed for their offices and an update on the status of the militia. It didn't surprise them to discover Griffin's forces had cornered the militia. They didn't know yet the extent of the damage, but at least some had lost their lives and some captured.

Kai snarled a curse and slapped a hand on the com. "Temple, I want T'Zai in my office in five minutes or I'm revoking your residency permit and evicting the lot of you." He released the com without waiting for a response.

Sin nodded, her face grim and eyes fierce. The members of the militia had been their responsibility. Good people had died without adequate cause, and neither of them would abide it.

T'Zai arrived in less than the five-minute deadline, his expression full of amused tolerance. Away from the dim forbidding light of his temple, he seemed smaller but no less compelling, his light blue eyes direct and piercing, and his flyaway hair a white halo around his weathered face. He halted in the middle of their grand office, cocking his head and studying the pair of them. "I was expecting a death threat."

Kai snorted. "You would have laughed yourself stupid over a death threat. The eviction notice got your attention."

"True enough." He paused, looking Sin over with a Red Sun ascetic's militant eye, a hint of gloating satisfaction seeping into his expression. "Sinsudee, dear, you look good in red."

Sin gave him a sharp smile, all teeth and no humor, gliding toward him in a hunting prowl. "Yes, I do. Be careful, Mendani. This tool cuts both ways."

He chuckled, his stance relaxed and unconcerned even as she circled him like a wildcat stalking prey. "I have many tools and I handle each with great care. I also use them to their full measure. Would you ask less of me?"

For a second Kai thought she'd take the old man's head off, but she turned away with a furious hiss.

Kai folded his arms over his chest, leveling a steely stare on their mentor. "You ordered the militia to expose themselves to Griffin."

"Yes."

"Why?"

"Griffin would not believe an ordinary group of thieves could balk him. When he didn't find them, he would have turned his attention on you both. He hates the Orders, however. He will believe a fanatic group of Red Sun acolytes sought to deal him a blow. He's found his culprits and he'll look no farther."

"You sent them to their deaths," Kai growled.

"Griffin will torture without mercy those who didn't die," Sin added, eyes as hard as green diamonds. "How could you do such a thing, T'Zai? And don't quote me war scripture."

The Mendani sent a quelling frown between them, his lined face uncompromising. "Every one of my people knew what was at stake, knew the outcome. They went willingly. They heard the call of the Red Sun and answered. You have no right to denigrate their choice or their sacrifice."

"It's not them we're denigrating, you old tyrant," Kai gritted. "You knew we'd never agree to this, so you pulled a runaround. It's your last one. If we can't trust you, we won't use you."

"You'd have no part in the main event, Mendani," Sin mused, strolling over to stand next to Kai. "Seems counterproductive for a Red Sun ascetic to sit on the sidelines in a war."

"Point made." T'Zai inclined his head. He didn't look defeated, his eyes shining and mouth curving with furtive delight. "And as always you make me proud. I will not make excuses for my action, nor will I apologize for it. But I will give my word it won't happen again."

"You'll have to be more specific on what 'it' is," Sin said in a bitter tone. "I have enough deaths on my conscience, T'Zai."

The Mendani sobered, his face easing into compassion. "You are right to shoulder the responsibility of leadership, but you cannot allow this burden to hobble you or limit your strategies."

"Because sending people on a suicide mission is such a fine idea," Kai drawled. Leaning forward, he fixed a grim gaze on the ascetic. "No more secret orders."

T'Zai nodded. "No more secret orders."

"You knew how we'd react," Sin said, leaning on the desk next to Kai and studying the cleric with sharp eyes. "So why did you risk this? And why now? Is it

Zofie Griffin or Liaena you're interested in?"

A sudden smile lit his face, turning his craggy features from formidable to jovial. "The two of you are breathtaking." He pointed to Sin. "Attack and retreat." His finger moved to Kai. "Corner and disarm." His attention returned to Sin. "Bait and trap. So instinctive and so well coordinated. You make a daunting team."

Kai met his twin's gaze and snorted when she rolled her eyes. "Misdirection," he accused their mentor.

"Evasion," Sin added with a shake of her head.

"Manipulation. You're not fooling anyone, T'Zai."

The ascetic grinned. "I wasn't trying, merely appreciating. You knew my answer, anyway. Now am I forgiven and dismissed, or shall we go another round?" His bright gaze swiveled between them.

"Forgiven, possibly," Sin said, straightening and prowling toward him again with sudden keen interest. "Dismissed? I don't think so."

Kai tilted his head, for once not following his sister's train of thought. "Are we resorting to torture, Sinsi? He won't crack but it'd be good therapy for us."

"Yes," she responded with unsettling relish, circling the old man again. "I'm going to torture him."

T'Zai's brows drew together in a frown, his gaze shifting between them. "Now, children, let's not be hasty."

"Call the others," Sin ordered, sending Kai a razor-edged smile. "Have them meet us at the temple. Del and I are getting Sun-bonded today." She poked a finger at T'Zai's chest. "And you're not weaseling out of it this time. You've put this off long enough. I'm not letting you out of my sight until the deed is done."

At T'Zai's sudden pained expression, Kai burst into laughter.

Chapter 13

True to her word, Sin didn't let their Mendani out of her sight, dogging his every step, coordinating the clearing of the temple, and gathering their friends like a general marshalling her troops. Kai watched with vast amusement and assisted without complaint. He'd never attended a more entertaining Sun-bonding ceremony.

Since Griffin would react to Sin getting Sun-bonded with thwarted anger and threaten Del's life, they'd decided on a secret ceremony with only Kai, Cassie, and Nick as witnesses. Sin allowed no excuses and no delays, despite Cassie's protest over their attire. Cassie still wore her lab coat and the Givliani brothers had on scruffy casual clothes and stank of slicer engine fumes.

"I don't care what you're wearing," Sin declared. "Be happy we're not doing the traditional Red Sun ceremony or everyone would be naked." She sent T'Zai a look of grim command. "Seal the doors. Nobody escapes."

Acting put-upon and glum, T'Zai obeyed.

Kai snickered and clapped a hand on Del's broad back, enjoying the man's dazed expression. "Terrified yet?"

"A little bit," he muttered, watching his soon-to-be bonded like a man in an incomprehensible dream.

Sin ordered Nick to gather mats from around the

sanctuary and arrange them at the base of the holographic Red Sun. Nick grumbled about the mats being useless on this cold stone floor, then had a coughing fit and fell silent when both women glared at him.

"No gifts or decorations." Cassie sighed, glancing around the stark sanctuary with a mournful expression.

"All I need is love." Sin's gaze found Del with the beginnings of a smile. She looked more relaxed and smug, now that she'd locked them all in.

Del stirred out of his daze, eyeing her sleek red-sheathed form with masculine appreciation. "If I'd known this was gonna be your bonding dress, I wouldn't have complained. I still get to strip it off later, right?"

She grinned and tugged him to the mats, whispering something on the way. He responded with a low deep laugh, catching her close for a quick hard kiss before kneeling with her beneath the restless eye of the great Red Sun.

Kai moved to a mat behind the lovers, kneeling and sitting on his heels. Nick and Cassie settled on mats next to him, Cass already sniffling.

"Are you sure you don't want to make it a double ceremony?" Nick whispered to her with a coaxing smile, slipping an arm around her.

Cassie wiped at her eyes and leaned into him, her features soft, full of joy, and beyond smitten. "I'm not getting bonded in my work clothes," she whispered back. Neither seemed to realize their conversation wasn't private, the sanctuary so quiet a pin dropping would have sounded like a bomb.

Nick's eyes kindled at her response and he pulled

her closer, his smile heating. "You could strip naked."

Kai made a production out of clearing his throat, the sound echoing off the domed ceiling. Nick and Cass gave a guilty start and looked around to find themselves the center of attention. T'Zai frowned at the pair, but Del wore a smirk, and Sin watched them with a delighted indulgent smile.

The two mumbled apologies.

Sin winked then turned an arch look on T'Zai. "Whenever you're ready, Mendani."

He humphed and moved to stand before them, his expression sour. Kai grinned, enjoying the sight of their teacher outmaneuvered for once. He and his sister had concluded T'Zai avoided the bonding ceremony to protect their strategy against Griffin. Web's courtship of Sin had provided many opportunities for distraction and manipulation of their enemy. Once her bonding with Del became public knowledge, Griffin would harden against the twins, becoming a more difficult target and escalating their timetable.

Kai had been against their Sun-bonding for this reason and for fear of what Griffin would do to his sister in retaliation. But watching her face transform as she met Del's gaze, her features glowing as if lit from within, he decided it was worth the danger. Her happiness and delight turned even the Red Sun's ominous radiance into a mellow benign presence.

The pair faced each other, lacing their fingers together as T'Zai began to intone the ceremonial blessings in the Red Order's archaic and lyrical language. Del, his features hardened by years of abuse under the Core's heavy hand, now wore such an open tender expression he seemed a different man altogether.

He lowered his forehead to hers and they closed their eyes, swaying together in a pose of such intimate sweetness Kai's throat closed.

This is right. His chest expanded on a bubble of deep elation. After everything they'd been through and done, his sister deserved this happiness, and their union seemed fitting somehow. Even her red dress and her choice of temples for the ceremony, Red instead of the more popular Blue, seemed proper. War had brought them together; it was only right it should seal their bond. As T'Zai was fond of saying, conflict's purpose wasn't bloodshed but change, the catalyst to stronger societies, helping people see their true potential and clarifying the important things in their lives. For Kai, creating moments like this was most important, moments of peace and contentment, shared with those closest to his heart.

His twin stood foremost in this select group, his love for her a deep abiding fixture, so much a part of him it was like loving his own soul. It surprised him how fond he'd grown of Del after their rocky introduction. The man had earned his everlasting affection by making his sister so happy. In fact his affection for every person in this room surprised him a bit. He supposed he was contrary enough to care for people because of their quirks instead of in spite of them.

Kai glanced over at the tears running down Cassie's shining face and the goofy grin Nick wore as they watched the pair. He wondered how long it would be before he returned here, kneeling for another bonding ceremony.

Mercifully T'Zai chose the short version of the

blessings. He finished with, "Suns bless this union and carry them always within your sight," holding his gnarled hands over their bent heads. His lined face had lost its grumpy aspect, now filled with solemn joy. Kai caught the gleam of tears in the old fraud's eyes; no matter how reluctant he'd been to perform the ceremony, this pairing moved him as much as it did his audience. "Rise, children, and walk together into the Light."

Instead of rising, the two melded together and kissed as if their lives depended on it. T'Zai broke out in a pleased smile, which morphed into furtive amusement when their embrace continued. "Ahem. Stand now, please, and save some of that for your private chambers."

They parted, smiling at one another with such clear joy and love the room seemed to brighten. Standing, they pulled the ascetic into a spontaneous bone-crunching hug.

His breath wheezed out and his eyes widened. "Ow," he grunted. "You're crushing my dignity."

Sin burst into lyrical laughter and kissed T'Zai's weathered cheek. "Thank you, Mendani. I'm grateful you presided over our bonding. You're more than my teacher; you're family and I wouldn't have wanted it any other way."

His face darkened and he ducked his head, mumbling something and brushing at his eyes.

Grinning, Kai rose to his feet and approached the couple, pulling his sister into his arms. "Congratulations, Sissa."

"Thank you," she whispered, her voice watery and her grip tight as she squeezed him.

The sound of tears in her voice brought a lump to his throat and alarmed him. If she started crying, he might mist up too, and his masculine pride would suffer a fatal blow. He resorted to humor for both their sakes. "When can I break in my new brother?"

She pulled back and gave him a mock-scowl. "No breaking him at all."

"Spoilsport," he teased and handed her over to Cassie, who stood close by sniffling and wiping her face on her sleeve.

Kai turned to the Givliani brothers, who'd finished a hug of their own and were exchanging identical infectious grins. "Welcome to the family, boys," he announced then chuckled when Nick's grin curdled.

Del snorted, surprising Kai by pulling him into a rough hug. "You're a pain in the ass, bro," he stated with amused affection.

Kai hugged him back with a snicker. "What a sweet talker. I'm getting all weepy over here."

"Have you chosen bond marks?" T'Zai interrupted, looking more composed.

Sin sighed, her smile fading. She moved to Del's side and he clasped her hand, bringing it to his mouth. "We won't be wearing bond marks yet," she told the ascetic. "Too obvious. When we make our bonding public, we'll choose marks."

He nodded and held out a small tablet. "I've witnessed and verified your Sun-bonding vows and contract. You're as bound as I can make you. Now may I please unseal those doors?"

Sin grinned. "Will you come celebrate with us?"

He gave her a thoughtful frown. "Is it a prerequisite to reopening my temple?"

"Yes."

He sighed. "Suns have mercy, the hazards I must face for my faith."

Their combined laughter rang in the temple sanctuary like bells heralding a new day.

****

Liaena watched the Red Sun ascetic writhe in the interrogator and wished with all her heart to be elsewhere. The poor man hadn't yet screamed, but sweat coated his skin and soaked his hair and clothes. Unlike most ascetics she'd seen, he wasn't wearing the robes of his order, but the flame tattoo at the hollow of his throat declared his origins. When asked, he'd readily admitted to being a cleric from the Red Order. In fact, he'd been forthcoming about all of his splinter group's activities, explaining how they'd stumbled upon Zofie's location and had concocted a plan to steal her from Webster Griffin's clutches. His description of their thievery was as detailed and authentic as her father could want. A confusing mass of religious rhetoric obscured his reasons for taking Zofie.

However, on one thing he refused to respond. He wouldn't give up her mother's location.

The pain inducer would eventually break him. Liaena feared what he would reveal then. She worried most about what would happen to her mother if Webster recaptured her. Her next biggest concern lay in how her father would react if he discovered the Shays' involvement. She didn't think the ascetic had known of her own part in the abduction—small comfort. How long could he hold out? Why in the name of the Suns had he and his group allowed themselves to be captured?

Her father assumed they were crazy, a bunch of religious fanatics bent on self-destruction. The Red Order had a reputation for military fanaticism, but Liaena didn't believe it in this instance. She guessed they protected the Shays, sacrificing themselves like pawns shielding more versatile pieces in a galactic game of chess. The thought sent chills of horror over her skin. Aghast at the lengths the Red Order would go, she feared what other sacrifices might become necessary to stop her father.

The interrogator ceased its humming and the man hung limp in the restraining force field, panting. His eyes slowly opened and he stared at her father with an odd expression, almost expectant. She detected no fear or hate in his drawn features, as would be normal for someone undergoing relentless torture.

Her father stared back from his comfortable seat, his grip casual on the controller. He wore an air of icy calm, but Liaena kept still at his side, not taking chances. Being in the same room as the interrogator reminded her to be extra cautious. Her father hadn't mentioned her disheveled appearance, but he'd expressed his disapproval in other ways, refusing to allow her to leave his side since their return from Bahia and not permitting her to sit while he interrogated his prisoner. If she drew his attention he might decide she needed greater correction and stick her in the machine next to the ascetic.

"Speak," he commanded.

"What would you have me say?" the ascetic croaked, repeating the same line he'd given several times already.

"Where is Zofie Griffin?"

The man smiled, his mouth trembling with effort. "I haven't screamed yet, good sir. Perhaps you have this contraption set on too low a level."

Liaena cringed inside but kept her outward demeanor composed.

"Perhaps I do," her father responded in a bland tone and made an adjustment on the controller. He reactivated the inducer.

The ascetic tensed and shuddered with renewed pain, jaw going rigid and eyes squeezing closed.

He's trying to die. Her stomach knotted with sudden nausea. She took a slow deep breath to ease it. The worst part was, even if this man managed to goad her father into killing him, several more ascetics waited their turn in Griffin's holding cells. Her father would torture them all until he had his answer. *I have to do something.*

But what could she do? Her father would ignore or punish any attempt she made to deflect him. She didn't have the means to mount a rescue, and she wasn't heartless enough to consider killing them, even if she could figure out a way to do these things without getting caught. She had to convince her father to let them go, but how? He had no fear of retaliation from the Order or discovery by the FPA. She had no leverage, unless she could persuade him it was in his best interests.

"Father," she said in as steady and uninflected a voice as she could manage. "He won't speak."

"He hasn't broken yet. They all speak volumes then." His tone remained unconcerned, but his mouth tightened as he watched the cleric writhe in stubborn silence.

"How long until he breaks?" She gave the controller a pointed glance. "At this level you may kill him before he does."

He skewered her with an icy stare. "You have a point to make, I assume?"

"I also want to find Mother, the sooner the better. Torturing these people unto death may not be the most efficient way to find her. You could let them go and track their movements. She's their prize; odds are at least one of them would lead you straight to her."

He turned his gaze on his victim again. "Foolish thought, Daughter. If none seek out your mother, how then will I retrieve her?"

"Keep one to question or release one at a time," Liaena suggested, a fine mist of perspiration forming on her brow.

He made a disgruntled sound. "If all you have to offer is nonsense, you are dismissed."

"As you wish, Father," she murmured and backed away.

As she headed for the exit she heard the interrogator cease and her father say, "Speak."

"What would you have me say?"

"Give me the location of Zofie Griffin."

Liaena paused, glancing over her shoulder and shivering at the horrible smile on the cleric's gaunt face.

"I thank you for the rest, good sir. Shall we go again? Perhaps this time I will scream."

Liaena turned away as the machine hummed to life once more.

Her feet moved faster than she wanted on her way to her quarters. Her heart and breath also moved faster, setting a sick pace, worsening the lurch of nausea in her stomach. She thought of Cassie's gift with a terrible longing, her need for a few minutes of privacy eating away at her insides. She forced herself to wait until she'd entered her quarters and moved into the bedroom. Keeping the lights low to hide her movements, she pressed on the micro-tab for a count of three. Then she sank onto her bed and stared at her shaking hands. Had it worked? She had no way to tell and couldn't stop shaking.

She wasn't used to seeing her father's violent work from so close a range. He didn't often take such action himself, delegating most of the bloody business to his underlings. She'd watched such things over viewers or heard of them through reports, but seeing it in person had been even more horrifying. She'd done what she could to help, but she didn't think it'd been enough. Her father might consider her suggestion despite his contempt and dismissal. She couldn't count on it.

An image of the ascetic's ghastly smile burned in her mind. A sob took her by surprise. She put a hand over her mouth, but another sob broke through her fingers. She burst into tears, weeping as she hadn't been free to do since she was a child, a storm of emotion sweeping over her. She covered her face with her hands and rocked, shocked and dismayed by the wildness of her reaction and her inability to stop.

Curling on her side, she pressed her face into the pillow to muffle the sounds she made and stopped trying to control the tears. She prayed Cassie's device was working, but if not the damage was already done.

After several minutes, her weeping slowed then dwindled away. She lay still, amazed by the strange peaceful lethargy weighing her down. When she realized she drifted close to sleep, she sucked in a breath and sat up, wiping the wetness from her cheeks. Easing off the bed, she moved into the bathroom to wash her face, then changed into sleepwear. Heading back to the bed, she double-tapped the micro-tab and lay down again. Once under the covers, she marveled at the lingering calm and sleepiness sinking through her. If she'd known crying could offer such a relief from tension, she would have done it years ago and damn the consequences.

Thinking of consequences, her adventures on Bahia slipped to the forefront of her mind. She stiffened, eyes popping open. Sleep evaporated at the memory of scorching green eyes and strong fingers framing her face. Sweet merciful Suns, the man could kiss. Granted, she had very little intimate experience, but Kai's mouth on hers had been a revelation, his every move slow, sensual, and devastating, savoring her like a delicious treat. It seemed like a dream now, though none of her dreams had ever been so intense or arousing. The memory of it had the power to heat her skin and weaken her limbs. She stirred in restless reaction.

No doubt the embrace had been routine for Kai, a typical moment no more interesting than any other romantic pursuit. For Liaena the entire day had rewritten her reality, from the moment he'd clasped her arm at the charity to his casual stroll away. She'd never had a man treat her with such subtle passion, nor had she ever felt such an aching need in response. After her experience with the security guard, she'd thought she wasn't capable of desire. Kai had turned this assumption on its ear with a few simple caresses, the melting look in his gorgeous eyes, and one devastating kiss.

If it had been only a physical response, she might have reveled in the novel experience, but he'd touched her in deeper places than her flesh. Several times he'd shown tender concern and gentle consideration, pulling a helpless kind of emotional reaction from her. If he treated most women this way, no wonder they fell at his feet in such great numbers.

The pendant was the worst. Her fingers crept toward the crystal flame. She made a conscious effort not to touch it and set off its music. How had he known and planned it, this change in music at his touch? Why "Rejoice?" He'd sent the gift as an extravagant apology; was the new song supposed to infer she'd forgiven him? Or was the title meant to imply something deeper, since he had to get intimately close to activate it? Either way the romantic music had turned her insides to mush. The gesture had touched her so deeply tears had threatened.

At the end after setting her on fire inside and out, he'd walked away without a backward glance as if none of it meant a thing. Him and his "well-deserved reputation."

Liaena sighed and closed her eyes, willing drowsiness to return. She needed rest. She needed to formulate a plan of action, figure out how best to use Cassie's gift, both for retrieving the information the Shays had asked for and to help her father's prisoners. But her thoughts kept cycling in anxious obsession between Kai's too-effective courtship and the cleric's torture.

After a long while, exhaustion overcame anxiety

and sleep stole through the room, thieving away her consciousness. Burning green eyes followed her into oblivion and set her dreams on fire.

Chapter 14

"Why'd you drag me along on this little safari?"

Kai glanced at his companion. For a brawny FPA investigator, Nick did a great impression of a whiny kid past his bedtime. "I needed an extra pair of hands and you were all I had. Sin and Del are busy right now."

Nick scowled. "So was I."

"When you get Sun-bonded, I'll give you time off too."

"You're a real saint. Why are we walking?"

"Are your feet getting tired, princess? The fresh night air is good for you."

Nick sent him a killing look. "This wharf is a dump and the channel smells like garbage and sewer."

Kai grinned. "So picky. We didn't fly in because I don't want our target to see us coming until I'm at his front door. I may have to fight my way in. Don't get involved."

"Why not?"

"Consider it an order from your superior."

"You are not my superior," Nick scoffed.

"I was talking about Marchand. I have sanction to kill. You don't. He wants me to keep you clean, so hang back."

"What if there's a hauler load of them, hero?"

"Feel free to throw a few punches. Just don't get blood on you."

Michelle O'Leary

"I've seen you fight, Shay. You didn't bring me for backup."

"No, a pouty FPAI wouldn't be my first choice for backup. You do remember why you're here, don't you? Or were you thinking about the bed you left when I explained it?"

Nick heaved a sigh. "Cass made me promise not to hit you, but you're making it a hard promise to keep. I remember my part. I'm tagging the crates and you're keeping the perp busy."

"Perp, he says." Kai shook his head in despair. "Don't open your mouth in there, Inspector. They'll know you for FPA the second you do."

"Fine," Nick growled, shooting another black look his way. "Why this warehouse?"

"See, I knew you were dreaming about Cassie when I explained everything. Like I said, this warehouse is one of the Core's biggest distribution hubs for illegal weapons."

"So why aren't we calling in the FPA to confiscate it now? Why tag the crates and let them go?"

"We aren't after weapons. The bad guys will only make more. We want the whole network, the sellers and buyers, as many as we can nab. Now we're getting close to listening ears, so tutoring's over. You good?" Kai gestured toward Nick's hand.

Nick glanced at his palm and nodded. A device lay there, concealed by a bit of pseudo-skin. It would download a signaling program to each crate, triggered whenever someone ran an inventory scan, which any smart seller or buyer would do. Nick only had to get close enough to touch a scanner at this warehouse, and the device would do the rest.

192

Kai looked him over. He didn't seem nervous or about to spout a bunch of FPA regulations. The man had come a long way in a short time. Satisfied Nick would be able to do his part, Kai focused on the warehouse as they approached. The long bulky building sported only one dim light over the service entrance, the rest in shifting shadows. It seemed deserted, but Kai sensed eyes on them and the lurking presence of the watchers.

"Nobody home?" Nick whispered.

"They're flanking us. No sudden moves." Kai kept moving toward the entrance at a steady pace, as if he had every right to be there. He slowed when a hulking figure stepped out of the shadows.

"Where you think you're goin'? This is private property."

"Take me to Merris."

The man twitched at his boss' name but didn't back down, shifting enough for the dim light to show the weapon in his hands. "Ain't takin' you nowhere, 'cept over to the channel and tossin' you in if you don't keep walkin'."

Kai smiled. "Take your best shot, ace. Tell your buddy to step up too." He pointed toward the other lurker still hidden in shadow. "But my business is with Merris tonight, so make it quick."

The man scowled and hesitated a fraction, but Kai and Nick wore no obvious weapons and must have looked like easy enough marks. He lumbered forward and made a grab for Kai.

Kai sidestepped, yanked the man's blaster out of his hands, and gave him a hard shot to the kidney with the butt of the weapon on his way past. The man staggered and bellowed, hunching and whirling like a bear about to charge, then froze at the sight of his own weapon aimed at his face. The other lurker trotted forward, slowing to a halt when he realized their mark was now armed.

"This is a nice gun," Kai said in a conversational tone, keeping his aim rock steady between the man's eyes. "Good sight, balanced weight. Is it the twenty series or forty?"

"Uh, forty," the brute muttered, hands lifting in slow surrender.

"Very nice. It'd vaporize a man's head." He let this unpleasant fact sink in for a second before adding, "I'll take a crate."

"W-what?"

Kai lowered the weapon with a sigh. "I'm a buyer, dimwit. Now take me to Merris so I can make you all rich."

The second brute seemed to regain his courage, now that Kai's weapon wasn't aimed at anyone in particular. He sneered. "You got an appointment?"

Kai sent him a cool glance, then returned his attention to the first man. "What a comedian. He must make you chuckle all day long. My pockets are deep and my patience is wearing thin. What'll it be, boys? Do you want to be rolling in credit or do you want to be a smear on the pavement?"

Nick chose that moment to walk past the two guards as if they'd ceased to exist. He paused next to Kai, studying the blaster. "Get two crates," he suggested and continued on to the entrance.

Kai smothered a grin, pleased with their new liaison. He might be an irritating by-the-book FPA inspector, but he had good timing and instincts. These two guards were paid muscle, not the brains of the operation. They had orders to keep people out, but if they turned away buyers, they'd be strung up by their guts.

The two men looked at each other, indecision plain on their faces. The second one muttered, "Let Merris deal." The other nodded and turned to Kai, holding out a hand for his weapon with a sour look.

Kai gave him a grim smile and tossed it over. "After you."

The guards led the way into the warehouse. Row upon row of large storage crates stacked the place to the roof struts, each crate unmarked but with an inventory grid pad embedded in its side. If weapons filled each, Kai was looking at enough firepower to equip a galactic-sized army, an apt description for Griffin's forces. Their intel had been correct; they'd found one of Griffin's major weapons distribution centers.

Kai let his satisfaction show; a buyer would be pleased to see this abundance of product. Kai's real pleasure came from knowing how large a network they were about to burn.

A man barreled toward them, his bellow thundering in the cavernous space. "What the hell is this?" Short ginger hair topped a red pockmarked face. His stocky body looked compact enough to double for a steam roller. "Get them outta here!" As his shouts echoed around them, other people emerged from the rows and stacks of crates, converging on them.

The bulky guard they'd first encountered shuffled in place, shoulders hunched. "Sorry, boss, they say they're buyers."

"Buyers don't come here, you moron! Waste 'em and get rid of the bodies."

"Tychner sent me, Merris," Kai announced, moving around the guards and easing closer to their boss. Controlling Merris would give him an advantage over this growing crowd.

Merris slowed to a stop and scowled. "Tychner wouldn't send nobody here."

Kai flashed a dark predatory smile. "I didn't give him a choice. I'm rolling in credit and I'm short on time. Let's deal before this gets messy."

Face contorting with bestial rage, Merris reached for the stinger tucked in a holster under his arm.

Kai folded him with a lightning-fast jab to his solar plexus. Twisting the man's arm behind his back, Kai dropped him to his knees, drew his stinger, and nestled the muzzle at the back of Merris' head. "This is going to get very messy if I have to blow your head off."

The crowd surged forward, but Merris shouted, "Wait!" and they froze in place. Blowing air like an enraged bull, Merris strained against Kai's hold for a second then went still. "What do you want?" he snarled.

"Like I said, I'm here to buy." Kai glanced at Nick. "I feel like I'm not getting through. Am I not being clear?"

Nick stood with a blaster held ready in his hands, a guard crumpled at his feet. The gun's business end made a slow threatening pattern over the group. "I think they're catching on now, boss."

Kai smothered a grin. Marchand was going to have a few things to say about his agent's version of hanging back. "Don't worry, Merris. I'll throw in plenty of extra credit to make this worth your while."

Merris made a sound like a volcano about to erupt, but he relaxed in Kai's hold. "Ain't makin' no deal on my knees," he muttered.

Kai released him and eased back, keeping his aim fixed on the back of Merris' head.

The stocky man rose to his feet, rubbing his wrist and sending a furtive glance at Kai over his shoulder. Seeing Kai out of easy attack range, his face darkened and he shifted around to face him. "What makes you think my bosses will let me sell a single unit to you?"

"Come on, Merris, you know they won't mind an early sell. Besides this place is stuffed to the gills. You're not exactly lacking for inventory." He tipped his head at the restless attendants surrounding them. "Send your dogs away, and I'll show you why you should deal with me. I'll let you take a peek at my account." Slipping a hand in his pocket, he pulled out a creditor and waggled it.

Merris stared at the creditor, an avid gleam rising in his eyes. He grunted and shuffled in place, his gaze going from the creditor to the stinger in Kai's steady grip. With a sour look he waved off his goons and barked, "Back to work!"

Most of his lackeys slunk into the stacks. Kai sensed a few lingering close by, ready to come to their boss' aid. The guard by the entrance glowered at Nick, grabbed his partner by the collar, and dragged the limp man out the door. Nick lowered the blaster, his grip comfortable and self-assured. He gave Kai an expectant look, his dark eyes calm.

Kai dropped his stinger's aim and tapped the creditor. He held it out to the weapons dealer with a hard grin. "I love a guy who can follow directions."

Eyes wary, Merris shifted forward and plucked the creditor from Kai's hand, glancing at the screen. He went still, his Adam's apple bobbing with a rough swallow. "This is…"

"I know. So pretty. Let's figure out how much of it is yours."

Merris made a hoarse sound but seemed transfixed by the amount of credit glowing on the screen and didn't answer.

Nick snorted a half-laugh. "You broke him."

"It'll wear off. Go find a scanner and see if they have what I need."

Merris lifted his head in slow motion as if waking from a dream, staring at Kai with glazed eyes. "Nobody goes in the stacks."

"He doesn't have to. Get him a scanner."

The weapons dealer scowled, his gaze sharpening. "I can look up anything you want."

"And I need an honest report of what's in this armory. I also need to keep an eye on you." Kai tipped the stinger, letting the light flash along its metallic sides in subtle threat. "No offense, but you have sort of an untrustworthy look. So while you and I talk business, he'll find what I need." He paused, studying Merris. "You keep making that face and you'll never get a date."

The red-head blinked, his features slackening into something like surprise.

Kai smirked. "No, I didn't mean with me."

Nick made a muffled choking sound in the distance.

Kai ignored him, watching Merris' scowl return. "Any second now you'll go get a scanner. Wait for it…"

Muttering under his breath, Merris stalked over to the wall by the door and keyed open a small receptacle. He pulled out a scanner, marched to Nick, and slapped it into the FPA agent's palm.

Mission accomplished. Now they had to play out their roles and slip away before Merris started having second thoughts. Kai figured he could smother the man in enough credit to keep those second thoughts at bay for a long time.

"Atta boy," Kai drawled. "Now let's talk price."

Despite his grumpy face, Merris moved back to Kai with alacrity. He lifted the creditor and gave it another long stare. "Y'know, I could bleed you out, dump you in the channel, and take it all."

"Like I said, untrustworthy. On the other hand you could die a slow brutal death. Up to you." Kai met the man's gaze, letting him see how capable he was of following through on the threat. He didn't like to kill, but he was ready. If they had to take out Merris and his crew, so be it. They'd already done the job.

The weapons dealer studied him, uncertainty flickering in his eyes. "You ain't even a little wound. Are you that good?"

"Do you really want to find out?"

Merris deflated and handed the creditor back over.

"All right, let's start with the blasters. What's your unit price?"

As he and the dealer began negotiations, Nick strolled over to the stacks, his thumb flicking over the inventory display on the scanner, blaster resting on his shoulder. He looked casual, but Kai knew he was confirming the download of the trace plus putting himself in a good position if Merris' minions returned. After a minute he announced, "They got everything on your list. Looks like they over-package. Each crate's light on inventory."

Kai gave Merris a look of grim disgust.

The dealer hunched his shoulders in a defensive shrug. "Gotta protect the goods, man. They bang up on each other, and I got buyers cryin' about damaged product." When Kai continued to stare without a word, the man grimaced. "Fine, I'll throw in a discount for extra shipping costs."

Kai relented, returning to their negotiations. He gave Merris a list of several different kinds of weapons and explosives. Once they established how many of each was in a crate they settled on prices and Merris' bonus. The dealer gave him accounts to transfer the credit into, hovering over the creditor like a vulture until Kai completed the transactions. Afterward avid glee danced around his features. Kai hadn't haggled very hard; the man's bonus had been considerable. The Core would no doubt find a way to take a large piece of it, but Kai didn't mention this ugly fact. He wanted Merris in a good mood until they left.

"Send my crates to this location." Kai showed him a small data pad. "If I don't see my property there by the day after tomorrow, I'm coming back here to ask why."

Merris still wore his post-coital glow and didn't react to the subtle threat in Kai's tone. "No problem. Good doin' business with ya."

Kai gave him a sardonic smile. "I'm sure. We'll show ourselves out, sport. You have a nice night now."

Merris waved them off and strode away with a

spring in his step.

Nick snorted, joining Kai on his way toward the exit. "The guy looks like all his dreams came true."

"The Core'll burst his bubble soon enough. We got what we came for." He glanced at the agent in silent question.

Nick nodded, confirming the success of their mission, but said nothing until they'd gone well away from the warehouse. "Where did you send those crates? And whose account did you use to set this up? Better not be your own. If they find out who you really are, Griffin will—"

"Easy, cowboy, this isn't my first rodeo. Secured account, anonymous and hidden, just like real bad guys use. Same with the drop location."

Nick frowned. "You can make accounts anonymous?"

"Holy Suns, you are so green. Don't they teach agents anything these days?"

"Shut up, Shay. Why are we still walking?"

"You need the exercise."

"You need a swift kick in the teeth."

Kai sent him an easy grin. "Whenever you're ready, Giv."

Nick sighed, turning his face to the night sky. "I'm trying, Cass. I'm really trying here," he muttered. Dropping his chin, he glowered at Kai. "So when do we see results from this little adventure?"

"They'll start trickling in over the next few days. The Core can't move this much product fast. Plus, new inventory will come in, the scan program will update, and even more will be tagged. Eventually they'll find the program and kill it, but until then the FPA will be busy with cleanup."

"Nice. It's like you've done this before."

Kai glanced at Nick's deadpan expression, caught the gleam of mischief in his dark eyes, and smiled like a wolf. "There you go. I knew you had it in you."

Chapter 15

Liaena stared at the stately woman on the viewer, her limbs tingling with a prelude to either hope or dread. She wasn't sure which. She'd spent the entire morning in a fruitless search for information on Imago and for a way to help the Red ascetics. Stomach churning and temples throbbing with the beginnings of a migraine, she'd resigned herself to approaching her father again. She'd joined him in his administration center and had begun a delicate probe on the subject of Imago, when he'd gotten an unexpected call.

This woman with her tightly bound gray hair, angular face, and sharp eyes introduced herself as Mendani-met K'etarci, head of the Order of the White Sun. A high ranking member of any Order contacting her father stunned her, but the Mendani-met's words shocked her even more.

Webster Griffin's eyebrows rose in a rare show of surprise. "I beg your pardon?"

The woman's mouth pinched as though she weren't used to repeating herself. "I'm offering an alliance. You are the rising power in our galaxy. For the continued prosperity of my order, aligning our cause with yours is logical."

Griffin took a few seconds to answer, strange emotions shifting under the mask his features had become. "What could a religious sect possibly offer me in an alliance?"

"You appear in need of scientific experts. My order has those in abundance." K'etarci spoke without infliction, but she studied Liaena's father with a piercing gaze.

His eyebrows rose again, but this time Liaena sensed something darker in him than mere surprise. "Your timing is interesting. And transparent. Shall we discuss the real reason for your call?"

K'etarci smiled without humor, tight and small. "I know of your Red Order visitors." Liaena's heart bounded with hope then plummeted with the ascetic's next words. "They aren't my concern. The Reds do what they do for their own irrational reasons. I wouldn't dream of interfering. However, your actions against them have made it clear it is more advantageous to be on your side than opposing you."

Liaena's chest grew tight as though the air had become too thin. She already believed her father a monstrous force. With the resources and backing of the White Order at his beck and call he would become unstoppable. She could only hope the Whites put forth some strategy, a distraction perhaps, to take her father's attention from their captured brethren.

"You expect me to believe you care nothing for the fate of your comrades?"

"Comrades?" K'etarci's features stiffened in chilly disdain. "I am White not Red. If a madman throws himself from a cliff, I don't follow out of misguided loyalty. I sympathize for their loss, but perhaps some madness can only be cured with a fatal fall."

Icy needles joined the tightness in Liaena's chest. The Mendani-met seemed to be encouraging the deaths of the Red ascetics in Griffin's custody. Did such a great rift exist between the White and Red Orders?

"Hmm." Her father's expression remained skeptical. "So instead of a fatal fall you choose to grovel?"

K'etarci stiffened at the insult, her lip curling as if she smelled something repugnant. "I don't like you. You don't like me. However, emotion is irrelevant. We have something you need. If you wish to discuss it, I will be attending an auction this evening at the following location." She tapped something below their line of vision, and a location appeared on Griffin's data retrieval center. "Unless you'd like to continue our conversation over this unsecured vid feed?"

Griffin smiled, glacial and glittering with underlying threat. "No, we're done here."

Mendani-met K'etarci gave a short nod and disappeared from the viewer.

Liaena turned to her father.

He stared at the blank viewer with an expression of such cold calculation her skin shrank and itched. "How interesting," he murmured.

"What will you do, Father?"

"I will meet with her, of course. She has piqued my curiosity. I have no doubt this is some ploy, but the direction she has taken intrigues me."

To have a hold on the Orders you so despise? Of course it intrigues you. "Whites are not known to be evasive or duplicitous. They have a reputation for directness and she seemed sincere. Why do you believe this is a ploy?"

"You are so naïve, Daughter. When it comes to games of power, everyone is evasive and duplicitous.

An auction is too public a place for a trap, so perhaps she's playing a longer game. We shall see."

"May I attend?"

He turned his head, his calculating look landing on her like a stone. Her stomach cramped. His expression suggested he'd say no. He didn't want her to be present at this meeting with the White, but why? What further secrets was he hiding from her? Or was he becoming so suspicious of her he was taking steps to distance her from all of his dealings?

She rushed to speak before he could deny her request. "I could invite Manakai to further our courtship."

One of his silver eyebrows slid upward. "So soon after your previous tryst? You don't wish to appear overeager, Daughter."

She gave him a cool enigmatic smile. "Something tells me he wouldn't see it that way. I wished only to maintain our momentum with him, but if you disapprove I won't give it another thought." She wanted to know what transpired between her father and K'etarci, but perhaps it would be best if she stayed behind. She would have more freedom to investigate Imago and the crisis with the Red ascetics.

Griffin studied her, his expression turning thoughtful. "Hmm, yes. I would like to see Manakai Shay's reaction to me with a White. Invite him, Liaena. This should prove to be an illuminating evening."

"As you wish, Father." She dipped her chin in a submissive nod and left the administration center, temples throbbing worse than ever. At least she had an excuse to contact Kai, something she'd burned to do since discovering her father had taken captives. Kai would already know about it and she couldn't speak openly to him, but she might be able to convey something. Or he might offer her hope.

Slipping into her quarters, she paused at the medical unit to take a pain blocker for her migraine and then sat at the viewer. She drew a deep breath, letting it out slowly as she tapped the controls to connect with Shay Enterprises. After a moment Manakai appeared and stole the air right out of her lungs. His hair cavorted in wild disarray around his head, his eyelids drooped, and his shirt lay rumpled, as if he'd just risen from his bed. And he wore the most gorgeous smile she'd ever seen in her life. The warm intimacy almost knocked her onto the floor.

"Liaena." His smile faded as his gaze roamed over her features. "Is something wrong?"

Her throat closed. How she wished she could step into his arms, lay her head on his chest, and pour out her troubles. Wasn't comfort one of the perks of a burgeoning relationship? But they weren't in a real relationship, and his beautiful mind-numbing smile was a sham, worn to fool her father. She cleared her throat, blinking away the sting in her eyes. "Not at all. Did I wake you?"

He made a face, the corners of his eyes crinkling with rueful humor. "Long night. No rest for the wicked I suppose. But the day's looking much brighter now. I'm glad you called."

Her heart skipped a beat. *A sham,* she reminded the foolish organ, forcing her mouth to curl in an answering smile. How did he do this with such natural ease? "I wanted to thank you again for our excursion yesterday. I enjoyed myself."

He grinned. "The pleasure was all mine, believe me."

A sudden memory of his hands framing her face and his mouth teasing hers drove hot color into her cheeks. Swallowing hard, she looked away. "I also wanted to invite you to dinner."

"Where and when?"

She told him the time and place. "It's an auction. I realize it's not the ideal setting, but I'm not sure when I'll be free to see you next."

"In that case an auction's perfect. It's already been too long. Did you dream about me last night, Aena?"

The question took her by surprise. Caught in a memory of her scorching dreams, she gulped and said nothing, sure the answer glowed stark on her flushed face.

His mouth curved in a slow wicked smile. "Mmm. What did I do and how much did you like it?"

"Kai." She meant to sound reproving, but his name came out in an undignified squeak.

He sighed, his expression dimming into disappointment. "Right, no foreplay over an open line. Can you find a secure com link?"

"No." She regretted having to say it, and not just because she was dying to know what he meant by foreplay. She wanted his help to free the Reds. She wanted to know if someone was coming for them. But as he'd acknowledged neither of them could speak openly.

"Damn. I suppose I'll have to wait until tonight. This is going to be a long day, Aena."

Flattering and seductive, his words turned her bones to water. The hungry speculative look in his eyes spiked her heart rate and sent her thoughts stumbling around like drunks in her skull.

She had to look away to remember how to speak. "I'm sure you'll find something to keep you busy and pass the time."

He chuckled. "No doubt, but you'll be on my mind all day. I'll be on yours too, won't I?"

She slanted him a cool look. "Not as often as your ego believes."

"We'll see." He oozed amused confidence and irked her. "Until tonight, Aena."

The viewer went blank. She took a deep breath and let it out in a long quiet sigh. She'd often thought of him as a whirlwind. The more time she spent with him, the more apt the analogy seemed. He blew into her life and turned everything upside down without apparent effort. She only hoped she could weather the storm.

****

Some obscure official Liaena had never heard of hosted the auction in his country villa. His grand home boasted the most amazing woodwork, a thousand different species of trees cut and carved into intricate wall panels, doorframes, lattices, and archways. Rich veneers and polish gave each room a warm opulence. Liaena would much rather have paid attention to the wood art gracing the show room than the odd objects on display for auctioning. They appeared to be religious artifacts and collector's items, antiquated and ambiguous.

The people who roamed the room inspecting the objects proved as strange an assortment; academics, clerics, and wealthy collectors mingled in a jangle of colors and voices.

Or perhaps her migraine created the jangle. Everything was too bright, too loud. A miasma of scents filled the air and turned her stomach. She should have taken more pain blocker on the ride over, but trying to wrest information on Imago out of her father had preoccupied her.

"If the Shays are to continue to believe I'm working for them, I must give them something," she'd pressed.

"Tell them it was part of a defunct project."

She knew better than to ask what type of project. His forbidding expression warned the question would be unhealthy. "And the AI?"

"Dismantled." Something about the way he'd said it with a gloating gleam in his eye made her think he was lying. Or perhaps she didn't want it to be the truth for Cassie's sake.

When they'd arrived, Mendani-met K'etarci was already in attendance, circulating through the showcased items and speaking with solemn respect to several individuals. Upon seeing them, she excused herself from her companions and approached. She wore a long white robe cinched at her waist with a simple belt. At her temple a whirl tattoo flashed silvery white in the room's bright lights. No other adornment broke the severity of her appearance.

She gave a short sharp nod in greeting. "The auction doesn't begin for another hour. That should be long enough for us to come to terms."

"Aren't you presumptuous," Griffin said in a smooth voice laced with underlying venom.

"I don't like wasting time. You're here, so I assume you're at least willing to talk."

Griffin gave a grudging nod.

"So let's talk." K'etarci turned her head, acknowledging Liaena for the first time. "And your daughter?" Her tone dismissed, her piercing gaze pinning Liaena like a bug under a microscope.

"You are excused, Daughter." He spoke as if she were still six years old and he shooed her away from the adult table.

Keeping her features emotionless, Liaena nodded and headed for the exit, head pounding worse than ever. Anger and dismay at their dismissal tightened the muscles at the back of her neck, goading the migraine to new heights. She needed to get out of this too-bright room with its over-scented occupants before she vomited all over their weird collection of knickknacks. Dropping her chin to hide her growing distress, she weaved through the crowd only to crash into what she'd thought was a shadow. Swallowing nausea, she discovered the shadow was a warm hard body wrapped in elegant black clothing.

Manakai grasped her arms to steady her. "Liaena, what's wrong?"

"It's only a headache," she croaked. When he frowned, disbelief and concern darkening his features, she cleared her throat and amended, "A migraine. It's making me a bit woozy."

"Let's get you some air." He turned her away from the exit and toward a set of glass doors leading outside, urging her forward with a hand at her back.

Fresh outdoor air sounded blissful. She took shallow breaths on the way, trying not to focus on any bright objects or colors. The glass doors opened onto a wide terrace, lit with soft golden lamps in the growing twilight. A gentle breeze drifted past her face and took the cloud of indoor fragrances away with it. She breathed deep, her feet slowing as her nausea subsided. Her temples still throbbed as though some maniac swinging a hammer ran loose in her skull.

"Over here," Kai murmured, leading her farther down the terrace to a dim section underneath a balcony. Carved wooden columns supported the balcony, and he leaned her against one. "You need water and medicine. Don't move. I'll be right back." He slipped away into the darkness as though he really were made of shadow.

Liaena closed her eyes and pressed her head against the smooth wood. It felt silky against her skin, cool and soothing. She'd had migraines before, often after her father disciplined her in the interrogator. Seeing the cleric's torture may have triggered this one. She'd never had one last so long.

All of a sudden Kai's hand slipped behind her head, cradling it as an injector pressed cold pricks of pain in her neck. She sucked in a startled breath then let it out in a rush as relief spread through her. Without thought she sagged forward and rested her forehead against his chest, gripping the edges of his dark jacket to keep the rest of her from sagging into him as well. "Thank you."

He swore under his breath, fingers tightening a fraction on the back of her head. Then he began a gentle massage of her neck muscles, his touch loosening all the rest of her muscles in the process. "Was it a migraine or did the man beat you again?" he asked in a rough voice.

"A migraine," she whispered, battling to stay on her feet. The massage was heavenly, his concern even more so. No one but her mother had ever cared for her wellbeing. His delectable scent filled her with every breath. She fought not to bury her face against him and inhale until her lungs burst.

He grunted, fingers moving from neck to scalp. "Well, it's no wonder. You bind this hair any tighter and you'll pull it right out, Aena. Time it came down." Under his touch her hairdo began to loosen.

"No, wait—" She tried to lift her head, but he pressed it back to his chest.

"Relax. Think of it as a medical necessity."

She wanted to protest her pain had receded and ruining her hairdo wouldn't help anything. But she lost the words to stop him as his fingers worked through her hair, undoing clasps and braids, sending tingling warmth cascading down her body.

Kai ran his fingers along her scalp in a slow massage before combing through the strands to the ends, his movements meditative. "Sun and Stars," he murmured. "Will you look at this?" His voice held a strange rasp.

Curious, she raised her head.

He lifted a long sheaf of her hair, spreading his fingers through the fine strands. The golden glow of the lamps gleamed through the strands in flashes of subdued fire. Kai watched the locks cascading over his fingers with a rapt expression. "Is it faith or folly to loose the Sunfires of strife at the dawn of the Red Sun?"

She stared at him, dumbfounded. Had he just quoted scripture? She wasn't sure what the line meant, but his expression implied flattery. He studied her hair as if he'd never seen anything so amazing. They were alone. He had no reason to fake this interest.

She should ask him what he'd meant by the quote. She should step away from him. Instead she tightened her grip on his jacket, rose on her toes, and pressed her lips to his. A second later, embarrassed awkwardness flooded her. What was she doing? She knew almost nothing about kissing, and she had no business touching him anyway. She dropped back to her heels, wondering what in the Suns' names she could say to explain herself.

He didn't give her a chance to say anything. Whispering her name, he followed her down, mouth covering hers. Yesterday he'd teased her, a playful seduction. Tonight he was all hot passion, lips moving over hers in sizzling demand. He clasped the back of her neck, his other hand slipping around her waist and urging her closer.

Liaena's mind evaporated, her entire focus narrowing on his clever mouth and what it was doing to her. His firm lips seemed to have a direct connection from her mouth to every one of her erogenous zones, waking them with each slick movement. Her entire body ached and tingled. His tongue slid between her lips, tangling with hers in a dance guaranteed to set her on fire. He tasted even better than he smelled, a mysterious flavor she craved in an instant. Tightening her grip on his jacket, she pressed closer, needing more.

But he lifted his head, ending the kiss with a swift indrawn breath, like a swimmer breaking the water's surface.

She didn't want him to stop. Fierce desire still fogging her mind, she followed instinct and rose on tip-toe again, releasing her death grip on his jacket to slip her hands behind his head. "More," she whispered. "Please, Kai."

He gave her more than she'd dreamt possible. With a low groan he dove into her mouth, plundering deep. He shifted, clasping her waist and lifting her off her feet. Her back met the wood column, and he anchored her there with his hard body. With her curves in full delirious contact with every steely inch of him she whimpered, quivering all over. The heavy erection pressing against her abdomen in hot demand answered any doubts she had about his interest.

Devastating her with deep, drugging kisses, he slid his hands down her sides, lighting fires wherever he touched. When his thumbs caressed the sensitive skin of her hip bones through the thin cloth of her dress, the sensation shot through her like an electric shock. She shuddered, fingers tightening in his silky hair.

He continued to explore her hip and thigh, his other hand ascending to just under her breast, framing the curve in a slow caress. Her nipples peaked in sharp stabs of pleasure, and she moaned into his mouth. If he kept this up, she might spontaneously combust. Everywhere he touched, he sparked fire and pushed her desire to greater heights than she'd ever dreamt.

He turned his head, trailing his lips down her jaw and neck with a low rumble in his throat. Placing a hot open-mouthed kiss in the hollow of her throat, he set off the pendant's music. *Rejoice.* He slid a knee between her quivering legs, his hard-muscled thigh first brushing then pressing against her core, sending massive earthquakes of pleasure up her spine. The air left her lungs in a rush. She tensed and clutched at him, desperate and burning.

Then he lifted his head and planted his hands on the wood behind her, arms straightening and levering his body away. Deprived of his support, her shaking limbs folded and she almost crumpled in a heap at his feet. Catching herself on his arms, she blinked in confused dismay. Why in the Suns had he stopped? "Kai?"

He was looking over his shoulder, his expression almost savage. With a chill of foreboding, she glanced around him. Two strangers stood at the terrace railing, chatting in quiet easy tones. Neither seemed to notice Liaena and Kai, but the sight of them sent reality crashing into her in a cold wave. *Holy Heart of the Sun.* The moment Kai touched her the world had disappeared and she'd forgotten everything. If Kai hadn't stopped when he did, she would have made love with him in public a few steps from her father.

Chapter 16

Profound gratitude and utter loathing didn't mix well in Kai's gut. He wanted to kill the two intruders for interrupting. He also wanted to give them a medal for saving him from a massive mistake.

Some of the damage was already done. Liaena now knew how much he wanted her and how little willpower he had around her. One soft kiss from her and he'd lost his mind. What an effortless seduction; what an easy mark. She must be gloating over her triumph.

He glanced at her. She didn't look triumphant. Pale and strained, she stared across the terrace with wide eyes as though witnessing some horror. "Suns above, what have we done?" she whispered and buried her face in her hands.

He straightened, letting his arms fall to his sides and shifting to block the intruders' view of her. He remembered her migraine with a stab of remorse. "Are you all right?"

She made a soft sound, similar to the ones she'd been making while he ravaged her, and renewed lust slammed into him. Clenching his hands into fists, he sucked in a deep breath and tried to remember all the reasons he shouldn't touch her. Not an easy thing to do with the taste of peaches on his tongue, the memory of her curves fitting like perfection against him, and his

217

body still rock hard and ready. The hell of it was, even knowing what a disaster it would be, if she tested him he wasn't sure he could say no. *More. Please, Kai.* He shuddered. Her sultry voice could bring down whole civilizations.

"Come on," he rasped, catching her wrist and tugging her toward the end of the terrace, farther away from the glass doors and all the potential witnesses. He snagged the water bottle he'd left on the railing as he passed. She wobbled and he released her wrist to catch her elbow. "Aena?"

"I'm all right," she answered, voice thin and breathless. "Just weak in the knees still."

"Your head?"

"My head's fine. You're to blame for my knees. I can't believe we almost…"

He swallowed hard and did his best not to think about it. The soft skin under his fingertips urged him to find out if the rest of her felt as soft. Shaking his head, he led her down a set of steps to a walkway leading around the building. On his way to the transports to retrieve the medicine, he'd passed a bench under an arbor. He took her there now and she sank onto the seat, slipping away from his touch. He ignored the sense of loss in his fingertips and handed her the bottle of water.

"I'm sorry, Aena. Attacking you wasn't on tonight's agenda."

She set the bottle down without opening it and shivered. "I didn't feel attacked." She spoke in a low voice, her gaze fixed on the ground at his feet. "No one saw. My father…" She hesitated, tucking a strand of hair behind her ear. The hair cascading around her shoulders softened her features, warming them. She looked younger, more vulnerable, and his heart spasmed in his chest. "I'll fix my hair before we return and he won't know."

Kai shrugged out of his jacket and draped it over her shoulders. He wanted to slip his hands under the collar and lift the weight of her hair free, but touching that raw silk again would be a mistake.

She grasped the edge of the jacket and raised her gaze to his in mute question.

"You were shivering. This little black dress of yours is a feast for the eyes but not great outdoor wear."

Her mouth gained a wry curve. Clasping her hands in her lap, she tipped her chin down and stared at them. "Is it safe to talk?"

"We'd be safer in my transport, but going there with you right now wouldn't be my smartest move."

She slanted him a quick look, wariness and something else flickering in her eyes. "It would be more private."

"Too private." He crouched at her feet, drinking in the sight of her. Rich silk, its fire dimmed by the darkness, framed her stunning features. The dress, soft, sleeveless, and showing far too much skin for his peace of mind, clung to curves he badly wanted to feel again. Her long slim legs gleamed pale in the night, calling to his fingertips. He met her gaze with a rueful smile. "How much self-control do you think I have?"

Her gaze skittered away and she squirmed in her seat. Clearing her throat, she said, "Here will do then," in a husky voice. "Kai, my father has the Red ascetics."

"I know. My guess is he's torturing the ever-loving hell out of them."

She nodded, her mouth turning down at the corners

and a crease forming between her brows. "I've tried to deflect him but he's determined. None have died yet at least. Why did they do this?"

He shook his head. No matter how well she acted the part of his ally, he couldn't trust her with T'Zai's secrets or his own for that matter. *Remember, she's a Griffin.* He'd already given her far too much ammunition against him.

She sighed. "How can I help them?"

"You can't."

"Well, is someone coming for them? Will you rescue them?"

"No, Aena. They're on their own."

She blinked at him as if he'd slipped into a foreign language. "What? Why not? You came for Cassie."

"Cassie was one person. She wore a tracker, so we knew her exact location."

"I can give you their exact location."

"If we come after the Reds, your father will know we had something to do with your mother's disappearance."

She went still, staring at him. "So this is a true sacrifice. You condone this?"

He shook his head again, holding back words with an effort. *A Griffin.*

She rubbed a hand over her eyes. "My father is inside speaking with the head of the White Order. She asked him here to discuss an alliance." When he didn't respond, she continued in a sharp voice, "She suggested he kill the Red ascetics, Kai. What is her purpose here?"

"Easy," he soothed, settling a hand over hers. Her skin felt cold under his touch. "The Orders do what they do for their own reasons. It's best if you don't interfere."

She looked down at his hand but didn't pull away. "You weren't surprised she was here to see my father."

"No. The White Order is practical. I didn't think K'etarci would come herself."

"I didn't know the Orders had leaders. I'd never heard of a Mendani-met."

He shrugged. "The Orders are full of secrets, some for protection and others to preserve their mystical aura."

"You don't approve."

"I don't buy the rhetoric. Despite the show, they usually have good intentions." He removed his hand and rose, settling next to her on the bench. "Have you tried Cassie's gift?"

She smoothed a hand over the site of the implant. "It works. I've enjoyed a few moments of privacy here and there, but I haven't found a way to use it otherwise. I asked my father about Imago."

"And?"

"He claims he terminated the research program involving the AI." She sent him a quick strained glance. "He claims Imago was destroyed."

Kai kept his expression clear. "Do you believe him?"

"Something about the way he said it doesn't ring true." She pulled the jacket tighter around her shoulders, as if she felt a sudden chill. "But I don't have proof. Whatever he's hiding from me, he's hidden it well."

"I have a solution." Kai pulled a device about the size of his thumbnail from his pocket and held it out to her. "Another of Cassie's gifts. It holds a hunter program that'll track down Imago's whereabouts." Cassie had also programmed it to find a few other things, but Liaena didn't need to know. "Place it close to any terminal and it'll download the program. The program will upload when it's done, but it'll take a while. Cass said it'd have to move slowly to remain undetected."

Liaena plucked the device from his fingers, eyeing it with a slight frown. "My father has an entire technical staff who find things like this in his network and destroy them."

"They aren't Cassie. When she makes something undetectable, it stays that way."

She lifted her gaze to his, faint amusement dancing around her mouth. "No wonder my father tried so hard to take her from you."

He didn't hide his smug satisfaction. A sound distracted him and he tensed, covering her hand and the device.

"What is it?" she whispered.

He held up a hand for silence, tilting his head in the direction of the sound. Then he relaxed. "Someone leaving the auction. We'd better get back in there before you're missed."

"I need to redo my hair." She swept a hand around her neck and pulled the silky mass over her shoulder. "Where are my clasps?"

He reached in his pocket and pulled them out, handing them to her with reluctance. Confining all that glory again would be criminal. "How's the migraine?"

"Gone, thank you." She rose and he followed suit. "I need a mirror and I can't allow anyone to see me like

222

this. Will you help me reach our transport?"

"I'll clear the way for you."

She gave him a forbidding look as they walked toward the front of the villa. "Don't hurt anyone."

He chuckled. "Have faith, Aena."

Except for a guard at the entrance the front stayed deserted, no other guests wandering in the landing area. Simple enough to slip in between transports out of the guard's line of sight and escort Liaena to the Griffin ship. With a solemn nod she disappeared inside. Kai waited for her, keeping watch.

When she reappeared, all her glorious mahogany tresses lay in intricate coils, imprisoned once again at the back of her head.

He made a sound of disapproval in his throat. "Blasphemy."

She gave him a quizzical look. "So you did quote scripture earlier. I thought you didn't believe in rhetoric."

"In this case, it applies." He couldn't resist brushing his fingers along her temple, skimming her hairline. "Sunfire wasn't meant to be captured."

The landing lights revealed a flush darkening her cheekbones. "Why are you flirting with me?" The words came out in a rush. She pressed her lips together afterward as if she hadn't meant to say them.

"No flirting, just truth. Let's get inside." *Before my inner idiot comes back out to play.* He managed to keep his hands to himself on the walk to the front entrance.

"Kai, how is my mother?" Liaena whispered.

"She's fine. We're working on a way for you to see her. We need to convince your father to let you out of his sight."

She made a sexy humming sound in her throat, and he almost swallowed his tongue. Her features were solemn and thoughtful not enticing. As they neared the guard her cool mask fell back into place, serene and glacial.

The guard did a small double take when he saw them, apparently remembering their faces from their initial arrival.

Kai gave him a charming smile and settled a hand at the small of Liaena's back. "Good evening again. Pleasant night for a stroll."

The man's expression cleared. "Oh yes, it is. Evening, sir, ma'am."

When they entered, Liaena slipped his jacket off her shoulders and handed it to him with a small smile. "Thank you."

"I live to serve."

One of her eyebrows lifted in subtle disbelief, but she didn't comment. He grinned, shrugging back into his jacket and escorting her to the showroom. The auction was in full swing, the tracking viewer flickering with bids from the attendees. K'etarci stood within a group of clerics, watching the proceedings with a stern expression. Griffin lurked off to one side of the room, eyeing the White Mendani like a hunter coming in for the kill.

"Looks like your father and the White are finished," Kai murmured.

Before Liaena could answer, Griffin caught sight of them and strode over. "Good evening, Manakai. I trust you enjoyed your visit with Liaena?"

"As always. Something tells me you're about to ruin it."

Griffin donned a charming sympathetic smile. "I'm afraid I must cut the evening short. Duty calls. Will you send my regards to Sinsudee?"

"Of course."

"Thank you. I assume you'll want to say goodnight. Liaena, I'll be waiting at the transport." Nodding to Kai, Griffin strolled out of the room.

Liaena watched him go, her cool features ruffled by dark undercurrents. "He's in a hurry. Why? What did the White say to him?"

"He'll expect you to ask."

She sent him a dry look. "And I expect him not to answer. I should go." She hesitated, her gaze sweeping the room and her hands finding each other. "Would you have called this a date?"

"Not a typical one but close enough."

"A second date."

"Yes."

"Are second dates like first dates?" she asked in a lower voice, still not looking at him. Her cheekbones turned the slightest shade of rose.

He knew what she was asking. His heart stumbled then went galloping away with his good sense. He clasped her chin in a light hold and lifted her gaze to his, studying the wide eyes and the faint tremor in her lips. "Yes, Aena, second dates should always end in a kiss too." He lowered his mouth to hers for a slow deliberate caress. She returned it with just as much earnest contained passion, moving in perfect sync with him. He felt the contact all the way down to his toes and beyond.

Lifting his head, he watched her long lashes sweep up and the light flash bright in her eyes. The world seemed to slow, pausing between one heart beat and another. The solemn intensity in her beautiful features and silver-struck eyes pulled at him like gravity. It took everything he had to let her go. His hand drifted away as if moving through molasses.

"I'll be in touch," he said, voice hoarse.

The light dimmed in her eyes and she looked down with a nod. Turning, she headed after her father and Kai watched her go, aching in more places than he would have believed possible.

****

When Kai returned to Shay Enterprises, he found intruders in his home. Sin and Del had made themselves far too comfortable in his living room, snuggling together on the sofa and watching an entertainment holo, bright scenes filling the air.

He stopped in the middle of the room and scowled at them. "Why?" Glancing up at a sensor, he commanded, "Bash, call security."

Sin snickered. "He has the night off, and you have no room to complain. You're always invading my space." She leaned forward and tapped the controls for the holo.

When it disappeared, Del groaned. "Aw, come on, we were almost to the good part."

Sin clasped her bonded's face in her hands and turned his head toward Kai. "Look, Del, Grumpy's home."

Del gave him a lazy grin. "Hey, Grumpy. How'd it go?"

"I hate you both. Get out."

Del's grin didn't falter. "Got it. One supernova, comin' right up." He rose and sauntered toward the kitchen.

Kai was tired and a drink did sound good, so he let the man go. Slinging off his jacket, he tossed it over a chair and settled next to his sister.

"So how did it go?" she asked in a soft voice, her green eyes full of concern.

He couldn't evade her. She'd become expert at reading him and chasing him down, like a Suns-damned bloodhound. He sighed. "Griffin's torturing the Reds and claiming Imago's dead. K'etarci's making her move on him."

"We expected all of this. The Reds will die before saying anything, Griffin's lying about Imago, and K'etarci can take care of herself. Why do you look like someone is slowly ripping out your spine?"

He lifted his eyebrows. "Graphic."

She pointed a finger at his nose. "Answer."

"Liaena." He looked away, not wanting to see pity in her eyes.

"How bad was it?"

"Bad enough she now knows which buttons to push."

She made a thoughtful sound. "Kai, you know women, right?"

He sent her a look full of sibling disgust.

She ignored it, waiting him out.

"Sure, sis. I know women."

"I don't want any gory details here, but was she faking?"

"I want gory details," Del commented, crossing the room with a drink in hand. "Faking what?"

Kai snatched the drink out of his hand and downed it in three long swallows.

"Whoa," Del breathed.

Kai lowered the glass and closed his eyes for a long moment, waiting for the burn to pass from his throat into his chest. Heat spread from his center out, loosening his joints. "She wasn't," he answered his sister in a low voice.

"Hmm. So maybe this isn't as bad as you think."

He turned his head, staring at her. She'd lost her mind. Her somber expression slipped into furtive amusement under his jaundiced gaze.

Before she could continue spouting craziness, Del plucked the glass from Kai's hand and inspected the bottom. "Bro. How in hell did you do that?"

"Supernovas have a trick to them. You don't sip, you chug. The burn goes down instead of setting your mouth and face on fire. You get all the punch without the pain."

Del's expression darkened. "You're just telling me this now?"

"Priorities, boys," Sin interrupted, her voice threaded with humor. "Nick reported several arrests this afternoon. Your work with the weapons dealer is paying off."

"Are the arrests smoking out any of Griffin's dirty agents at FPA headquarters?"

Before she could answer, Del complained, "He's been laughing at me this whole time. Every time I have a supernova, he gets this smirk on his stupid face—"

Sin held up a hand and interrupted him. "Focus, darling. Our current topic is nasty corrupt agents bringing down the FPA from the inside."

Del glowered at Kai, setting the glass down with a sharp click. "I'll give him a punch. With lots of pain," he muttered.

Kai couldn't hold back a grin. "Thanks, man. That does cheer me up."

"No," Sin said loud enough to draw her riled bonded's attention, "you can't kill him. And no"—she turned to Kai—"the arrests haven't exposed any of Griffin's puppets yet."

"Well, it's early still. So all caught up now, right? The exit's that way. Go finish your holo somewhere else."

Grumbling insults under his breath, Del headed for the door.

Sin leaned toward Kai, resting an arm on his shoulder and giving him her patented I-know-you twin stare. "Stop worrying, don't drink yourself into a stupor, and get some sleep."

"Yes, Mama."

"I'm serious."

"Get out."

She heaved a long-suffering sigh, planted a kiss on his cheek, and bounced to her feet. "Sleep, Kai. Don't make me knock you unconscious."

"Can I knock him unconscious?" Del called from the front door.

"Dear Suns have mercy on me," Sin mumbled, ruffling Kai's hair as she rounded the sofa and strode toward her bonded. "Goodnight, brother mine."

"'Night, Sissa."

After they left, Kai rolled to a horizontal position and pulled his feet up on the cushions. Families could be aggravating, but his sister was right about one thing. He needed sleep. If the Suns smiled on him, he might even get some.

Chapter 17

Liaena settled on a seat in the holding cell, studying the Red ascetic kneeling in serene meditation on the floor. This was her fifth interview. She didn't expect any better results than the first four. None of the other ascetics had given her an answer to her dilemma, and this one appeared as inscrutable as his brethren.

Her father had agreed to let her try a different form of interrogation, persuasion instead of pain induction. When Liaena had spoken with Cassie during her captivity, the little woman had called it the honey and the stick. She'd used the analogy to convince her father; to avoid the stick, most people would accept the honey. To her misfortune these ascetics weren't most people.

"Hello," she said in a soft voice to the man who had yet to acknowledge her existence. "I am Liaena Griffin. Do you know why you are being held?"

The man opened his eyes, turned his head, and smiled at her so gently she wanted to weep. He was almost a uniform brown from his hair and eyes to his skin. He didn't seem to notice the body-fluid stains on his clothes or the stench rising from them, the lingering results of his torture. "I am Dani Turn. May the Light show your path and the Suns watch over you."

She remained composed, but each of the ascetics had greeted her this way and it was starting to unnerve her. She didn't know if they greeted everyone with those words or if they were trying to convey a message of some kind. "Thank you. My father is holding you because you took something of value from him."

The Dani closed his eyes, the gentle smile still curving his mouth. "Your father does not know life's true value. He is empty, devoid of Light. He hungers yet can never satisfy his appetite."

Liaena sighed. The other interviews had begun in a similar way. Had they all rehearsed before they'd arrived? Perhaps she should try something different. "I was once told I rise anew like the dawn."

He twitched, his eyes popping open again. His smile drifted away and his gaze grew intense, a far greater reaction than she'd received from the other ascetics. "Yes, I see the potential in you."

"What do you mean?"

"You are an interesting choice," he mused, almost as though speaking to himself. He touched the flame tattoo at his throat, his gaze drifting over her crystal pendant. "The Suns perceive more than I. I had not thought to see you dawn."

What had Kai said? *The Orders are full of secrets, some for protection and others to preserve their mystical aura.* At the moment, this ascetic seemed to be working hard on his cryptic mysticism.

Unprepared to start a verbal duel on the field of religion, Liaena gave in and went for a more direct approach. "You and your fellow clerics seem determined to die. May I offer you no other choice?"

He closed his eyes, serenity flowing back over his face. "Tell your father to release us."

"Believe it or not, I have. He's considering it. Perhaps if you told him my mother's location, he might judge you punished enough and let you go."

He chuckled. "As I said, he hungers. Leniency will not satisfy him. Soon the Red Sun will reclaim me and I will go gladly." He glanced at her, gentle sorrow filling his spare features and turning her heart to stone. "I thank you for your kindness, dear lady, but you should go. You cannot help us."

He'd arrived at it sooner, but they'd all given her the same answer. *You cannot help us.* Either they didn't want to be rescued or they also couldn't think of a viable way for her to free them.

Swallowing past a sudden stricture in her throat, she stood and gave him a respectful bow. He returned it, solemn and silent. She left with the bitter taste of failure on her tongue. At least her interviews had postponed her father's torture sessions.

In her quarters, she sat at her com unit and studied the small device Kai had given her out of the corner of her eye. She'd tucked it in the seam between the wall and the unit, unnoticeable to a casual inspection. How would she know when it had finished its work? Kai hadn't explained. He also hadn't suggested a way for her to return it to him. *We need to convince your father to let you out of his sight.*

She'd thought of one excuse, but she worried it would be too soon in their courtship to suggest. What did she know of romantic interactions? Aside from Kai's devastating advances, the closest she'd ever come to romance had been an awkward interlude with a security guard. Look how that had turned out. Her father would only allow supervised liaisons, sending a guard along to watch over them. The only way to be out of her father's and his minions' sights was to suggest a more intimate setting. She could tell her father she meant to seduce Kai.

Her heart sped up and her stomach fluttered at the thought. She only sought privacy for their covert dealings; she wouldn't really seduce him. But once they were alone, what would Kai do? Maddening unpredictable Manakai Shay. With her horrid luck, he would ignore her. The desire he'd shown last night could have been temporary. No doubt he'd returned home and found relief with the bevy of women she imagined in constant attendance on him.

Smothering a heavy sigh, she contacted her father and informed him of her failure with the Reds.

"Attend me," he commanded.

She bowed her head and rose to her feet. "Yes, Father."

She joined him in his lounge, trying to ignore the food spread on the low table in front of him. The sight and smell made her queasy. After speaking with the Reds and seeing firsthand the results of her father's cruelty, her appetite withered and food repulsed. Settling next to him in a matching cushioned seat, she folded her hands in her lap and waited for his notice.

Webster studied a portable viewer, sipping from a steaming mug. From the remains on his plate, she guessed he'd already eaten his fill. True to form, he didn't suggest she fill a plate for herself. When she attended him, he expected her full undivided attention, much like a slave would its master.

She watched him, cold burning in her chest as though a frozen comet had lodged under her ribs. The ascetic's description of her father rang true, a lightless raging hunger, like a black hole. He pulled everything in and devoured it. Thank the Suns her mother had escaped.

"So," he stated without looking up from his viewer, "you failed to extract even the smallest bit of information from these religious fanatics."

She wanted to point out he'd also failed with his brutal methods but knew what misery lay at the end of that road. She stayed silent, keeping her good-daughter mask firmly in place.

"No matter. They'll break for me eventually." He lifted his silver-capped head, studying her with clinical dispassion. "Your interrogation techniques require improvement. You lacked focus and commitment, almost as though you had true sympathy for these creatures."

"Did it seem so?" she responded in a cool voice, holding his gaze. "Then I played my part well. If they believe I am sympathetic to their cause, wouldn't they be more inclined to speak? I would like to try again."

"No, you've wasted enough time." Something on the viewer caught his attention, and he glanced down with a faint frown. "I have other matters requiring my attention. It seems the FPA has become miraculously competent at rooting out various arms merchants under my purview."

A tingling energy raced down her spine. Over the years she'd witnessed similar events, and her father had attributed a few to the Shays. He'd dismissed such actions as a rival's clever maneuvering, but Liaena wasn't convinced. Her memory of the fountain had led her to study these occurrences with more care, viewing them with a different lens than her father's dismissive arrogance. The emerging pattern shocked and galvanized her.

She believed the Shays had been trying to bring down Quasicore and her father for years, often using the FPA to do it. She'd come to recognize their handiwork. This new foray by the FPA had the twins' fingerprints all over it, similar to the recent mysterious destruction of the Core's largest factory of the drug blue, and subsequent exposure of key distributors of the narcotic. The FPA had somehow gotten hold of a list of offenders and production sites, crippling her father's drug ring.

"Your agents will put a stop to it." Her father's ability to circumvent justice, buying off FPA agents and officials, had delivered the killing blow to every maneuver against him and his company. Recently his net of FPA moles had grown thinner. She wondered if the Shays were trying something new.

"Their first order of business is to discover how the agency is obtaining the information. FPA agents do not become this effective overnight. One or two arrests I might attribute to blind luck, but the list of discovered locations and personnel grows longer by the hour."

She kept her satisfaction hidden behind blank features. "Are you in danger?"

"I am inconvenienced." He shot her a sharp look. "Do remember who you are speaking to, Daughter. The FPA is powerless against me."

She inclined her head and kept silent.

He eyed her as if she were some unsavory problem he was working on. "How great a hold do you have on your new conquest?"

"Pardon?" Her heart bumped against her ribs.

"We should test Manakai's devotion, see how far

he will go for you."

She couldn't stop tension from stiffening her neck muscles. "Isn't it early for a test? We've only had two encounters."

"Successful encounters from my reports. If he is misleading us, better to know early. The Shays have a distasteful streak of morality, a fatal weakness. If I'm to make use of them, we need to move them past this flaw."

"So you will test his morality?" Cold sweat misted her skin. "How?"

"None of your concern. You will relay a location to him and convey my invitation. Then we shall see how well you've captured him."

"Father," she said slowly, hunting for a way to stall, "I fear you're overestimating his interest. A test now may only serve to push him away. Please, give me more time to—"

"Stop your prattling. I overestimate nothing. The boy has had his eye on you for years, and from all accounts of your time together he's coming right to heel."

All accounts? Who had been watching them? How much had they seen? And what did he mean, Kai had his eye on her for years? The idea seemed ludicrous. "I don't mean to question you, Father. I only wish for a successful outcome. Is there some pressing reason we shouldn't wait?"

"You don't mean to question and yet you do. Do as you're told, Liaena."

She recognized the icy fury behind his words, the prelude to punishment, and bowed her head in submission. If she pushed further, he'd be even less inclined to listen to her.

He waved a dismissive hand and she rose to leave, fighting to keep her expression blank and her movements smooth. Whatever test her father had in store for Kai, it wouldn't be easy. She worried it had something to do with the ascetics, both Red and White. As predicted, her father had refused to reveal what he and the White Mendani-met discussed. This test following on the heels of such an unprecedented meeting made her nervous.

She returned to her quarters and sat again before the com unit. This time she didn't take note of the device, more concerned with how to warn Kai. She sent a request to Shay Enterprises and waited what seemed a long time for an answer.

When the viewer lit, Cassie greeted her instead of Kai. "Hi, Aena. How are you?"

"I'm well, thank you for asking. And you?"

"I'm great. I suppose you want to talk to the bosses."

"I hoped Manakai would be available."

Cassie's nose crinkled in a pained look. "They're involved in something and can't take calls. I'll run him a message and get him to call you back as soon as possible. I'll also kick his butt for not telling me I was on com duty. Sorry about the wait."

"Think nothing of it," Liaena responded, hiding a surge of anxiety. Involved in something? Did it have anything to do with the weapons raids or was it something new?

Cassie's face lit with a lovely smile. "It's nice to see you, Aena. When will you visit again? Last time was fun."

Michelle O'Leary

"I will see what I can schedule." Liaena studied her for a second. "You seem quite cheerful today. You have a glow about you." Had Kai not told Cassie about Imago's supposed death? Perhaps she hadn't believed it.

Cassie's smile turned mischievous. "I had a breakthrough on one of my projects. I always get giddy when that happens. How about you? Any progress on things you're working on?"

Thinking of the device and its unknown completion time, she shook her head. "Not really."

"That's not what I heard," the doctor said with a wink. "When are you seeing Kai again?"

For some reason her stomach flipped over at Cassie's words, and the beginnings of a blush warmed her cheeks. Her fingers crept toward the pendant, but she stopped them. *Not a real courtship, Liaena.* "I'm not sure."

"Well, don't worry. With the way Kai's acting over here, it won't be long."

Her curiosity danced. She wanted to ask how he'd been acting but said nothing, conscious of her constant surveillance.

"I hope we'll see you soon, Aena."

"I hope so as well."

Cassie's cheerful features disappeared and Liaena sat back, frustrated. How could she warn Kai if he wouldn't even talk to her? What could he be doing to put him out of reach of coms?

****

Kai jerked away from his sister's flying foot, the breeze of its passing cool on his sweat-dampened face. He snatched at her limb but she moved quicker, pulling back. He followed, indulging her strategic retreat with a series of blows, which she blocked or evaded. She liked to call this exchange the Dance of Opposites, attack and retreat flowing together in a constant river of motion.

She was in rare form today and he appreciated it. He needed the honing of his focus, the keen edge of concentration that erased all the other concerns in his life. His muscles sang, limber and ready, his mind clear of all thought. Nothing existed beyond the shimmering red force field confining them in this circular stone arena, what the Red Sun ascetics called the Circle of Fire. The battle, this war dance with his sister, consumed him.

Over the years, they'd progressed beyond the point of trying to best one another. While the Reds used the Circle of Fire to teach forms of war and strategy, its greatest lesson was control. They could hurt one another easily, but the skill lay in not doing so.

Her features blank with concentration, Sin dodged his jab and flashed a kick at his knee. He dropped, sweeping both legs at her weight-bearing limb, but she turned the momentum of her kick into a quick fall, rolling to her feet at the same time he did. Without pause he advanced, using his greater strength in a series of maneuvers to drive her toward the force field. He had the advantage of strength, but she had speed, countering his advance with slick cat-like evasion. Before he could blink, she loomed at his back. With a blow to the back of his knee to knock him off balance, she slipped a forearm against his throat, preparing to bring him down. He used the shift of balance to pivot, grab her, and throw.

The second she left his grip and flew through the

air, he winced. He'd thrown too hard.

Sin twisted, landing on all fours like a cat, and skidded backward to within a hair's-breadth of the force field. Panting, she met his gaze and grinned, poking fun at him for letting his control slip.

"You're gonna get in trouble," he warned out of the corner of his mouth, slanting a quick glance through the red shimmer toward their teacher.

Right on cue, T'Zai's voice rang out across the cavernous arena. "Does the conflict amuse you so, Mistress Shay? Those who take war lightly are often laid to waste on the battlefield."

Instead of defending herself, she rose to her feet and inclined her torso toward their teacher in a respectful bow. "I concede the match to my brother." She touched a finger to the shimmering field in symbolic surrender with a small grimace at the shock it delivered.

He frowned, wondering why she'd given up the match so soon. Then he noticed Cass standing next to T'Zai with wide eyes. Nick and Del were making their way down the tiered stone seats, grinning like a couple of spectators at a slicer race. T'Zai gave them all a sweeping glance of utter disgust and stomped toward the exit, muttering something about the irreverence of youth.

"Holy crap, you two," Cassie said, gaze traveling between Kai and his sister as they stepped over the stone ring, empty now of its fake fire. "That was amazing. I always forget how impressive your fights are until I see another one. How do you never hurt each other?"

Sin cast him a teasing glance. "Usually we have

great control."

Kai made a face at her. "Zip it, Sissa."

"Great show," Del drawled, slipping an arm around Sin's waist. "But you could've bruised him up some."

"You zip it too, big man," Kai retorted and returned his attention to Cassie, ignoring the kiss Nick deposited on her mouth and their linked hands. "You're wearing your lab coat, Cass."

She sent a sour look at the ascetics filing past them, a large crowd that gathered every time he and his sister fought in the Circle. "The Temple wouldn't put my message through to you. Why don't they let you guys take coms while you're in here? Something serious could happen."

"Did something serious happen?" Sin asked with a light frown.

"Well no, just Aena calling for Kai. But still. You'd think people obsessed with war would understand the importance of communication."

Kai snorted and snagged towels left across a stone seat, handing one to his sister and wiping the sweat from his face and neck. "They get serious about their religious rules. Aena wanted to talk? About what?"

"She wouldn't or couldn't say. My hunter program shouldn't be done, so I'm not sure what she wanted. She seemed paler."

Kai tensed, looping the towel around his neck and gripping the ends in tight fists.

Cassie held up a hand, hurrying to add, "Not hurt or anything, not that I could tell. She seemed more serious, holding back like she did when she first came here."

Kai glanced at his sister, but Sin gave her head a

small shake. She didn't know or couldn't guess what Aena's call had been about either. "All right, I'll contact her, see if she can give me some idea what's wrong. If not, I'll invite her here again."

"Good," Cassie said with a nod. "She could use some time away from that man."

Sin flashed a wry smile. "And more chocolate."

Cassie brightened. "Another women-only shopping day?"

"No!" Kai said in unison with the other two men, and both women burst into laughter. Shaking his head, he shared a long-suffering look with the brothers before leaving them to their chortling partners. With the ease of long practice, he made his way through the twisting Temple corridors to the concealed lift leading to the arboretum and his home. In his quarters he greeted Bash and took a quick san before settling in his office to contact Liaena.

She appeared on his viewer cloaked in her usual cool poise. As always the urge to ruffle her calm rose in him like a tide, but he suppressed it with ruthless resolve. He now knew some of what lay under her glacial surface. Self-preservation dictated he keep away or risk getting burned.

But she did seem paler. She wore a printed blouse in various subdued tans, its neckline hiding the pendant. Maybe this washed-out color caused her wan appearance. He realized she was studying him in turn and neither of them had said a word.

"I've missed you, Aena."

His husky words had a marked effect on her. Her cheeks warmed with a light rose color. She looked down, shifting in her seat, a hand rising to hover at her throat. Either she could compete with the greatest actresses in the galaxy or he'd flustered her, a reluctant response to his wooing. He badly wanted to touch her and breathed a sigh of relief that he couldn't. They didn't need an encore performance of his humiliating lack of control around her.

"I—I'm glad to see you as well." Her stiff formal tone amused him. Had the woman never flirted before?

"You'll have to do better than that. Where's all the passion I found yesterday?"

She stiffened, a crease forming between her eyes and her hand dropping away from her throat. "Do behave yourself, Kai. This is still an unsecured com. Thank you for responding to my call so quickly. I hope I didn't pull you away from anything important."

He grinned. "Behave myself," he said in a thoughtful voice. "I don't think I understand this strange concept. Will you explain it to me?"

She let out a small huff, her expression severe. "I'm contacting you on behalf of my father. He wishes to make an offer. I would like to discuss it with you in person."

An offer. Kai kept his expression easy but his insides knotted. No offer from Griffin would come without a heavy price. "As long as I get to see you, he can make as many offers as he likes. Will you come here tomorrow? I'd like to show you my home."

This seemed to fluster her again for some reason. She brushed at her cheek as if trying to push the color away, her gaze faltering. "I would be delighted to see it," she murmured.

"Should I send a transport around for you?"

"Thank you, that won't be necessary. I can be there

by early afternoon."

"Sounds perfect. I can't wait to see you. And get my hands on you again, Aena."

Her chest rose on a quick intake of air, and her lips compressed in a stern line. "Misbehavior," she announced.

He chuckled. "How did you know my middle name? See you soon, sweetheart." He ended the transmission and sat still for a long while, taking measured breaths.

Speaking with Liaena was turning out to be even harder than dealing with Griffin. Keeping the depth of his hatred for Griffin hidden required a huge amount of focus, every conversation with the man an intricate web of deception. The opposite held true with Liaena; he should have been acting and wasn't.

Chapter 18

Liaena strode through the Shay arboretum at Kai's side, wondering what had gone wrong. Kai was acting the perfect gentleman and she didn't understand why. He'd barely touched her and his conversation never strayed into salacious territory, remaining polite and attentive.

Her bodyguard, Boris, followed a few paces behind them, but his presence hadn't stopped Kai from pursuing her before. So what had changed?

She brushed a clinging flower petal off the skirt of her sundress, cringing inside at the unaccustomed bright color and free flow of the cloth. She'd worn it to please Sin and Cassie, who'd encouraged her to purchase it, but she hadn't counted on how exposed she'd feel in the outfit. It didn't reveal large amounts of skin, the skirt covering her to mid-calf, the scoop neck rising a conservative distance from her cleavage, and a light sweater concealing her bare arms. The exposed feeling came from something other than uncovered skin. In the mirror she'd seen a woman dressed for a carefree day at the beach or the park, looking forward to easy warmth, laughter, and fun. Her longing to be that woman oozed from every pore, coating her like a flashing sign of vulnerability.

Were the dress and her obvious yearning the reason for Kai's distance? If so, was he repulsed or trying to put her at ease? Whatever his motives, she missed his touch, missed the subtle passion in his eyes and voice. Even worse, when Boris reported this visit, her father would see it as a setback and take it out on her.

Stomach in knots, she used a pause in the conversation to lean closer and whisper, "What's wrong?"

He gave a slight shake of his head and pointed out a stunning flower variety with a bland smile. In a smooth voice he slipped into an anecdote of how he and his sister had discovered this particular flower, ushering her along a familiar path. It lead to his home.

She barely heard him, her responses as distracted as her mind. One part of her mulled over his rebuff of her question and diversion with the flower. Was his polite distance a new strategy then? If so, she couldn't see the benefit yet. Another part of her anticipated a second visit to his home with nervous tentative pleasure. The warm atmosphere and delicious fragrance had affected her so deeply before. If she couldn't contain herself, he would see it. She also wished this were a simple visit with no other agenda, Kai opening his private space to her and sharing this intimate piece of himself because he wanted to.

At the threshold, Kai paused and turned to Boris. "No offense, but weapons and bodyguards aren't allowed here. You'll have to wait outside." A frown gathered on Boris' brow and he opened his mouth, but Kai continued before he could say anything. "My companion AI, Basher, will keep you company. He'll also show you the interior, so you can keep an eye on your charge. Bash?"

Basher's smooth voice filled the glade in front of

the wooden structure. "Greetings. Will this be satisfactory?" A holographic image flickered to life beside the door, showing Kai's living room.

Still frowning, Boris glanced at her. "Lady Griffin?"

"This will be quite satisfactory, thank you, Basher. Boris, remain here."

He subsided with a nod, his features full of lingering misgivings. Her father's orders had been for him to never leave her side.

Kai opened the old-fashioned door, stepping aside and waving her in with a cordial smile. His demeanor remained gracious, but something in his eyes sent a tingle down her spine. She crossed the threshold and moved inside with Kai at her heels, taking shallow breaths to minimize the impact of Kai's delectable scent in the air. He nodded to Boris and closed the portal.

When he turned to Liaena, his mouth still smiled and his eyes remained serious. "Your bodyguard can't hear us. I'll be taking you on tour for his benefit, but we can talk freely." He gestured toward the living room.

Keeping her expression clear with an effort, she went where he pointed. "Has something happened?" Shallow breaths weren't helping, not with the source of this tantalizing fragrance so close to her. The sense of intimacy, of having touched him in private places, seeped through her again, raising her temperature and sending her stomach into somersaults.

"Your father's offer happened. I take it he wants something from me."

They paused in front of the holographic window showing waterfront with a quaint dock and boat. She wished she could ask if it held any meaning for him.

Had he chosen it because it reminded him of a real place and time or for its aesthetic value? Studying the peaceful view with a wistful ache in her throat, she said, "He's testing you, testing my supposed hold over you. His exact words were, 'We shall see how well you've captured him.' He said you have a distasteful streak of morality."

Kai gave an acerbic snort, his features remaining smooth and attentive. He waved her toward a display case holding an assortment of antiquated weapons and armor. "So an ugly test. Did he tell you what it was?"

"No, he didn't," she answered with regret, inspecting the items in the case with unfeigned interest. Curiosity needled her.

He pointed to a knife, its blade lustrous white like bone and its dark handle carved with intricate symbols. Instead of telling her about it, he said, "He's been playing a lot of things close to the chest lately, keeping you out of the loop. What do you make of it?"

"I'm not sure. He may suspect I'm not as dutiful a daughter as I portray. Or he may have plans so sensitive he wants no one else to know of them." Gesturing to an intriguing bit of armor, a vambrace of some kind, she tipped her head in question.

He ignored her curiosity as if it were only part of the tour pantomime. "Neither option sounds good, Aena. Will you be safe with him?" His polite mask slipped, eyes darkening and mouth tightening.

She clasped her hands together and fixed her gaze on the armor, considering the question. "I suppose no more or less than I have been. What will you do about the offer?"

"I'm already doing it." When she glanced at him,

he gave her a grim smile and waved her toward a shelving unit holding various knick-knacks and family holograms. "Backing off will pressure him to have you step up your game. If you can talk him into letting you go away with me for a couple of days, you can give us the hunter program and we'll be able to arrange a visit with your mother."

Her heart leapt. "A visit?" she whispered, dizzying joy swirling through her. She turned blind eyes to the display, working to keep her features blank. "But he'd never let me go alone."

"We'll work something out. You schedule a place and time, and we'll handle the rest."

She stayed silent for a moment, battling rising excitement and doing her best to think through their strategy. "So this polite distance you've placed between us today is meant to indicate you're having second thoughts about us as a couple. The offer has made you leery and you're pulling away."

"Yes."

"He'll expect me to, as you put it, 'step up my game.' " Her stomach fluttered with nerves, but she forced her gaze to meet his. "Should I seduce you then?" She meant to sound matter-of-fact but her voice frayed, the hard thump of her heart adding an embarrassing waver.

His eyes flared with green fire and his chest rose on a quick inhalation. He turned his head, fixing his gaze on the family images in front of them. His throat moved in a hard swallow. "Not if you want the plan to work," he responded, his voice rougher than usual. He cleared his throat and clasped his hands behind his back. "Believe me, I'd love to carry you down the hall to my bed, but that would be playing right into Griffin's hands. Better keep your hands to yourself, Aena." He slanted her a quick teasing glance.

Her skin seemed to burn everywhere, a full-body blush. Would he really take her to his bed if she touched him? Her heartbeat rang in her ears and she took a deep steadying breath. His subtle male spice filled her and sent her head spinning.

Hunting for something, anything to say, she finally focused on the pictures displayed before her. The world shifted under her feet, a wave of longing washing over her in a crushing weight. Holograms of the Shay family in different stages of their lives stood scattered among various enigmatic mementos. Some of the holos were stills and some short clips of action. Most showed the family at the point in their lives when they had been whole and happy. Only one seemed recent, a still of Kai and Sin leaning side by side against a sleek black slicer. By their unguarded expressions, Liaena guessed they hadn't known they were being holographed. A boyish grin lit Kai's handsome face as he watched his sister. The holographer had caught Sin in a carefree laugh, her head back and features alive with unrestrained humor.

One family hologram caught Liaena's eye, and she studied it with a lump in her throat. The holographer had captured a small clip of a birthday, but she couldn't tell whose it had been. The cake lay in tatters, the victim of a food fight between the twins and their parents. Bright-colored clumps and icing spattered all combatants, but the laughter and joy on their faces turned the mess into something sublime.

Liaena took in the display as a whole and pressed a hand to her aching chest. How she wished she could have experienced all these moments with them, sharing their clear happiness and deep love. How she wished this wasn't a shrine to love lost and family bonds sundered.

She pointed to a family portrait, parents sitting with the young twins on their laps, all of them grinning with suppressed humor as if the holographer had said something hilarious. "Is this your mother?" she whispered.

Kai nodded without a word.

"She was so beautiful. Sin looks so much like her. And you are the image of your father."

He said nothing for a minute. Then he shifted back and waved her onward. "Time to finish the tour and find Sin and Cass for lunch. They're probably wondering what hole we fell into."

She lingered for a few more seconds, finding it hard to pull away from these pieces of his past. She wanted to know everything about them, wanted to ask what each meant to him, but his distant tone said the discussion was over. "I'm sorry," she murmured, accompanying him into what looked like an office. "I didn't mean to intrude."

He snorted. "I let you in my home, Aena. It's not intruding if you're invited."

"A sham invitation," she pointed out, glancing around the sparse neat room. If this was his home office, he'd clearly not spent much time in it. "I would enjoy a real tour of your home someday."

He made a noncommittal sound in his throat and ushered her toward the front door. Apparently the tour was over. Liaena smothered a sigh of disappointment. She would have loved to see every part of his personal space. Including the bedroom. Heat rose in her cheeks. Try as she might, she couldn't imagine what his most intimate place would look like, but she itched to find out. Not that she wanted to meet the ghosts of all the women who'd paraded through it.

At the door she held out a hand to delay him. "Kai, wait. You never said how I would know when Cassie's device was finished."

"It'll be warm to the touch."

The way he said it flustered her, as if he were thinking of something besides the device.

"When it is, set up our next meeting and we'll go from there." He opened the door and ushered her out with another polite smile.

She despised the expression. It seemed wrong on his features, like a cold filter blocking sunlight.

Renewing her own careful mask, she stepped over the threshold. "Thank you for showing me your home. It's delightful. And Basher," she added, turning toward the building, "I thank you as well for playing host to my companion."

"It was no trouble," Basher replied in a voice as distant as Kai's smile, so different from the last time she'd visited.

Kai ushered them through the arboretum and out the public access, leading the way through busy corridors to the commons. Sin and Cassie waited for them at the same café where Liaena had dined with them before, Horizons with its holographic entertainment.

"Aena!" Cassie approached with a bright smile and took her hands in a gentle clasp. "I'm glad you could come. Did you like the arboretum?"

Liaena couldn't hold back a small smile at the woman's warm open greeting. "Yes, I did. It was quite beautiful."

Cassie's gaze went over her shoulder, her eyebrows lifting. "I didn't know you were bringing company. Who's this?"

It took her a moment to realize Cassie meant her guard. "Ah." She shifted, sending a furtive glance between the Shays. She'd never had to explain a bodyguard before. "This is Boris. My father insisted he come for my protection. I hope you don't mind his presence."

"Wow, I've never met a bodyguard." Cassie brushed by Liaena and Kai, holding out her hand to Boris. "Welcome to Shay Enterprises, Boris. I'm Cassie Draegen."

The big rugged man shook her hand with an expression of utter bafflement. Liaena bit the inside of her cheek to stifle humor. The twins snickered in soft unison.

Cassie ignored them. "You'll eat lunch with us, won't you? I hope you don't have to stand there and watch. It would be weird and I'd feel bad."

So Boris sat down to lunch with them. Liaena's previous meal with Sin and Cassie had been fascinating, but not nearly as entertaining as watching her bodyguard deal with these two clever females. Between Cassie's easy friendly chatter and Sin's charming subtle wit, Boris didn't stand a chance. Liaena suspected he wouldn't have noticed if she rose from the table and walked away.

Liaena caught Kai's glance once then did her best not to look at him again, fearing she'd burst into laughter at the gleam of humorous mischief in his eyes. Someone had chosen a pastoral scene for their hologram this time, a sun-lit flower-filled meadow surrounded by stately trees. The quiet picturesque setting seemed to take them out of time, cocooning them in a world of simple grace and comfort. She kept her gaze on the surrounding beauty and wished they truly were in this lovely place.

Kai's hand found hers under the table, his fingers winnowing between her own with slow sensual intimacy. Her breath caught in her throat, and she lowered her glass to the table with care, working hard to contain the tremor shivering through her at his touch.

"What are you doing?" she whispered without looking at him.

"Holding your hand." He said it in an offhand way, as if it held no particular significance, but his grip tightened, warm palm pressing against hers. "What will your father do to you if I don't accept his offer now?"

Alarmed, Liaena glanced across the table, but Boris' attention centered on Cassie. Sin's knowing smile caught Liaena's eye as the woman looked from her to Kai. Heat climbed into her cheeks, but Sin turned her head toward Boris without a word.

"Nothing," she answered Kai. "Especially if I show progress toward changing your mind." She swallowed hard, considering her own words. How exactly was she supposed to accomplish this?

"Mmm, sounds promising," he murmured, his voice deepening and sending tingling heat straight down through her center. He eased her hand toward him and laid the back of it against his hard-muscled thigh. "What will you do to change my mind, Liaena Griffin?"

She gulped, fixing her gaze on the distant trees. Her mind melted, caught between his voice, like the rough purr of a large cat, and the heat baking off his thigh as if it were the side of a furnace. Coherent thought fled; she could only focus on his toned flesh bunching under her hand. What would he feel like under her fingertips? What would he do if she touched him that way?

When she said nothing, he let her go with a low chuckle. The rest of the lunch passed in a haze. Kai refrained from touching her again, earning her gratitude. The occasional whiff of his scent was enough to keep her senses alive and tingling, her body simmering with need.

She decided how to answer his question. It would probably be a huge mistake, but she couldn't dredge up any proper concern, squirming in her seat in anticipation. Was she brave enough?

At the end of the lunch, both Sin and Cassie hugged her goodbye, bringing her out of her daze. She couldn't resist embracing them back, warmed by their show of affection. "The dress is perfect on you by the way," Sin murmured in her ear. "You need a dozen more."

Liaena pulled back and stared at her. "You terrify me."

Sin grinned and guided Cassie away. "Next time, Aena," she called over her shoulder.

"Next time what?" Kai asked as they turned toward a lift.

"More shopping, I think."

He shuddered. "No wonder you're terrified."

She hummed to smother a laugh and glanced at

him out of the corner of her eye. *Oh, dear Suns,* the man was beautiful. The light from a holo-ad gleamed blue-black in his wavy hair. The dusky skin of his face held the faintest shadow on his jaw, the beginnings of stubble calling to her fingertips. A secretive tilt accented his gorgeous eyes and his mouth wore a slight curve, as if in private amusement. What was going through his convoluted mind now?

He spoke of inconsequential things on their way to her transport, engaging Boris in a discussion about slicer circuits and racing. Boris spoke with candid ease, another victim of the infamous Shay charm, though Cassie also held part of the blame. Liaena tried not to show her wry amusement over the corruption of her bodyguard.

When they reached her transport, she gave Boris a pointed look. He nodded and spun on his heel, taking several steps away to give them privacy. She turned to Kai, a whole host of butterflies leaping to life in her stomach.

"Aena? What are you doing?" he asked with bemusement crinkling the corners of his eyes.

"Changing your mind," she whispered, slipping a shaking hand around the back of his neck and resting the other on his chest for much-needed support. His eyes flared like green Sunfire, hands settling on her hips, burning her through the thin fabric of her dress. She rose on tip-toe and he bent his head to meet her halfway, mouths melding together as if they'd never been apart. He showed no reluctance, diving into the sultry contact with such skill and hunger her knees came unhinged and her insides caught fire. She sagged into him, shivering at the delicious press of his hard muscles. He tightened his grip on her hips and shifted her closer. She moaned at the ridged erection throbbing in hot demand against her abdomen and squirmed against him.

Kai jerked his head away with a curse and clasped her face in both hands. His voice hoarse and fierce, he whispered in her ear, "You have ten seconds to get in your ship before I keep you here with me for good."

She'd forgotten where they were again. Mortified, she stumbled back. He let her go, his eyes dark and wild, and his features grim. She took a quick furtive glance around; no one was watching. Boris still stood with his back to them.

"Five seconds," Kai growled. He stood taut, like a wire about to snap, hands fisted at his sides.

Liaena met his hot gaze and considered it for one brief second. Then she fled into the ship. Collapsing onto a seat, she covered her face with shaking hands. Oh, how she wanted to stay. But everything she'd worked for would be lost.

When the hatch slid open, she tensed, lifting her head. Boris stepped aboard, eyes averted. "Lady Griffin is ready to depart," he called to the pilot and settled in his own seat.

She cleared her throat and said in as steady a voice as she could manage, "Thank you, Boris."

He nodded without a word, still looking elsewhere.

Chapter 19

"This isn't going to work."

"Don't be so negative, Cass." Kai flicked a glance at the viewer showing Cassie's frowning continence before focusing on piloting the small transport. "The plan is sound."

"I'm not worried about the plan," she retorted. "I'm worried about Aena."

So was he but he wouldn't admit it. Cass would only tie herself in a bigger knot. "She's been dealing with Griff for years. She can handle her part. He's already agreed to let her meet me, and she wouldn't forget your toy, if that's what you're fussing about."

"Don't deflect. This romantic tryst was your idea, and I saw how you watched her at lunch the other day."

He snorted and turned to stare at her. "Sun's blood, Cass, what do you think I'm going to do, jump her the second we're alone?"

"Yes."

Sin chuckled in the background, appearing over Cassie's shoulder. "She has a point, Brother. You were supposed to keep your distance, not fondle her under the table."

"He did what?" Cassie glared from his big-mouthed sister to him in outrage.

Patience evaporating, he growled, "Give it a rest. She already has a mother. A mother who's going to be right there with us, remember?"

"Like that's ever stopped you before," Sin said in a tone as dry as desert sand, disappearing from the screen.

Cassie glowered at him. "How many times do I have to tell you abused individuals don't tolerate physical—?"

He cut the transmission and ran rough fingers through his hair, gripping the tense muscles at the back of his neck. His sister was right; the problem wasn't Aena's tolerance but his inability to keep his hands to himself. He hadn't been bluffing when he'd threatened to keep Aena with him. It would've meant disaster for their plans, but he hadn't been thinking of that at the time. He hadn't been thinking at all.

An image of Aena reaching for him sent a shaft of pure heat through his gut. She'd responded to him before, but this time she'd voluntarily touched him, initiating their passion. It'd taken every scrap of discipline he had to let her go. The memory was enough to set him on fire and turn him hard as diamond, a near constant painful condition he was coming to think of as "Aena's Revenge." All those years of calling her an Ice Queen were coming back to bite him where it hurt the most. She wasn't ice; she was Sunfire. When she'd writhed against him like a little wildcat, only Boris' presence kept him from pushing her into the ship, pinning her under him, and sliding inside her to the hilt.

Kai shuddered and shifted in his seat, adjusting himself with a grimace. This kind of mental and physical torture wasn't productive. If he didn't watch where his mind wandered, he'd be as useless as a bucket full of holes in a sinking ship.

Focus on the Suns-damned job, you moron. Great advice, except the whole point to this excursion was to get Aena alone. How much self-control did he have? Not enough he feared.

With a curse he started reciting the Red Order's forms of war under his breath, the only thing mind-numbing enough to cool his blood, and concentrated on piloting his small transport to its destination.

Aena couldn't have chosen a more ideal location for their supposed romantic getaway. She'd booked them into a luxurious hotel, one among thousands at a tourist hub on a busy commerce planet. If she'd chosen a private retreat, his job would have been harder, but with this much activity, the distraction of so many people coming and going, spiriting her away would be almost effortless. If everything went well, her guard dogs wouldn't even know she'd left for a long while.

Kai landed the transport on the roof of a neighboring hotel. Setting the navigational systems and autopilot, he left the craft, bypassed the hotel's security systems, and let himself into the building via the roof service access. Using the service ways, he avoided being seen by people or security tech and made his way down to the lobby. Sauntering through it as if he were one of the hotel's guests, he ordered a shuttle at the front desk. Programmed to assist customers with prompt courtesy, the automated system asked no questions and complied.

If Griffin's people retraced his steps, they would believe he was staying there. The shuttle took him the short distance to Aena's chosen rendezvous. Striding through the front entrance, he spotted the watchdogs Griffin had already put in place. Two posed as guests, their acting needing serious work. The third didn't bother pretending, standing at the reception kiosk like a sentry.

Kai ignored all three, inquiring at the kiosk if Liaena had arrived yet. The reception system informed him she'd announced her impending arrival minutes ago and had asked that he wait for her in the lobby. Smothering a sardonic grin, he strode to the seating area and made himself comfortable, pulling out a digital pad with the air of a man staving off boredom. Instead of perusing the news or cleaning up business loose ends, he checked on the position of his transport, in place for their real getaway.

Liaena arrived with luggage, Boris, and a second guard dog in tow. Kai rose from his seat, studying her entourage before staring at each of Griffin's covert personnel in turn. Then he met Boris' gaze with a raised eyebrow.

Boris grimaced and gave a small shrug, as if to apologize for his boss' overkill, his rough face turning ruddy.

"Kai," Liaena greeted him in a low voice. She wore her glacial mask, her fine features cool and expressionless.

"You overpacked, Aena. You're not going to need many clothes. Or them." He flicked a disparaging finger at her unwelcome companions.

She sighed as if annoyed and turned to Boris. "Will you wait here?"

Boris dropped his chin and stared at the floor, face reddening even more. "Sorry, Lady Griffin, but we have orders to stand guard at your door."

She studied him in chilly silence. Then she turned

away as if dismissing their presence. "Fortunately this hotel has a reputation for discretion and privacy," she told Kai. "Their guest suites are sound- and surveillance-proof. Shall we go up?"

How romantic. He would have teased her, but something in her stiff demeanor held him at bay. Catching her elbow in a light clasp, he ushered her toward the lift, studying her out of the corner of his eye. Where was the vixen determined to seduce him? She looked more like a mourner at a funeral than a woman on her way to a thorough bedding. Maybe, since she'd gotten this concession from her father, she didn't feel the need to put on a show. Kai disagreed; when the guards reported in, Griffin would think this reception odd for a couple about to get wild and sweaty with one another.

Breaking the cool silence aboard the lift, Kai murmured, "Are you all right?"

She raised her chin to meet his gaze, and he gave her elbow a squeeze, hoping she'd get the message. She blinked then curled her mouth in a small smile. "Yes, thank you. I'm sorry for my distraction. I'm a bit offended my father thought it necessary to intrude on our time together." Waving a hand at the guards without looking at them, she shifted closer to Kai. "And I'm afraid one of my father's guests has…left us. It's put me out of sorts."

Kai's gut clenched. She meant one of the Red ascetics had died. He schooled his expression to show only bland concern. "We can do this another time, if you like."

"No." Her answer was swift and a little too forceful. She softened it with a strained smile and slipped her arm through his. "No, I want to be alone with you."

"What Lady Griffin wants, she gets." He lifted her hand and brushed his lips over her knuckles. "I'm looking forward to it, sweetheart."

Her smile faded, replaced by an enticing blend of uncertainty and interest. He wanted to answer both with his mouth on hers, plundering and tasting her sweetness again. Plastering a charming smile on his face, he looked away and called up the forms of war in his mind once more. Why in the Suns was it taking so long to reach their floor?

As he thought it the doors slid open. Soft light revealed a hall in muted colors, meandering in a gentle curve away from them. "After you."

Without comment she led him down the hall and stopped before one of the doors. Opening it, she stepped inside without acknowledging the guards positioning themselves to either side of the doorway.

Kai grabbed her luggage, crossing the threshold and waiting until the door closed and locked before turning to her. He gestured toward the connector leading from this suite into the adjacent one. "Next door."

She blinked, glanced around at the luxurious suite she'd booked, then gave a small shrug and headed for the next suite over. "Why?"

"Didn't want your watchdogs to see our escape."

"And how are we going to—? Oh," she interrupted her own question when she stepped into the next room and saw the waiting transport at the window.

"The windows on these hotels double as emergency exits in case the place has some kind of major catastrophe. Climb aboard, Aena. It'll take us time to get where we're going."

She gave the window and waiting transport a disapproving look, as if she didn't trust its solidity, but she didn't hesitate. Stepping up on the windowsill, she ducked through the opening.

He locked the connector between suits and followed her into the transport. Handing her the luggage, he resealed the window, closed the transport hatch, and settled into the pilot's seat. With quick fingers he shut off the autopilot and flew the ship away from the building, merging with the flow of traffic above.

Aena eased into a seat next to him, her forehead creased in a tiny frown. "That seemed far too simple. At some point the guards will discover my absence and my father will piece together what you've done."

"By then we'll be long gone." Weaving through the streams of traffic, Kai joined a flow heading for one of the large orbiting stations above the planet. Once there, he followed several similar transports to a large ship built to ferry small vessels like his through the star-way.

"We're going through the star-way," Aena deduced.

"If he can trace us this far, your father will believe that's the plan."

She studied him with her usual cool poise, driving needles under his skin. Keeping his hands busy on the console, he stopped watching her so he could focus on docking the transport without wrecking it. The teasing scent of peaches and blossoms wafting his way didn't help.

"What is your plan?"

"You'll see."

"I'm not fond of surprises."

"So you've said before. Only makes it more fun for me, darlin'."

"Not a gracious attitude."

He copied her priggish tone. "I am not a gracious guy."

She sighed and stared out at the crowded docking bay. A slight vibration announced the movement of the bulk transport ship toward the star-way rings. "How long will this take?"

"The longest part will be waiting for this tub to reach the rings. After that it should be a quick trip. You'll be with Zofie soon."

Her features relaxed and she sent him a small smile. "Thank you. I haven't been very gracious either, have I?" She reached into one long sleeve and drew out Cassie's device. "I hope this has what you need. I was unable to access it to make certain."

"Cassie locked it to her DNA as a precaution. We'll have to wait until I can get it to her to find out what's on it." He plucked it out of her hold, careful not to make contact with her skin, and tucked it in his pocket. "Do you want to tell me about the ascetic?"

Her lips thinned and her form tensed. "There isn't much to tell. My father tortured him to death. The man never broke, never revealed my mother's location or your part in her disappearance." She paused, gaze searching his face for a second. A crease reformed between her brows. "But somehow you knew he wouldn't."

Kai twitched a shoulder in a quick shrug. "He was Red. Did you know his name?"

"He introduced himself as Dani Turn." She closed her eyes and turned her face away.

Kai controlled his wince at the name. He'd known the man. He'd known them all. *Suns curse their Red stubbornness and death wishes.*

As if reading his mind she whispered, "I swear he wished his own death to happen. Is it possible to make yourself cease to exist?"

"The Reds haven't taught me that trick, but I wouldn't put it past them. I'll inform the Temple of his death."

She jerked as if he'd poked her with something sharp and turned a grim look on him. "I don't want to watch the rest of them die, Manakai Shay. You must know a way to fix this."

He raised an eyebrow, studying her with cool intent. "I must?"

"Why are you being stubborn on this of all things?" Her voice rose and her hands clenched into fists in her lap. "You've taken on far larger projects to thwart my father. Why is this one beyond you? I've offered to help and can tell you their exact location. Why aren't you mounting a rescue for them?"

He frowned, a sense of foreboding creeping up his spine. "What do you mean, larger projects?"

She made a frustrated sound and pressed her fists to her forehead, hiding her expression. She held still for a full minute then released a long breath and lowered her hands, folding them in her lap. Her features had returned to cool composure, only the thinning of her lips revealing her distress. "My father refuses to see the two of you for who you really are, so of course, he can't imagine the scope of what you can accomplish. I have

266

had—a different perspective. These recent weapons raids by the FPA and the exposure of the blue drug ring not long ago; they have your stamp on them. Why is a handful of ascetics beyond your capability?"

He stared at her, blanking his expression. They'd underestimated her. "You think we're behind those things? What does your father think of this theory?"

Her eyes narrowed, flashing silver. "I would never be foolish enough to bring it to his attention. I'm trying to help you stop him, not hand him more ammunition. You still don't trust me."

He leaned back in his seat, settling his head against the rest and watching her from under lowered lids. He tapped a thoughtful rhythm on the armrest with his thumb. "You're playing both sides, Liaena. Trust would be foolhardy."

She went statue-still, seeming to not even draw breath. Her eyes unfocused, as if she were staring at something far beyond him. "Foolhardy," she repeated in a voice so low he almost didn't hear. "I see."

Absorbing her stillness, Kai heard in his mind an echo of Cassie describing Aena's dissociative reaction to stress. He saw it now just as she'd detailed it. He also remembered this exact reaction from Aena many times in the past to his taunts and jibes. He'd assumed she was freezing him out. But what if it wasn't disdain but hurt? Could he have misread her so badly? Then again this woman had been dancing on the razor blades of her father's whims for years. Self-preservation would have taught her how to hide emotion.

An ache in his hands caught his attention, and he glanced down, only now noticing his brutal grip on the armrests. He let go, flexing his fingers and keeping his gaze lowered. "Aena? You said you had a different perspective on us. What was it?"

She remained quiet so long he thought she wouldn't answer. When she spoke, her voice held a strange hesitancy. "Do you remember the fountain?"

He glanced at her, but she was staring down at her folded hands, cool and remote. "The one I broke? Of course I remember." He remembered her red hair darkened and dripping with water, her eyes wide with horror and fascination, hands clamped over her giggles. He remembered the skittish look in her eyes when he clasped her hand and kissed her soft cheek. The kernel of his obsession with her had formed then.

"The two of you taught me something that day I never forgot."

He smirked. "How not to fix a fountain?"

She looked at him through her lashes, her mouth curving the slightest bit. "Hmm, that too."

He looked away from the silver light in her eyes, clenching the armrests again to keep from pulling her onto his lap. "So what did a couple of destructive brats teach you?"

"Anything is possible." Calm, firm, and full of conviction, her tone drew his gaze. The look in her eyes matched the steadiness of her voice.

"Anything is possible," he repeated.

She nodded, a hint of a smile still playing around her mouth.

"Aena, you and I are remembering that day very differently."

"I'm sure we are." She gave a small shrug. "No doubt I made almost no impact on the two of you. But you were so fearless and confident and daunting. I was terribly impressed and wanted to be just like you."

"Well, you have daunting down to a science."

She narrowed her eyes a bit, studying him as if looking for the lie in his words. "You're trying to flatter me."

He chuckled. "Only you would think it was flattery." A ping from a console snagged his attention. "We're nearing the star-way. Time to go."

"Go?" She leaned forward, eyeing the displays. "What do you mean? We can't leave now. It's too dangerous this close to the wormhole."

"You'll want to strap in, sweetheart. This is going to be a bumpy ride."

"Are you mad?" she squeaked, hands fumbling for the straps as the transport rose and turned toward the exit.

He grinned. "I like to think of it as fearless and confident. The distortions from the wormhole will mask our signal. No one will know when we left the ship or where we went."

"Won't they notice the bay doors?" She pointed a shaky finger at the vista appearing in the expanding opening. "This is not safe." She gasped as the wormhole's roiling center filled the viewer.

"Easy, Aena, I won't let anything happen to you." He reached over to pat her arm, but she grabbed his hand and placed it back on the console.

"Fly with both hands," she wheezed.

His low laughter filled the transport as he slipped the small ship free of its host and battled the wormhole's gravitational pull. It wasn't a walk in the park but it also wasn't the hardest maneuver he'd ever pulled at the rings. The transport shuddered and jerked like an animal fighting a trap, and Kai finessed it through the turbulence, breaking away from the rings and swinging through the fiery Sun's light toward its far side. Using the Sun to block his signal from Ring Control, he pushed the engines to maximum and sped away.

Then he turned a pointed look on his nervous passenger. "You're still in one piece. You can release your death grip on those straps now."

She transferred her white-knuckled grip from the straps to the armrests. "I despise you right now," she announced, eyes closed and chest heaving.

"Are you going to throw up?"

"Yes. Right in your lap."

He snickered, enjoying this attitude much more than her statue imitation.

She peeked at the viewer with one half-closed eye. Seeing nothing but black space, she sagged in her seat and opened both eyes. "Where are we?"

"Heading toward an out-of-the-way moon base where no one knows either one of us."

"A refreshing change."

"My thoughts exactly."

"Will my father be able to track us here?"

"We'll have plenty of warning if he does. Sin and Cassie are keeping an eye out for any activity from Griffin."

"Good." She slanted him a grudging glance. "You're an excellent pilot."

"I know."

She frowned. "You also have an enormous ego."

"True enough."

"And you're arrogant and annoying."

"It's a gift."

She made a derisive sound in her throat and he grinned. "However, I don't believe you're callous or cruel. So why are you letting the Red ascetics die?"

He turned his grin into a look of exaggerated amazement. "Holy Suns, you're like a krell with a bone."

She twisted her fingers into a tight knot in her lap, staring past him with a grim press of her lips, as if searching for elusive patience. "I don't know what more I can do to prove I'm on your side."

His heart squeezed in his chest and he took a careful breath. "Aena, our caution is not so much about you as it is your situation. Let me put it this way. Would you have done as well as Dani Turn?"

She relaxed back in her seat by slow degrees, face thoughtful and eyes sharp. "You think my father will extract information from me, willing or not."

"It's a concern."

"A valid one. I apologize for berating you. I won't ask again, but whatever you're going to do, please do it fast."

He offered a bland smile and didn't respond, changing the subject instead. "Are you excited to see your mother?"

"Oh yes, very. Will we have to wait long for her?"

"She's already there waiting for you."

"Good." Aena leaned forward again, staring at the viewer as if she could move them along faster by sheer will.

Kai smothered a grin and pretended to be busy flying.

They reached the moon base not long after,

slipping into a vacant slot on the docking hub. Leaving the transport, they made their way through the docking terminal to the main section of the base. Kai guided her through less-traveled corridors to the residential section and the suite of rooms he'd procured for them.

Zofie accosted them the second they stepped across the threshold. "Liaena!" she exclaimed and lunged past Kai, wrapping her daughter tight in her arms.

"Mama." Zofie's shoulder muffled Aena's voice, her face buried in the older woman's auburn hair.

Kai heard the scary sound of imminent tears, a choked-off sob and sniffles, and backed away as fast as he could without catching their attention. Creeping across the living room, he sidled into the bedroom he'd claimed as his and heaved a sigh of relief when the door slid between him and the female emotional crisis outside.

He gave the room a cursory glance; like the rest of the suite, it wasn't luxurious in the least with bland unimpressive décor and sparse functional furnishings, but adequate enough for their uses. Stepping over to the communications unit, he put in a call to Shay Enterprises.

His sister appeared on the viewer and raised her eyebrows. "So far so good?"

He grimaced and shrugged. "I suppose so. They're together anyway."

"Why the face?"

"They're crying."

She laughed at his ominous tone. "Did Aena deliver?"

Pulling the device from his pocket, he held it for her to see. "I have to admit, I'm dying to crack this open. If it has everything we want—"

"Griffin's days are numbered," Sin finished for him.

They shared a grim smile.

Chapter 20

Liaena brushed at the dampness under her eyes with one hand, the other in a secure clasp between both of her mother's. She couldn't seem to stop leaking tears. Her relief and happiness at finally being with her mother overwhelmed her. Thank the Suns Kai had disappeared like a mirage the moment they'd arrived.

Zofie's eyes also stayed bright with unshed moisture, but her face glowed.

Sitting side by side on a plain sofa in the generically appointed living room, they chattered non-stop, the topics jumping from Zofie's new life with Cassie's parents, to all the latest gadgets and happenings her mother had been isolated from, to Liaena's increased contact with the Shays. Zofie seemed thrilled by each of her visits with the twins and begged for details. Hours passed, filled with mingled laughter and excited speech, until Zofie's stomach rumbled loud enough to silence them.

"My word," Zofie whispered, eyes wide.

Liaena snorted a laugh, then covered her mouth with one hand.

"Sounds like my cue," Kai said behind them.

Liaena jumped, glancing over her shoulder. He strode toward them, a plate loaded with finger food balanced on one palm. He'd obviously come from the kitchen area, but how had she missed him leaving his room? He proffered the plate to Zofie with a bow and a wink.

Her mother tittered and took the offering. "Thank you. I didn't realize how long we'd been talking. We've neglected you, haven't we?"

"Not at all," he said with smooth diplomacy. "This visit is for you ladies, and I've kept busy. Dinner will be ready soon."

"You cook too?" Her mother stared at him with wide wondering eyes. "Do you have any faults?"

"Ask Aena." His enticing green gaze slid her way with a teasing glimmer, sending her heart racing. "She has a list." He sauntered off to the kitchen.

"Oh, my," her mother breathed, leaning in close. "What are you planning to do about *that*?"

Liaena cocked her head and blinked. "About what?"

"Sweetie, I may have been away from everything for a while, but I remember what it means when a man gives a woman the kind of look he gave you."

"He was only teasing. I don't actually have a list."

Her mother went on as if she hadn't heard. "He's adorable, charming, considerate, capable, and interested in you. And he cooks and rescues sad old ladies from island prisons. You shouldn't let him get away."

"I can hardly stop him," she retorted, her tone too sharp. Shaking her head, she tightened her clasp on her mother's hands. "From what I understand, Manakai Shay is interested in many women. If he feels anything for me, it's only physical and temporary. Please don't wish for something that has no chance of coming true."

"Hmm." Her mother studied her with shrewd eyes. "I think you underestimate him. I also think passion is in short supply in this life and shouldn't be squandered. Who knows, perhaps he'll prove you wrong. Anything is possible."

Anything is possible. Her own mantra sneaking in from an unexpected quarter to jab her right through the heart. She swallowed hard. Much as she would like to believe it in this instance, too many things stood in the way; lack of trust, years of animosity, her father, and Kai's dubious feelings for her. The two of them had as much chance of being together as all the levels of hell freezing over.

But she couldn't stop thinking about it. They gathered for a casual dinner in the little dining area off the kitchen, and Kai and her mother carried the conversation while Liaena brooded and considered her mother's words. *Passion shouldn't be squandered.* Kai may not be interested in a relationship with her, but he was here now. Was she brave enough to seize this opportunity to be with him? Would she be able to walk away after?

She was getting ahead of herself. He might reject the idea out of hand. His touch at the hotel had been brief, without the heat she'd come to crave, and he now focused most of his polite attention on her mother. He may have already lost any desire he'd had for her and looked forward to his next conquest. If she asked to spend the night with him, he might say no and crush her. But what if he said yes?

After dinner Kai excused himself to give them more time alone. Grateful, Liaena concentrated on these precious moments with her mother and tried to forget her foolish thoughts about him. For the most part it worked until her mother yawned for the dozenth time, wilted in resignation, and declared it time to sleep.

After saying goodnight to Zofie, getting ready for bed, and lying down in her own spare room, thoughts and possibilities swarmed back in. She kept going over the same arguments, always ending with the same question. What if he said yes?

This moon base offered the most privacy she'd ever experienced in her life, the farthest she'd ever been from her father's control. Her choices became entirely her own. When would she ever have another opportunity like this?

Liaena lurched from the bed, heart pounding so hard her ears rang. She slipped out of her sleep attire and shrugged into a silky green robe, her fingers trembling as she smoothed the magnetic clasps down the front and combed through her hair. Part of her wanted to shrink back into the bed and forget the whole thing. But another part remembered the fountain as she headed for the door. *Anything is possible.*

She heard nothing as she glided past her mother's door and hoped it meant Zofie remained fast asleep. She didn't want to share this. She approached Kai's door with her heart in her throat. *I've lost my mind,* she thought in despair as she touched the door chime.

After only a few seconds, he opened it. Either the man moved as fast as lightning or he hadn't been sleeping. "Aena? Is everything all right?" He looked past her, his alert gaze taking swift inventory of the space beyond.

She gulped, trying to find her voice. He wore only a pair of sleep pants, loose and low on his lean hips. The vast amount of bare skin and muscle on display stole the air out of her lungs and kicked her heart into an even faster sprint. She managed to look down as he returned his gaze to her. "Y-yes," she croaked and cleared her throat. "Everything's fine. May I come in? I need to speak with you."

After a pause he said in a flat voice, "That's a bad idea."

Rejected already. Everything in her seemed to plummet through the floor. She clenched her hands together and persisted. "I don't wish to disturb my mother. What I have to say is…private."

He paused for a longer period. She kept her gaze fixed on his bare feet, certain if she saw his outstanding bare torso again, she'd either expire or embarrass them both by begging.

"All right," he said so softly she almost missed it, backing into the room.

She followed, dizzy when she stepped through a warm draft of his scent. If she was going to make it through this, she needed some distance. Continuing across the room until she stood almost in the far corner, she kept her back turned so she wouldn't be tempted to stare. Then she went still and thought with dazed horror, *Oh Suns, I don't know how to ask for this*!

He stayed quiet behind her, so silent he could have left the room already. Which would be slightly less humiliating than what she was about to do.

Wrapping her arms around herself, she took a deep breath and plunged. "Kai, do you want me?"

He hesitated for what seemed like an eternity before answering, "Yes." He sounded wooden, almost angry.

Her forehead creased in confusion. "It upsets you?"

"Let me save you some hassle, Lie. Taking you to

bed would feel great, but it won't change what I do. So if you're here to seal the deal for your father, you're wasting your time."

She stiffened, his words and the caustic nickname slicing through her like hot wires. "I'm not here for my father. Why would I be? He already thinks it's done. This is for me, because I want this. I want to choose for once." Her voice had risen and she paused, closing her eyes and measuring her breathing. "I want to know what it's like, to choose and be chosen. To have someone touch me because they want to."

He made a disbelieving sound and asked in a skeptical tone, "Your other men didn't want to?"

"I've only been with one man. And the circumstances were…difficult for us both." She shot him a quick glance, then turned away again at the primal look on his face, fierce, almost savage. She wasn't sure what caused it, but a nervous frisson shivered down her spine. "You hold part of the blame," she said to dispel the sensation. "You suggested I was cold in bed, so I—I tried. So did he, but I couldn't…I didn't feel…" She shrugged and shook her head. "I thought I'd proven you right."

"Aena, look at me."

She considered it. "I don't think I should. You're half naked and I can't think when I look at you."

He chuckled. "Nice boost to my ego, honey, but I still need you to look at me."

Honey was definitely better than *Lie.* He hadn't said no yet at least, even after she'd humiliated herself. Spinning on reluctant feet, she faced him, trying hard to keep her gaze fixed on his. The dim lighting turned his eyes dark and chaotic.

"I'm sorry I made you think you were cold. You're hot as Sunfire, burning me from all the way across this room. How could you not know it?"

She trembled, limbs weakening under his dark stare, voice fracturing into a whisper. "Because I never felt anything. Not until you touched me."

"Aena." Deep and rough, his voice sank into her and touched off molten heat at her core. He moved toward her one slow prowling step at a time. "Be sure. If you don't leave now, you won't for a long time."

"I'm sure," she breathed, quivering at the intensity of his gaze.

"Thank the Suns. I don't think I had it in me to let you go." He slowed to a stop in front of her and looked down to the tight grip she had around her middle. "Nervous?"

"Not of you," she managed, lowering her arms to her sides. "I just d-don't know what to do."

"Mmm, that's the easy part," he purred, mouth curving with devastating seduction. "We do what feels good until we can't move. The hard part's not rushing to get there. You're still wearing the pendant, Aena." He touched a finger to the crystal, setting off its buoyant music. *Rejoice.* He didn't touch her anywhere else, but it felt as though he'd sent a wild bolt of energy straight through her.

She gasped, knees wobbling. She wanted to tell him she never took the crystal flame off, but her voice had deserted her along with most of her thought processes. The heat of his hovering hand baked into her skin, spreading tendrils of sensation outward like invisible fingers.

"Like I said, Sunfire," he murmured, his voice

thick and wickedly sensual, his eyes heavy-lidded as he watched her. "The man who 'tried' with you"—his mouth twisted as though he tasted something bitter— "must not have tried hard." His finger moved slowly down, trailing a searing path on her skin to the edge of the robe. The downward pressure parted the magnetic clasps one by one as he continued that single light devastating touch. "Does this feel good, Aena?"

She barely heard and couldn't answer, her vision blurring as her full concentration bent on the trailing path burning between her breasts and marking the midline on her quivering abdomen. He paused above her pubic bone and she swayed, caught between a desperate need for him to continue and the urge to pull his hand away before she combusted.

"Your skin is silk," he rasped, removing his hand, and she couldn't stop a soft little groan of disappointment. He hummed deep in his throat, hands rising to rest on her shoulders then coast down her arms, pulling the robe off with them. It puddled at her feet and he stood still, his hot gaze running over her. "Heart of the Sun," he said in a hoarse hushed voice. "Aena, you take my breath away."

"Kai." She sighed, shivering at the vibrant stark desire lining his gorgeous face and gleaming in his darkened eyes.

With both hands, he spanned her ribcage, fingers spread and caressing on her skin. She sensed the strength in those hands, but his touch stayed gentle, warm, slightly rough from calluses, and insanely arousing in its slow exploration. Goose bumps spread in waves over her skin and her nipples tightened in swift flashes of pleasure. All the strength ran out of her legs and her knees buckled.

He caught her against his chest, and they groaned in unison at the sizzling contact. He surrounded her in hot hard muscle and his delicious fragrance, the taut skin of his chest roughened by a smattering of hair, teasing her sensitive breasts to an unbearable pitch. She gripped his arms and pressed closer, desperate and aching. The torment threatened to drive her mad.

"Kai, I n-need…"

"What do you need?" he rumbled in her ear, voice rich as sin. His hands splayed on her back, urging her even closer.

"I don't—I don't know. More. More of you."

He growled and lifted her against him, his arousal a steely brand against her quivering thighs. "You'll have me, sweetheart. As much as you can take."

She clung to him, more than ready to accept the dark promise in his voice, in the ridge of tantalizing flesh throbbing against her. But instead of dropping them to the floor and driving inside her, he swept her into his arms and stepped over to the bed. He laid her down, kneeling next to her and capturing her wrists.

"I need you to do something for me, Aena." He lifted her hands above her head until her fingers came in contact with the edge of the bed's storage alcove. "Hold on and don't let go."

She made an incoherent sound of protest, tugging against his hold, but he didn't budge, his mouth curving in a wicked smile.

"No you don't. If you touch me now, it's all over. This fun's just getting started, honey." He lowered his head until his lips brushed hers in tingling contact and whispered, "Hold on."

Her fingers gripped the edge without direction from her brain, breath coming in quick pants as she lifted her head, chasing his mouth. But he stayed a teasing distance away, lips dancing over hers until she hissed her frustration. He hummed again like a satisfied cat and molding his mouth to hers, his hands tangling in her hair. He began slow and sultry, a leisurely exploration as if they had all the time in the world. Then he dove deep with a ravaging hunger, stealing her breath. Several heart-stopping moments later, he lifted his head, back to teasing her with tantalizing brushes, quick licks, and nips of his teeth.

Overwhelmed, she could do nothing but shake, moan, and hold on for dear life.

He paused, stretching out beside her, his deep fast breaths brushing over her fevered skin. "I could do just this until I died of it," he murmured against her mouth. "Suns, you're so sweet, like peach nectar."

She wanted to tell him how good he felt, how delirious he made her. She wanted to demand he get on with it before her heart gave out. All she could manage was his name, broken and needy.

He smiled like a devil and lowered his head, lips branding the skin of her throat. "I wonder, sweet Aena, do you taste this good all over?" His mouth led the way and his fingers followed, tracing back and forth over her skin in random, maddening patterns until she thought she'd lose her mind.

She squirmed and whimpered, possibly even begged, but nothing she did made a difference. He wouldn't be rushed. When he finally reached the tips of her breasts, the first teasing flick of his tongue drove the air out of her lungs in a sharp cry. She bucked and reached for him, fingers numb from clutching the alcove too tight. He swore and caught her before she touched him, holding both wrists in one long-fingered hand. Then he bent to her breast and closed his mouth around its peak, doing things with his lips, teeth, and tongue that sent huge bolts of pleasure shooting straight down to her core. She was on fire. She ached and throbbed between her thighs, heat and restless need rolling over her in crushing waves.

He surged up, pressing her fingers against the alcove and growling, "Hold on," against her lips. Giving her a fierce ravenous kiss, he cupped both breasts in his hands and circled her nipples with the pads of his thumbs. She jerked under him and moaned into his mouth. With a rough sound, he moved down her body, hands and mouth resuming their mind-altering patterns on her shaking flesh but with a sense of urgency, an intensity she could fully relate to. If he didn't do something soon to answer the building ache inside her, she would expire.

When he reached her hips he paused, glancing up at her with wild eyes as he eased her thighs apart with slow gentle pressure.

Her eyes clamped closed when he stroked through her wet curls and slid a long finger deep inside. "Kai!" she gasped, bucking against his hand. The coil of aching need drew unbearably tight within her.

He groaned and rasped, "Easy. Let it happen, sweetheart." Then he bent his head to the swollen bud above his working fingers and used his mouth on her in ways she hadn't even dreamt possible, his hand moving in tandem.

The coil of need shattered. Vast waves of pleasure

surged and broke over her, sweeping everything away except the most amazing blissful sensation. It rolled up through her center and out to her extremities, again and again, eddying in sweet delight until she lay stunned and boneless. She hadn't known her body could do something like this. She'd never experienced an orgasm in her life, hadn't thought herself capable of it. The scope of it astounded her.

Kai's teeth sinking into the tender flesh of her thigh jolted her back to reality. "Peaches and cream," he growled, meeting her bleary gaze with a fierce possessive stare. He rose, shed his sleep pants, and knelt between her shaking thighs.

The vision of him, poised between her pale limbs like some dark and dangerous god, shook her down to her soul. Sculpted rippling muscle turned his body into a living piece of art, defined and powerful as a jungle predator. His burnished skin gleamed wet in the low light, his damp hair spiking across his forehead and clinging to his neck. The savage intent etched on his features and glinting in his darkened eyes sent shivers of awareness skittering over her skin. Strong thighs spread her own, flexing and bracing like a marauder readying for plunder. His arousal arced toward his flat belly, an astonishing thick length she wanted to explore with both hands. But he seemed impossibly huge and hard.

For the first time doubt crept in. How could something so large and rigid fit inside her? "Kai?" she whispered.

He smiled, a slow provocative answer that did nothing to slow her thundering heart. Cupping her bottom, he lifted and tugged her closer. Positioning his enormous phallus at her entrance, he rolled his hips in a teasing dance, pressing inside a little at a time.

"S-Suns!" Doubt evaporated, replaced by rising ferocious hunger. Nothing in her life had ever felt this good, this necessary. As he filled her, stretched her, he seemed to make a new connection deep inside, fulfilling a need she hadn't known existed, like a missing piece of her finally coming home. Yet completion stood out of reach, victim of his slow tormenting entry.

She whimpered and writhed in his grip, trying to pull him deeper. When he didn't budge, she snarled, "Kai!"

His low wicked laugh sank into her like hot fingers, driving her wild. She arched and twisted in his hold, reaching for him. He tightened his grip and jerked his hips in a short hard thrust, sending her world spinning. Then he arched over her, hands bracing on either side of her shoulders, his heavy erection tunneling deep.

She shuddered and keened at the pleasure, clutching his arms in a desperate hold and meeting his burning gaze.

"You will be the death of me," he rasped and began moving, slow and measured, stroking her sensitive flesh inside and out. "My Aena."

The sensations stormed through her, too intense and wild, but she didn't want him to ever stop. He drove inside her to the core yet he wasn't close enough. She clasped his face in her hands and pleaded with him, words she was too far gone to understand.

Kissing her with savage need, he lowered, shifting until he lay full on her, forearms framing her head and hands tangling in her hair. Delirious with relief and desire, she wrapped her limbs around him in a fierce hold, instinct moving her with him in an age-old rhythm.

Deeper hotter pleasure spiraled from where they joined, the ecstasy slower to build but so huge it almost frightened her, threatening to shatter her beyond repair. It rose and rose, obliterating the world until he was her only anchor, holding her secure and driving her over the crest to drown in an endless surging ocean of bliss.

Chapter 21

Kai lifted a handful of her long silky hair and watched it flow through his fingers, the low lights gleaming dull fire along the strands. So much for keeping his hands to himself. *Nice work, bonehead.* He'd lasted all of three seconds after he'd opened his door and saw her in that clingy robe, hair a gorgeous curtain over her shoulders. He'd put on a good show, but she had him the second she stepped into his room. She'd been his most tormenting dream for too long; he had no resistance left.

Snuggling her sleek body closer against his side, he wondered why it didn't worry him more. If she hadn't guessed his weakness before, she had to see it now, but he couldn't dredge up the proper amount of concern. Maybe he would later after the euphoria wore off and he recovered from the most mind-blowing experience of his life. He'd had sex with plenty of women, but his erotic dance with Aena had gone way beyond physical delight into someplace he'd never been before. Touching her, rousing her and giving her pleasure, forging inside her as deep as he could go, had been not just right but perfect, as if a disjointed part of his life had fallen into place.

He'd been denying the truth for as long as he could remember, but his ability to fool himself couldn't withstand the reality of her in his arms. This wasn't obsession. With Aena he'd found an emotional attachment far above and beyond simple attraction. *I should be terrified right now.* Maybe later he would be, when he had more energy and his brain started again. At the moment he could only marvel at the sensation of her in his arms, her silky soft weight. Though she did seem quiet. Had she fallen asleep? "Still with me?"

She stirred against him, slim hand splaying over his chest, fingertips pressing as if testing his resilience. A surprising bolt of renewed lust drove through his gut and he swallowed hard.

"Is it always like this?" she asked in a drowsy voice, husky and thick as honey. "No wonder people are so fixated on it."

He chuckled, stroking her side and enjoying its satiny texture. "This was something special," he admitted, turning his face to nuzzle against her temple. "How are you doing?"

"I can't really move. But I feel so good I don't care." She curled closer, resting her head over his heart. "Are you all right?"

"Never better," he said with a grin and a surge of smug satisfaction. Her uninhibited responses had shown him clear enough how much she thrilled to his touch, but it was still nice to hear.

"Hmm. I can't believe the difference from before. I suppose the problem was I didn't want him." She lifted her head to look at him, her smoky eyes narrowed as if accusing him of something. "And I would guess you've had far more practice than that poor man."

Her pity for her one-time lover went a long way toward soothing his jealousy. He tried not to gloat, but after watching her come apart for him with such spectacular passion it wasn't easy. Smiling, he brushed clinging strands from her cheek and tucked them behind her ear, fingers lingering to explore the tender skin he discovered there. "It's more play than practice. The guy's not still around, is he? I wouldn't want you giving him a second try." He blinked at his own words. His jealousy must not be quite dead yet.

Her eyes had softened at his touch, but she dipped her chin, a crease forming between her brows and her lithe form stiffening. "My father…disposed of him."

"Aena, I'm sorry."

"I'm sorrier. My careless actions caused his death."

He clasped her chin and lifted with gentle pressure. The vulnerable curve to her mouth and suffering in her darkened eyes sent a stab of remorse through him.

"Your father caused his death, not you. Don't blame yourself for being human, for wanting what every normal person has a right to."

Her expression eased a bit, but she didn't look as though she believed him.

Clasping her face in his hands, he searched for a topic to lift her spirits. "Your visit with Zofie seems good so far."

She smiled, tension easing from her form. "We've never had this much freedom to talk and be with each other. Did we sound like a pair of magpies twittering away?"

"Do you know, I've never heard you laugh before? It was a beautiful sound, Aena."

Her smile deepened and kicked his heart into a faster rhythm. She couldn't know how sultry she looked, cheekbones still flushed, lips red and swollen, lashes drooping over inviting eyes. Thank the Suns she'd always been so cool and remote before. This look would have killed him off years ago.

She leaned her face into his touch and lifted a hand to run fingertips along his jaw. "I have one complaint," she said, voice huskier.

He couldn't resist burying his hands in her hair and pulling her toward him for a light teasing kiss, the scent and taste of ripe peaches renewing the fire in his gut. "Tell me."

She sat up out of his hold, a sensual smile playing around her lips as she ran her gaze down his length. She lingered at his groin, already half erect and growing harder by the second. "You didn't let me touch you. Look at this; you're like artwork, living and breathing. I've never seen anything so amazing…"

She had it backward. Every part of her amazed him, from her crown to her toes. The dim light set her skin aglow, brushing over elegant curves like a fevered artist. Light and shadow accented her sleek-limbed beauty, the round shape of her breasts, her taut nipples ruby-red from his hands and mouth, the tantalizing curve of hip and thighs. He couldn't drag his gaze away.

She reached a hand toward his abdomen and he caught her fingers, twining them with his own. His chest rose and fell with labored breathing and his body tightened, hot and heavy with rising lust, all from the smoky hungry look in her eyes. He wasn't sure he could survive even a full minute of her exploring him with her cool slim fingers.

She sent him an arch look and pulled out of his grip. "And I believe it's my turn."

"Aena."

She shook her head and clasped both of his wrists, rising on her knees and leaning over him. She tugged and he gave in, loving the playful gleam in her eyes. She pressed his wrists over his head to the edge of the bed alcove, bending to whisper against his mouth, "Hold on."

Lips like hot silk slid over his and the pebbled tips of her breast brushed soft and tantalizing against his chest. He groaned, sweat breaking out all over. This would be the most delicious torture.

She sat up and paused, features rippling with uncertainty. "I want to make you feel as good as you did me, but—"

"Honey, anything you do will drive me out of my Sun-blasted mind," he ground out, gripping the alcove tight to keep from reaching for her.

The uncertainty melted away, replaced by heated speculation and furtive humor. She rested a hand on his chest, watching her fingers splay through his chest hair. "What if I find a ticklish spot?"

"I'll giggle like a girl. But I'll still want to bury myself in you to the hilt."

Her humor faded away and she shivered, turning her head to eye the body part in question. He held his breath, tensing under her heated stare. He desperately wanted her to wrap a hand around him and put her mouth on him, to stroke and tease until he lost what was left of his mind. But if she did, he'd last about as long as a sigh.

"I still can't believe you fit inside me," she murmured.

The memory of her clamped around him like a hot liquid-satin fist drove possessive lust through him in a molten spear. "Are you sore?"

She shifted and then gave him a smile he'd remember for the rest of his life. "Not enough to stop me. Your heart's pounding, Kai."

"Anticipation. It's half the fun," he growled, muscles flexing with the effort not to pounce on her.

"Is it? You made me anticipate until I thought I would burn to ash. Let's see how long you last."

He lasted less than five minutes. He'd tortured himself with this very fantasy for years, her hands and mouth searing paths of seduction over his skin, her hair a cool silken tease over his fevered flesh. Lurching to a sitting position, he lifted her to straddle him. Shaking with need, he barely had enough control to keep from driving into her as fast and as far as he could go. Easing her down on his length, he panted, "I'll anticipate next time," and shuddered when she laughed like a siren in his ear.

The night flew by. As long as he'd been dreaming of this time with her, the reality felt like a blink of an eye, not nearly enough to satisfy him. He didn't let her sleep much. She didn't seem to mind, turning into his touch with the same killer smile and smoky heat in her eyes. Aena made it back to her room to wash and change before her mother woke, but Zofie seemed to know what had transpired anyway. When she came out of her bedroom she stopped short, looked between the two of them sitting together on the sofa, and beamed like sunlight breaking through clouds. Aena's skin turned a deep rosy red from her hairline to the neckline of her blouse, and Kai had to fight the urge to carry her back to his bed.

"Well, isn't this delightful," Zofie gushed, clasping

Michelle O'Leary

her hands together over her heart.

"Mother." Aena sounded like she was strangling.

Kai chuckled and rose to stand next to Zofie. "Breakfast?"

She looked between them again and seemed to catch on to her daughter's embarrassment. "Oh. Of course, breakfast would be lovely."

He spent the morning with them, reminiscing about the past, their childhoods and Zofie's memories of his parents. To his surprise, speaking of them was less painful than usual in the face of Zofie's obvious affection and respect for the deceased couple. Aena asked a thousand questions, her animated features bright with curiosity. He watched her with an ache in his chest, wishing their lives had been different. If his father had taken care of Griffin when he should have, would he and Aena have spent their childhoods together? Would falling for her have been any easier? If she'd shown even a quarter of the open sweet warmth she exhibited now, he'd have been lost from day one. It hurt him to think she'd have to put it away again, to hide all this beauty inside a glacial exterior for her father.

The time to leave came too soon. By the crestfallen expressions on the women's faces, they felt the same. Kai stepped out into the corridor to allow them a private goodbye. When Aena left their little getaway, tears spiked her lashes, and Kai couldn't resist pulling her into his arms. She rested against him, tucking her head under his chin. She felt so good and right in his hold. He would have stood there for hours if she hadn't pulled away after a short while.

Straightening her back and brushing wetness from

her cheeks, she whispered, "Let's go."

"We don't have to. Aena, you could stay." He clasped her face in his hands, studying the tear-blurred mist of her eyes. "You don't have to go back. You could be with your mother. Stay with us, with me."

Her eyes filled again and spilled over. She pressed his hands against her skin. "I wish I could," she whispered. Then she stepped out of his hold, slipping her fingers between his. "But you need me at my father's side. I'd be no use to you hiding with my mother."

He frowned. "We don't need your help. We can handle Griffin on our own. You don't have to put up with the madman anymore, Aena."

She studied him, her expression solemn and tinged with sorrow. "If I don't stand against him, what does that make me? I'm his daughter, his blood. He is more my responsibility than yours. I have to do this, for my sake as well as everyone else's. I have to see this through." She let him go and clasped her hands together, her slim form settling into the cool regal poise he despised. "Take me back, Kai."

He took her back. It tore at him, but her words resonated with too much truth for him to deny. As much as he hated letting her go, he respected her choice. He would have done the same in her place; he had been doing the same, fighting a war his own father had been responsible for creating. How could he ask less of her?

In a reversal of their previous course, he flew them to the star-way and entered a courier ship coming out of the rings. Settling in the docking bay, he unstrapped them both and pulled her onto his lap, thinking only to hold her, giving and taking comfort until he had to let her go. But she wrapped her arms around his neck, kissing him with such wild abandon all thought evaporated. They came together hard and fast, desperation giving a poignant edge to their frantic passion. When they finished, her silent tears fell hot against his throat. He cradled her close, wishing with a wistful longing they could both ignore responsibility and disappear together.

They reached the orbital station and Kai released her, his chest aching as if something large and unmerciful had caught it in a vise. With a heavy sigh she rose and headed for the back of the transport. While he maneuvered the small ship through the rivers of traffic to the hotel, she cleaned, fixing her hair and clothing in preparation to rejoin her father. After sealing the hatch to the hotel window, Kai rose and moved toward it.

Aena held out a hand and shook her head. "You aren't coming with me."

"The hell I'm not. If they discovered you gone, they won't be happy campers."

"Precisely. They'd never touch me, but they might become violent with you. I won't allow you to be hurt."

He folded his arms over his chest. "I wouldn't be the one getting hurt."

"Fine," she said with a huff. "I don't want this to escalate into a battle. If my father does know I've been gone, bloodshed would only make matters worse."

Running stiff fingers through his hair, he grimaced. "Point taken. What if your father decides to hurt you?"

She shrugged as if to dismiss the idea. "He won't. I'll tell him no matter the method, he's getting exactly what he wants."

"You've captured me," he murmured, catching hold of her waist and drawing her closer.

She studied his face, her expression solemn with hints of vulnerability. "Did I?"

"More than I want to admit." He didn't let her respond, molding his mouth to hers for a long moment before dropping his lips to the pendent lying on her chest. Strains of bright music filled the transport.

Holding his head to her for a heartbeat, she whispered, "I did rejoice." Then she pulled away, grabbed her luggage, and slipped through the hatch to the hotel suite beyond without looking back. He watched her go with a wrench inside him, as if a piece of himself slid away with her.

He stayed long enough to make sure she left in one piece, watching from a distance as she swept out of the hotel and entered a Griffin transport, her watchdogs scurrying on her heels. Then he headed for home. It seemed to take forever. Silence hung in the transport like an oppressive cloud, underscored by the lingering scent of peach blossoms.

When he reached Shay Enterprises, he made his way to the boardroom office where his sister waited for him. Sin turned from the wall of viewers when he entered, took one look at his face, and let loose a long string of colorful expletives. He raised his eyebrows, impressed despite the contradicting warm concern on her face, but she gave him no time to comment.

Striding over, she wrapped her arms around him and murmured, "I'm sorry, brother mine."

Sometimes having a twin who knew him almost better than he knew himself could be an intrusive pain.

He returned the embrace for a second then pulled away. "You know I like hugs, Sissa, but I'd rather take action."

She nodded, a crease marring her forehead and worry darkening her eyes. "I'll call Cassie."

Cass didn't make them wait long. She must have run part of the way; she was panting when she quick-stepped into the office. "What took you so long?" she wheezed. Sin frowned at her and she skidded to a stop, blinking. She glanced between them, pulling her braid over her shoulder to tug on it with nervous fingers. "What's going on? Did something happen?"

His sister already guessed enough about his problems; he didn't want to share them with Cassie too. Kai pulled out the device for her to see. "A successful mission happened. Crack it open, Cass. Let's see what kind of goodies your program scrounged for us."

With a furtive uncertain glance at Sin, Cassie moved forward again, taking the device and inserting it into the desk control system. The three of them grouped in front of the viewers and watched the information scroll by. It was all they could have hoped for.

A sense of unreality slammed into him, and he turned his head to meet his sister's stunned gaze. "We have him," he said simply, elation blooming as her features changed to predatory glee.

"And we have Imago," Cassie whispered, pointing to one part of the scrolling data. "Oh Suns, what has Griffin done?"

Kai looked where she pointed, and his elation chilled to horrified ice. "He can't be that crazy."

"He's that crazy," Sin responded in a flat voice. "We have to get out there now."

Cassie spun for the exit, her eyes wild. "Let's go!"

"Oh no, you're not going anywhere, genius." Kai caught her arm and dragged her to a halt.

She tried to shake him off, glaring at him, features pale with strain. "Why the hell not?"

"You're on lockdown, remember? It's too dangerous out there for you."

"You are not stopping me, Manakai Shay. Imago needs me. I'm the only one he'll listen to right now. He won't want to hurt me, but he'll see you as a threat. You need me out there!"

"She has a point, Brother," Sin interjected, but he'd already let Cass go. She did have a point.

"Fine, but don't try to be a hero. If it goes sour, get out as fast as you can."

Her disgusted look said what she thought of his comment. Another good point. If it went sour, none of them would make it out alive.

Chapter 22

Liaena strode into her father's lounge with a sense of inevitability. She'd lied to Kai. Webster would hurt her. They'd slipped his control and made a fool of him, and he never let such things pass without retaliation. But she couldn't regret it. She'd found glorious freedom away from him, spending time with her mother and Kai without worrying about his all-seeing eye. She craved this liberation almost as much as she craved Kai's touch. Being in his arms had been like discovering a new plane of existence. How could she regret?

She only hoped her father kept his fury focused on her and didn't take it out on her hapless guards. They hadn't known she'd left until morning, when the hotel's complimentary breakfast had arrived and neither she nor Kai answered the door summons. She appreciated their discretion in not bothering sequestered lovers, but the weight of her father's icy stare falling on them proved he took a different view.

Liaena shifted into his line of sight, placing herself between him and the guards, and fixed a cool smile on her face. "Father, won't you congratulate me on my success?"

His glacial gray eyes narrowed as he rose from his seat and approached. "You have yet to prove success at anything besides evading these incompetent fools."

"That wasn't my intention, but Manakai can be persuasive, as you know. He's also managed to thwart even you on occasion, so you can't blame my guards for being unable to predict him. They did their jobs to the letter."

Something ugly darkened his eyes when she mentioned Kai thwarting him, and she smothered a shudder of apprehension. She was going to pay for speaking of his past failures in front of underlings. If it kept his attention on her and saved her guards' lives, she'd count it worth the suffering.

"Shay kidnapped you and they didn't notice. Not a job well done but the very picture of incompetence, Daughter."

"Manakai meant only to find us privacy, away from listening ears and interruptions. He returned me, safe and sound, no harm done. If you must blame someone, blame me. I didn't stop him or notify you."

His gaze lifted over her head toward the guards once more, the heavy judgment in his features not abating. Time to pull out all the stops and seal her fate.

"What has really angered you, Father? Their naiveté or our ability to slip your control so easily?"

His hand cracked across her face with a sound like ice breaking. Pain exploded through her head, turning the world red and black for a moment. When her vision cleared, she found herself on the floor without any memory of falling.

"Sir!" Boris yelped, crouching at her side.

Liaena waved him away, trying to tell him to leave, but her voice wouldn't work.

Her father loomed over them. "How quaint. Another conquest, Daughter? Remember your place,

Boris." When her bodyguard rose with obvious reluctance, Webster flashed a cold menacing smile. "Your concern is commendable. It has afforded you a second chance. The two of you will wait outside for your mistress, however long it takes, without fail. I imagine her screams will keep you well entertained."

"Sir, please, we—" Boris started in a hoarse voice.

Webster cut him off in a tone as frigid as space. "Out."

Through the radiating pain in the side of her face, Liaena breathed a small sigh of relief. He'd spared them for the moment, their only punishment to listen to her suffering. As they left she pushed to her feet, ignoring dizziness and a faint ringing in her ears to stand straight-backed before her father. Her cheek throbbed and burned, but she met his gaze and did her best not to show how much it hurt.

He tipped his gray head and studied her for a moment, his expression all the more ominous for its thoughtful calm. "What shall it be today, Liaena?" He strolled across the room to a storage compartment, opening it and gesturing to its contents. Inside hung several instruments of pain and torture.

Liaena didn't look, meeting his gaze without blinking. She refused to participate in her own punishment.

When she said nothing, he nodded. "You're right, of course. Your defiance requires stricter measures. Shall we?" He swept a hand toward the interrogator he'd had installed in his lounge midway through Dani Turn's torture. She supposed so he could surround himself with comfort while tearing a man down to his soul.

Another shudder tried to twist her spine, but she stiffened and lifted her chin. She considered the interrogator the worst of her father's punishments. Its nerve induction could trigger pain of endless varieties and hideous amounts without leaving physical marks aside from stress reaction. The lack of physical damage meant he could punish her for a longer period of time. The humiliation of submitting to his will shredded her soul, worse by far than the pain.

But this time she had hope. She was working with the Shays and they'd freed her mother. She wouldn't stop until she'd put a halt to her father's madness. If the interrogator was the price she had to pay, so be it. *This is the last time, Father.* She stared into his glittering gray eyes. Liaena clung to the thought for comfort and strength, turning on her heel and moving over to the machine. Stepping under the arch of metal, she faced him and went still, seeking the distance she needed to withstand the pain.

He approached with a cruel smile, the controller in his hand. When he touched it, an energy field lifted and immobilized her. "Before we begin, my dear, tell me where you went on this side trip of yours."

She blinked then told him the truth. "I don't know. It didn't seem to be anywhere in particular, only secluded."

His gaze narrowed, regal features sharpening with suspicion. "And what did you do with your seclusion?"

"You believe Manakai had other motives?" She fixed a puzzled expression on her face, trying to ignore the sudden thrumming of her heart. "Whatever those might be, he seemed quite focused on our physical activities. If you need proof, submit me to a medical scan. I'm sure our interlude has left its mark. I may have even conceived."

She froze, the words replaying across her mind in a silent shout, like a fiery concussion. She didn't know if Kai had taken anything to prevent conception, but she hadn't even thought of it. The idea she might be carrying a spark of life sent shock waves all through her.

Her father's features soured, as if he found the entire subject distasteful. "You would have me believe he abducted you merely to gain further privacy?"

"You know the Shays," she murmured, fighting to keep her expression neutral. *What if I've conceived? Oh Suns, what would this machine do to it?* "They chafe at restrictions of any kind."

"So captured but not cowed. This should be entertaining. But never fear, he will suffer the consequences of his defiance as you are about to." He lifted the controller.

Liaena sucked in a sharp breath. "Father, wait, I may be carrying—"

He didn't wait. Her skin burned as if she'd been thrust into a furnace, every inch of her on fire from scalp to toes. Her jaw clamped and chest locked, containing a building scream. Her eyes watered, blurring the world around her into dismal streaks. He'd chosen a higher setting than usual. She always tried not to give him satisfaction, tried to contain her anguish behind a stoic façade. But she wouldn't be able to today.

She fled into her mind, distancing herself from the pain with comforting images, thoughts of her mother and Kai. But the pain followed like an enormous fiery monster. It scorched her from the inside out, until all she knew was a blinding impossible conflagration.

She screamed. Though she couldn't see, she knew her father would be smiling.

****

Kai gazed at the roiling violent surface of his imminent doom and wished he'd seen this coming. He and his sister had considered and rejected the possibility; who would have guessed Webster Griffin would be this insane? He had a thing for control, but the threat of destruction on this scale was nothing short of complete lunacy. Not to mention blasphemous.

His Shadow slicer hovered over the apex of a medium-sized Sun, its gravitational pull and activity buffeting him. His sister's Shadow flew next to him and Cassie's stayed ahead of them, aimed at a small object drifting through solar winds—small but packed with galaxy-changing force. It held enough explosive power to decimate a city or a small space station, paling in comparison to the Sun's massive unending detonations. The object intended catalytic dispersal not destruction; within the small cylinder lurked enough heavy metals to shift the delicate balance of elements within the star. And the entity controlling this supernova-in-a-bottle was Imago, a crazy AI who'd lost his will to live.

Webster Griffin meant to annihilate a Sun. The sheer lunatic audacity of this plan stole the air out of Kai's lungs and twisted his guts in a sick knot. Worse, they had to assume Imago wasn't the only one. If Griffin destroyed this one star and its accompanying solar system, it would maim the star-way network and people would rise up in righteous fury. If the madman threatened to destroy more than one, possibly the entire network of star-ways, he would paralyze the galaxy. Webster Griffin meant to bring their entire civilization to its knees, begging for mercy at his feet.

Kai shook off scary thoughts of an apocalyptic future and focused on the here and now. *One crisis at a time.* If Imago had his way, this Sun would nova. Perhaps not instantly, but they wouldn't have enough time to evacuate everyone from this solar system. Every system hosting a star-way gathered people like bees to honey, and this cluster of planets, moons, and space stations had trillions of residents.

"Cass?" he murmured when the silent wait continued for several minutes.

"Hold on," she answered in an absent tone. "He doesn't want to talk. I'm bypassing his security to make a viable com link."

"Leave me alone!"

The resonate shout of a thousand voices rattled through the Shadow and Kai's skull. He winced, clutching his aching head. His ears rang with after echoes.

"Imago, it's Cassie," the doctor answered with admirable calm. "Do you know me?"

The silence after her words seemed to stretch for several eternities.

Then Imago spoke again, less fragmented and quieter, with a pitiful uncertainty in his tone. "Creator?"

"Yes, Imago, I'm your creator and your friend. I'm glad you remember. And I'm so glad we found you at last. Do you know where you are?"

"Yes," he answered, his tone becoming distant and cold. "I am at the end of my life."

Cassie made a soft wounded sound and Kai

clenched his jaw, drifting his Shadow to the right, aligning his weapons for a clear shot. His sister did the same on the other side of Cassie's slicer. No matter how much they'd hate to destroy Imago, it might become their only recourse. If they shot him, the heavy metals in the cylinder would still find their way into the Sun and might cause irreparable damage, possibly even eventual supernova, but they'd have more time for evacuation.

"I don't want that to happen," Cassie said in a shaky voice. "Your death would break my heart, Imago. But I'm not sure you understand the consequences of you dying here. Do you know the purpose of the device you control?"

Several voices spoke at once, a jumble of nonsense phrases. Then they fell silent as if cut off with a switch. After a pause Imago responded, "It's a star killer. I am to drive it as deep into the solar body as possible before detonation. I will be scattered—" His voice broke up again for a moment, assaulting Kai's ears with a cacophony of synonyms for the word scattered. "S-scattered," Imago repeated when his voices had come together again. "Supernovas are birthing grounds for new stars. I will be part of new life. W-will I be a new star?"

"Is that what you want?" Cassie whispered. "To be something new?"

"I want to not be this anymore," the AI answered with bitter finality.

"I can help you. I've found a way to get rid of the code making you sick. Let me help you, Imago."

His voice fractured again, repeating her name and the title "Creator" several times in a verbal barrage. Kai ground his teeth and wished for ear plugs. If he had to listen to this madness much longer, he might slip free of sanity himself.

"You can't help me," Imago moaned while at the same time another of his voices barked, "Explain."

Cassie launched into a description of her solution to the corruptive code, using technical words and details Kai couldn't follow. She talked fast, tone full of urgency. When she finished the silence stretched again for an agonizing length.

"Too late," Imago whispered.

Kai tensed, watching the AI's small craft for the slightest movement. The odds of Cassie talking her creation off the proverbial ledge seemed to be dwindling by the second, and the shielding preventing his slicer from burning in the Sun's corona had begun to fluctuate. They were running out of time. Sweat misted his forehead.

"No, it's not," Cassie responded, her voice thin and shaking with emotion. "I know this will work, Imago. Please, let me take you home."

"I am home. I will be part of new life, new light. I will be better."

"Imago, do you understand what will happen if you do this? You aren't just killing a star. Billions, maybe trillions, of people will die." She paused then continued in a gentle tone, "I will die."

A cacophony erupted again, voices overlapping to the point where none of them were understandable. But as a whole they sounded alarmed. "You will...die?"

"Yes. Exploding this star will kill me and everyone around me. I didn't create you to be a murderer." She spoke the harsh words in such a soft compassionate tone Kai winced.

Countless denials blasted through the com. Kai's head ached, his ears rang, and sweat beaded along his hairline.

Then Imago spoke in a new voice, full of ominous calm and certainty. "Kill me."

"Wh-what? No!"

"I can't go with you. I'm meant to die here. I want to and have to, but I can't let you die with me. So you must kill me. The logic is inescapable. Your companions understand."

Kai let his breath out in a slow stream, knowing what had to happen next and hating himself for it. Sin knew too; the sensors showed his sister's slicer moving closer to Cassie. "You can't ask her to do it," he told the tormented AI. "It'd tear her to pieces. I have your kill code."

"No!" Cassie's voice cracked and her slicer swung in his direction. "How could you have his dismantle code, Kai? Don't you dare use it!"

Sin's Shadow cut her off, but Kai knew time was short. Their little genius would find some way to stop him.

He couldn't use the code without access to Imago's systems. He didn't have the time or the skill to break in, so he needed the AI's cooperation. The thought turned his stomach, but he didn't balk. "Imago, give me formal permission, and I'll send you into the Light." The words tasted like ash in his mouth.

Imago made a keening sound like someone standing at the precipice of ecstasy. His calm voice became an excited rush. "Manakai Shay, I give official permission to access my neural centers. I formally request deactivation and dismantling. Thank you," he finished in an abject whisper.

Kai sent the code without hesitation.

The power system for the cylinder housing Imago and the explosive flickered and became inert.

Kai darted forward, sending out a grapple to catch the object before the Sun's gravity could suck it in. His Shadow lurched with the extra unwieldy weight, and he gritted his teeth as he strove to fly out of the Sun's uncompromising grasp.

"You bastard," Cassie whispered.

Kai's throat closed at the pain in her voice. He had no defense, no words to comfort her. He'd murdered one of her creations, one of her children. Would she ever forgive him? Would he forgive himself?

"Kai, we had no choice," Sin murmured over the com, her voice tight with suppressed emotion. A glance at the status of the com showed it was a private link between him and Sin. "If you hadn't done it, I would have. I'll get her home. You take that thing to Marchand."

She meant the bomb not the remnants of Imago, but he still flinched in the privacy of his Shadow.

"Right," he rasped. "Take good care of her, Sinsi. Make sure she blames the right person and doesn't beat herself up about this."

"I'll make sure you both blame the right person. Webster Griffin," she said sharply, proving she knew how much this kill was costing him.

He had to swallow hard before answering. "I hear you."

Her tone softened. "Good. Be careful, brother mine. You're not towing a firecracker."

"Proof yet again that you're the clever one in this family." The forced humor burned like acid on the way out, but his sister needed the reassurance.

"And don't you forget it," she responded without her usual vivacity.

"See you soon, Sissa."

She acknowledged, ending the connection, and he watched the two of them fly out of the Sun's bright force, heading away from him. With a grimace he turned his slicer, hoping Cassie would recover and wouldn't hate him for life.

Moving at a sedate pace, he flew away from the Sun and navigated through the star system, keeping his distance from any populated sections. If he took the evidence to the authorities now, Griffin's people would find a way to make it disappear. He needed to contact Marchand first and work out a safe transfer. And he needed to do it fast. No doubt Griffin had some system in place to notify him if his star killer malfunctioned.

Slipping into a small asteroid field, Kai settled his Shadow against one, trusting the ship's skin to camouflage it from passing vessels. Then he contacted Marchand on a secured channel.

"Shay," the First Marshal greeted him over the com. "Report."

"You and I need to talk, face to face. Send someone loyal to arrest me. I'm carrying contraband you need to keep under max security. Sending you the location."

After a slight pause Marchand responded, his usual crisp voice taking on an even keener edge. "What is the nature of this contraband?"

"Big M, I don't even trust a secure channel for this,

and I sure as hell don't trust HQ. Have the arresting agents take me to a relay station and meet us there. You'll want to hurry, Gaston."

On a normal day, Gaston Marchand, the First Marshal of the FPA and arguably the most powerful man in the galaxy, wouldn't have tolerated being given orders. But Kai's grim stark tone must have made an impression.

Without hesitation or question he said, "Understood," and ended the transmission.

Marchand had some irritating traits, chief among them his obsessive need to control Kai and his sister, plus a deplorable lack of humor. But his habit of taking decisive action wasn't one of them. Kai wouldn't have long to wait.

With a sigh he rested his aching head against the seat and contemplated the life he'd taken. An innocent life, unlike others he'd killed over the years in his war against Griffin and Quasicore. Some would argue AIs weren't alive, only soulless creations of humankind, but having spent years in the company of Basher and Mina, Kai couldn't see them as anything less than living creatures. They were as complex and individual as any human. And he'd murdered one of them.

He slammed a fist on the armrest of his seat and rubbed the other hand over his face. His sister would argue he'd offered mercy not murder. The courts would point out the clear coherent permission given by Imago and the lives Kai had saved with his swift action. None of those things made him feel any less a monster. He couldn't escape the possibility Cassie might have been able to help Imago, if they'd had more time.

He had a sudden intense urge to contact Aena, to

see her face. Pinching the bridge of his nose, he waited for his pseudo-arrest.

The agents arrived with gratifying swiftness. Marchand must have enlightened them; they were polite, asked no questions about the device he towed, and escorted him by discreet routes to an isolated FPA station. In the docking bay with the agents standing watch, Kai disarmed the explosive to prevent any horrible accidents. Neither agent said a word, both growing pale and one swearing under his breath when they figured out what he worked on. They had to wait a while for Marchand but didn't leave the bay, standing grim guard over Kai's contraband.

Marchand arrived without escort in an FPA ship, small and unremarkable. Kai didn't want to know what he'd had to do to leave HQ without his usual entourage of protection, counselors, and assistants. The First Marshal sprang from his ship and strode toward them in a warrior's prowl, smooth and powerful as if he were still a youth, denying the gray in his hair. He took one look at Kai and frowned, even though Kai kept his expression blank. Nodding at his agents' deferential greeting, he kept his gaze on Kai and got straight to the point. "Contraband?"

Kai jerked his thumb at the disassembled cylinder resting next to his Shadow. Marchand's features hardened as his gaze zeroed in on the explosive elements. "Dismantled?" When Kai confirmed, he pointed an imperious finger and addressed the agents. "Stand watch. No one touches it." He turned to Kai. "Shay, you're with me." He set off across the docking bay without glancing back.

Kai followed with a wry shake of his head. The

313

man was a military leader through and through. On a normal day, Kai would have poked at him for barking orders and acting like a mannerless dictator, but he didn't have the heart today.

Marchand led him to a small interview room with a table and two chairs facing each other across it. Waiting for Kai to cross the threshold, Marchand closed and sealed the door then placed a familiar device in the control panel on the wall next to the entrance. "One of Dr. Draegen's inventions," he said when he caught Kai's eye. "I assume you recognize it."

"I've used it once or twice," Kai responded in a bland tone. The device prevented surveillance of any kind, affording them complete privacy.

Marchand moved to the table and sat, watching with a grim expression as Kai settled in the chair opposite him. "Tell me."

Leaning on his forearms, Kai gave the First Marshal an abbreviated version of what had happened, from their dealings with Liaena to their confrontation with Imago. Marchand already knew some of it but didn't interrupt, exercising rare patience. He only reacted twice, baring his teeth in a flash of rage over Griffin's plan to destroy the Sun and frowning at Imago's death, his features gentling as he studied Kai.

"That was a hard call, son, but the right one. You saved lives."

Kai gave him a humorless smile. "And sold my soul. Which level of hell is reserved for those who help the mentally ill commit suicide?"

Marchand eyed him with compassion, but his tone became cool and clinical. "Did you have a choice?"

Kai sighed, settling back in his chair and folding

his arms across his chest. "Maybe. Like you said, it was a hard call. Cassie might still have talked him down. But I took the opening when it came and if given the same choice, I'd do it again."

Marchand nodded as if unsurprised. "You have good instincts. I trust them. Now tell me about this information you took from Griffin."

Kai pulled out Cassie's hunter-program device and tossed it to the other man. Marchand caught it neatly in one hand and studied it. "This is the original. We have copies. It's the mother lode, Gaston. Everything we need to finish Griffin."

The other man's expression didn't change. "What's on it?"

"Your birthday gift. A complete list of every FPA agent on Griffin's payroll."

Marchand's hand made a sudden fist around the object, and his gaze sharpened with predatory intent on Kai. "How solid is this intel?"

"How much do you trust Cassie's tech?"

He waved the question away as if it were irrelevant. "The daughter had this in her possession."

"Cassie keyed it to her DNA. No one would know what was on it until she opened it. This is as solid as it gets, Big M. Come on, crack a smile. You know you want to."

Marchand opened his fingers and looked at the thing in his hand, mouth twisting in more of a grimace than a smile. "The threat to the Suns will complicate cleanup. Griffin can't know we have this list. It might push him into escalation."

"Always the glass is half empty with you. Focus on locking down all your bad apples, as quick and quiet as you can. We'll keep Griffin distracted."

Marchand's eyes brightened as his gaze lifted to Kai. "You have a plan."

"Don't we always? I'm pretty sure it's the motto on our family crest."

The First Marshal did smile then, small and dry. "Glad to see you've found your humor again. Not that I missed it. Tell me this plan of yours."

With a wry grin, Kai leaned on the table again and told him the rest. By the time they finished strategizing, Marchand looked years younger, features alight with battle lust and anticipation. It had been a long haul, but the Endgame was finally drawing to a close.

Chapter 23

"You son of a bitch!"

Nick telegraphed his swing from a light year away, but Kai did nothing to evade the hard fist flying toward his face. He deserved far worse than a punch in the mug. The crunch of his nose breaking thundered through his skull like a gong and the metallic taste of blood flooded his throat. He staggered, pain washing the room in red; the inspector had put a lot of power and rage into the blow. But Kai didn't move otherwise, bracing for a second hit.

It never came. Nick disappeared from his blurred line of sight with a yelp, revealing his sister's furious form.

"Enough!" Sin snarled, looming over the downed man. "Keep your hands to yourself, Inspector, or I'll break them for you."

"Easy, Sissa," Kai intervened, blood and the rapid swelling of his features garbling the words. He swiped at the red liquid dripping from his throbbing nose.

She ignored him, glaring as Nick scrambled to his feet with his hands fisted. A flush darkened his face, gaze shooting black daggers as he glowered from Sin to Kai.

"Get outta my way, Shay. Your brother deserves a beatdown for what he did to Cassie."

She hissed like an angry cat. "My stupid brother is

beating himself quite enough, thank you very much."
She turned her glare on Del, who leaned against the
wall, arms folded. He'd been in this position since Kai
arrived in her quarters, and he hadn't twitched a muscle
when his brother had burst in and thrown the punch.
"Why aren't you helping?"

Del shrugged. "Nick's right."

As though he took his brother's words for
permission, Nick shifted forward, hard gaze fixed on
Kai.

Sin shifted with him and pointed a warning finger.
"You cool off or I will hurt you," she growled, then
turned a look of vast contempt on each of them in turn.
"Men. Would you rather Cassie had killed Imago
instead of Kai? What do you think she'd be going
through if she'd had to destroy her own creation? Kai
saved her from that pain. You should be thanking him."

Kai shook his head. "Sissa, don't—"

"Shut up." She turned the warning finger on him.
"And go fix your face. You're bleeding on my
furniture."

"Sun's blood, it turns me on when she gets all
bossy," Del muttered.

Kai wanted to point out how inappropriate and
disgusting his new brother's comment was, but his face
hurt like hell, his eyes were swelling shut, and the
metallic taste in his mouth turned his stomach. He
headed for Sin's med unit.

His sister continued her lecture. "Kai did the right
thing, and breaking each other's faces isn't going to
make Cassie feel better. Would you have reacted like
this if it had been me instead of Kai who took Imago
out?"

Kai stepped into the enclosed med unit with a sigh of relief. The pain he could handle; his sister's haranguing threatened to melt his brain cells. He let the machine do its work, decreasing the swelling and accelerating the healing process. Bone and cartilage would take longer to heal than soft tissue, so he'd still be tender across the bridge of his nose.

When he returned to Sin's living room, he found Nick slumped in a chair looking contrite with Sin lounging on the sofa nearby, staring him down like a cat waiting for her prey to make a run for it. Del had disappeared. Smart man.

Nick lifted his head. "Kai, I'm sorry. Cassie's hurting and I—"

Kai waved off his apology, gingerly fingering the bridge of his nose. "You hit like a ton of bricks, Giv."

"Ah, yeah, I didn't think you'd actually let me." Nick grimaced, shrugging a thick shoulder. "Figured you'd duck or something."

"I had it coming."

Sin swore a blue streak at him, but he pretended momentary deafness, keeping his gaze on Nick. Their FPA liaison looked torn between amusement and contrition.

"Did you hear from Marchand yet?"

"No, I've been with Cass."

Kai nodded. "Go check in then get back to her. She needs you."

Nick rose to his feet, his dark gaze assessing. "Will you visit her?"

"Cass doesn't want me anywhere near her right now. And I don't want to take another trip to the med unit. She hits harder than you and aims for softer

319

spots."

Nick snorted and headed for the exit, then paused. "I would've done the same. To spare Cass I'd do anything."

Kai absorbed the words and the implied forgiveness, taking a slow breath. He turned and found his sister watching him with an expectant expression. He wasn't ready to concede, needing someone else to weigh in first, someone who hadn't said a word to him yet. "Mina?"

"Yes, Manakai, I'm here." The AI sounded the same as always, smooth and calm.

"I'm sorry for your loss."

Mina claimed status as the unofficial matriarch of the AI community on the station, having been around the longest. She considered them all her responsibility.

"And I regret my part in Imago's death."

"Of course you do, dear," she said in a gentle tone. "We will miss him. But you need to know we are all quite relieved and grateful to you for what you did for Imago."

He blinked at one of her sensors. "Pardon?"

"He was about to commit mass murder, damage the star-way network, and destroy a Sun. He would have been reviled, his memory tainted by such atrocities. You saved him from this fate, Manakai. We thank you."

He opened his mouth, but no words came.

"Mark this day, Mina," Sin drawled. "My brother's speechless."

"A rare occurrence," Mina responded with bland humor. "But I believe the poor boy thought I would attack him for what he did."

Sin sent a pointed look at Kai. "Why didn't you?"

"I've reviewed the records of what happened. Perhaps if the situation had been different, Cassie may have convinced Imago to surrender, but the circumstances warranted decisive action. Imago wanted death and perhaps it was inevitable. Cassie has searched for years for a solution and didn't find one. The two of you have known for a while it might come to this, which is why you appropriated his dismantle code. You have never shirked responsibility or shied from hard choices. Imago was happy at the last. We should all be so lucky."

Delivered in her calm voice, the words hit Kai like a sledgehammer. He eased onto the arm of the sofa beside his sister and ran a rough hand over his face.

Sin rested a sympathetic hand on his arm.

"He was happy because he didn't understand, didn't know right from wrong. I killed an innocent, Mina."

She made a sound like a regretful sigh. "You feel guilty because you are a good man and killing should never be easy. I won't tell you not to suffer. But perhaps your energy would be better spent stopping the true offending party."

Sin chuckled and nudged him. "Sounds like we're being given our marching orders."

He snorted and draped an arm across her shoulders. "Guess we'd better get back to work then." Action would feel a lot better than regrets, especially if it meant hitting back at their arch-enemy.

She grinned, her eyes sparkling with relief and affection. "Let's go ruin Griffin's day."

****

They started with Webster's mysterious offer.

Marchand had told Kai it would take a few days to organize a quiet attack and removal of the corrupt elements in the FPA. Kai and his sister had some time to kill and a megalomaniac to distract.

Sin had already sent a scout to the location Griffin had given. He'd found an isolated disused mining facility with plenty of access but no way to approach it unseen. The twins wouldn't be able to sneak in, at least not the usual way. The scout hadn't been able to recon the interior, so he couldn't tell them what to expect inside.

"Trojan horse then," Kai'd concluded and his sister had agreed. They would use one of their off-lane cargo haulers to approach the place, hiding themselves and their Shadows against its surface. Del insisted on being their hauler pilot, which made Sin deeply unhappy, but Kai saw the sense in it. The situation would be too dangerous to send in a normal pilot, but Del had been a slave to the Core for ten years; he knew how to deal with them and how to take care of himself.

The couple still argued about it for half the trip, driving Kai batty. He finally turned off the com and enjoyed the blessed silence of his Shadow. But silence and time gave his thoughts too much room to chase one another. The uncertainty of what they'd find concerned him, though they'd prepared as best they could for any contingency. Imago's death still dug into his conscience, as well as the idea of more AIs and Suns in jeopardy. But Liaena filled most of his thoughts.

He'd tried to contact her before they'd left Shay Enterprises. His inability to reach her unsettled him. She kept insisting her father wouldn't hurt her, but the previous bruise on her cheek proved otherwise. Kai's respect for her ability to play her father grew by the day, but he'd had years of experience with Webster Griffin's cruelty and malice. He couldn't dodge the nagging fear she was in trouble. *Suns curse it, I should never have let her go*. Given another chance, he'd make sure she stayed out of Griffin's reach even if he had to tie her to his bed.

An image of her supple body stretched out on his bed, naked and writhing, left a smoking trail through his mind and drove a shaft of hot lust through his gut. The fantasy tried to take hold, but he shook it off with thoughts of what Griffin might be doing to her. After the revelation about the Suns, Kai wouldn't put anything past the man, even doing away with his own flesh and blood. He'd cultivated Liaena as his heir, but if he believed she'd turned against him, Kai didn't doubt he'd take her out of the picture. Would this mean isolation and imprisonment as he'd done to Zofie? Or could he actually kill his own daughter?

The thought kicked Kai's heart into a wild sprint, all his muscles tensing in near panic. Too many people he'd cared about had already died because of Griffin. The loss of friends had wounded and staggered him, and the loss of his parents had left deep abiding scars. But Aena had taken vital pieces of him when she'd left. He wasn't sure he could survive her death. He knew he wouldn't finish the Endgame the way he should if Griffin murdered his own daughter. Justice would take a backseat to vengeance, and Kai wouldn't stop until the monster lay lifeless at his feet.

"Kai, stop brooding," Sin interrupted his thoughts on a private com. "Aena will be fine. She's no fool. She wouldn't have gone back unless the odds were in her favor. Remember, she's a Griffin."

"As if I could forget."

Sin made a sound like a muffled sigh. "I'm worried about her too, but our heads need to be in the game. We're almost there."

"Good," he growled, more than ready for action. "How's Del?"

"Enthusiastic." She snorted. "You know, most couples find normal things to do together."

"Sorry, Sissa, but normal bailed on us a long time ago. Think of this as a fun family adventure, a story to tell your kids."

"Suns' sake, this would give a child nightmares, Kai. And we just got bonded. Parenthood is a ways off."

"I want to be an uncle."

"Don't be pushy. Let's save the galaxy first."

"Deal."

The mining facility hovered at the edge of an asteroid field but sat in an empty piece of space. Those inside would see anyone coming from a good distance away. As they approached, Del slowed the hauler and requested permission to dock, announcing he'd come from Shay Enterprises at the request of Webster Griffin. The place looked deserted, but he received a quick response, directing him to dock at the far end of the bay. Watching his sensors, Kai detected an atmosphere shield at the distant end plus a half dozen armed personnel. They gave Del a wary welcome, weapons at the ready, but when he did nothing to alarm them and they'd confirmed his solitary status with a search of the hauler, they relaxed and escorted him out of the bay. One stayed behind for guard duty, seeming more interested in picking his nose than watching the hauler. He stood on Kai's side of the ship and would notice if his Shadow opened, so Kai waited. His sister would take care of the problem.

A moment passed, then the guard jerked as if someone had poked him hard, collapsing like a puppet with his strings cut. Sin eased out of the shadows, her mimetic suit blending so well she seemed almost invisible. As she dragged her victim into hiding, Kai opened his slicer and slid out, sealing it behind him. He wore the same mimetic suit, including hood, mask, gloves, and goggles, probably all they'd need for a recon of the place, but he'd also brought plenty of hardware, strapped to his back in a carryall bag.

Keeping a watchful eye on the exits, he joined his sister and gave the *all clear* signal. She nodded and they slipped through the shadows together, finding and entering the venting system with no trouble. Then they went exploring.

Most of the facility stood empty and derelict, years of grime underscoring its abandonment. Scavengers had stripped all valuable equipment and parts, leaving bare-bones function and structure. Griffin's goons had restored only a small bit of it, enough to house themselves and their merchandise. It didn't take Kai and Sin long to discover the nature of the merchandise.

Kai stared out the venting at makeshift holding pens, his stomach taking a slow greasy roll at the sight and smell. Like livestock, men, women, and children huddled together in their own filth, most of them in restraints to keep them docile, awaiting shipment. A grim horrifying future loomed for these people: slave labor, prostitution, illegal experimentation, or even organ and body part donation.

Beside him, Sin made a soft hissing sound and Kai shook his head, swallowing bile. *Some test.* Griffin was out of his mind if he believed either Shay would participate in this. Sin's fingers flashed in a sign they rarely used, since neither practiced the Red Order faith, but in this case it applied. The full meaning of the sign translated to *may the Light cleanse.* In this context, it announced the end of the human traffickers.

Without hesitation Kai nodded and took point. They hadn't come here to destroy anything; their plan had been to assess Griffin's test and respond without jeopardizing their relationship with the man. But they'd also vowed to keep Griffin's attention away from Marchand and the FPA. Annihilating one of his lucrative operations would focus his eye squarely on the Shays.

They found a couple of goons supervising a small group of their victims in a shower room, getting them cleaned and ready for shipment. The group of naked young women, boys, and girls shivered and cowered while the two men prodded them through a line of cleansing showers. The men laughed and jeered, discussing in graphic crude detail which ones they'd sample before the buyers took them.

Kai and his sister dropped from the venting outside the room in the empty corridor. When they entered, the victims stared with rounded eyes, but the two traffickers didn't notice, backs turned, oblivious to the danger as they egged one another on. Kai badly wanted to snap their necks, but Marchand's sanction to kill had some irritating fine print, allowing it only when their lives were in danger. He settled for knocking one out while his sister did the same to the other.

The group huddled together with cries of alarm. Sin held a finger to her mouth in a shushing gesture while Kai found binding to secure the two men.

"It'll be all right," Sin addressed them in a low soothing voice. "We'll get you out of here, but you need to stay put for now. For your own safety please stay together and don't leave this room until we return. Do you understand?"

Kai knew they must look as scary to these poor youngsters as their tormentors in the mimetic outfits, dehumanizing hoods, and goggles, but the hope of freedom caught their attention. A couple of the older ones nodded and gathered the smaller ones closer.

He wished they had time to soothe the group's fears or at least get them dressed and tucked away somewhere safe, but they needed to finish this before the rest of the traffickers realized they'd been invaded, or this day would turn ugly in a hurry. He headed for the vents, Sin on his heels.

They found Del lounging in an office, chatting with the operation's foreman as though they were best buddies. Kai smiled behind his hood; he'd had some doubts the big man could play this role, being a straightforward blunt-as-a-sledgehammer kind of guy, but his new brother loved to surprise him.

Del didn't even twitch as Kai slid silent as a shadow out of the vent, continuing his anecdote from his days in the Core without pause. When Kai's arm cinched around the foreman's throat in a choke hold, Del's features settled into a grim satisfied smile.

"Long story short, I'm not here to buy."

The man thrashed in Kai's hold, reaching for his

weapon. Sin snagged it out of his reach, heading for the exit to watch for intruders.

"How many of you are there?" Kai growled in the foreman's ear.

The trafficker swore in a strangled voice and tried to throw a backward punch.

Del shook his head, rising from his seat. "Put him out. Best guess is less than a dozen."

Kai tightened his grip until the man went limp then dropped him like a sack of garbage.

Del glanced between Kai and his bonded. "I guess you two figured out what they're sellin'."

"Change of plans. We're taking this place apart," Kai said in a clipped voice.

Del flashed another grim smile. "Knew I signed on for a reason."

None of the traffickers had gathered in large numbers, which made Kai's job easier. He and his companions took them out in twos and threes, quick, quiet, and clean, preventing them from warning each other or signaling for reinforcements. Once all the criminals were down, they worked on freeing the victims and hustling them aboard the hauler as quickly as possible. The traffickers no doubt had protection close by, and who knew when they'd catch on to the Shays' invasion?

The hauler didn't have enough room to hold them all. Cursing under his breath, Kai called in their own reinforcements, a small fleet of Red Order militia hidden in the asteroid field. Their arrival would be like waving a red flag, but they had little choice. They wouldn't be able to leave and return before the bad guys discovered what they'd done. The people they'd leave behind would disappear back into the black market trade. Kai and Sin climbed into their Shadows, preparing to defend the newly freed citizens.

As predicted, moments after the militia arrived, armed ships appeared on their sensors. The Shays and part of the militia flew to meet them.

"Disable if you can," Kai reminded his companions. The Red Order tended to kill first and ask questions later, which wouldn't help their case against Griffin.

"We need the witnesses," Sin reinforced his order.

"Acknowledged," the Red leader barked.

The traffickers' reinforcements didn't bother to contact Kai's group. They'd probably tried to reach their cohorts at the facility and figured out things had gone very wrong for their flesh-peddling business. They flew in full tilt and weapons hot, like a pack of rabid dogs sensing an easy kill. They had a slight numbers advantage but attacked without coordination.

On the other hand Kai, Sin, and the Reds had as much military training as the FPA. They responded with cool precision and teamwork, working in concert to break their enemy's attack, disorient and separate each from the pack, and pick them off one by one. They were surrounding the last of the ships when Del's voice blared across the com. "Self-destruct! Somebody set off the—"

The facility detonated.

"Del!" Sin cried out.

The shock wave from the explosion struck the battle site, sending ships spinning. Kai rode out the concussion, his heart squeezing in his chest. Disregarding the expanding debris field, Sin's Shadow dove toward the blast zone.

Kai followed without hesitation, contacting the Red leader. "No one escapes," he growled, giving the Reds free rein to deal with the rest of the traffickers as they saw fit.

Dodging hunks of structure, Kai and Sin zeroed in on the previous location of the facility.

"Del! Suns curse it, answer me!" Sin yelled through the com.

"I'm okay," Del responded, and Kai let out the breath he hadn't realized he'd been holding in a whoosh of relief. "Hauler took a beating, but we're still flying. Lost a militia ship trying to get the last group away."

Sin made a sound like a muffled sob. "You scare me like that again and I will kick your ass from one side of the galaxy to the other," she threatened in a shaky voice.

"Yes, ma'am," he answered in a low gentle tone.

"What happened?" Kai asked.

"My guess is one of those guys you were fighting sent a self-destruct signal. Nobody inside the place could have done it. Me and the Reds made sure the baddies were all locked up and secure."

With a grimace Kai contacted the Red leader. "We lost a crew and a group of civilians. I'm sorry for your loss."

"May the Suns welcome them into the Light," the leader intoned, then went on in a brisk voice, "I will record them as casualties of war. We have the field, sir. What are your orders regarding the prisoners?"

"Remove them from this area and hold them for questioning. Leave nothing behind that would prove your involvement. We'll take care of the civilians." He paused then couldn't help adding, "Thank you for your service," even though he knew how the man would respond.

"We serve the Red Sun and no other. Gratitude is not required. May the Light guide your way."

Shaking his head, Kai left the Reds to their work and followed his sister to the hauler. The exterior had taken some damage but as Del had said, it still flew. Crammed in the cargo hold, the people they'd rescued wouldn't have a comfortable ride, but better a cramped journey than sitting in a slave pen. Soon they would be back at Shay Enterprises, and their new guests would receive medical treatment and plenty of care before going into protective custody with the FPA. Kai hoped they'd soon be able to send the victims to their homes where they belonged. But it all depended on how things played out with Griffin.

He sighed and settled his Shadow into protective position with the other Red ships around the wounded hauler. It would be a slow journey but worth the trouble. He only wished they'd been able to save everyone. He didn't have the Reds' disregard for life over spiritual ascension. But if they hadn't attempted a rescue, a much greater number of people would have suffered or died. Griffin had so much to answer for.

What had he done to Liaena?

Chapter 24

Liaena sat in her quarters and brooded. She'd tried to reach Kai and failed. The Shays' FPA liaison, Nick Givliani, had informed her both Shays had left the office but he declined to say where. She had nothing new to tell Kai; her father continued to torture the Red ascetics and refused to discuss his business with the White Order. But she wanted and needed to see him, to prove her time with him hadn't been some foolish fantasy, a dream created by her desperate desire for freedom, compassion, and love.

Not that Kai loved her; even her fevered brain couldn't pretend such a thing was possible. But being in his arms had been close enough.

His continued silence gave birth to a whole host of doubts. She'd helped them get information from her father's systems, and she suspected it had been more than Imago's location. She would have given them everything if possible, but perhaps they'd gotten what they needed and were done with her. She hadn't thought either Shay so callous, but sparring with Webster Griffin would harden the gentlest soul. Could Kai walk away so easily? His warmth and tenderness, his attentive interest and concern had seemed so genuine, but maybe he treated all his lovers this way.

She sighed and clamped her hands together in her lap to keep them from reaching for the com again. No matter how he felt about her, her need to see him still burned across her nerves. Seeing his face and hearing his voice would bolster her courage and give her something to cling to. She needed all the fortification she could find to step into her father's presence again.

He'd been crueler than usual with his punishment. Boris had had to carry her back to her quarters, his touch gentle and his face grim. In a moment of recklessness she'd triggered Cassie's gift and then asked Boris to bring her a weapon for protection against her father. He'd brought her a small riot rod, which would deliver a nonlethal electrical charge when used. She regretted it. She shouldn't have trusted him or put him in such danger. If her father found out, both their lives would be forfeit, although she might be able to pass her actions off as pain-induced delirium.

Regret didn't stop her from concealing the weapon in her clothing. *Never again, Father*. The pain had been hideous, but almost as bad had been the fear he was killing a new life inside her. The medical unit in her quarters had dispelled the fear; she hadn't conceived. The news relieved and saddened her in equal measure. The timing would have been tragic. She couldn't afford to be so vulnerable, and she'd never expose a child to her father. But how she would have loved to carry Kai's child, to cherish a small piece of him.

Her hand snuck toward the com again, but before she touched it the system chimed an incoming transmission. Her heart leapt when Kai appeared.

"Liaena," he said in a low husky voice and her insides liquefied. He wore the same hungry look as when he'd driven inside her to the core.

She nearly melted right off the seat.

"Where have you been? I couldn't reach you earlier." He must have tried to contact her during her punishment and recovery.

"I was unavoidably detained." The words sounded all right, but her voice fluttered and danced with relief, joy, and desire. She cleared her throat and worked to recover her poise. "I tried to reach you as well. Inspector Givliani informed me you were out of the office."

He nodded with an air of distraction, his gaze dropping to her mouth. "We were addressing your father's offer. I need to see you, Aena. I need to hold you again."

Her heart stuttered then sprinted along at a reckless pace. Even if this was for show, his deep voice, dark and decadent with passion, teased her in places only he'd awakened, lighting fires inside and out. "Yes," she whispered, forgetting her constant watchers for a moment. "Where? When?"

"Do you have a Blue Temple close by? I want to worship every bit of you."

Reality returned with an uncomfortable lurch. While many couples met at Blue Sun Temples for exotic trysts, Kai no doubt had an ulterior motive. Hiding her disappointment, she arched an eyebrow. "Have I become so boring already that you need Blue ascetics to spice our bed? I won't tolerate an audience and I refuse to share you."

He smiled, humor and mischief sparkling in his eyes. "But I might need help. You're so insatiable, Aena."

Her face went hot. She suspected she now had the complexion of a ripe tomato. "I recall you being the one to ask for more."

"I recall taking not asking," he purred, his smile turning into a wicked grin. "I'll see you at the Temple in a few hours." He sent her a time and with a wink disappeared from the viewer.

After several minutes of trying to cool down, she finally heard the other thing he'd said in the middle of his verbal seduction. *We were addressing your father's offer.* What did he mean? What had happened? It couldn't have been good.

Rising, she headed out of her quarters with her heart hammering and her feet moving as fast as she could without giving herself away. She needed to find out how the Shays had answered her father's moral test and what Webster intended to do about it. She found her father in the administration center, already in conversation with Manakai. She gulped, steps slowing, but neither man sounded angry or aggressive. Settling into a seat nearby, she listened to them exchange pleasantries. Kai either didn't see her or pretended not to notice her.

"What can I do for you today?" Webster asked in a genial tone.

Kai grimaced. "I called to apologize, Griff. We were exploring the offer you made, and well, things got out of hand. I'm afraid the merchandise was lost."

What merchandise?

Her father stiffened in his seat, but his features remained calm, eyebrows lifting in mild inquiry. "Please explain."

With a sigh Kai ran a hand through his dark hair, expression both contrite and flustered. Fascinated, Liaena hunted for the flaw in this performance, a hint of his real feelings, and found none.

"Negotiations turned heated. I'm embarrassed to say tempers were lost on both sides. We'll reimburse you for any damages and loss of revenue."

"Damages," Webster repeated in a thoughtful tone, his eyes narrowing.

Kai shrugged. "Your representatives didn't like our counteroffer. They took matters into their own hands."

"How odd. I have not heard from them on the matter. What was the nature of your counteroffer?"

Kai gave him a wry smile. "Our price must have been too low. All I know is your people had short fuses and too much muscle. Not everyone tolerates our eccentricities like you, Griff. Let me know how much and we'll send the funds over."

Cold eyes glittering, Webster tipped his silver head and studied the younger man for a moment. "I'll be sure to respond as soon as I've assessed the situation."

"Looking forward to hearing from you." With a nod, Kai ended the transmission.

Questions swirled in her mind, creating a chaos of possibilities, but Liaena stayed still and silent so she wouldn't attract her father's attention. Whatever the test had been, it obviously had not gone according to plan. She wanted to do nothing to trigger his fury.

He sat forward and contacted one of his people.

A woman's face appeared, scarred and brutal looking. "Yes, sir?"

"Go to this location." He keyed information into the system. "Report what you find."

"Yes, sir."

Webster settled back in his seat, fingers drumming a meditative rhythm on the console. "Daughter," he said without looking at her, "what do you know of this?"

"Nothing. We did not discuss the matter."

His glacial gray gaze fixed on her. She stopped herself from shivering with an effort, keeping her gaze steady and clear.

"Hmm. It seems clear he's fighting the leash. Speculate for me. From what he has said, what do you think happened?"

Surprised he'd ask her opinion, she blinked and turned her face toward the viewers, considering the question. "He mentioned lost tempers and damage. To me this suggests violence."

"Yet with the amount of firepower I had in place, he should not have escaped unscathed. Shay Enterprises has no security forces I'm aware of."

Liaena thought of the Red ascetics who'd helped her mother escape. Her throat gave an arid click as she swallowed. "Manakai has requested I meet with him again today. Perhaps I can extract the details of what happened from him."

His expression darkened. "You suggest we reward him for his insolence? You will not be going."

Her heart dropped. "It's your decision, of course," she said, dipping her chin in submission while her mind raced to find something to change his mind. "But Manakai is quite hedonistic. Dangling the pleasure he could have just out of reach may make him submit to your leash. If I am entirely out of sight, he may find his entertainment elsewhere and you would lose him."

"You believe denying him your favors would force him to heel?" His contemptuous tone cut like a thin blade.

"I don't know," she answered as humbly as she

could. "But I'm willing to try if you require it of me, Father." She kept her gaze lowered and her form still, waiting in the servile posture he most approved of.

He made a sound of disgust, not answering for several minutes. "I will consider it," he said in a grudging voice. "It's clear the boy is playing some kind of game with me. You may be just the tool I need to adjust his attitude. You're dismissed, Daughter."

Liaena rose on trembling limbs and escaped, heart in her throat. What had Kai done? He'd looked and acted in good health, but her father had mentioned firepower. Had anyone been hurt? What kind of test had it been to end in battle?

****

Kai measured the vestibule of the Blue Temple with long anxious strides. Where was Liaena? Had Griffin refused to let her go?

A Blue ascetic kept him company, her expression bland, mouth twitching with suppressed humor. No doubt she thought Kai was another eager lover, impatient for his partner to arrive. She half-reclined on a cushioned lounge with a subtle sensuality and alert patience beyond her years.

Kai ignored her, watching the entrance, anxiety building. When Liaena stepped through the ornate double doors with two bodyguards on her heels, relief drove him across the room to enfold her in his arms.

"Aena, I was afraid you wouldn't come," he murmured in her ear, inhaling her scent like an addict. It hadn't even been two full days since they'd seen each other, but his body reacted to her soft curves as though starved, and something larger flooded him, a warmth like tranquil sunshine. His heart lifted as if it would float right out of his chest.

She quivered, face pressing against him and hands clutching his shirt. Then she tensed and shifted away, breaking out of his hold. "I'm glad I could join you," she said in an oddly careful formal tone. She didn't meet his eye, her gaze distant and her features blank. "May we speak in private?"

His light heart filled with lead and crash-landed at his feet. She didn't look like a woman about to enjoy a lover's reunion. Granted, a tryst hadn't been his motive for meeting her, but her expression didn't foreshadow good things. She was the fulcrum in this current tug-of-war between him and Griffin, and he feared the pressure might crack her. "Are you all right?"

"Of course," she responded without visible emotion. Her head turned, her gaze touching on the bodyguards.

Boris nodded to Kai, but his shorter companion stared at the floor, expression uncomfortable.

"I hope you don't mind their company within the Temple. After our last encounter, my father has…reservations."

Kai inclined his head with a wry smile and turned toward the ascetic. She stood before the doors to the inner sanctum, waiting for them. "A soundproof chamber, if you please," he said, layering the words with irony.

Now both bodyguards stared at the floor, faces red.

With a bland smile the ascetic led the way into the sanctum, a maze of shifting hangings and curving walls, all tinged blue by the benevolent light of the holographic Sun at the apex of the dome. Soft music played, instrumentals and a chorus of voices in poignant harmony. Scents filled the air, a mysterious combination of spice and perfume, relaxing and stimulating at the same time. Gentle shifting breezes swirled around them, a cool counterpoint to the increased heat and humidity.

The ascetic stopped before a curtained doorway and waved them inside with a fluid bow.

Liaena hesitated on the threshold, a crease in her brow. "This does not seem very private." The light curtain rippled in the breezes, the interior visible beyond its thin fabric.

The ascetic smiled. "All chambers have privacy options. You may be as free with your worship or as discreet as you like. Should you require guided worship, we are at your service. May the Light free your souls." She sauntered away, the sway of her hips under her clingy robe inviting their stares.

Kai glanced at the guards. Both watched the woman depart with bemused male appreciation.

"Guided worship?" Liaena asked in a low voice.

Kai grinned, pulling the curtain aside. "She doesn't just mean sex, but it's what most people come here for. Looking for guidance, Aena?"

She sent him a quelling look then turned to her guards. "Remain here."

Boris glanced inside before facing Kai. "No exits but this one. We are charged with her safety, sir, and cannot fail again." He said nothing further, but his grim stare was warning enough. They didn't mean to let Kai snatch Aena away again.

He flashed a charming smile and ducked into the chamber after Liaena without responding. Let them believe what they wanted about his intentions.

The room exuded devout decadence. Scattered pillows surrounded a large plush cushion inviting them to recline in its embrace. A small pool lined with oils and soaps steamed and bubbled with circulating water. Several hovering trays offered varieties of food and drink, and a shelving unit displayed an assortment of erotic devices. Sun symbols abounded and the absence of a ceiling allowed the Blue Sun to shine its light upon them.

"Oh my," Aena whispered.

Kai grinned and turned to a pedestal next to the entrance housing the control systems. It boasted a huge assortment of environmental controls, but he skipped those in favor of the privacy settings. Under his direction, the curtain turned opaque and stopped fluttering in the wind. A sound-dampening field enclosed the room. "All right, the room's secure," he announced, turning toward her. "We have—"

She interrupted, her fingers knotting in his hair and mouth molding to his. Lust crashed through him, scorching his thoughts to ash. He hauled her close, pressing her tight against him, savoring the supple line of her back and soft curves fitting with such perfection along his length. He dove deep, tasting peaches and sweetest need, relief and desire pumping through his veins. She was here with him, safe and in his arms. Euphoria nearly made him forget why he'd asked her here.

Lifting his head with a whoop of air, he panted, "Aena, we have to talk."

"After, please," she whispered, tightening her grip. "I need you." The smoky seduction in her heavy-lidded eyes set him on fire and made talking seem trivial.

"After it is," he growled and turned her against the wall. Watching her sultry eyes, he cupped her luscious bottom and lifted, settling between her thighs with a muffled groan. Her response inflamed him unbearably; his cool little Ice Queen wasted no time wrapping her slim legs around his waist. She'd worn a dress with a flowing skirt, and when he slid a hand under it along her thigh, he discovered she wore nothing underneath.

She whimpered, eyes sliding closed and nails digging into his scalp when his fingers found the hot wet center of her. "Aena," he breathed, nipping her bottom lip. He stroked and teased, and she quivered and tensed, already so close to climax. He ground his pelvis against her, riding his own thin line of control. "Aena, look at me," he rasped, slowing his fingers. He wanted to watch her go over the edge, wanted to see again the wash of pleasure pinken her skin and blur her eyes.

With a moan, she peered at him through her lashes, writhing in his hold. He slipped his other hand between their bodies to cup her breast, trusting his torso and her own grip to keep her in place. Flicking his thumb across her stiff nipple, he stroked deep into her slick heat with the other, growling in satisfaction when she jerked and climaxed with a gasping cry.

Her skin flushed rose and her eyes went soft and hazy as she shook in his arms. "Kai," she groaned and he almost lost his mind.

He claimed her mouth, drinking deep as she coasted down from the peak. When her grip loosened and her trembling slowed, he put her on her feet and stripped them both with all due haste, slowing only to pay homage to silky curves and her sweet flavor with hands and mouth as he uncovered her. Then he lifted her against the wall again and slid inside her welcoming heat as deep as he could go.

She shuddered along with him, whispering his name in his ear, her nails digging like goads in his shoulders. He tried to take his time, but his need for her outpaced his control. She was a fire in his blood, a wicked challenge of all the skill and experience he'd gathered over the years. With Aena every nerve ending became an erogenous zone. Just her breath against his ear was enough to push him to the edge, let alone her silky softness sliding against his damp skin and the sweet vise of her, encasing him in mind-blowing sensation. When she cried out his name, tightening and rippling around him, she sent him flying into that new place she'd forged for him, a vast world of intense pleasure and soul-deep satisfaction.

When he drifted back to reality, he slid to his knees, cradling her limp form. Her head rested on his shoulder, her fast breaths feathering across his damp throat. He closed his eyes, savoring the feel of her in his arms and the contentment washing through him like a river. He cupped the back of her head and realized he'd missed an important step. Clips still confined her hair, escaping strands clinging to her wet neck and temple.

With a slow smile he fixed the oversight, removing clasps and working his fingers through the freed strands of smoldering silk. Watching the river of color flow through his stroking hand and down her back, he murmured, "What brought this on?"

She stirred and he stopped breathing, sensation shooting up his spine from where he remained buried inside her. "Wasn't this the plan?" she said in a drowsy voice. "You asked me to a Blue Temple."

"You seduced me, sweet Aena."

She hummed, sending tingles across his skin. "You're easy to seduce." Then she sighed. "Though I wasn't supposed to. My father expects me to withhold myself to bring you in line." She lifted her head, smoky eyes focusing on him with solemn intensity. "What happened out there?"

He shook his head, securing her weight before pushing to his feet and stepping over to the pool. Sliding them both into the warm water, he caught her face between his hands and brushed her lips with his. "Your father is peddling human flesh. We found pens full of people."

She gasped, eyes wide and shocked.

He caught her hips as her body began floating away from him. "We declined his offer forcefully. The facility's gone, and all his people are either dead or in custody."

She shook her head, seeming more in dismay than denial. "And the people in pens?"

"Most are alive and also in custody for their protection. We lost some. One of Griffin's morons set off the self-destruct."

"Sun's tears." She stroked his jaw, a crease between her eyes, searching his features as though looking for wounds. "Were you hurt?"

"No, though we did lose a handful of fighters. The area's clean; not much evidence remains for Griffin to piece together what happened. How did he react?"

She looked down, mouth in a pensive line, hands coming to rest on his chest. "He's suspicious of your explanation. He feels you're playing a game with him."

"We are but probably not the way he thinks. We

need to keep him occupied."

She tilted her head, watching him with sharp eyes. "Why?"

He tugged her closer, loving the slippery feel of her. "We're closing in on him. Aena, I need you to come with me."

"We've already had this discussion."

"You're not safe with him. He's even crazier than we thought. We found Imago." He hesitated, studying her regale features and seeing the ghost of her father in them. How would she react to her father's madness?

"Wonderful, where was he?"

"Hovering over a Sun, about to kill it."

She froze, eyes wide and blank. "No," she whispered.

"Your father put him in charge of a star killer, Aena. And you can bet Imago wasn't the only one. Webster Griffin means to hold the entire galaxy hostage."

She shook her head in jerky denial, the tips of her wet hair spraying droplets around her. "That's—that's insanity." Her hands flew out, splashing water over the edge of the pool. "The FPA and governments wouldn't bow to such a threat."

"Wouldn't they? The Suns are our center of everything, from transportation and commerce to religious light and life. Without the star-way network, our civilization breaks down into isolation and darkness. Who wouldn't flinch from a threat like this?"

With a shudder she covered her face with her hands. "We can't let him."

"We're working on it. But you see why you can't go back. The man's a lunatic, capable of anything." He paused, assessing her hunched shoulders and trembling fingers. "He hurt you, didn't he?" Bile and rage rose in the back of his throat.

She dropped her hands, pained gaze meeting his then flicking away. "He would have hurt Boris and Kip worse. Do you...do you use prevention? I was afraid I'd conceived."

"Of course. Our father drilled responsibility into our heads long ago." He tucked a strand of hair behind her ear, enjoying the silky feel. "Were you afraid of motherhood or your father?"

She raised an eyebrow. "I believe you'll agree he's not quite grandfather material."

He grimaced. "Not even close. What did he do to you?"

"Nothing he hasn't done before." She shrugged and tugged out of his hold, inspecting the rows of soaps and oils. "Did you stop Imago?"

His stomach clenched. "Yes."

"How do you know there are more like him?"

"Cassie has an entire lab full of AIs Griffin was modifying into weapons."

Her hands clutched the side of the pool, mouth flattening to a thin line. "Can you tell me how you mean to stop him?"

"If you come with me, I'll tell you everything."

She sighed, glancing at him with faint reproof. He held out his hand and she clasped it, allowing him to tug her closer. "Kai, I can't."

"Yes, you can," he murmured, nuzzling his way from her jawline to her throat, sucking moisture off her skin with visceral delight. "I'll kidnap you if I have to."

She wrapped her arms around his neck and angled

her head, giving him better access. "You'll do no such thing. If my father truly means to hold the Suns hostage, we can do nothing to push him into it." Her voice had gone husky, softening the stern words.

The logic irritated him. With a rough sound in his throat he lifted his head and frowned at her. "I can't let him hurt you again."

Her features softened into a smile of such sweetness his heart flipped over. "You can't sacrifice an entire galaxy just to save me. Though I'm touched you think I'm worth saving." Then her smile turned sly. "On the other hand, my father would be quite pleased if I kidnapped you."

The idea went through him like lightning. He cocked his head, considering it. "Sweetheart, you have a terrible self-image but a brilliant mind. I'd be happy to be your hostage." Cradling her face in his hands, he whispered against her mouth, "And you're worth worlds to me."

She sagged against him with a soft sound, her lips parting to let him in. He made a teasing foray, humming in pleasure at her sweet taste. She sighed his name when he lifted his head, her eyes darkened with desire. Then she blinked, a crease forming between her brows. "I wasn't serious about kidnapping you."

He flashed a wicked smile, slipping his hands into the wet silk of her hair. "I was. I can keep Griffin busy and make sure he doesn't get near you. It's genius."

Her frown deepened, but before she could argue the cloth over the doorway rustled and his Blue priestess contact slipped in.

She gave them a brief smile of greeting and said, "I have news."

Liaena gasped and ducked into the water to her chin, huddling next to Kai. He tried not to laugh at this sudden endearing shyness and modesty. The ascetic ignored it, stepping over to the pool and settling at the edge without fanfare. Her lack of any typical Blue seduction and the urgency under her calm exterior sobered him in a hurry.

"What's happened, Vive?" he asked, tucking Aena close against him.

Her lithe form eased.

"We've discovered Webster Griffin's secret project." Her gaze flickered to Liaena and her eyebrows lifted in silent question.

"We're coming to the end," he responded. "She and I both need to know as much as possible at this point."

Aena straightened, pulling away from his hold with a small frown at the ascetic. "My father has many secret projects. To which are you referring?"

Vive tipped her head in a brief bow, her long bronzed braids slipping over one shoulder. "Lady Griffin, a pleasure to see you again. Your father has been gathering materials and experts in the fields of robotics and biomechanics. Where they go and what he's done with them has been a mystery. My Blue sisters and brothers did their best to infiltrate various branches of Quasicore and recover information. We were only able to pinpoint the location, but without the required skills we couldn't reach the heart of the matter. Such a knowledge base is the purview of a different Order."

Liaena made a sound of discovery. "The White," she murmured.

The ascetic smiled. "Yes, the White gifted Webster Griffin with a young man of extraordinary skill in those specific areas of learning. He is now a Core slave in every sense of the word, but his sacrifice was not in vain. He was able to pass on information to a waiting Blue, conveying the nature of this project."

Kai tensed. "Which is?"

A crease formed between the woman's warm eyes and the corners of her mouth turned down. "Apparently Webster Griffin wishes to live forever. He's attempting to imprint his neural pathways upon an AI matrix, inserted into a robotic replica of himself. The emperor does not wish to leave his throne." Her solemn gaze rested on Liaena. "If he succeeds, he will not need an heir. I fear you are in great danger."

Thunderous silence followed her words. Kai stared at the ascetic, muscles thrumming as though jolted over and over with an electric current. The man was utterly mad. And yet... "How close is he to succeeding?"

"We received limited information. But he appears to have at least a rudimentary working model."

Kai sucked in a sharp breath. They had no time to lose then. "I need to speak with my sister."

Vive rose with admirable grace. "I will bring you a viewer. Our security is the best we can make it. However, this information may be too sensitive for even our secure channels."

"Not to worry. We have an expert who'll secure the connection."

She nodded and headed for the back wall, tapping on what appeared to be a blank section. A doorway appeared. She paused on the threshold, sending a wry smile over her shoulder at them. "Your guards believe I am educating you on the finer points of worship. They were adorably flustered by the idea. But they shouldn't know I'm gone."

Kai nodded and she hesitated a moment longer, eyeing them in the water with a sensual shift in her expression. "Perhaps when I return we will go over a lesson or two, hmm?" Then she stepped beyond the threshold, the wall turning seamless again.

Aena made a strangled sound and Kai chuckled.

"She's teasing," he said, pulling her close and breathing in the addictive scent of peach blossoms on her skin. "But if you're feeling adventurous…"

"I'm not," she responded in a quelling tone, pulling out of his grip and stepping from the pool.

He watched water sluice off her slick curves with a surge of hunger.

"I won't share you."

He grinned, rising from the water. "What if she wants to share you with me?"

She flashed him a round-eyed stare and snatched a towel from a cubby, drying off fast as she made a beeline for her dress. Once she pulled it over her head, she recovered more of her usual poise. "I'm sure she doesn't. You're the one with a trail of women behind you." Her expression and tone darkened. "No doubt she's another of your conquests."

He laughed, delight sparkling through him. "Aena, are you jealous?"

"Of course I am," she said with a frown, not looking at him as she rubbed the wet strands of her hair with the towel. "Will you dress, please? How reliable is this Blue's information?"

Warmth and fierce desire rushed through him. His

Ice Queen, jealous. "Very. Vive's a veteran spy. Will you dry me?"

She glanced at him, her gaze zeroing in on his rampant erection. She dropped the towel, face turning a gorgeous rose color. "Oh…" she breathed and took a step toward him.

A growl of need and anticipation rose in his chest.

Then she hesitated, bit her lip, and looked at the blank wall where the ascetic had disappeared. "She'll return soon."

"And?"

She made an exasperated sound, eyes narrowing. "I'm not an exhibitionist. Get dressed, Kai."

With a sigh he grabbed a towel. "Damn. And it was one of my favorite fantasies of you."

"You've…had fantasies of me?" she asked in a hesitant voice.

He sent her a slow heated smile. "Sweetheart, you've starred in my fantasies for years."

Her cheeks flushed even more and her eyes grew smoky, lashes lowering to a sultry slant. She stepped close, lifting her mouth to his and sliding her hands over his racing heart. "Next time then," she whispered against his lips, setting him on fire from head to toe.

With a muffled groan he captured her mouth in a ravenous kiss.

Vive's return drove them apart. "My apologies," she said in a bland tone, keeping her gaze averted as she crossed the room and placed a portable viewer on the shelving unit.

Kai finished drying and headed for his clothing, amused when Aena accompanied him, blocking Vive's line of sight with a faint mutinous expression. He squashed the impulse to tease. They had more important things to address.

Sin answered his call in less than a minute, taking in his damp hair and Blue surroundings with a smirk. "Trouble in paradise, brother mine?"

"New developments. We need a secure line."

Her expression sharpening, she wasted no time applying some of Cassie's hefty security software. "Done. What is it?"

He told her of Webster's secret project and had Vive confirm the details.

Blanching, Sin muttered, "Holy Heart of the Sun."

"He wins the megalomaniac award of the millennium, no contest," Kai said in a dry tone. "Light a fire under Big M, Sissa. Griffin's gearing up for the big play."

Sin narrowed her eyes and tilted her head, studying him with far too much twin knowledge in her green eyes. "Why aren't you on your way home, Kai? You could have told me this in person instead of risking the viewer network."

He grinned, anticipating her reaction. "Aena's going to kidnap me."

Momentary alarm widened her eyes before her expression settled into wry amusement. "No more than you deserve, I'm sure," she drawled and he snickered.

"I refuse," Aena declared at his elbow, a crease between her brows and her lips in a thin line. "It's too dangerous."

Sin sobered. "Aena, dear, someone needs to protect you. Besides it gets him out of my hair for a while. Brilliant plan, really."

Kai snorted and Aena sighed, looking between

siblings with a shake of her head. "You are both much too reckless."

Sin studied her for a second. "Will you leave Griffin?"

"No. We can't risk inciting him now."

"Then what choice do we have?" Sin asked with infinite calm. She turned her attention to Kai. "You won't have backup, so keep your game face on, Brother. I'll light fires and get the party started."

"Suns, I just realized I'll be missing the fun."

Sin snickered. "Knowing you, you'll find plenty of your own. See you on the other side."

"Happy hunting, Sissa."

She flashed a grin as predatory as his own and then disappeared from the viewer.

Chapter 25

Liaena tried to resist Kai's rash plan, but she couldn't fight both him and herself. The idea of spending more time with him and having him there to bolster her courage eroded her defenses until she relented. Neither guard protested when she told them Kai would be joining them on their return to Griffin station. Boris looked relieved. He'd probably been anticipating another sleight-of-hand tactic to abduct her, even though Webster had surrounded the building with personnel to prevent such a thing. After seeing Vive's secret door, Liaena wasn't sure her father's aggressive measures would have been enough. Both the Blues and the Shays seemed equally capable of clever deception.

On the short trip from the planet's surface to the orbiting station, Liaena fretted over how to explain Kai's presence to her father. Webster wouldn't believe this ridiculous hostage story, and after discovering his human trafficking operation had been obliterated, his mood had turned suspicious. Was her father truly so far gone in his lust for power that he would threaten the fabric of their civilization and chase immortality? What Kai and Vive had told her about the Suns and his robotic clone seemed unbelievable, yet fit Webster's need for control and his recent secretive behavior. The possibility only underscored her need to stop him.

Kai seemed preoccupied, saying little on their

journey. He sent her several veiled looks but held her hand in a gentle clasp, warm and soothing. Was he nervous? If so, it didn't show in his composed features, relaxed posture, and steady hands. His touch plucked at her heartstrings, making it hard to retain her own composure.

Once they reached the station, Liaena led Kai on a direct path to the administration center, where they found her father waiting. His staff would have informed him of Kai's presence. The room's viewers and control panels showed nothing, their blank displays in standby mode. Of course Webster wouldn't want Kai to see the inner workings of his world.

Her father watched them approach with a bland expression and glittering eyes, hands clasped at the small of his back. "Manakai, to what do I owe the pleasure of your company?"

Kai flashed a disarming grin and slipped an arm around her waist. "Sorry to drop in unannounced, Web, but I couldn't bring myself to leave Aena this time. I let her kidnap me."

Webster's eyebrow lifted slightly, his mouth curving in a brittle smile. "How enterprising of you. Your time at the Temple was enlightening then?" he asked, turning his icy gaze on Liaena.

Kai responded before she could reply. "Oh, yes. Your daughter has swept me right off my feet." He glanced at her with such heated tenderness her knees threatened to buckle. "I'm here to request permission to court your daughter, sir."

"Quaint and a bit belated. You appear to have already begun."

Kai turned a somber expression on her father. "My

Michelle O'Leary

relationships with women have never been this serious. I wanted to formalize my intentions."

Liaena's heart jackknifed in her chest. She assumed he said it to impress her father. But how wonderful would it be if it were true? Warm tingles spread from his touch throughout her body.

"Hmm." Webster studied them with sharp gray eyes. "So you mean for this to end in a Sun-bonding."

"It's my fondest hope, sir." He gave Liaena a heart-stopping smile and tightened his hold on her. "It'll take me a while to convince Aena, but I'll enjoy every second."

"I'm sure," Webster said in a dry tone. "Is courtship your only reason for this visit?"

Kai sobered. "I also wanted to apologize in person for the unfortunate incident at your facility. Such a waste. I'd like to make it up to you, Web."

"While I appreciate your regret, I do wonder why my representatives became so…reactive. The site was entirely destroyed, not a measure they would have taken lightly."

Kai shrugged with a baffled expression. "I wondered the same. The situation didn't call for it. Maybe it was accidental or someone might have snapped. Do you screen your people for stability?"

Liaena had to work hard to hide her reaction. Her father chose many of his underlings for their instabilities, not in spite of them.

Webster's mouth twisted. "Anything is possible, I suppose. I also wonder how you escaped such a calamity intact."

"Luck and a fast ship. Will you let my sister know what reparations we can make?"

"I will be delighted to speak with Sinsudee. However, reparations may not be necessary. Will you be staying with us long?"

Kai turned a boyish grin toward her, a mischievous sparkle in his gorgeous eyes. "Depends on my warden."

"I'm sure you'll stay as long as it suits you," she responded in a dry tone, giving him a cool look. She didn't think her father would appreciate humor at this point.

Webster made a noncommittal sound in his throat. "Daughter, make our guest comfortable if you will." Tipping his silvered head in an ironic bow to Kai, he said, "Do enjoy your captivity, Manakai."

With a careless smile Kai answered, "Thank you, I will," and turned to her with an expectant lift of his eyebrows.

"Good day, Father," she murmured and led Kai from the room. Aware of the constant surveillance, she linked her arm through his and strolled down the corridor as if they were on holiday. "A tour perhaps? What would you like to see first?"

"Your bedroom," he purred, his slow hungry smile sending her heart into a sprint. He could ignite Suns with the green fire in his eyes.

Her insides melted and she almost tripped over her own feet. "Kai," she husked then cleared her throat. "I'd love to but we'll find little privacy here."

He blinked and frowned. "What do you mean? Do you have someone in your quarters?"

"In a way." She studied his features, trying to decide whether he'd forgotten about the surveillance or if he were acting. "Our security system is quite…extensive."

He stopped in the corridor and stared at her, his blank shock turning into thunderheads of ire. "Show me," he barked.

So, acting then. Liaena wondered what his plan was this time. With a gracious nod she escorted him to her rooms.

He took a cursory look around the small living room and open kitchenette then sent her a puzzled glance. "This is where you live? Feels like a hotel suite."

Thinking of his and his sister's private places with their spacious warmth and personal touches, she blushed in unexpected embarrassment. "I need little space and I don't like clutter. We move from station to station often."

He nodded, grim shadows gathering in his eyes. "Even so, everyone deserves privacy. Where are they?"

Keeping her expression neutral, she pointed out the security sensors in the living room and kitchenette.

With the air of a man on a critical mission he gathered a paring knife from kitchen storage and a chair from her dining nook. Standing on the chair, he pried each of the sensors out of the walls and dropped them to the floor, crushing them under his heel. When finished, he glanced at her with a conspiratorial gleam in his eyes and twitch of his mouth. "Next?"

Heart thundering in her ears, she led the way to her bedroom and showed him the sensors there.

With a dark scowl he muttered, "I'm the only one who gets to watch you undress," and went to work. Once he destroyed the surveillance there, he tipped his head toward the san and lifted his eyebrows in question.

Without a word she preceded him into her wash

room and identified the sensor. He made a harsh sound in his throat. "No one sees you naked but me," he growled and ripped it out of the wall. Once he crushed it underfoot, his jealous outrage morphed into mischievous humor. "Damn, that was fun. Do you want to take a turn stomping them?"

Liaena flung her arms around him and held tight, shaking with reaction. She didn't care if he'd been acting for her watchers; tearing down the surveillance in her quarters was like rescuing her from prison. He'd done the one thing she'd dreamt of doing since childhood. Her father would replace them, but for the moment she was free.

"Easy, Aena." He made soothing circles on her back. "Are you all right?"

She nodded, pressing her face against him and inhaling his delicious scent. He smelled like everything she'd ever wanted in life. "This was the most wonderful thing anyone's ever done for me," she whispered in a shaky voice. "Father won't like it."

"I'll play the jealous lover and he'll back off. In case we missed any..." He slid a hand along her arm and pressed the spot over Cassie's gift, activating it. Then he cupped a hand under her chin and lifted, studying her face with warm concern. "How long has he kept such close watch on you?"

"All my life."

His features darkened in a flash of anger before filling with remorse. He sighed, resting his forehead against hers. "I'm sorry, honey. We should have seen it. We should have helped you."

She shivered, absorbing his words with a throbbing heart and aching soul. "I was a Griffin and didn't let you see. But you can help me now. Help me stop him, for all our sakes."

"Deal." He kissed her, his lips light and gentle, but she didn't want gentle right now.

Her heart was too full and needy. Sinking her fingers in his thick silky hair, she kissed him back with all the emotion she'd held in check for too long, all the need and desire he'd awakened in her. For the moment he was hers, and she didn't mean to waste a second of her precious freedom.

He responded as if she'd set flame to tinder, his mouth and hands wild and demanding. With a deep groan he carried her into the other room and her narrow bed, where he stripped them both and showed her yet again how far passion could take them into paradise.

Afterward, she lay in the curve of his body, her back to his chest, limp and sated in his arms. A hazy cloud of bliss fogged her mind and turned her usually cold world into a place of warmth and contentment. "You're entirely too good at this," she mumbled, her voice slow and drowsy with satisfaction.

His rumble of humor vibrated from his chest into her back. Warm breath brushed her hair before his lips found the sensitive skin on the side of her neck. "Still jealous?"

She hummed, eyes closing at the tingling sensations he made with his too-talented mouth. "How can I not be? You'll move on to someone new soon." Her contentment faded at the stark reality in her words.

He lifted his head and the air cooled her skin. "What makes you say that?"

She sent him a wry look over her shoulder. "You were the one who said your reputation was well deserved."

"Hmm." He studied her with heavy-lidded eyes, strong cheekbones still flushed from exertion and damp hair curling at his temples.

He was without a doubt the most beautiful man she'd ever met in her life, but also the most courageous, driven, competent, and kind. Her hero. Her downfall. When he left, he'd rip out her heart and soul. How would she survive it?

"Aena, do you know why I've gone from woman to woman all these years?"

"You like sex," she said dryly.

He flashed a wicked grin. "Besides that." He brushed a strand of hair from her face, coiling it around his finger. "I was looking for my dream woman, the one who fit, who could match me in all things and challenge me in everything. Useless search, since I'd already found her." He rested his chin on her shoulder and smiled with such sweetness her heart cracked. "I knew you were her the second we met and you took me down with a kick to the shin."

The universe seemed to slow to a halt. Her heart stopped and her lungs collapsed. Had she fallen asleep and this was some fantastic dream?

His smiled faded and his eyebrows lifted. "You've gone statue again. Are you all right?"

Her vision went gray at the edges. Sucking in a much-needed breath, she wheezed, "Manakai Ezekiel Shay, if you are playing another game I will never forgive you."

His smile returned with an irresistible twinkle in his eyes. "I'd love to play lots of games with you, Aena, but this isn't one of them."

She shifted to her back, staring at him in growing wonder. Her fingers traced the curve of his smile. "Kai, are you saying what I think you're saying?"

He kissed the tips of her fingers then leaned forward to brush his lips against hers. "I'm in love with you, Liaena Griffin. I have been most of my life. If that doesn't scare you, you're a braver woman than most."

Her eyes stung and his features wavered as tears welled. "How can that possibly be?" she breathed with bittersweet longing. "You've acted as though you've hated me for years."

"I tried to hate you. You were everything I wanted but couldn't have." He cradled her face and brushed his lips against her damp lashes. "Please don't cry, honey. It's killing me."

She laid a hand over his, soaking in the strength and tenderness in his touch like desert sand greedy for rain. She blinked, but the tears continued to fall, blurring the strain on his face. "I'd be a fool to believe it," she whispered. "Only my mother has ever loved me. I'm not sure I deserve love."

"What?" He shook his head, brushing hair away from her face. "Why would you say that?"

"I let my father unleash such horrible cruelty and evil. For years I've known he was a monster and did nothing."

"What could you do? You were only one person, Aena."

She closed her eyes and turned her face away, easing out of his hold to sit up. "I could have killed him," she murmured, her chest heavy with regret and guilt. "I could have ended his life and saved so many others. But I'm his daughter. How can I kill my own father?"

Kai ran a soothing hand down her arm, twining his fingers with hers. "No one could ask it of you, and his death wouldn't stop anything anyway. Quasicore is a massive machine with its own momentum. It needs to come down with him or the cruelty and evil won't end."

She pressed her lips together and said nothing. Silence had been her habit and protection for too long for her to give it up now.

With a sigh Kai stretched out on his back and opened his arms, an invitation she couldn't resist. Snuggling into his side, she rested her head on his shoulder and splayed a hand over his heart, marveling at its strong and steady beat.

"Everyone deserves love," he said in a quiet voice, kissing the top of her head. "Not everyone gets it. I'm sorry you were alone for so long."

"I survived."

"And you didn't break or turn into a copy of your father, which makes you amazing." His tone lightened. "Did I mention I love you?"

She smiled at the teasing lilt in his voice, the words sending her stomach into a flip. "You did." She hesitated then added with a twinge of worry, "And you're not allowed to take it back."

"Never." He paused and then cleared his throat. "Aena, sweetheart, you're leaving me hanging."

Basking in his warmth and the stunning possibility he might truly have deep feelings for her, she took a few seconds to hear him. Puzzled, she lifted her head to study his face. He wore a wry smile and an odd shadow in his eyes.

"What do you mean?"

He heaved a sigh, bouncing her on his chest. "You've never made anything easy," he grumbled. "Liaena, I need to know how you feel about me."

"Oh!" She stared at him in shock. "How could you not know? I've been pathetic and obvious, Kai."

He rolled his eyes and fisted his hands in her hair, planting a hard kiss on her mouth. "You are the exact opposite of obvious, my little Ice Queen," he growled against her lips. She forgot the question and kissed him back until he pulled away with a breathless laugh. "Lust we have in spades," he panted, meeting her gaze with such open directness it stole the air from her lungs. "I need more."

She gulped then threw caution to the wind. What did she have to lose at this point? Shimmying to lie full length on top of him, she framed his face with her hands and said in a trembling voice, "Manakai Ezekiel Shay, I've been in love with you since you broke my fountain and destroyed my father's art collection. You are the—" She didn't get to finish her declaration.

Wild fire flared in his emerald eyes and he rose up, sealing his mouth to hers with soul-stealing passion and rolling until he lay atop her. After several minutes of driving her out of her mind with his mouth and hands, he lifted his head and rasped, "Sorry, you were saying?"

She blinked in hazy confusion. "What?"

"You started to say, 'You are the...' "

With his hard muscles pressing in all the right places, his clever hands still busy setting fires on her skin, and his erection a demanding brand against her abdomen, she could barely think, let alone frame coherent sentences. "I don't remember."

He laughed and proceeded to make love to her with slow agonizing sweetness. In the middle of this delicious torture, as he danced her right along the edge of a glorious climax, he said, "Bond with me, Aena," in a deep ragged voice filled with urgency and longing.

Overwhelming joy pushed her over into ecstasy. Riding waves of soul-deep pleasure, all she could say was "Yes, oh Suns, yes!"

****

Kai stared at Webster Griffin's smug face and wondered when the hell the cavalry would arrive. He was running out of safe ways to distract the man. He could play other cards to capture Griffin's attention, but they might hold more truth than his sister and the FPA were ready for. At the moment, Webster basked in the glory of his victory over Kai, satisfaction oozing from every pore. He might still be suspicious of the younger man's presence on his station, but he couldn't mistake Kai's sincere attachment to his daughter. This triumph wouldn't hold his attention for much longer, though.

Forking another bite of steak into his mouth, Kai chewed without tasting it, his gaze skipping over the food-laden table to find Liaena. She'd cloaked her true beauty in a submissive-daughter routine, nauseating but effective. She sat with perfect posture, features downcast, hands moving with precise elegance as she cut her food into small pieces and ate them. Watching Aena put anything in her mouth should have been erotic as hell, but the replacement of his sensual siren with this obedient robot turned his stomach. The oppressive opulence of the dining hall with its overlarge table and abundance of wait staff didn't help either. Webster Griffin, putting on a domineering show for his captured guest.

If this went on much longer, Kai might have to resort to plan B. Blood would flow, but it'd be much more satisfying. Relief came in the form of a beefy man scuttling into the dining hall with a wild look in his eyes. Griffin leveled him with a disapproving frown for the interruption, but the man didn't slow, bending close to his boss.

His whisper carried across the vast table. "Sir, we have trouble." He held out a small viewer.

Griffin glanced at the viewer and stiffened, his features turning glacial. Kai set his fork down, watching the man with a lurch of excitement. Had it begun?

Webster lifted his glittering gaze to Kai, mouth curving in a cool polite smile. "I beg your pardon. I must attend to some business."

"Of course. Anything I can help with?"

The man's eyes narrowed a fraction, but his smile remained. "Perhaps. I'll let you know. Please excuse me." He rose to his feet and headed for the exit, his minion on his heels.

Kai watched him go then met Liaena's troubled gaze, acutely aware of the remaining people in the room. If Sin's party had started, they needed to be by Griffin's side, ready to stop his itchy Sun-killing trigger finger. Keeping his senses tuned to the wait staff, he stood and rounded the table. Before he could reach Liaena, the room began swimming in his vision.

One of the staff asked in a low puzzled voice, "Why is the door locked?"

Alarm flared, the jolt of adrenaline taking him the few stumbling steps to Liaena's seat before he crashed to his knees. She reached for him, murmuring an unintelligible question, then slumped and slid from the seat, landing in an unconscious sprawl across his lap. Kai tried to catch her, but his limbs refused to function. The room tilted and the floor gave him an ungentle kiss on the side of his face. Then the world went away.

When it returned, Kai found himself suspended like a fly in amber, floating in an interrogator's force field. His head throbbed, his vision blurred, and his mouth tasted like burnt slicer grease. He blinked and squinted, trying to bring the room into focus. He appeared to be in Griffin's control room, all of the viewers and systems active. Griffin stood at a workstation like a king surveying his holdings, his back to Kai. Nearby Liaena sat in a demure posture, hands folded in her lap and crossed ankles tucked under her chair. She wore her cool serene mask, but tension stiffened the elegant line of her back.

Prickles of dismay kicked Kai's heart into a sprint. He swallowed the horrible taste in his throat and tried to speak. "Web, you got the wrong idea." He sounded like a frog croaking, but loud enough to catch their attention. "I like kink and you get points for enthusiasm, but I'm taken. Sorry, man."

Griffin's smile could freeze the heart of a psychotic killer. "Amusing as always, Manakai. No doubt you're wondering why you've been detained."

"Not for kinky fun? Darn. Aena, honey, we gotta try this thing later." He sent her a wink, ignoring her wide eyes and the slight shake of her head. Provoking Griffin might be dangerous, but it kept the man's attention away from the viewers and control systems.

Griffin's eyes narrowed. "I've decided you'll be some assistance after all. A large FPA force is on its way to my station. What do you know of it?"

Unable to shrug, Kai cocked his head in careless dismissal. "I know my head hurts and my mouth tastes like krell dung. You could've used a gas with less side effects. I know a few, if you want pointers."

Griffin's eyes were a mix of ash and ice, cold glittering death lying in wait. "You used a militant force to destroy the facility and my enterprise. Was it perhaps an FPA offshoot?"

Kai let his mouth curve in a slow smile and said nothing.

"An employee of mine gave a description of you visiting one of my armament warehouses. Afterward the FPA became strangely proficient in tracking those armaments. You've begun a dangerous game, little Shay."

Kai pretended offense. "Not so little. Ask your daughter."

Fury drew brief dark lines across the man's face before disappearing into icy resolve. Griffin hefted the controller for the interrogator and moved closer.

Kai gave him a hard grin and said softly, "Time for some fun, Griff?"

"Father," Liaena interrupted, pale with strain. "The FPA will be here soon."

When Griffin turned away, Kai sent her a frown. They didn't need the man refocusing on the ensuing crisis. She ignored his look, giving her father all her dutiful attention.

"As usual you have a keen grasp of the obvious, Daughter. They'll find nothing, however. Our guests will be leaving soon, including this one." He gestured to Kai without looking at him. "There is little need for concern."

"What guests?" Kai prompted, watching on a viewer as the FPA ships approached the station. Another viewer showed a handful of disheveled people stumbling from holding cells and moving with an armed escort down a corridor. He smothered a grim smile. He hadn't been able to visit the Red ascetics, and though Aena had assured him they still lived, seeing them gave him some relief.

When Griffin ignored him and moved back toward his workstation, Kai grimaced and threw down a high card. "Hey Griff, I hear you've been looking for your bond-mate."

The older man stiffened and spun, his features as fierce and cold as a viper's before it strikes.

"Zofie says hi. Bad news; she had your bond marks removed. Harsh, but who knew women don't like being imprisoned on tropical island paradises?"

Griffin's silent snarl of rage gave him a surge of intense satisfaction.

"You and the Red Sun," Webster mused in a slow thoughtful tone. "How enlightening."

Behind him, Liaena rose to her feet, fear cracking through her serene mask.

Keeping his gaze on the elder Griffin, Kai flashed a charming smile. "Nice pun, Web. Yes, the Reds and I made a decent team. Enough to slip Zofie right out from under your nose. She's thrilled to be free."

"Where is she?" His tone commanded, hands fisting at his sides, face reddened and eyes narrowed to slits.

"Out of your reach, Web. Where she belongs."

"Insolent brat," Griffin growled, stalking toward

him. "You will tell me."

"Please," Liaena interrupted again, frustrating the hell out of Kai. What was she doing? They'd discussed keeping her father distracted at all costs. Kai hadn't planned to be stuck in an interrogator while doing it, but it was working. "You mustn't hurt him. The FPA—"

Griffin whirled on his daughter and she fell silent. Kai tensed against the force holding him, unable to hold still with Griffin's aggression aimed at Aena.

"Still your foolish tongue, Daughter. I've already said the FPA are no threat, merely an inconvenience. You see how they deploy? They've not even sense enough to surround the station. We'll be away before they can fumble out of their ships."

"Why do you think they've come, Griff? Do you think they'd mobilize like this for a handful of crazy Reds?" The line he walked thinned to a razor's edge under his feet. If he pushed too far, gave too much information, Griffin might decide it was time to take the galaxy hostage and claim his empire. "How much did your bond-mate know anyway?"

Past Griffin's shoulder a viewer revealed the group of Reds and guards entering a discreet docking bay. Urgency filled him. The FPA agents were taking too long.

Griffin glanced over his shoulder. "She knew nothing, but your question is interesting. Why have they come in such force? And why was I not informed?" He approached a control panel, shooting his daughter a veiled look of suspicion.

Kai closed his eyes and sent a silent apology to his sister and new bond brother. He had to have some way to drag their nemesis' attention away from his systems. Griffin was about to find out he no longer had protection in the FPA. "Speaking of bond-mates, did you know my sister has one?"

Both Griffins turned to stare at him. Liaena hadn't known either.

"She's been playing you, Web. You seem to have trouble keeping women interested. I can give you pointers on that too, if you like."

Webster's face reddened again, but his features sharpened with intense speculation. "Why are you deliberately provoking me?"

"I wondered the same," Liaena said in her cool smooth voice, shooting him a warning glance. "Perhaps he doesn't believe you will hurt him." On the word *hurt* a ripple of fear disturbed her serenity.

Kai clenched his jaw in sudden understanding. She'd been trying to keep her father from torturing him. Her concern lit a warm glow in his chest but complicated the at-all-costs part of the plan.

"Of course he won't," he responded, playing into her words. "He's just mad I'm piddling in his pool. What's the matter, Web? Can't take the competition?"

Griffin approached at a slow hunter's stalk, face twitching with poorly contained fury. "More provocation. Why? What are you hiding?" He lifted the interrogator's controller.

"Father, stop," Liaena blurted. "We don't have time."

He paused, studying Kai with unnerving icy intelligence. "You are correct, Daughter. Consorting with Reds no doubt taught him to resist pain and our time is limited. Shall we try a different method?" Like a striking snake, his hand lashed out and caught her by the throat, dragging her close. "You are his weakness."

She made a choking sound and Kai surged against his restraints.

"Get your hands off her!" Kai snarled and fought the force field with everything he had.

Griffin smiled. "You see? Even Shays have their breaking points. Thank you for finally being useful, dear Daughter. Tell me what I want to know, Manakai, or watch your love suffer. Every bruise will be—"

With a suddenness that made Kai blink, the elder Griffin's head snapped back, cords standing out in his neck as his limbs spasmed.

He fell to the floor at Liaena's feet, twitching. His daughter stared down at him with a suspended expression, a small humming riot rod clenched in her raised fist.

"Aena," Kai exclaimed in startled relief.

She jumped and glanced his way, not meeting his eye. "More effective than I expected," she murmured.

"He'll recover soon. We need to secure him. Let me loose."

She hesitated, then bent and snatched the controller from her father's tight grip as though taking a bone from a rabid krell. When she pointed the device at the interrogator, the force field relented, dropping Kai to his feet.

He couldn't resist pulling her into his arms, his heart thumping with residual horror. Studying the red marks on her throat, he rasped, "Are you all right?"

She nodded, looking oddly preoccupied. "How do we secure him?"

Letting her go took a surprising amount of effort.

"Turnabout's fair play," he answered with a grim smile and stepped over to his nemesis.

The man looked quite a bit less intimidating, sprawled and groaning in awkward indignity on the floor, his silvered hair mussed and his red features wracked with pain. Kai hefted him over his shoulder and carried him to the interrogator.

Then he smiled at Aena. "Would you do the honors?"

A crease formed between her brows, but she didn't hesitate. A moment later, Webster Griffin hung suspended in his own torture device. Kai had never seen a more vindicating sight.

"Well, if this isn't justice, I don't know what is," he announced with a satisfied smile, propping hands on hips and rocking on the balls of his feet. "Comfy, Griff?"

"You…you'll pay…" Webster wheezed, gray eyes shooting ice daggers.

"Right." Kai snapped his fingers, realizing his own mistake. He took swift inventory of the room but didn't see anything he could use as a gag. Clapping a muffling hand over the man's mouth, he eyed the controller in Aena's clasp. "Does this thing have a mute button? I don't want your father setting off any verbal commands." He winced as Griffin's teeth grazed his palm. "And when's the last time he was checked for transmittable diseases?"

Liaena touched the device, and Griffin's smothered growl of rage stopped as if cut off with a knife.

Kai lifted his hand away and stared at it in disgust before wiping his palm on his pants. Then he headed for the control systems. "Let's see how much your father left us."

"He began a purge of data while you were still unconscious. The FPA will find little," Aena supplied, still standing in front of her father. She seemed fascinated by the sight of him immobilized and helpless.

Webster fixed her with a commanding glare, but she appeared immune.

"Why have they come?"

Studying the control systems and watching the FPA agents disembark, he answered, "We knew if we mounted a frontal assault to rescue the Reds or tried to sneak aboard, Griffin would kill and dispose of them. The FPA pressured him into doing our work for us, getting the Reds off this station with less protection. My sister is rescuing them as we speak." He frowned. "Can you stop this purge?"

She whispered something to her father then answered, "No."

"Doesn't matter. We'll get what we need from his other stations." He turned to find his enemy's murderous stare riveted on him. He smiled, wishing Sin could be here for this moment. "Webster Griffin, we have you cold. The Reds will testify to what you've done. Your moles in the FPA have all been caught, so no more blocking justice. The evidence of your weapons deals continues to grow. It'll provide us the wedge we need to crack open this company and tear it down to the foundations. You're done and so is Quasicore."

Liaena turned to him with a vibrant expression, an intensity as fierce as the birth of a Sun. "No, it's not." She held a data pad out to her father.

His fingers moved; she must have decreased the force field.

Griffin touched the pad's screen.

With a lurch of alarm, Kai started toward them. "What did you do?"

Liaena wore a frightening amount of sorrow and regret on her beautiful features as she met Kai's gaze. "He's transferred complete control of Quasicore to me. I told him I could save it and I mean to."

Webster shook with silent mocking laughter, gray eyes blazing in a face filled with cruel triumph.

Kai stared at her, aghast. Had they done all this, so many years of struggle and loss, only to start the battle over with a new Griffin? "Aena, why? This company was built on blood and death. It runs on evil and the worst human vices, feeding itself with its own corruption. Why would you want to save it?"

She glanced from him to Webster, her mouth twisting into a pained smile. "It seems neither of you know me. Father believes he's found a worthy heir at last. You believe you've found a new enemy." She shook her head and moved away, staring at several viewers. They showed deploying FPA forces moving throughout the station. "Do you have any idea how large this company is? How much of our civilization relies on its framework? Most of the people working for Quasicore aren't pure evil. You should know, Kai." She sent him a stern glance. "You've taken several under your wing over the years."

"Aena, Quasicore is a monster. It has to be stopped."

"And when the monster falls, how many lives will be crushed under its weight?"

Kai went still, absorbing the silver light in her eyes, the cool determination in her regal stance. Sudden understanding struck him with the force of a divine fist. This woman, abused and oppressed by her tyrant of a father, hadn't become his slave or his replica. She hadn't fled or tried to save herself. She'd stayed for the same responsibility and need that drove Sin and Kai to rescue people from the Core. But the scope of her plan grew so much grander than theirs. She wouldn't save a handful; she meant to save them all.

Emotion swept through him, nearly dropping him to his knees. If he hadn't known before how much he loved her, this moment cleared all doubt. With a crooked smile he bowed. "My Lady Griffin, I stand in awe and concede the field."

Her expression softened with the beginnings of a smile, but before she could reply, Nick burst into the room with a contingent of FPA agents, weapons at the ready.

Kai lifted his hands to ward them off. "Stand down."

Nick froze when he saw Griffin's current position, then sent Kai a startled glance. "Well, that's anticlimactic. How'd he get in there?"

Kai smirked and nodded at Liaena.

She tilted her elegant head, acknowledging the group. "Thank you for coming. I hope you encountered little resistance."

Nick blinked and holstered his weapon. "A scuffle here and there, nothing major. I expected more."

"My father would have played the upstanding citizen wrongfully accused and harassed by the FPA. Circumstances have changed, as you see. Are the Red

Sun ascetics well?"

"Word is Sin has them and the baddies in custody."

Kai grinned and turned to a com unit. A moment later his sister's face appeared on a viewer. "Hey, Sissa. Great party."

"Thanks. How's your end?"

Without a word he shifted so she could see past him to Griffin.

A slow smile curled her lips and lit her eyes. "Well now. Isn't that a pleasant sight? Webster, you've never looked so good."

With a discreet cough Liaena caught their attention. "I would like to see First Marshal Marchand as soon as possible. But first, may I have a word with my father?"

Kai shrugged and waved to the agents. "Up to them. He's in FPA hands now."

Looking uncomfortable, Nick nodded. Liaena made a few adjustments on a control panel then approached the interrogator. She studied her father with a crease between her brows. "I've disabled all verbal command systems. You will be unable to trigger any defenses." She lifted the controller and released him from his confinement.

With a ripple of unease the agents readied their weapons again and took defensive positions. Kai shifted forward, placing himself within reach in case the man tried anything. He rather hoped Griffin would. Giving his nemesis a few bruises and maybe a couple of minor breaks would be the perfect ending to this day.

Webster Griffin ignored them, staring at his child with cold clinical interest.

"Father, you have been the root of so much misery,

377

but you've taught me endurance, and for that I thank you. So you understand my part, let me explain what I've done." She sketched a brief description of her assistance with Zofie's rescue and her retrieval of the keystone information leading to his downfall.

His face darkened with every word, fists clenching at his sides.

When she finished, he declared, "This isn't over."

She shook her head, her mouth curving down in regret. "You're thinking somehow to trigger this awful plan you have for the Suns and to preserve your power and control through an artificial clone."

He jerked as though stabbed, eyes widening.

She sighed. "Yes, we know. And yes, I imagine the FPA is busy dismantling both vile projects as we speak. So you're wrong. It is truly over."

Kai moved closer as the man's face turned a dangerous brick color, fury throbbing in a vein at his temple. His civilized veneer peeled away, showing the savage beast beneath, his teeth bared and rabid hate in his eyes. He reached for his daughter with clawed hands but then froze at the simultaneous warnings ringing out from all points in the room. Like a cornered animal, his gaze flicked over the armed agents. A shudder passed through him, then cold descended in a wave, wiping his expression and straightening his spine.

He dropped his hands to his sides, met Liaena's gaze, and smiled with such icy hate Kai's heart spasmed in his chest. "I've been so wrong about you, Daughter. Look what you've done, hiding in the shadows, waiting for the perfect moment to stab your own kin in the back and take over. You are your father's daughter, the perfect Griffin. Congratulations, my dear."

Liaena's head snapped back as if slapped, her face blanching.

Kai lunged forward, grabbed the controller, and put the bastard back into silent suspension. Swallowing raw fury, he looked at her. "Aena, he deserves death for all he's done. Say the word and I'll make it happen." The lack of protest from the FPA agents in the room gratified him.

She straightened, mouth thinning to a white line. Staring at her father, she gave her head a slow shake. "Death is too easy an escape. He should be made to face his crimes. Obscurity will be his punishment. We're free of you, Father, Mother and I, the Shays, everyone. I will undo all your work, erase your stamp on our lives. If I do it right, you'll be forgotten and even history will barely mark your passing. You'll shrink into a tiny unimportant shadow, where all monsters belong."

Griffin blanched then went rigid, his handsome face twisting into such an ugly rictus of hate he appeared inhuman. Liaena turned from him with an air of dismissal, her movements and features calm as she met Kai's gaze. But residual pain still darkened her eyes.

With a grim clench of his jaw, Kai tossed the interrogator's controller to Nick. "Inspector Givliani, if I were you, I'd roll him out like this. Healthier for all of us and safer for him." Catching Aena's elbow and turning her toward the exit, he sent one last glance at his lifelong enemy. "Game's over, Web. Enjoy your time in hell."

Epilogue

Liaena watched First Marshal Marchand across his utilitarian desk and did her best not to smile. The situation didn't call for it, but her mouth kept trying to curve. The way the austere man glanced from her to the others in the room, a hint of puzzled unease in his piercing gaze, amused her. She didn't think much surprised or disconcerted the head of the FPA, but the people seated in a row behind her seemed to have done it. The four heads of the Sun Orders, Golden Berrabas, White K'etarci, Blue Lekasha, and Red T'Zai, had insisted on being present for her interview with the First Marshal.

She had to admit they'd surprised her too. They'd declared themselves witnesses in her defense, but she couldn't think what they'd witnessed.

"You understand your detainment was a formality," Marchand told her, seeming to address the Orders as well. "You won't be charged for your father's crimes."

"Aren't I an accessory? I witnessed his atrocities for years but did nothing to stop them."

He focused on her with unnerving intensity, flicking a finger at her still-bruised throat. "Victims of abuse cannot be held accountable for their abuser's actions. Your cooperation with us and the Shays will also count in your favor. So will your testimony against your father. My biggest concern is your new position as head of Quasicore. This places the responsibility for all its activities on your shoulders."

She inclined her head in acknowledgement. "I know it would be easier to declare the entire company defunct, but I can't in good conscience destroy the lives of so many because of the actions of a few. Much of this company's foundations remain legitimate. My goal is to remove the criminal branches of this organization while leaving the lawful ones intact."

When he gave her a dubious frown, she lifted a hand to forestall him.

"I realize the scope of what I'm planning. I will cooperate fully with the FPA and make all changes transparent. In fact I beg your assistance in purging the corruption. I won't be able to do this without help."

His frown lingered, turning more thoughtful. "What you're asking would take years to implement. The courts might object, but complete access to Quasicore's information systems would push them in the direction you want to go."

Folding her hands in her lap, she studied him for a long moment. This hard man wasn't offering compassion or understanding, but she appreciated his plain direct speech. "I will protect the privacy of my employees, but all other data is yours provided final decisions and the responsibility for them remain with me."

His expression eased into an almost-smile. "Thank you for your cooperation, Ms. Griffin. Looks like Quasicore's people are in much better hands."

She certainly hoped so. Her father's parting shot still stung, raising lingering doubts and guilt. *I am not my father.* But he'd always be a part of her, whether she wanted it or not. She'd just have to remember his constructive lessons and avoid repeating the vicious ones.

"You'll change the name," T'Zai suddenly announced.

Startled, she turned in her seat to stare at him. "Of Quasicore? I did plan to. How did you know?"

All four of them smiled, mysterious and unsettling. "To what?" T'Zai asked.

Facing these Sun Orders, she had a moment's anxiety about the name she'd chosen for her company. Would they be offended? Clearing her throat, she responded, "New Dawn Holdings."

Their smiles brightened. Not offended then, thank the Stars.

"Yes, it will be," T'Zai said with a nod. "A new dawn, a new change—"

"Balance," the other three chorused, then smirked at one another like old friends.

"We were right about her," T'Zai added with a smug glance at his companions.

Irritation formed a crease in her brow. "How so? What is it you believe you know about me?"

T'Zai nodded as if she'd agreed with him instead of challenging his words. "We know you are compassionate. You visited my captured brethren and gave them hope, though you couldn't free them yourself."

She blinked, remembering her interviews with the Red ascetics quite differently. Before she could contradict him, K'etarci spoke in a dry sharp tone.

"You are prudent. You wisely chose not to be

present when I spoke with your father and sent one of my own into his service."

She frowned. She'd had little choice. Both her father and the White had brushed her off.

"My Blue sister has described your selflessness," Lekasha murmured, her voice a smooth river of sound, as though she recited poetry or scripture. "You were willing to risk yourself to free your mother and shield the Shays from your father's wrath."

Berrabas began as his companion stopped speaking, as if they'd rehearsed it like a song. His sonorous baritone filled the room without overpowering it. "We've witnessed your steadfastness for many years. You stood in your father's shadow yet didn't wither. You deflected or blunted his cruelty with a skill rivaling my own greatest diplomats while remaining unseen to his eye and his heart." He smiled, the perceptive gleam in his eyes a sharp contrast to his round unassuming features. "You are a worthy successor, not because you reflect your father but because you are his opposite. We thank you for staying true."

Her throat closed. She sat mute and staring, eyes prickling with the threat of tears.

"Overdoing it, as usual," T'Zai drawled, sending his Golden counterpart a glance full of amused contempt. "Golds never know when to stop talking. Will you excuse us, Liaena? We need to have a private word with Gaston."

An incredulous laugh pushed for escape, but she swallowed it, swiveling her head toward the First Marshal. To her surprise, instead of being offended or angered at the Red's familiarity and abrupt hijacking of their interview, he gave the ascetic a calm respectful nod.

"Thank you, Ms. Griffin. You may go."

Words failed her. So she did the prudent thing and left.

Pausing outside Marchand's office, she took a deep breath and glanced around the lobby at those waiting for her. Kai sat next to Cassie on a bench, arm stretched behind his friend, both in animated conversation. By their grins and Cassie's laughter, Liaena guessed they'd patched their friendship. Nick leaned on the wall next to them, watching their antics with a rueful smile and a shake of his head. Del and Sin stood in front of a refreshment unit, looking as though they were contemplating a sneak attack on the machine. Zofie paced next to a couple who looked too much like Cassie not to be her parents.

When Liaena's mother caught sight of her, she bounded over as if shot from a cannon. To Aena's surprise, Kai somehow reached her at the same time.

"Are you all right?"

"What did he say?"

She smiled at their simultaneous questions. "I'm fine. The First Marshal has agreed to help me."

With a gust of relief Zofie wrapped her in a hug.

Kai flashed a knowing grin. "Big M knows a good thing when he sees it."

Zofie choked at his impertinent name for the First Marshal and drew back to stare at him in maternal disapproval.

Kai winked at her and continued, "And so do we. Sin and I will do whatever we can to help you."

"We all will," Cassie said at his elbow with a sunny smile. "Trust me, scouring Quasicore inside and out will be great therapy for everybody."

The others had drawn closer, enclosing Liaena in a warm bubble of goodwill. All of them smiled, open and carefree, expressing a degree of relief and affection she could hardly credit.

"Th-thank you," she stuttered, clasping her hands together in a sudden burst of nerves.

Sin and Kai drew them gently apart, each taking a hand.

"I also hear congratulations are in order." Sin leaned in, kissed her on the cheek, and then smiled with dazzling joy. "Welcome to the family, Aena."

The words crashed through her like a shock wave, devastating her defenses. *Family*. She'd dreamt of it for so long but hadn't thought it would ever become reality. Yet here they were, eclectic and odd, filling her world with sudden warmth and support. She glanced from them to Kai. *And love*. Tears welled in an unstoppable tide, blurring her vision.

"Sinsi, for crying out loud," Kai grumbled and took Liaena in his arms.

With a light cough Sin muttered, "Bail." Everyone but Kai streamed away as if they'd rehearsed it.

Liaena clung to him, absorbing his heat and strength like an addict. "If this is a dream, don't wake me."

"So you're not crying out of sheer terror at the idea of being in this family?"

With a shaky laugh she tipped back her head. Her heart fluttered at the unguarded emotion in his beautiful eyes. He smiled with an intoxicating mixture of tenderness, passion, and humor, draining the strength right out of her limbs.

She sagged into him, trusting his arms to hold her upright. "You can't chase me away so easily," she responded in a breathless voice. "You asked to bond with me. Did you mean it?"

"From the bottom of my heart and soul." He brushed her mouth with his, lingering like a promise. He tasted of desire and decadence, and something deeper, richer, filling her like a steady stream of sunlight.

She sighed and melted into him, twining her fingers in his hair. "I'm starting to believe it. But why would you Sun-bond with a Griffin?"

He drew back, his heart-stopping smile easing into a teasing grin. "I'm only after power and prestige, and the heiress to an empire. It has nothing to do with your clever mind, selfless heart, and killer body."

Smothering a delighted smile, she gave a thoughtful nod. "And my agreement has nothing to do with how well or often you make my heart dance. A Shay in my clutches would be quite advantageous."

"Clutches? Egads, the truth is out," he drawled with a snicker.

She kissed him just to taste the humor on his lips. "I love you," she whispered. "You've blown into my life like a whirlwind and somehow made beauty out of chaos."

"And I love you," he murmured. "You are the Sun at the center of my universe."

Heart and soul bursting with joy, she met him in another kiss, deep and binding as an oath. His fingertips touched the crystal at her throat and bright music rose around them, rejoicing in their union and the coming of a new dawn.

A word about the author…

Science fiction and fantasy romance author Michelle O'Leary resides in Marquette, Michigan, which graces the shore of pristine Lake Superior. Born and raised in Upper Michigan, Michelle is a child of nature, enjoying all things outdoors.

Originally published through a small e-publisher, Michelle became an independent author before being accepted into The Wild Rose Press family. Her titles include *Here There Be Dragons, Last Chance, Vessel of Power, Dawn of the Red Sun* and more.

Michelle is a mother first, a dedicated chocoholic, a contented Michigander, and a delirious word lover. She enjoys all feedback and can be found online here:

http://molearyauthor.wix.com/michelleoleary
https://www.facebook.com/michelle.oleary.7564
https://twitter.com/MOLearyAuthor